CW00382558

# Peter's Out
## How the Catholic Church Ends

This revisionist history of the future might lower cholesterol and create or increase penile girth.

ALBERT SO

Copyright © 2019 Albert So
All rights reserved.
ISBN: 9781520940311
Imprint: Independently published

# DEDICATION

For K.V. and M.S.
Congratulations on your unsuccessful suicides

# WARNING!

Do not skip the endnotes. The endnotes are an integral part of the plot.

Consider yourself warned. (Snicker)

# 1

## DON'T GULP YOUR
## HOLY WATER SWEETIE PIE

Little baby Peter entered the world with his immortal soul fouled by the corruption of original sin.[1] For thirty-two tense days after his birth on June 6, 1960, the destiny of Peter's teeny little soul teetered on the brink of Limbo.[2] If Peter's parents waited too long to baptize him and he died, they would be guilty of committing a mortal sin.[3]

Peter was the youngest of nine children. The Bondeo brood packed into the family station wagon heading to church looked like a circus car jammed with midget clowns. A face pressed up against a window would suddenly disappear then quickly be replaced by another. Peter was an anomaly in this rambunctious gaggle.

Peter's parents sat in the front seat wearing expressions of resignation tinged with pride. Miles from happy-go-lucky, they were serious without being grim. This is where Peter inherited his humorlessness.

Occasionally a car would pull up next to them at a stoplight and the people inside it would stare, obviously impressed with the pride of kids. Most folks considered large families cute back then.[4]

Those were innocent if not somewhat dumb times. Good Catholics had large families. Peter's mother, Mary, often would not wait for the silent question mouthed from the other car. "How many?" She would flash the necessary fingers followed by a weary, patient smile.

She and her husband, Joseph looked a little wearier than usual that morning. It was after all, a chore to dress eight resistant kids in their Sunday best (On a Saturday? Mom!). The new infant was the exception. Peter was as agreeable and complacent as a salesman with a signed contract and an advance check in his pocket.

Peter was the only one of his eight brothers and sisters who was a quiet baby. Mary was not about to spoil a good thing by asking a doctor why the baby never cried. For that matter, Peter never really laughed, smiled or chortled.

Mary could hold him over her head and coo at him all day long and Peter simply looked back at her quietly. No giggle or squeal like the other kids. Peter breathed. He ate. He pooped. Peter was about to make a rare expression of feeling.

Peter's father, Joseph parked the car in the church parking lot. [5]

The kids clambered out of the Rambler, but maintained a certain semblance of control. After all, they were at church. Even though it was a Saturday, they knew they better calm down.

Peter's brothers' and sisters' first names started with the letter 'P' as well. That was the way people entertained themselves during the Eisenhower administration. Mary and Joseph called the first three Pamela, Patrick and Paul. Realizing they were on a roll, they decided to get cutesy with Paula.

Pembroke and Priscilla constituted a brief formal sounding stage. Paco added an international flare. Petunia rebelled against her odiferous handle by being a bit of a stinker.

Peter was named Peter because someone reminded Mary and Joseph that Catholic children were supposed to be labeled with the names of saints. They hoped naming Peter Peter would atone for any transgression they might have committed.

Calling the baby Peter was also a little inside joke between Mary and Joseph. Joseph remarked with mock jealousy that the baby's pecker was already bigger than his. Mary found herself clucking in wonderment every time she changed his diaper.

Father Pablo Olivera, the priest at Saint Michael's Church & Catholic School, was busy in the back of the church at the baptismal font exercising an expression of twitchy patience.[6] Father P.O.[7] was busy being distracted by everything in general and one thing in particular.

The font looked a lot like a big birdbath made from marble. A pretty fancy birdbath, gilded with gold, ornate piping, there was also a ring of fungus just above the holy water line.

That was one of the things on the long list of Father P.O.'s list of on-going distractions. He wondered why the damn, busy body nuns didn't clean up that crap.

The family fussed about in the back of the church. A couple of the older P's whispered know-it-all orders in each other's ears. A stern look from Mary put that to rest.

Matteo Bondeo, Peter's godfather-to-be, sat in the last pew making goo-goo eyes at little Petunia. She and Paco giggled and squealed a bit. Unlike his stick in the mud brother Joseph, Matteo was goofy. His wife, Johanna, fixed him with a stare that could freeze a puffin's pecker. The two had no children of their own. That is why Matteo was so happy-go-lucky and Johanna took every opportunity to bitterly point out every possible shortcoming of Matteo's.

If Peter's parents died while he was still a kid, his godparents were supposed to see to it that he received a proper Catholic education. Not that it mattered.[8]

In about a dozen years, Peter would be capable of telling Matteo and Johanna a thing or two about how to be a good Catholic. Not that he would.

During the baptism ceremony, Matteo and Johanna, as stand-ins for teeny Petey, were supposed to renounce Satan and all his designs. The church was wise enough to realize that a person who still poops in his pants was not old enough to make such a statement on his own.

Father Pablo was not one to bother with theology or too much mumbo jumbo either. He poured a little of the skuzzy water on Peter's forehead then skated by with the basics for the remainder of the ceremony.

"I baptize thee in the name of the Father, the Son and the Holy Ghost." That was all he said before plopping Peter into Matteo's arms. It did not matter to the priest who Matteo was. He was standing closest. Matteo had never held a baby. He promptly dropped Peter in to the baptismal font.[9] Peter screamed and sputtered several times before Mary had the presence of mind to pull him out. How was she to know it was not something the priest does intentionally? No matter. Peter was now a Catholic.[10]

# 2

## FATE'S ENVELOPE SEALED
## WITH DEATH'S SPITTLE

Peter first pondered the possibility of pursuing popehood at a very young age. Pope was not his initial preference. Sister Evelene, a bit player with enormous impact in this epic, dragged him by the ear in that direction.

Everything about Sister Evelene's classroom was authoritarian. She realized decades earlier that given half a chance first-graders would walk all over you. Her frequently spat motto frequently included spray. Hence the moniker: Old Foamy.

"Shut up and sit still. Maybe you'll learn something."

Sister Evelene saw to it each and every morning that the five rows of ten desks each lined up meticulously along the worn, well-waxed tile floor. If not, she ordered the students to push them to within a cat's hair of alignment.

There were rules. No looking out the window at the gray-blue Lathrop Village overcast. No squirming, no fidgeting. With few exceptions, such as when reading or writing, students sat ramrod straight and looked directly at her. No slouching. Only Lutherans slouched. The children's perception of Lutherans was universally consistent if not necessarily accurate.[11]

Grade school children were not allowed to dress like whores and gigolos, hence the dress code was strictly enforced. Boys wore navy blue pressed slacks. The school issued royal blue long-sleeved dress shirts emblazoned with the Saint Michael The Archangel Catholic School emblem: A fist clenching a flaming sword also dripped blood.[12]

As a former archangel, Lucifer used to be God's best friend up in Heaven. Then one day he got the idea in his head that he would like to be in charge. God sent Mikey to slew Luci and throw him into Hell. That is the only recorded attempt to overthrow God in Heaven. It is unknown if safeguards have been taken to keep it from happening again.

Black Oxfords shined. Sister Evelene ordered those who came to school wearing scuffed shoes to stand in their socks facing the corner while holding the offensive shoes. Loafers were for lazy people. That is what Sister Evelene said.

The girls wore navy blue jumpers with the same logo. They also wore royal blue long-sleeved blouses distinguished with an ironic "Peter Pan" collar. Children wore the same uniforms regardless of weather. When it was cold, the nuns allowed a standard, genderless, navy blue sweater.[13]

No bangs allowed. Hair never dared to tickle a forehead. Instead girls used rubber bands only-no fancy barrettes-to pull their tresses back in pigtails. Ponytails were not allowed because they were considered seductive. Boys were forbidden to put their hands in their pockets.[14]

All sat in alphabetical order, boys on one side of the classroom, girls on the other. No talking, whispering or touching allowed. Note passing was a fantastic rumor of what the ignorant barbarians in the public schools did.

You want to chew gum? Well Sister Evelene had a cure for that! She maintained a large glass jar containing wads she had confiscated over the years. Since these were first-graders with no previous experience, they had no idea gum chewing in school was a sin.

She ordered offenders to take it out of their mouths and set it aside. Then, since they wanted to chew gum so badly, she "allowed" them to take a piece out of the jar and put it in their mouths and chew it for the rest of the day! Since waste was also a sin, the fresh piece was dropped into the jar to be saved for the next non-conformist.

The children accepted this tyranny with complacent nervousness. Which was just as well since they had no choice. Do what the nun wants and escape with your skin was the easy to learn first lesson.

On this particular morning, Sister Evelene pulled a fast one. As usual, her students unloaded noisily from the buses, hushing the moment they went inside the school. They hung coats on labeled hooks and put lunch boxes squarely in assigned spots.

Sister Evelene smiled at them. A few brave kids chanced a sidelong glance of wide-eyed disbelief. Unsettling. Sister Evelene never smiled.

She usually looked more like a vulture: gaunt, with sunken, ashen cheeks and swollen, weary eyes with their challenging, watery stare. When standing, she stooped arthritically. In their six months under her wing, a critical smirk was the closest she ever came to a smile. This smiling vulture was creepy.

The smile was a marketing ploy. Sister Evelene had something to sell. She was about to convince at least a couple of these little seven year-olds to become priests and nuns. She had to convince them today-now-before the sins of the flesh distracted them. So she had to be nice. Being nice meant smiling. Her lips started to stick to her drying teeth with the effort.

"Hurry up. Sit down." She licked her lips. The smile returned. Good thing she only did this once a year.

"Who knows what a 'vocation' is?" She enunciated in her thin baritone. Sister Evelene may have been a dinged up antique, but her voice worked fine. The class responded with silence. Except for Mark Minor, the class clown. Mark's chubby paw waved obnoxiously.

"Disneyland!" He piped. Why wait to be recognized? The class put massive effort into swallowing their giggles. Mark smiled, proud to have done what he had to do: inject a little life into the proceedings. Mark led his peers in wit development, but was conveniently dopey regarding classroom protocol.

Sister Evelene waited until the commotion died down, then … a little longer for effect. She stared at him.

"All right, Fatso." She nodded her head almost imperceptibly to the left. Nothing more needed to be said. Mark sulked over to the corner in the front of the room and turned his back on the class. The two had done this dance previously. Sister Evelene looked oddly pleased as she refocused on the class.

"Vocation. Not vacation. Nobody knows?" Lots of little negative headshakes.

"Everybody has to do something for a living. Men can be president or a policeman or work in an office. Women can get married but they must have babies. That can be what they do for a living and that is good in the eyes of God. They might even go to heaven when they die.

"But some people are special. God looks down on some people and gives them a wonderful gift. A vocation. A vocation is when God chooses you to serve him as a priest or a nun."

A hand appeared. This time it was Diane Gillette. Though cooperative in her own winky way, Diane was miles from being like one of the lemmings surrounding her. Diane did not so much raise her hand as just sort of put it out there. She demurred from the standard twelve o'clock position. Diane's raise was closer to say … nine-thirty, with the hand waggling limply from the wrist. The gesture looked as if she expected to have her hand kissed.

"Is that Miss Smarty-Pants with a question?"

"Why is being a nun better?"

"Good question. The answer is because of my vows to God of poverty, chastity and obedience. Taking those vows is the only way to reach a perfect love of God. And I know because of my vows that when I die and go to Heaven, that I will be closer to God." Sister Evelene stood and surveyed the class.

"Wouldn't you like that? A special place in Heaven after you die?"

Game, most of the class nodded yes.

The exceptions were Peter, Diane, and Mark. Diane had several career paths routed, none of which included nun or mom. Mark also had a pretty cool idea, but his thoughts were more involved with his imagined involvement in a Jimmy Durante television special than with an upper bunk in Heaven.

"Fatso!"

Mark was in the midst of asking "Schnozola" how many boxes of Kleenex he went through when he had a cold. Regretfully, he abandoned the peals of laughter in his fantasy.

"What are you going to do for a living? Turn and face the class, you tub of lard."

"Huh?"

"What are you going to do for a living?"

"A job you mean?"

Sister Evelene responded with her trademark smirk. That did not tell Mark anything. Not that he needed much encouragement.

"Oh. If you mean a job? I want to be a disc jockey like on WXYZ. You know? 'Wixey-100'? Or maybe a comedian like Jimmy Durante. Hot cha, cha cha cha!" Her stare withered Mark's jiggling and enthusiastic impression of the bulbous nosed comic.

She wagged an arthritic finger in his general direction. "Face the corner chubby." Sister Evelene stood and shuffled slowly down the aisle towards Peter's seat. What was going on inside this curly-haired noggin?

Peter was not paying attention. He was busy playing a little game he invented the first day he sat in a school desk. The lid was on a slight incline from the student. Towards the top a little ridge was cut out. That was where students put their pencils when they were not writing. Peter would flick the pencil from the bottom of the desktop so that it would roll up and lodge itself in the little groove. Initially he only used his index finger. As his talent quickly accelerated, he began using his other fingers and thumb. Soon he added his left hand to the pencil-pushing repertoire. Nearby neighbors found it neat that no matter which digit Peter used, from any part of the desk, the pencil would have just enough steam to roll up to the ridge, then pause-as if it had come up short-before dropping in. He never missed.

"Well, Toe-head? Are you going to tell the class why you think you are too good to become a priest? You have a better idea what to do for a living?"

It was a frightening challenge for any seven year-old to be that close and forced to look directly at the face of Sister Evelene let alone express themselves. This was especially difficult because he had been daydreaming and had not really caught the question.

In self-defense, Peter's focus inched slightly to the right of the nun's face. There, over her left shoulder, his eyes found the two pictures that hung above the chalkboard on the front wall of the classroom. The same two pictures that hung in the front of every classroom in every Catholic school in the world. Peter knew who they were. There was a picture of Pope John XXIII and a picture of Jesus Christ.

The current Pontiff seemed to grimace impatiently in his papal refinery. John looked as if he would be a lot more comfortable burping and farting garlic in a sleeveless t-shirt and a pair of fading boxers, maybe contemplating a bocce ball instead of the Holy Trinity.

Peter would try to open that particular escape hatch momentarily. Instead, he found solace in the other picture: the doe-eyed, sad and somehow hurt expression of the longhaired Savior. He offered his answer.

"I want to be a Jesus." It was not the challenge Sister Evelene took it to be. It was just the simple attempt of a young child to give the right answer.

"You wa-." In her younger days, Sister Evelene would have knocked the offender down on the floor with one quickly placed whack. But she was in her eighties now, and time had slowed her previously lightning fast judgment/punishment reflex. Instead, a boiling metal sensation gripped her stomach. Her bladder weakened and leaked a drop or three. She snorted dryly several times and finally came to her senses. She grabbed his ear and twisted.

She twisted as hard as she could then released, grabbed and twisted again. The blasphemous little cretin did not respond. Concerned that Peter might be adjusting to the pain quicker than even the sturdiest mutt, Sister Evelene let go and grabbed the other ear with her other hand and twisted until she felt her fingernails start to dig into skin. Peter stood up.

She dragged him by the ear to the front of the room and after throwing him against the blackboard, released him. She had not lost quite all of her spunk.

"Stand there and face the board!" She was so enraged she could barely look at him. She slumped into her chair wearied and wheezing. The class stared in awe at her power. They also enjoyed relief with a dash of smug to see someone else the victim.

"How dare you." She hissed into her desktop. Sister Evelene pulled out her handkerchief and dabbed at a nonexistent bit of saliva that had not formed at the corner of her mouth. She did that occasionally.

"How dare you desecrate Our Lord." Normally, the next move would have been to force Peter to make an Act of Contrition for his sin.[15]

The problem was that he had not been taught what that was or how to do it and would not learn until the second grade. Sister Evelene was at a loss for a punishment. Leaning over the top of her desk and staring at it did not help her rapidly deteriorating thought process.

She set aside her hankie and her hand began to levitate thoughtfully in patterns across her desk, as if led by an invisible Ouiji device. She did that occasionally too.

"Sister? What did I do?" Peter was still facing the board, still not crying.

"Shut up." That resuscitated her some. However, the sincerity in his voice reminded her that he was a child and maybe he did not know. If she didn't teach him, who would?

"Come here. Stand right here by my desk. Stop staring at me. Look at the face of Our Lord. Look at Him. See how you have hurt him? Now. Tell me what you are going to do for a living?"

At first, Peter only knew what he was not going to say. He hesitated only slightly.

"Could I be the Pope?"

Sister Evelene exhaled exasperation as she pulled open the drawer of her desk. Not a good sign. Not much of a chance she was reaching for a pencil or fresh stick of chalk. The metal ruler gleamed and clanked slightly on the way out.

"Yes. You can be the Pope. Put out your hands. Palms up. Straight out." Having seen enough, some of the kids closed their eyes. Some peeked through squinting eyelids or between fingers. Diane watched. Mark set aside his fantasy of being asked to sit in for an ailing Shelly Berman on The Ed Sullivan Show.

"Yes. You. Can. Be. Pope."

Still Peter did not cry. That antagonized Sister Evelene. The awareness of his wrongdoing had obviously not sunk in.

"Turn your hands over. Palms down." Whack.

"You can be Pope?" Whack.

Peter shuffled his feet in a slight dance of pain and confusion. A tear appeared. A seed was planted.

"Are you sorry?"

That question at least afforded Peter an out. "Yes Sister. I'm sorry." More tears formed and then fell. A pathetic sniffle followed.

"It is going to be a very long time before God forgives you for this sin. You had better pray very hard for forgiveness. You had better hope that you don't die before He forgives you. Only a very holy person can be the pope. You have committed a very grave sin. If you want to be holy, you must pray to God to forgive you every day. Until God tells you. Until you hear his voice forgiving you. Don't just stand there. Go back to your desk you big crybaby."

Peter looked at his reddened hands, still held in front of him as he walked back to his desk and sat down softly. Two seats further down the row, the blasé hand hung out.

"Take out your penmanship books."

"Sister." It was not an inquiry. "Sister." Again! She did not even give Sister a chance to tell her to shut up. The class turned cautiously, astonished, anticipating another bloodletting.

"Now what."

Diane rose and sauntered haughtily towards the nun's desk. She was a seven-year-old Isadora Duncan gliding languidly, chin held high, fingers caressing her neighbors' desktops. As she passed, invisible scarves trailed. The little upstart leaned slovenly against the nun's desk and offered her hands.

"I want to be pope too."[16]

10

Sister Evelene had never heard of any girl popes. Right then she was hearing something like a freight train roaring in her ears. She felt several ice picks in her chest. Her vision of the class grew darker and darker, but, eerily, her eyes were pointed at Peter.

"…be…pope…" She was dead before her face hit the desktop.

***

After the Medical Examiner's hearse left that day, Peter skipped the bus ride home and went to the church, which was connected to the school. Solemnly, he approached the railing that stood guard around the altar. Empty with echoed silence, the hall of worship held the odor of burned incense and sweating Catholic hides.

Beyond the altar, across the sanctuary, against the far wall of the church hung a life-sized replica of Jesus Christ permanently nailed to a real wooden cross in all His gory glory.[17] He gushed plastic blood from His ceramic hands, feet, chest and noggin. His eyes turned in anguish to the sky. His inflexible mouth wondered silently why His Father had left Him to die and what was the point? Beneath this crucifix was the real event: the tabernacle with the monstrance on top.[18] If God was anywhere in the building, this was the place. So Catholics, Peter included, believed. He knelt on the marble step at the base of the railing that bordered the sanctuary and prayed. His eyes fixed on the monstrance.

Peter had not learned the formal, memorized prayers yet. That made no difference. Neither did the cold, hard marble against his young knees. This was something he had been told to do. By a dying nun no less.

# 3

## FIRST CONFESSION.[19]
## FIRST COMMUNION.[20]
## FIRST BLOOD.

It had been almost a year since Diane Gillette raced to the nun in the next classroom screaming at the top of her lungs that Peter had murdered Sister Evelene and her dying words told him to be the pope. That news spread to the rest of the school like ants in an unsprayed honey factory.

Peter's reputation was transformed from a nondescript kidlet into a full-tilt pariah. Who in the heck would want to hang out with a creepy kid like that? Bad raps last a lifetime in grade school.

Evil weasel or not, Peter planned for his first Confession and First Holy Communion along with the rest of his second grade class. Confession could not have come soon enough for Peter. He murdered Sister Evelene. He knew that. Murder was a mortal sin. A mortal sin was the same thing as stabbing Jesus in the side with a Roman lance as he hung dying on the cross. Peter was compelled to confess his crime to a priest before he died or he would go straight to Hell and burn for eternity.

Technically, he had already asked for God's forgiveness out of simple instinct. This was done in his mind though, while praying, not spoken aloud in a confessional with a priest to formally forgive him. Since her death, he had told God several hundred times that he was very sorry for killing Sister Evelene (which he was) and that he sincerely would not do it again (which he would not).

Peter learned about sincere acts of contrition during instructions about going to confession and subsequently made a sincere act of contrition at least once per day ever since. For most normal sinners, telling it to a priest should be icing on the cake. However, Peter knew that getting into Heaven was complicated.

The possible ineffectuality of the sincere act of contrition gnawed at him because it was too easy. He yearned for harsh punishment. He knew it was necessary. Peter had received no punishment for the mortal sin he was certain he had committed. He worried his soul was not in a state of grace.[21]

Peter's childish ignorance of the Catholic facts was a tremendous burden for a little kid to carry. He knew just enough to be confused or to overcompensate. With that in mind, it should be easier to understand the consternation Peter experienced entering the confessional for the first time. This warm, dark and cozy booth would be a lousy place to be trapped. Maybe his sin was unforgivable. Maybe after he confessed the murder a steel gate would slam shut barring escape through the curtain. Then the wall would disintegrate in flames. Then the Devil would appear, hell-bent on plunging his pitchfork into Peter. Maybe, instead of an understanding confessor not quite visible on the other side of the little sliding door, a decayed and cackling Sister Evelene would appear. Peter was seriously considering standing up and sneaking out when the little door whacked open.

"Confess." Wary, annoyed, this was not the voice of Sister Evelene. It was Peter's conduit to Christ, Father P.O. This was the pharmacist with the right prescription for his despair, the janitor who would sweep away his sins, the washerwoman who would suds his soul.[22]

"Bless me Father for I have sinned." Peter felt a surprising twinge of confidence. Though Father Pablo was gruff, Peter knew from the pictures in his religion textbook that Jesus floated above them both at that very moment. His arms were outstretched and He was ready to listen to any tale and forgive. He could not see Him, but he knew He was there waiting to escort His little lost lamb back-

"Confess. This your first time?" Impatient? I'll say.

"Yes, Father."

"What'd you do? Fought and quarreled with your brothers and sisters? Lie to mom and dad?" It might have been compassion motivating Father Pablo to suggest possible sins to make the errant lamby cake's time a bit easier. More likely that the priest knew there was a whole class of fifty-eight eight year-olds yet to come, all of them squirting in their shorts in anticipation of their first confession. If he did not prime the pump, he would be here until next Wednesday.

"Yes, Father. And murder."

13

"Murder? Oh, really. Who?"

"I murdered Sister Evelene last year in the first grade, Father." Peter heard Father Pablo make a strange noise. It never occurred to Peter that he was inspiring mirth.

"How'd you do that? Stab her? Shoot her?"

"No, Father. When I committed another mortal sin. When I told her I wanted to be Jesus and then I told her I wanted to be the pope, she got so upset she died."

"First of all, everybody should try to be like Jesus. That's not a sin, son."

"Not like Jesus, Father. I told her I wanted to be a Jesus. For a living."

"Well, you can't be Jesus. You can be like Jesus. You can follow his example. But you can't be Him. Even if you tried to be, it still would not be a sin. Did sister explain that to you before she died?"

"No, Father."

"Well, she was probably just about to. Do you understand now?"

"Yes, Father. I can be like Jesus."

"Just to be clear. Jesus is the Savior. The Son of God. Something no human being can ever be. You see? That position has already been filled. However, you should always act the way Jesus did. Be charitable and humble, make sacrifices and be good to others. Understand me?"

"Yes, Father. Father?"

"Yes?"

"Father, I know it's not a sin, but I just wanted to know, is it okay to like Jesus?"

"You should love Jesus with all of your heart, soul, mind and body. As He loves you.

"Yes, Father."

"Now about you being the pope?"

"Yes, Father?"

"Be my guest."

"Yes, Father."

"Now. About this murder. Did you want her to die? When you said you wanted to be Jesus for a living, did you say that to kill her?"

"No, father. But when I said it then she died and Diane Gillette said I killed her."

"Who do you believe, Diane Gillette or me? I'm telling you that Sister Evelene died of old age. It doesn't matter if you were there or not, the woman would still be dead. It was her time to go and God took her."

"Then I committed another mortal sin, Father."

"Lord." Father Olivera's amusement withered.

"I lied to God when I made a sincere act of contrition and told him I killed Sister Evelene."

"Did you intentionally lie to God?"

"No, Father. I made a sincere act of contrition."

"Then you didn't lie."

"But I didn't tell the truth, Fath-"

"Listen. Don't split hairs with God. You're forgiven. Any more sins?"

Nothing.

"I'll tell you what. I'm going to forgive every sin you have ever committed even though you haven't confessed it. Since this is your first time. If you remember a sin later, you can always come back and confess it anytime. However, just in case you missed one, consider yourself all right with God. Sound fair?"

"Can I still receive my First Holy Communion?"

"Tsk. Yes of course. For your penance and because you gave me such a hard time, say three "Our Fathers" three "Hail Marys" and three "Glory Bes." I absolve you from your sins in the name of the Father, the Son and the Holy Spirit.[23] Amen. Go and sin no more."

▪▪▪▪▪▪▪▪▪▪▪▪▪▪▪▪▪▪▪▪▪▪▪▪▪▪▪▪▪▪▪▪▪▪▪▪▪▪▪▪▪▪▪▪▪▪▪▪▪▪▪

Peter and the ninety-nine other First communicants were equally apprehensive about chowing down on Jesus. Whispered rumors buzzed around a hornet's nest of fear. What if you forgot to confess a mortal sin and received anyway? What would happen? Would you explode? Turn into a Devil?

Many of the children concerned themselves with the concept of transubstantiation. If the host really, really were Jesus, would that make the host taste like blood? Or worse yet, old rotting flesh?

Speaking of which, Sister Termanatem, the roly-poly septuagenarian who conducted the second-graders through their First Communion training, got no thrill out of scaring the shit out of eight-year olds. Lord no. She had been doing that for too long to get any kicks out of it. On this particular day, the nun was giving them tongue lessons.

"Don't stick it out at the priest like he's you and some goose friend out on the playground." She demonstrated then explained. "Simply open your mouth like this. Do it now." One hundred and one mouths opened. "Make sure the host is on your tongue before you close your mouth. Biting the priest is a mortal sin. Making him drop the host is also a mortal sin.

"Do not CHEW Our Lord once he is in your mouth. I repeat: Do not chew the host. That is a mortal sin."

That morsel of info invariably drew a gaggle of surprised protests: "Not chew it? How can we eat if we don't chew? My mother makes me chew something fourteen times before I swallow!"

Sister Termanatem's response?

"The host should not even touch your teeth. That is a venial sin. Make sure your tongue is wet before the priest puts it on your tongue. That'll keep the host from sticking to the roof of your mouth. And don't have your mouth full of spit either. Just so it's moist. The priest will say a prayer in Latin to you and what do you say?"

"Amen." One hundred dispirited voices answered.

"So. Open your mouth. Move your tongue forward across your bottom teeth ever so slightly. The priest puts the host on your tongue. When you pull back your tongue, keep your mouth open wide or else the host will hit your teeth, fall off your tongue and onto the floor. And what is that?"

"A mortal sin." Communion was starting to look like a soul-threatening chore.

"If you should make the host fall on the floor, do NOT pick it up. Only a priest can touch the host. Not even nuns can touch the host after it has been consecrated. In an emergency, say if the priest is a cripple and can't bend over, and there are no nuns around, if you are the only one who can pick up the host, do not touch it directly with your hands. Use a piece of clean cloth and then burn the cloth later.

"After you receive, walk slowly back to your seat. Slowly! This isn't the Indy 500. Show your respect for what is happening. Keep your hands in a prayerful position and bow your head. You have just received the Body of Christ. So act like it. However, you should swallow the host as quickly as possible. It will melt."

A chorus of surprised and amazed "Oohs" briefly interrupted Sister Termanatem.

"Yes. So you want to get Jesus inside your soul as soon as you can. The more host you get down the more grace you receive. If you don't swallow any, then you may as well have not gone to Communion at all, for all the good it will do you.

"When you are back at your position in the pew, kneel down immediately and thank God for this precious gift. Adore and worship Him. Ask Him to make you a better person. To do better in school. To always obey your teacher and parents. After you've done all of that, you may sit. Quietly!"

What else could a kid possibly need to know?

It was a dark and stormy day. Peter's parents bought him his first suit for the occasion. Every boy in the group had a new suit. The girls wore what looked like little wedding dresses. All white, of course none of this beige or cream crap. People who stuck out were showing off and therefore committing a sin.

They lined up all twitching frills and starched discomfort in the first five pews. The boys, with slicked back hair, fought the fidgets on one side. The girls, annoyingly prim and proper, held court on the other.[24] Their beaming families sat behind the two groups. The ceremony went without a hitch. Except for Peter. Peter had a little problem. He spit out the host.

Not that he ever intended such sacrilege. Far from it. The prospect of his First Holy Communion totally enchanted Peter. The other children walked reverently ahead of him. Peter felt as if the whole church was glowing with God. He should have been concentrating more on Sister Termanatem's instructions. Especially the part about the wet tongue.

As he knelt at the altar railing, Peter's excitement vacuumed every last molecule of moisture out of his mouth. It was so dry he could barely open it. Here comes the priest already! Before he knew what had happened the host was on his tongue and the priest was moving away!

Peter rose from his knees, stood and began to walk back to his pew. He realized his mouth was still open. He closed it. The host felt huge on his tongue. His teeth, a venial sin waiting to happen tightened their perimeter around the Sacred Prisoner. To make matters worse, the only instruction he remembered was the one he needed the least.

"Swallow the host as soon as possible."

At that point a mouthful of dirt and rocks would have gone down easier. Peter's tongue lashed the host to the back of his throat directly against his gag reflex.

Not all of the wafer landed on the floor. A couple particles went up his windpipe. A little chunk jammed its way up his nose. Sister Termanatem, still the supervisor, was the first on the scene. She expected at least one of these dumb bunnies to have a problem like this. Termanatem blocked Peter from going any further. She held him at bay until Father P.O., halted the ceremony and came over for cleanup operations.

Two hundred and four eyes watched in wide-eyed astonishment as…FATHER P.O. ATE THE SPIT OUT HOST! He then escorted Peter back to the altar railing.

"Kneel down." The priest again mumbled the Latin words inquiring if Peter wanted to accept the Sacred Body of Christ.

"But Father!" Peter whispered so fervently he felt faint. "I just committed a mortal sin. I have to go to confession before I can receive!"

"First time doesn't count."

Peter did not yet know what a genius was, but he thought Father Pablo must be one.

As if the murder of Sister Evelene was not reason enough for Peter's classmates to turn thumbs down on him, after he hurled Our Lord all over the church floor they washed their hands of him. Peter did not help matters any. When he was not busy being attentive in class, he was busy praying. And not always in church. God was everywhere, he had learned, including the playground, the cafeteria and the boy's bathroom. All were fair game for areas of worship.

Another thing Peter and his peers lacked in common were the territories their minds inhabited when they traveled to the land of Daydreams. His schoolmates dove head first into fantasy worlds inhabited by Daniel Boone, Nancy Drew, Tom Swift or Leave It To Beaver's mother. Peter dog-paddled in a pool of worry over his future.

He knew he would not be pope for a few years, but occasionally the burden of the responsibilities he would assume hypnotized him with panic. Peter developed a bizarre, papal torture chamber for himself. While the other twelve year-olds pinched, pulled hair, passed love notes or gas, Peter spent his morning bus ride to school vexed by his vision of terror.

During the typical rerun of a prime time papal daymare, Peter found himself suffocating in heavy cream-colored satin, fingers clanging noisily with gold and jewels, his head gouged by a papal crown. His mouth felt full of paste as he prepared to address the masses shivering expectantly below his balcony. What would he tell them? Unable to intellectualize it at that age, Peter nonetheless was aware that there was something wrong with the Church.

The teeming horde packing Saint Peter's Square dressed in Roman rags. Peter's understanding of Italian fashion was limited to gladiator movies he had seen on television. They reeked of cooked cabbage, a meal he forced himself to eat to help the starving children in China.[25]

Would this herd-yes, cattle were on the scene too-drag him down and crush him under hoof? If they should decide to torture him, would he be strong enough to resist?

Dragging finery and wishing for sackcloth, Peter approached the patriarchal portico. Before stepping out, he made a quick check for boogers.

"Ew! He's pickin' his nose!"

The kid stink of the present hit Peter like yesterday's tuna sandwich stored in an airtight rusty, official Zorro lunch box. The aching reality of the bouncing bus was offset by Greg Fent's announcement to all the world of Peter's attempt at mucous munching.

As the self-proclaimed (And who would argue?) King Bully of Peter's neighborhood, Greg's goal in life was grander than just beating up on loogie-picking sissies. This future weight trainer was driven by an all-consuming need to intrude.[26]

"Find any snails in there, Saint Peterless?"

Peter let his active hand fall slowly to his lap then down between his legs where he wiped his embarrassing treasure on the already crowded seam under the bus seat. Then, in his best imitation of Christ-like confounding manner, he closed his eyes and put his hands together in fervent prayer.

"You may strike me now." Peter knew that he was not going to die at that moment. He knew just making the offer made him closer to God. It is also possible that his elementary understanding of saintly psychology led him to believe that making the offer would emotionally move Greg so greatly he would not only back down, but turn holy too.

19

Unfortunately, Greg appreciated the invitation. He may have performed senseless, often random acts of violence, but he was not a completely mindless bully. Before he prompted pain he usually sketched, if not completely mapped out, a defense strategy against the inevitable adult intervention. This one was foolproof. "But he told me to slug him!"

"Thanks for the invitation Your Fartliness."

Then Greg punched Peter in the nose. This not only hurt, it put Peter in a quandary. He could not fight back the tears, and he certainly could not fight back either. Nor could he clean himself up in spite of the slow liquid warmth he felt seeping from his right nostril.

Just like Jesus with Satan barking at his heals for forty hungry days in the desert ("If you are really the Son of God turn this rock into a loaf of seven-grain.") the quickly approaching delirious Peter dodged the impulse to respond. His saintly self-image would not allow him to snort the snotty blood mixture either. Peter's "Lives of the Saints" (A recent First Communion gift and "the best present ever."), though full of inspiration was curiously short on tips.[27]

Two seats back on the other side of the Saint Michael the Archangels Catholic School Bluebird sat Diane Gillette. She was about to make unintentional atonement for being a stoolie back in first grade.

Unlike Greg's roundhouse, which a visually impaired person could have seen twenty yards off, Diane's broadside retaliation with her "I Dream of Jeannie" school bag was as swift and effective as a Teddy Roosevelt charge.

"You stupid hyena! Why don't you pick on someone your own size?"

Stunned from Diane's whack and quickly starting to smart from the embarrassment of his moment of glory now darkened by a girl, Greg did not know what to do.

Marge helped. Nothing moved the cantankerous lumberjack-coated bus driver to action more than monkey business.

"Siddown." Her beady bloodshot eyes threatened doom in the overhead mirror.

"Don't make me pull this bus over, er yerl be sorry." Being forced to remove the constant Lucky from her mouth made Marge surly. Marge was one of the few people who scared Greg. This time her remonstrance allowed him to exit what had somehow turned into a humiliating situation.

"You hear me liddlelady? You too big shot."

Diane sat on the seat next to Peter.

"Does it hurt?" She asked with more exasperation than concern. "You shouldn't do that. Ask for it like that."

Peter coddled Diane with his eyes. Boy, he sure was weird.

"I'm suffering like Jesus." As good Catholic children were taught, they bowed their head quickly at the mention of His name.

"I want to be more like Him." Peter bowed. Diane did not think it was necessary to bow for pronouns.

"He-" (Peter nodded.) "-wouldn't ask some jerk to slug him." Diane insisted. "Please wipe your nose. It's starting to look gross." She proffered her hanky.

Peter wiped and the incident was ended. Oh sure Greg was obligated to punch Mark Minor as he strode to the back of the bus. Mark was looking at Greg and therefore an accomplice to Peter. As a result, he was "asking for it" too. For better measure, Greg punched a couple of arms attached to bodies wearing faces he found disagreeable.

Contrary to expectations, Diane would not trumpet Peter's case to the principal. Why bother? Peter would just stand there. Marge? Marge figured a sock in the snout might do the little saint some good.

# 4
## MINOR'S MASS AND NAKED VIRGINS

About the same time that Peter became an altar boy, he started to "say" mass.[28] Not in the church of course. Peter made his efforts at transubstantiation in his bedroom or, in warmer weather, the garage. Real wine and hosts were both out of the question. Peter made do with a parfait glass of Welch's grape juice and a small finger bowl of crisp Ritz crackers.

Ignorant of Church condemnation of the idea, Peter insisted that Diane preside as an altar boy.[29] Sometimes when Peter offered "solemn high mass" Diane served as second priest.[30]

Playing saying mass went on for years on a fairly regular basis of at least once a week. On this particular occasion, Mark was off somewhere sharing an intimate moment with a quartet of Twinkies, leaving Peter and Diane stuck with the forces fit for only a lowly 'low' mass.[31]

With all his real-time experience as an altar boy, Peter had most of the priests' gestures and procedures for the various mass levels down pat. The ceremony, mock or not, was not complete without full adherence to the rituals including those done in the sacristy out of the public eye.

Like an exacting pilot running through the pre-flight checklist, Peter's every movement mimicked the real thing. It was done speedily, but properly. Peter had seen the priests adorn the vestments in preparation to say mass.[32] While he didn't know what Latin pronouncements were uttered during the vestments vesting, he could do a pretty decent Latin mumbo-jumbo.

"Domine consumay auditorium ad quid pro anima, anima meum in eggsus benedictus." He whispered as he put on his terry cloth bathrobe over his shorts and t-shirt. The robe followed code because it was white. Luckily it had buttons, since Peter needed the sash to drape around his neck like an untied tie.

The closest thing to the real thing in the ensemble was a pint-sized chasuble. His grandmother had constructed it for him out of real white silk. She had the presence of mind (She had created it just prior to dipping into senility.) to add two strips of blue forming a cross on the front. Peter draped a thinning hand towel over his wrist and the homemade costume was complete.

Peter's Saint Joseph's Daily Missal had all the Latin words of the mass in it with English translation on the facing page. It just wasn't big enough to give the right effect. The family bible however was plenty big enough. It had wide, solemnly colored ribbons glued into the bindings—permanent bookmarkers —that Peter could dramatically flip back and forth just like the priests did when they were "celebrating."

Mark arrived later than expected from his date with Hostess. His jacket was disheveled and smudged with fresh spring grass stains. His cheeks were rosier than usual. Signs of a struggle?

Mark's father gave him a hair cut every month. He would half drag his son kicking and screaming to the garage and plop him on a stool. Mark's father, totally lacking in any tonsorial talent or patience, would then buzz Mark's head with a set of old electric barber's sheers, which had not been sharpened since he bought them ten years prior. Mark was due for a head mow any day now. He'd have to clean the Twinkie out first. He sheepishly wiped at his hair in response to stares from Peter and Diane.

"I had a little talk with our booger nosed friend, Greg, the Creature from the Black Lagoon. Chee wiz the guy acts like a real Protestant sometimes."

"Did he hurt you?" Diane was always ready to slug someone for Justice.

"Don't say anything or do anything okay? He'll just do something worse later."

"We'll say a prayer for him." Guess who.

"Yeah sure. Let's pray he dies today and goes straight to heck."

"Mark, you used profanity. That's a sin."

"No way! 'Heck's not a sin. Hell maybe."

Diane giggled. Mark figured he had the crowd.

"Listen. Let's just skip the mass, okay? Maybe we could play "Adoration in The Grotto?"

Diane glanced at Peter expectantly.

"After."

It wasn't as if the mass took that long anyway.[33]

Most apparitions occurred in out-of-the-way places in a bucolic setting that included a brook, stream, or-the best-a grotto. The spot Peter, Diane and Mark had chosen was perfect for an apparition though there wasn't really much room for a church. That was probably why Mary remained a no-show.

They staged their apparition in a small clearing in the woods a ways off behind Diane's house. The three snuck along the side of the house and then out through the backyard. They furtively pussyfooted deep into the forest. "Adoration in the Grotto" was a souped up version of "Doctor." So it probably was not a smart idea to alert a lurking parent.

Two or three inches of Mark's wobbly butt cleavage became visible as he led them up and over an embankment. Once on the scene, they undressed quickly. The boys tossed their clothes into the bushes off the path and went to their positions. Diane laid hers out neatly in the sun. Then she mounted her pedestal, a good-sized rock midway up the next incline. She stood, arms raised, palms to the sky in admiration of the warm spring day, her eyes closed, her smile beatific.

Playing one of the shepherds, Mark, a lecher since birth, fell to his knees below her where the view was best. After several summers of this ceremony (held as often as he could instigate) he was still transfixed and fascinated by Diane's lack of a wiener. Her delicate folds mesmerized him. For Mark this was truly a religious experience.

Diane's pose differed somewhat from classic Madonna poses.[34] In addition to being naked, this contemporary virgin, instead of flattening her hands together in prayer, held her delicate digits up to the sky. There was movement too. She caresses the warmth, tickles it with some slightly voodoo/belly dancer-looking arm gestures. There is a grasping quality to her interaction. Simply put, Diane was weird. She still had that Isadora Duncan thing going.

Her face was no lipid reflection of the original model either. Her smile challenged the heat source itself for warmth and sincerity. Never mind the errant bit or two of parsley from today's chicken salad sandwich wedged between her teeth.

The legs were no virgin pose either. The toes were pointing out. Diane was pigeon-toed- no argument there. The condition later corrected itself during ballet lessons. Her legs were spread a little. No. The legs were spread about two feet apart.

Though only a spring chicken barely out of her shell, Diane was proud of her vagina. It would be another ten years until she tripped over the just-right word to describe it: sublime. Further she thought it was neat, made more sense, and was more practical, and OBVIOUSLY more pleasant looking. Not that she thought the boys' peni by comparison were ugly. They were goofy looking. There was a certain winsome meanness to Diane's pose. She was proud of her genitals and wanted to visually rub the boys' noses in it in much the same that she would do so literally when she grew older.

The politics of the matter were lost on Mark. The aesthetics were not. This grand view had come with a good deal of effort on his part. Joyful and slightly smug as she was about her own genitals, Diane was not the first one to suggest running out into the woods and dropping their drawers.

They began this ritual years earlier when they were "just kids." Mark was the culprit behind the original idea and then later the usual instigator. A kernel of respect for women was created when Diane yessed the idea without hesitation. Of course Mark had to talk Peter into it. Peter was under the impression that being naked for anything other than bathing was a mortal sin. Mark and Diane both put him straight on that account easily enough. The fact was though, that Peter, already at an early age, was a sucker for a logically made argument that included a discussion about faith and morals.

"Why don't we just say the rosary with our clothes on?"

"Because, bonehead, about a thousand people a day say the rosary to Mary and she never appears to them. We need to do something that will get her attention. I'll bet you nobody prays to Mary with their clothes off!"

That sold Peter. Diane sat nearby smashing daisy petals between a thumb and finger, smirking.

The religious connotation was a stroke of genius. Since it hinted at holiness, you should do it over and over as often as possible (Or as often as Diane was game.) because it was actually something that would bring you closer to God. So Mark had reasoned successfully.

Was this sexual then? Mark and Peter remained just as flaccid as snoozing snails. There was no denying the excitement though. Mark was transfixed. He was saving the scene for a later time when inspiration was needed. He memorized every detail. He noted every goose-bump and freckle. It was the only time in his life when he would pray the Rosary with sincere reverence. It was a challenge to speak though, since he was nearly dumb with awe at such a flagrant flaunting display of what you just plain normally never got to see. Mark stared so hard his eyes watered.

Unwittingly, Diane was contributing to Mark's appreciation of women. Years later as an adult, Mark was transfixed by a sense of wonder at the sight of any naked woman.

But what about the Holy Roller? Is this any way for a person of future infallibility to behave? Though not the gleeful eroticist to be, like his fellow bean sprouts, Peter was drawn in by religious art and the occasional scandalous glimpse of Eros it offered. Sometimes during class he would sneak his "Lives of the Saints" out of his satchel and just stare at the pictures for as long as he dared.

Of particular interest was Saint Anne. The nun enamored of God and tortured by a false-god worshipping horde of Babelists, or whatevers. He was drawn to the four-color depiction of her standing proudly before the crowd of leering heathens, her veil torn and wimple askew,[35] one shoulder bared (!). Peter would stare at the shoulder and wonder and wonder and wonder some more.

There could be little doubt that on this day there was something sensuous going on though. Adulthood was much closer than they realized. The gentle summer-to-come breeze tickled places usually covered by ready-for-the-hamper clothing. The sun was shining on places were the sun don't normally shine. It exhilarated all three.

Unfortunately, the wind was not hefty enough to wipe the air clean quickly enough when Mark let one rip.

In a wink, Diane's expression changed from Donna Reed to Gidget.

"Ew! Mark!"

"What? A little slice of cheese never hurt anybody."

"Yeah, well, I'm escaping before my skin turns green."

With that Diane turned and clambered up to the top of the hill. Peter followed and settled down next to her on the initially chilling grass. Mark looked at their clothes. He was momentarily concerned they might be swimming too far from the dock. Then not wanting to miss anything he threw caution to the wind and climbed breathily after his two friends.

"Hey. Wait up. I got some Roquefort you might like."

Mark stood above his two reclining friends and surveyed the area for any possible sign of grownups. As producer of this scene, he was more concerned about security. His parents were stricter too. If caught, his punishment would be more painful and prolonged.

After having secured the area (looking around nervously just like Vic Morrow did on the TV show "Combat") Mark plopped down on the other side of Diane. She of course, lay there with legs spread comfortably apart, glorifying in her self and the sun.

"Hey Diane look! Now I'm a girl too." Mark had squished his genitals between his legs.

"You should be so lucky."

He let them pop back out.

"Phew. I'm a boy again."

He pushed them back in between his legs.

"Oh no! I'm a girl again."

Peter and Diane were having no part of Mark. Even without an appreciative audience, Mark refused to be daunted. He continued.

"Ever hear Eddie explain how babies are made?"

That did get a tired glance and a cluck from Diane.

"Eddie, you know Eddie the kid who talks funny?"

"He has a harelip." Diane explained patiently.

"A what?" Mark guffawed. "A harelip?" This was the funniest thing Mark ever heard. He attempted an argument.

"He doesn't even shave yet."

Again the withered glance from Diane.

"A harelip doesn't have anything to do with hair."

"Well why's it called a harelip?"

"I don't know. There's just something wrong with his mouth. His tongue, I think."

"That's for sure." Mark thought about Eddie and his speech impediment for a moment.

"He says Ws for Rs. It's pretty funny. You know Raymond Charlotte? He says 'Way mund'. He was yelling about it on the playground the other day. And he was saying 'Way mund Shah what is a lie ooh. For liar. What a hoot."

"It's not funny Mark. You shouldn't make fun of people who can't talk right. How would you like it?"

"I know. But it's still pretty funny anyway." Sidetracked by the dichotomy the story had taken, Mark almost forgot his original point. Even when it did come floating back to him he decided instead on a different tact. Mark always preferred goading to other forms of communication.

"Hey Peter. I bet you don't know where babies come from."

"From God." That was quicker, more succinct sounding and considerably more difficult to argue than what Mark had anticipated.

"Oh. Yeah. I guess. Sorta." Seeing he had run up against the wall of inerrability, Mark gave up.

"So anyway that's what Eddie was all mad at "Way mund" about. They were having a fight about how babies are made. See the lip isn't the only thing that don't quite work right on old Eddie." Mark took on an amazed conspiratorial tone.

"He thinks a mom and a dad make a baby by rubbing their fannies together. Hah! Ain't that a hoot?

For lack of a response, he concluded.

"So Ray tried to set him straight, and Eddie got all mad and everything."

Mark plunked backed in the grass. It couldn't have been the story. It must have been the audience.

After staring at the clouds, feeling the wind tickle his naked skin, putting his hands behind his head, putting his hands on his stomach and tapping a formless rhythm, Mark became restless. After all, he hadn't said anything for almost fifteen seconds.

The thought that he could be studying Diane instead of staring at the sky tapped him on the shoulder. Rolling over on his side, he pretended to pick at the grass while actually staring at Diane's maturing mound.

"Holy cow! What's that?" An innocent enough question, though not usually when directed at someone's genitals.

Diane raised her head slightly with another annoyed little cluck and looked where Mark was staring: her pubis.

"You know what..." Diane's annoyance trailed off as she witnessed the march of time making tracks between her legs. Her first pubic hairs, like the first greenery all about them, was sprouting daintily. The sun was at just the right angle to highlight the advancing troops below.

"... Oh." she concluded.

"What is it?" Mark insisted incredulously.

"It's hair..." Diane gulped.

28

"Peter look at this. How long has it been there?" Peter leaned up intently on one elbow and joined the inspection. Diane simply swiveled her head back and forth, not comprehending.

"Wow... is it on the inside too?" Mark, ever eager for a closer look was almost believable in this attempt at bewilderment.

Diane slapped him lightly on the arm as she sat up, evidently intent on finding an answer to the question.

"You want some help?" Mark was just so considerate.

"No I think I can manage."

Gently Diane separated her lips as all three bent down for a close look.

"Mark! You're blocking my light."

"Oh sorry." Mark quickly accommodated.

"I don't see anything. It seems to be just around the top part."

"What about the inside?"

Mark was very pleased that the thoroughness of his concern led Diane to cautiously insert her middle finger. She moved it down towards her perineum then twisted it around and slid it up the other side. She was back at the top, started to take her finger out, then instead pushed it back all the way inside.

"Oh..."

"Find something?"

"Sort of..." Diane exhaled deeply then removed her finger.

"What did you find? Are you okay? You look kinda funny."

"Never mind Mark."

"Wow look at Peter's Peter. Peter's got a boner!"
Sure enough, there it was: several stoic inches of propagation bursting at the seams.

"Wow, Peter. Talk about wood! That's a whole lumberyard!"

Certainly confused and nearly paralyzed by his first intimate arousal, Peter barely managed to shake his head. Getting up and leaving would only lead to a display of prominence. Staying where he was kept him on display as well.

Sensing his discomfort, Diane broke things up.

"Let's just lay in the sun."

It had never openly occurred to them that they were doing something wrong with these naked frolics. But there was always some type of danger of something lurking over the proceedings. Even Mark was quick to comply. Though, thanks to Diane's innate wisdom they realized that some type of line had been crossed.

"Phew. I need a cigarette."

Diane turned, a lazy smile tinged by the hair falling across her face. A characteristic gesture: she wiped it back behind her ear.

"You smoke cigarettes?"

"Oh yeah. All the time." Mark shrugged.

"I get em from Marge." Marge, in her attempts to keep a butt glowing at all times, wound up littering the bus floor around the driver's seat with fallouts. It made for easy pickings for Mark and the other scavengers.

As may be gleamed already, Mark never needed more than the hint of encouragement for anything. Quickly, his chubby body bounced down the hill. He scrounged his shorts then puffed back up and plopped down

"It kind of got busted." Mark offered the half Lucky, one tip shredded.

"It'll light easier this way."

Mark stuck the butt about half way into his mouth. Where to strike his kitchen match was more a slight inconvenience than a problem. Mark wandered around grazing the grass with his toes until he found a rock. He plopped down.

"Phew! Bad habits are exhausting."

He still had the torn fag in his mouth as he struck the match successfully against the rock. Then, like any true novice, he removed the Lucky from his mouth and held it to the match. The shreds took fire.

"Oh good. Sometimes it takes awhile."

He lay back beside Diane and held the cigarette at arms length.

"Aren't you going to smoke it?"

"You want to try it first?"

"No. You go ahead. I'll watch."

Mark brought the smoldering butt to his lips.

"Ahh. Pretty good."

"I think you're supposed to inhale. Not blow on it."

A glowing spark of ash fell off the tip. It startled Mark and Diane.

"Maybe you better put it out before you start the whole woods on fire."

"Yeah, well just one more puff. I really need it."

Mark inhaled. Not using the usual traditional smokers method of drawing the smoke into the mouth and inhaling from there, he pulled it directly into his lungs. The terror of his retch was that whether inhaling or exhaling the toxic sour smoke still clawed his windpipe. Gasping and wheezing, he finally had no choice but to cough. And cough some more, until tears came to his eyes and spit to his lips. Eventually he got it all out.

"Wanna drag?"

"No. Thank you."

"Okay. I'll save the rest for later."

"Diane!"

Her mother's shout from a distance brought instant terror. Like unfortunate deer caught in the blazing headlights, like the owl's "who?" at the snap of a twig, the rabbits went scurrying for cover. Back behind a fragrant burl berry bush, they pressed against each other cowering.

"Diane?" The voice was inquisitive with an undertone of warning.

Peter still had a boner of course. He was on both knees. Diane had somehow crouched back into him. Diane looked at Peter. She smiled. The smile was painted with excitement, fear, and tinged with a softness he did not understand. Peter ejaculated into the grass.

"Diane!" a little more insistent as she drew closer, Diane's mother came into view but stopped stock still some distance away. There in plain as day view strewn along the path were puffs of underwear, socks, shoes, a shirt and jeans.

"You guys wait here." Before they could respond Diane was up and casually sauntering towards her mother.

"Hi Mom! What are you doing here?"

"Diane-?" Her mother struggled briefly to disguise her response at her child now just sort of hippity hopping towards her. Naked.

Mark and Peter could make out no more of their conversation than a stressed word here and there.

"... doing ... clothes? Someone..."

As part of her full frontal attitude assault, Diane marched towards the head of the path. She was headed for her clothes up near the grotto rock. In doing so she steered her Mother away from the boy's clothing.

She stepped daintily into her underwear, and then before casually putting on her blouse and shorts, said something stern to her mother.

Mrs. Gillette brought one hand to her mouth, and turned ever so slightly away from her daughter. Was this a display of embarrassment? Shame? Sure looked like it.

Diane laced her shoes tersely. She seemed to be bawling out her mother, whose shoulders now slumped. Her arms, previously akimbo, now hung limply at her sides.

Mark and Peter watched in wonder as Diane led her mother back down the path. It took Mark and Peter several minutes to recover. Eventually they dressed and skeedaddled. Peter still had a boner.

# 5

## PETER PEERS OVER THE PYRO PRECIPICE

Two weeks later Mark, Diane, and their families moved out of town. Both their Fathers had been laid off from different accounting offices (one receivable, one payable) at the American Motors facility in Livonia as the company struggled to avoid going belly up. They, like many of their fellow "Rambler" car company employees and families, scattered to other jobs with other companies in other areas of the country.

There was no big farewell scene between Peter and Diane. At the exact moment Diane and her family were driving across the state line, Peter and his mother were at Hudson's shopping for shoes in the Budget Basement. Diane was more excited about going somewhere new than she was upset about leaving. Peter was more excited about his new black Oxfords with the ripple soles (just like Father Pablo's!)

This is not to say that they were not affected by what happened that day. Whether or not some sort of special bond had developed among the three remained to be seen.[36]

There was an exchange between Peter and Mark: more of a confession actually. The two were just sort of talking. Mark scuffed at the sandy driveway outside his house. His toes drew meaningless designs. Mark stared at the ground for the most part, darting a glance at Peter from time to time as he tried to explain that he had "lost his vocation" so he would not be joining Peter at the seminary and because of admission deadlines would be attending the public high school instead. For a young Catholic in those days going to a public school instead of one run by Catholics was a lot like hitchhiking on the Highway to Hell.

"Anyways, I'm pretty sure I lost it. I just keep having dirty thoughts. I don't think a priest is supposed to think like that. And dreams too... I been having some ... really good dreams lately."

"Mark. God is always with us. But so is the devil. The bad thoughts will go away."

The truth and sincerity of what Mark said next, sealed his friendship with Peter for life. In spite of his penchant for religious pomposity, Peter was a sucker for truth.

"I don't want them to go away."

It also planted a little negligible niggling seed inside Peter's head. They both smiled. Then Peter's face creased with a frown. As far as he was concerned, there was nothing anyone should be but a priest.

"But what else could you be?" He projected.

"I thought it might be kinda neat to drive a truck."

"Will you still be a Catholic?" Somehow Peter equated truck drivers with non-Catholics.

Peter's question inspired a good deal of head scratching and ear digging from Mark. He was squirming with an even more difficult confession.

"I think I'm 'fallen–away.'"[37] I kinda… sorta…started…" Mark focused on the tree branch above them. The leaves slapped playfully at the sunlight. Nature reminded him of that day—the day—of the Last Adoration of the Virgin. Intoxicated briefly by the memory to the point of developing a chub, he continued.

"I kinda started jacking off. Not that much. You know, four or five times a day."

"Did you confess?"

"Oh right! To Father P.O?" Mark followed that with a self-conscious shrug. "Besides, I can't find it in the book. The confession book they gave us in second grade? Doesn't say anything about slamming the salami."

That was a good one. Peter was none too sure about how to confess it either. Not that it was anything he would have to consider for himself.

"It might be under 'Thou shalt not commit adultery.'"

"No. I think that's when you do it while you're married. Hey if it's not in the book then maybe it's not a sin."

Mark felt himself getting perilously close to starting a discussion about his masturbation motivation. He brought it to an end.

"So I guess I am 'fallen away.' I don't really feel any different. Funny. I mean I still go to church. But it's starting to get kinda boring."

"So you're not going to the seminary?" Peter referred to Dun Scotus Seminary in Southfield, Michigan. This was the high school Petri dish for priests to be. Both he and Mark had sent away for the catalogue. They marveled over pictures of the numerous little shrines on the campus. Around every corner and behind every bush lurked an invitation to be pious and prayerful.

Mark had been impressed with the cafeteria. One glossy picture featured an unabashedly chubby white-habited nun ladling some lumpy red concoction on to an equally anonymous and chubby seminarian's plate. At the time, this had thoroughly saturated his Friar Tuck ambitions.

"Eh… well … I guess I don't really have to decide right now." Mark evaded.

Peter had sent his application immediately after receiving the catalogue. He filled it out before looking at the brochures. He would go regardless of what heaven looked like. The affirmative response was quick.

Mark had demurred. Though his insistence that he had to talk to his parents about it was bogus—they would have packed his bags for him—an excuse for not doing something is not always readily available. Is it?

Peter did not need to be hit over the head with a brick. Mark's soul was a goner. Perhaps as a portent of wiser days to come, Peter also realized that it was Mark's decision to make and not his.

"You've been a good friend."

"It's not like I'm gonna die!" "Jeez! Hey cool shoes! Just like Father P.O.'s."

So. They sat under that early summer tree, one carefully deleting smudges from his new Oxfords, the other grinding ants with his bare heel.

This kid who would grow up to be a fisher of men was, as a kid, lousy at making friends. Eighth-graders intuitively understand that some one lost in prayer is not going to score many runs.

Though truly holier than thou, or anyone else with the exception of Jesus, Peter was not immune to the ungodly thought. Though he was steadfast and sincere in his spiritual ambition, he did receive a jolt that he perceived as leaving him leaning over the precipice, dangling over the open slavering jaws of the dark abyss itself. He had a sexual fantasy.[38]

Sister Juleen was born to give meaning to the word exuberant. She danced and flirted with the joys of life and her love of God. Small wonder our little Peter would become enamored.

35

Normally an attentive, excellent student, Peter went a step further with Juleen. He would sit chin in hand, elbow on his desktop, fascinated by every little detail she had to say in History class.

"The mission of Christopher Columbus was a mission of Christ and the church," she exclaimed fervently, her hands pressed passionately to her bosom.

With a little pirouette, she turned and bounced over to Greg (the impudent monster was always made to sit in the front. Peter and other well-behaved children sat towards the rear: a position of trust. Bad kids were up front so the teacher could keep an eye on them and to offer a more accessible reach for yanking ears or whacking knuckles with a ruler)

Juleen affected all the boys, including Greg, the local pipsqueak-punching barrister of evil. Though far from gaga, he would pay attention to Juleen. Instead of fly leg-pulling or intimidating other students he would look at the Sister. See? Sometimes it is a good thing for males to think with their testicles.

"Isn't that right, Greg?" How does someone more pure than Ivory soap manage such a simple, straightforward, seductive smile?

Scrunching his furry eyebrows, unsure if this was a trick question Greg, a bit stupid, but a cynic nonetheless, plunged forward recklessly.

"Wasn't he after… gold and stuff? I saw this movie…" Greg sensed his own hand tightening a noose around his neck. He trailed off with a shrug of indifferent embarrassment.

The diminutive Juleen pressed into his desk at upper thigh level. She did that a lot. She put her hand on his head then took her sweet, sympathetic understanding and rubbed his nose in it.

"But Columbus was Catholic wasn't he?" She toyed with him. En masse the class imagined her twirling their hair with her finger.

Greg's ears burned crimson. Similar color splotches formed on his cheeks. The rat cornered still refused to give the cat what she wanted.

"He was killing Indians and… stuff…" His stammer ended with something between a giggle and a whine. Though making a valid, historic point, the great Greg was about to see this sublime sexless seductress chew up his ideas and spit them out. He shivered in anticipation.

"It is true that they did defend themselves against savage attacks." She consoled. Her hand still raising the fever on Greg's head, Sister looked up at the rest of the class. Her smile graced the pound of puppies, each one eager to please, lick a hand, wag a tail.

"Peter?" At that age he preferred Pete, but Sister Juleen could call him anything she darned well pleased. Especially when *that* look came into her eyes. She straightened, held her hands in a light and fluffy gesture of prayer. Oh, she made holiness look like fun!

Peter stood. He always stood promptly when teachers called upon him. The good little soldier looked at her expectantly, respectfully.

"Was that right for Columbus and his men to defend themselves?"

"I'm not sure, Sister."

She melted. This angel melted her. This sweet boy, she knew he was already accepted to the seminary, this little tadpole priest, so cute, so darling, so adorable, and so *sincere* with this doubt.

"Why is that, Peter?" They were two lovers whispering, sharing a fear–shrouded intimacy. The church, the only vestige of what is right in the world… was this holy child about to find a chink in its infallible armor; an Achilles heal opposite end of the God Head; the Holy Trinity missing a marble?

She knew he was special, even approached a fancy that he was headed for something grand. And weren't the saints, especially, pursued by the most serious doubt, only to be made stronger by it? Yes, this poor girl, intellectually raped so young by her own modest innocent prayers was still subject to the ultimate demon: thinking.

"What about turning the other cheek?" He offered it simply, without challenge.

Inwardly the class gasped. Wow! What a good one! By a long shot, this beat the pants off "How many angels can dance on the head of a pin?"

There is a perception that these knuckle-whacking penguin brides of Christ were not receptive to confrontation, especially of the sort that challenged The Church. But Peter's query was so lacking in aggression that Juleen responded more to the form than content.

Like the chorus in a local opera production, Peter's classmates swiveled their heads back to Juleen. How would the

Queen of the Night respond to Sarastro's suggestion? Only Papageno (that would be Greg) tooted a brief tune in the midst of that otherwise dense, shocked, excited silence. He snickered. Then cowered pridefully.

Juleen smiled. The class at-eased without breaking ranks and actually relaxing. She faced him with something like admiration. Something like it.

J.F.K. was barely cold under his eternal flame. In those days, a woman who has sworn off earthly pleasures: money, sex and the right to question, does not admire an eight-grader. Not normally.

Juleen though, bloated with God's love, was also lean and hungry for life. Young and dedicated then, eventually, the lack of satisfaction from pressing herself against desks would lead her to find different methods to scratch her itch.

But there she was that day, the sanctified spin exposed as so much half-baked potato. She was thrilled. If secreting vaginal fluids were a method of physically displaying intellectual excitement, her cotton would be coated.

"That is a very good question, Peter."

The class sighed inwardly. Of course Mr. Goody–Goody wouldn't get his holy fanny in trouble.

"Maybe you should ask Father Pablo about it when he comes in to class for religion on Thursday."

"Yes, Sister."

"Please be seated, Peter."


It was a Tuesday just days before Peter and his fellow eighth–graders were to graduate. There was choir practice after school, which Juleen conducted from the organ.[39] Peter's responsibilities as head choirboy included setting out the music before rehearsal.

As he did so, Juleen climbed onto the bench set before the massive organ[40] with its display of stops and three keyboards. She reached underneath to throw the power switch.

At the back of the choir loft the pump and bellows slowly groaned to life. Juleen practiced silent scales as she waited for her beloved monster to come to life.

Bach was not allowed during any type of church service. Though dead for centuries, while alive, old J.S. was a Lutheran, and the church, setting aside its forgiving nature, could hold a grudge. But right now, save sister and pope-to-be, the church was vacant. No witnesses. It was time to be naughty.

Venting the pipes full, Juleen wailed into the famous D Minor Prelude.

"Nee yuh NEEE!! The opening mordent's Lon Chaney imagery smeared the stain glass beneath them with musical godlessness. By the time she laid out the fully diminished seventh chord the pews were rumbling and the very hosts stored in the tabernacle wilted.

A congregation can never fully appreciate the physical power of a grand pipe organ without having stood in its loft in close proximity to the bank of pipes. The whole body vibrates. The senses are overwhelmed to near numbness. Organs have been known to drive its driver giddy with musical power.

Peter quickly finished dealing out the sheet music, walking on waves of sound the whole time. He edged slowly to the grand console and then leaned against it as he watched Juleen play.

A short woman, Juleen would stretch like a rack victim to reach the needed foot pedal notes. Like most every musician, both talented and un-, she relished performing those facial and bodily contortions they all seem so fond of doing.

The only light in the dark loft came from the music stand lamp. Her kind, youthful, feminine features accepted its challenging glare gracefully.

"Me nomey nomey nomey nomey nomey…"

She pattered her way competently through the fugue, but then stopped suddenly. Stretching for the foot pedals of the Prelude had stretched the skirt of her habit restrictively, making it difficult to reach some of Bach's far–flung bass notes.[41]

With both hands, she swiped at her skirt bunching it loosely up on her thighs exposing her legs from just above the knees down. She smiled as Peter watched.

The sight of her inelegant brown dress moving up her legs, her hands sliding along her thighs were real. The thought that snuck into Peter's imagination was the sensation of those hands, delicate yet expressive sliding–now–in slow motion along those silken thigh highways. The flesh firm yet giving, the skin glistening with silken sensations waiting to be given.

Peter closed his eyes. With a brief glance away from her music, Juleen saw, and then smiled again. This wonderful boy was so obviously moved, even by a heretic like Bach! They were doing something evil together.

Closing his eyes only made matters worse. In the dark fetid world of self, her hands—Wait! What happened to her sleeves?!—

Ended at naked arms. Tiny delicate black hairs decorated the flesh of her forearms.

Peter opened his eyes but it made no difference. He was trapped in his fantasy.

The hairs lightened to white as they crept invitingly to her bare (!) shoulder. Her wimple had previously, gratefully, covered her luxurious mane. But now untapped the dishwater blond was strewn about like so much fresh soapsuds.

It exploded from her head in a lewd mesmerizing mess. Curls like shrapnel, lay about her gently jutting collarbone, wounding him with their lustrous and dangerous frivolity.

The granny glasses also evaporated and her eyes flashed like brown diamonds. Her nostrils flared with the phrasing of the music, her lips mouthed a secret unanswerable question: What would it be like to kiss KISS these. Kiss these.

The top lip was a seductively splayed V exposing the white glistening teeth and beyond… a magic tongue.

No. He shouldn't look! Peter whimpered to himself. But what difference did it make? The rest was sitting right before him. He had only to look down.

The breasts, real woman's breasts, with the same lustrously soft skin as the thighs, were small and almost fat–boyish. In reality Juleen was a bit stacked, but what did Peter know about boobs and how a woman could dress to hide them?

His fantasy continued its seductive flight across her flat firm tummy, desperately grabbing on to that navel like the hem of the Blessed Virgin herself.

"Stop Peter! Stop! Don't look! Don't look!" Must have been the little angel sitting on his right shoulder.

Tearing himself away from the organ (literally the mechanical one and figuratively the one made of earthly, sin–inducing flesh) he half–stumbled to the edge of the choir loft balcony. Desperately, he grabbed the railing and looked below.

The floor was just closing, but Peter did not fail to see below him the gaping chasm filled with flailing flame-broiled souls. Their unanswered screams—screams of despair, screams of the most terrified fear, screams of accusation—echoed then faded slowly, too slowly before gratefully fading.

The screams were gone about the same time the music finished. Peter abruptly, but politely, excused himself. He walked quickly to the rectory across the street, knocked on the door, and then waited patiently in the library for one of the priests to show.

40

Father Pablo got older and frailer by the minute. At that point in time he was pretty much just waiting around to die. He did not like to be disturbed from his afternoon nap, or for that matter, his morning or evening naps either. With eating and bodily functions an embarrassment, sleeping was his only pleasure.

"What do you want boy?"

"I have to confess a sin, Father."

Father Robert stared at Peter. The geriatric's jaw, usually open anyway, moved up and down a little.

"You're forgiven. Go and sin no more." He waved a papery-skinned Sign of the Cross in Peter's general direction, turned and began to shuffle back upstairs to his bed.

Not that Peter would ever *not* accept the credibility of any priest's forgiveness, but he had expected maybe a little sermon and a penance to fit the sin. The priest had assigned no penance, no punishment. Peter had not even told him what the sin was!

"But Father. I had an unclean thought." That didn't quite tell the whole tale. " I had a lot of unclean thoughts. All together."

Father Robert stopped. He stood stock-still. Not that he wasted many movements now a days.

"Do you bowl?" He turned slightly to face the boy.

"No father."

"Take up bowling. It'll take your mind off dirty thoughts." That was the same thing a priest had told Father P.O. ages ago when he made the same confession. The advice had worked marginally well.

"Yes, Father."

That is how Peter's bowling habit became so deeply engrained. He cut back a little on prayer and instead hiked to the bowling alley. His parents gladly gave him the money. They knew that since day one he had been dropping his weekly allowance in the "Peter's Pence"[42] box in the vestibule of the church.

Bowling also distracted his young, impressionable mind from facing the truth. The fantasy had made him feel good. Worse. It had felt right.

# 6
## SEMINARY BLOWS

Peter spent twelve years training to be a priest. This was no truck driving school. While at Duns Scotus[43] Seminary in Southfield, Michigan, he climbed mountains of philosophy and theology, crossed the barren deserts of literature and nearly drowned in the rivers and streams of Latin and Greek. There were no short cuts. Seminarians did not take crash courses in anything. When they graduated, they might still be fools, but at least they would be educated fools.

The course wound its way through four years of high school seminary, then four years of college then four years as a novice. It ground to a halt at The Big Day: Ordination: Holy Orders.

Prior to seminary, Peter had never been much of a chatty Charlie. Since when do angels yack? He was quiet as the proverbial church mouse and unassuming as one too. That changed drastically for a short period during his second year in seminary where a dramatic event brought him back to his prayerfully dulled senses.

Temporary, but true, Peter got cocky.

The period of explosive pimples and penises is never a pleasant period for any post-pubescent puck. No woman alive, dead, or yet born could ever imagine what it is like waking up every morning with a boner.[44]

You just try it! Morning after morning that blanket made into a tent by something so hard you could drive nails with it. Often times hard to the point of pain, it also seems clogged and ached with the need to explode. Not only in the morning, but also at noon and night and every waking minute in between, Mr. Johnson proudly waves a reckless, predictable propensity for rearing his head at the most inappropriate moment.

Most lads dive reckless and confused head first into the quicksand of testosterone. Seminarians, on the other hand, tiptoed precariously along the edge occasionally/unfortunately for some dipping just the edge-just a Canadian inch of toenail-into that squalid miasma.

Sex sucked in many a seminarian only to eventually spit him out into the real world. However, the honest reason was rarely stated. The need to satiate sexual desire was an obvious sign of weakness. How could anyone say aloud "I relinquished the opportunity to serve Christ-the part human part God guy- who allowed Himself to be NAILED TO A CROSS AND DIE-because my pee-pee wanted a nice place to park it?" More likely, the mumbled reason to astonished teachers and family was the cryptic "I lost my vocation." Nobody argued that one. If God can call someone, he can just as easily hang up.

Father Kirk offered an alternative to the sexless vow of the celibate. Simple. Break the rule silly!

Father Kirk taught religion, Latin and Greek. The appearance of Peter in Kirk's class reaffirmed the latter's belief in the existence of a supreme being, albeit one with Hellenic sensitivities. Peter stumbling over declensions was so provocative!

Kirk was a good decade ahead of his time when it came to being "out" with his homosexuality. No, it was not something he would actually utter or ever openly allude to. Hints though, were nasty fun.

Kirk teased the straight (Ha! Straight? Ha! They were celibates for Chrisakes! Ha!) with their own discomfort of him. He loved to dance and flit around them. Feel the repulsion when he touched a hand a little too long. Just a finger or two on a wrist for Chrisakes! Look at Father Squeamish squirm!

Kirk preferred them young, but not necessarily illegal. So, the only problem at the seminary was being forced to occasionally exercise a little restraint. Kirk would be the first to insist that he had no victims. His prior "attendants" (as he chuckled to himself during reveries of pals past) were "that way" or, on a few rarer occasions, "headed in that general direction."[45]

Kirk knew he was not the only religious person whose vocation was inspired by sexual preference (or initiation). Kirk loved the chance to surround himself with men: the smell of them or "flavors" he would muse. Discovering they were on his team never ceased to delight him.

Kirk was patient. He enjoyed his conquests. (Conquests! Ha! The Ancient Greek Wars should have been so easy.) There were exceptions to that and Peter was one of them. Kirk considered himself a decent spotter. With Peter though, he began to think he might have been beating his head into a brick wall. Peter, like the wall, being a bit thick (Oblivious is more like it!) when it came to understanding that he was an object of desire.

Kirk quivered off in the bushes like a wild beast with pulse pounding, ready to pounce then devour the gazelle. Yet he remained patient because he had convinced himself that Peter would eventually be his. Kirk was rarely wrong.

It was during Peter's junior year that Kirk's antsiness led to recklessness.

In the seminary, Peter's religion began to make more sense to him than it ever had during childhood. As a kid, floating, wispy, invisible angels and stories of gutted, headless saints, ear-twisting nuns and fear guided his spiritual view of the world. In the seminary, he discovered urges dictated by his developing intellect. He needed to understand. He uncovered answers-albeit Catholic versions.

Those insatiable adolescent energies corroborated the dogma with fawning teenage intensity. This humble pie bubbled with reasons why the Catholic Church was superior. God and Christ were The Big Cheese and Peter by association was exalted.

Peter was not and never would be comfortable with a know-it-all role. That is no way for a pope to-be to be and there is no doubt that was the way he was not. There was one brief exception when Peter's innate humility swerved. The rubber hit the road and Peter skidded a bit. Of course Kirk was involved.

Peter's elevated testosterone level grabbed his erect and throbbing faith and stroked it. Suddenly - more than simply believing - his faith made so much sense. Faith satiated every concern. The power of truth ignited his oily passions.[46]

During this time, Peter had friends, good friends, close friends. Three friends. True friends. As friends are wont to do, they both distracted him from and immersed him into himself. The four spent every minute they could together. Walking down the musty seminary halls, often they could be heard excitedly and emphatically debating some finer theological point. If there had been girls at Duns Scotus Seminary they would have looked at Peter, Vincent, Al and Frank and giggled.

The rest of their classmates referred to the four as "The Perfect Priests." The other clique was called "The Romans" an appellation resulting from their arrogant sinning and a predictably grim future salvation-wise. "Perfect Priests" took their vocations seriously. The others took their vocations for granted and often to the bank.

The former prayed slowly and with thoughtful reverence. Everything they did was a prayer of thanks to God.

"Thank you God for this flower" and "Thank you God for this glass of water" and "Thank you God for this old worn out toothbrush" and "Thank you God for this hangnail." They could say stuff like that and actually mean it.

For the most part, P.P.s found the seminary a Mecca where they could revel in the spirituality for which kids back home snickered. They did not need to die. They were already in Heaven.

Religion literally lined the walls. The cafeteria displayed a huge replica of The Last Supper. Full-sized statues filled cutout shrines every twenty feet in every hall. It was either coincidental ignorance or someone with a sense of irony who decided to put a statue of Saint Albinus, patron saint of those who suffer from kidney ailments, in the bathroom off the sophomore dormitory. Leave it to Peter to make the connection immediately.

It was also part of the tradition that after ordination, "The Romans," the delinquents from Christ-like behavior, were usually more popular with their congregations. They wasted little effort with the effrontery of holiness. Instead, they would race through the mass ceremony at a rate to make the prayers incomprehensible.[47] P.P.s on the other hand, would constantly be on the lookout for new words to stress and therefore inspire.

Romans told jokes during their sermons. Attendance was required. That was bad enough. No need to drag a worship service out all day and make the congregation suffer any more than it had to suffer already.

They were fun to have at wedding or funeral receptions because they would surprise and delight celebrators and mourners alike with a tremendous capacity for belting booze.

While the Romans participated in frequent circle jerks, the P.P.s bowled. The bowling alley lanes-all two of them-were in the unheated basement of Duns Scotus.

"They should not even be in the seminary. They should be learning how to pour concrete or install toilets." Frank shouted from the roost at the end of the alley. The pinsetter was a hotly contested position of humility. Of course the alleys were not automated. The alley was a necessity, not a luxury.

Peter was an exceptional bowler. Oddly, he was not a very good bowler. Yes, he could throw strikes and plenty of them. The shortcoming of his talent was that if he did not knock down all of the pins he would not knock down any. Strike. Gutter ball. Strike. Gutter ball. Strike, strike, gutter ball, gutter ball, then, perhaps as yet another example of Christ-like generosity, another gutter ball.

Peter, grim with a sportsman's concentration, readied to follow his last smashereeno with a sizzling pair of zips.

"Maybe we should pray for them?" suggested Al? Who spoke everything as a question? It was a habit he had picked up from Peter but carried to a homicide-inducing extreme.

"I've prayed for them until my lips were chapped." Said Frank.

"What should we do, Peter?" Al asked?

Instead of rolling his ball, Peter set it down. Frank abandoned his post. More than humility, he enjoyed a good philosophical discussion. They all drew up chairs to the scoring desk. The chairs were dilapidated school desks that for lack of a better place were being stored in the bowling alley. The musty long low-ceilinged hall echoed with the scrape of metal legs against the concrete abutment to the lanes.

Peter sat up straight in his chair, cupped one elbow in the other hand, which he put pensively to his cheek. So did Al? Hanging on a wall nearby, the picture of Saint Charles Boremeo also seemed to be expecting an answer.[48]

"We can set an example." Peter said. The others sensed it to be an incomplete thought and so waited. "Didn't Pope Pius XI say priests are another Christ? Or a continuation of Christ?"

"But actually, since we are not priests, since we have not been ordained, we are not really that." Frank, Mr. Technicality, interjected.[49]

"We're not ordained yet Frank. But shouldn't we get ready now?" Guess.

The basic antagonism between P.P.s and Romans existed in relative subterfuge at the seminary. The priests and brothers who ran Duns Scotus knew about it because they had either witnessed it or been a part of it during their training. So when things got too out of hand, all the current bands needed to do was figure out who was a former P.P. or Roman and squeal accordingly. Unfortunately, the sitting P.P.s did not yet realize this.

"He touched me." Vincent whispered.

The other three sat, stunned, not only that this could happen, but that Vincent would confess it. They were pals, but the friendship revolved around a nerdy obsession with their religion, not body talk.

"Who? Where?" Frank easily the bravest.

"Who else? The Emperor. Charlton." Tears filled Vincent's eyes though he seemed, oddly to the others, strengthened by the admission. "He pulled my- he grabbed me by the-"

Peter dropped his cheek and leaned forward slightly. So did Al? Every attorney needs evidence so Frank pressed onward indelicately.

"What did you do?"

"I prayed."

"Good. You prayed that was good."

"Not exactly. We were in the showers-well by the sinks. I was reaching for my robe and he pulled off my towel. And the other Romans were standing around watching. He started being a jerk saying- "Do you Perfect Priests ever get boners?" That was a big joke. Ha ha. Everybody laughed.

"Then he- grabbed my-it-and pulled… it. I had my eyes closed then because I was praying to the Blessed Virgin for deliverance. Then I became- I got- you know when you get up in the morning?"

A trio of understanding heads nodded.

"I. It." Vincent looked down then back up. His face contorted with failure. There was anger too. "Squirted."

It should be noted that up until that point at least, none of the P.P.s masturbated. All but Vincent had experienced occasional nocturnal emissions. Vincent had brief dreams of an indefinable but obviously sexual nature. He would manage to wake himself up as soon as the level of steam elevated and just before the boiler could alert the blow-off valve.

What Vincent did not know was that Charlton was a regular jerk-off champion. He would brag about it and was the usual instructor for incoming freshman.

Nobody was more surprised than Charlton though, with Vincent's immediate eruption. Charlton's intent (If a brainless slug can actually be capable of such.) as he approached that "little pimply chicken turd" was to just grab those pathetic excuses for family jewels and give 'em a condescending twist or two. Oops.

47

Charlton was not halfway into his tug when Vincent's microscopic wiener unfurled to its fully masted two inches. The pud-puller had expected resistance, or at least, that the pinpecker would move away. Anybody with balls would. Of course, with Vincent's passive nature, that was not going to happen.

The first copious gob blasted out toward the end of the second stroke and landed on the chest of one of the Romans six feet away. The bully realized and halted his unintended milk shake making. Charlton drew his underhanded assistance away just as Vincent's joystick released an astonishing four-inch in diameter bubble into his hand. It actually made a noise. "Skurggle."

Vincent withheld these details. For him, it was a great enough effort just to relate the essentials.

The P.P.s sighed. Frank figured retaliation.

"That has to be a mortal sin. We should get him kicked out of the seminary."

The silence that greeted Frank's suggestion also eventually buried it.

"There's strength in numbers? Maybe if we quit serving early mass? We could shower at the same time together?" Al's idea was not bad. However, it is amazing how easily a wimpy presentation can deflate the best of plans.

Vincent was less concerned about the future than the past. Presently, he looked directly at Peter.

"I committed a sin. Didn't I?"

Frank and Al began to admonish Vincent for even considering such a thing. He the victim of a bully. How ridiculous! Charlton's behavior was downright devious. Vincent was more like a martyr. They should call Rome! Tell them to start the paperwork for sainthood!

Their mouths were still flapping away chastising Vincent for his silly thoughts when they noticed Peter apparently was not with them on this one.

"Did you enjoy it?" Not even Peter knew where that question came from. It probably had something to do with reading several missives, which stated that sex is so tempting because it is so enjoyable.

Vincent flushed quicker than he had ejaculated. The rush of blood to skin's surface indicted and convicted him. Al and Frank's eyebrows arched in surprise before settling into Catholic judgment.

"Does that mean he's a hameosexual?" queried the ever-curious Al.

"Don't be dolf. It's homeosexual." Frank was also studying German.

Vincent bobbed his head in morbid acquiescence.

"I've sinned. I could never confess this. I have sinned. I am going to hell. I cannot confess this. Oh I am going straight to hell." He trailed off, feeling the flames lick as surely as he experienced what felt like the uselessness of his existence. His spilling tears crushed Al and Frank into weighty silence.

Peter stood, walked to the parquet platform, tiptoed his approach and threw another gutter ball. He was not buying any of the guilt part. Peter believed in Jesus, not judgment. This type of thinking may inspire a big, yawning so-what nowadays until it is remembered that this was years before homosexuality was considered acceptable behavior.[50] Peter was about to learn a lesson or two, too.

"Talk to Father Kirk." What an astonishing thing for Peter to say! Although the four were dense as bowling balls when it came to gay activity, complete duhs all, they were not blind! Father Kirk was sort of swishy. They would be lying to deny it. P.P.s were not blind to overhearing things. Just because they turned a deaf ear to gossip does not mean they would not hear anything with the other one.

"Why talk to Father Kirk? Won't he just try to talk him into...?" Pretty good question and a half, actually, from Al no less.

"There will be a greater reward in Heaven for a greater challenge faced and conquered. The truth of Christ will win out. Always. What would have happened if Christ had given in to His own weakness and fear in the Garden of Gethsemane? Instead, He accepted the chalice filled with his own blood and faced fear. He conquered fear and the death that is sin. His Heavenly Father offered His Son no escape. Vincent. Can you do any less?" Well. You know. If you are going to put it that way.

Vincent and Peter stood face to face not a foot apart. Peter finished with a hand on Vincent's shoulder. His friend. A very sincere gesture for both. Warmth and conviction radiated from the hand. In that moment of exalted personal drama, Vincent fooled himself into imagining he was some kind of obedient soldier. In reality, Peter was marching the chicken out to meet the fox.

Peter fooled Vincent. Unintentionally of course. If Vincent had maintained his wits about him, he may have sensed the

49

obvious. He was certainly smart enough to realize that the older, smarter guy, Father Kirk, was queer. He began to feel a little queer, as he began to look forward to it. Maybe instead he should just go to confession and forget about it. Maybe the anonymous confessor will offer another solution more effective than bowling. Like billiards.

However, Vincent did not think for himself. Such is the power of leadership. Into the valley of buttered buns rode the six hundred.

***

Kirk fried other fish as he waited for the right time to hook Peter. There were plenty of other options. Actually, Duns Scotus was a pond fairly well stocked with gay boys. Occasionally the priest would encounter a rutting stallion who would clumsily exploit Kirk's reputation with shy, slyness. Sometimes a doe-eyed dear showed up unexpectedly at his door. One day it was Vincent.

The main chapel at Duns Scotus was almost big enough to qualify for cathedral status. A soft cough would echo. The main altar stood with garish, thunderously heavy formality front and center. This "priest's workbench" was solid marble with the exception of a space, about the size of a breadbox, dead center on the top surface. In this cutout was another slab of marble a little smaller than a breadbox with another cutout dead center. In that cutout, no bigger than a hot cross bun rested an ornately decorated glass case trimmed in gold and lined with satin. Inside it: a bit of the body of Saint Anthony of Padua. Really. A splinter of bone no more than a thirty-second of a toothpick but still a first-class relic.[51]

Peter stared at it. This was as close as a person could get to a saint and still be alive.[52]

He had just stripped the altar of its linen coverings, and he always took this moment to look at the bone lying there teeny tiny on its teeny tiny bed of rotting, purple cloth. He wondered briefly, as he had many times if there were replacements for the aging rot somewhere. The thought quickly demurred as he returned to being mesmerized.

Peter's daily chores included cleaning up and changing the linens on the side altars.[53] Then there was the sacristy. It was unlikely priests would leave empty beer cans and pizza boxes

50

strewn about. However, most did have a bad habit of not hanging up their vestments, or worse, leaving them in a heap on the floor.[54] Since there were twenty or more priests at Duns Scotus during the period Peter attended, there were plenty of vestments. Most considered saying a daily mass as part of the morning ritual: shit, shower, shave, and say mass.

Vestments were color-coded based on the holy calendar with certain colors set aside for special occasions. The tabernacle[55] and chalices, all the priests' equipment, were covered with a matching, color-coded cloth.

All this stuff had to be stored somewhere. It could not just be left in piles out in the church collecting dust and the attention of garage sale fanatics, to say nothing of gold and precious jewel collectors.

It was very expensive too. A chasuble, the main drape or cover the priest wears, sort of a poncho but without a hood, this grandest of vestments could set you back five hundred bucks, easily. The mandible (not the jawbone) the thing draped over the priests arm just north of the wrist, would drain one-hundred-fifty smackers. Then you have your basic stole. Unless it's stolen, this long scarf was worth a good two-fifty.

Peter forced himself to volunteer to care for all the church finery, the silken vestments with their delicate embroidery, flaming patterns with weighty tassels, the gold chalices and plates, the crisp, ironed-to-a-shiny white linens, because they thoroughly repulsed him. He was in the process of developing an argument in his mind for why Jesus would not be caught dead or alive in such outrageous outfits when Kirk interrupted his reverie.

"You will wear those one day." Kirk had expected the lad to be startled and was a tad surprised himself to see Peter turn calmly and almost sigh.

"For the glory of God."

"Yes, of course, for the glory of God. It is also quite fun to play dress up. And you shall. Soon. In the twinkling of an eye." Kirk's voice and mannerisms were an awful lot like William F. Buckley, Jr. including the thing where he would keep sticking out his tongue just a little.

Peter began to finish folding the last of the chalice cloths. Kirk leaned against the cabinet counter and rubbed his chin reflectively, making a scratchy, stubbly sound.

"When you are ordained, Peter, do you plan to look like a fuzzy bear?" With this he gave Peter's cheek hairs a slightly too long caress with the back of his fingers. He quickly buried his disappointment at the complete lack of any discernable reaction. Kirk was miffed.

"And by the by thank you so much for sending Vincent to me. He says that was your idea? For him to talk to me about his little confrontation with those beasts?"

Peter, Al and Frank had barely spoken to Vincent in two weeks. He seemed to be avoiding them.

"I have taken him into my counsel. Under my wing. Vincent is very sweet."

Peter said nothing. He felt vaguely stunned though close to clueless as to what Kirk was talking about.

"This might sound a little funny. But. It almost seemed as if Vincent was a gift to me. That you sent me a gift." Kirk fiddled idly with a cincture for a moment then looked at Peter intently. Importantly.

"I thought maybe you sent Vincent because you were afraid to come to me yourself. Is that right? Were you afraid of me?"

"No, Father." Peter's brows knitted so tightly that he seemed to squint.

"Good. I do not want you to ever be afraid of me. You can talk to me anytime. If it is late at night, you can come and see me. We can talk about anything you want. Or maybe you just feel the need to be close. Do you ever feel that way? The urge to feel close? Maybe just close enough to lean against...? Kirk left the query dangling vaguely.

"No, Father." Peter was pretty clear on that account. The clouds were also starting to part on what Kirk was up to. Kirk wanted Peter to come to his room so they could touch each other. And not shake hands either. The neophyte moralist found his voice.

"I don't think that's right, Father. Men, especially men who dedicate their lives to Christ and his church should remain chaste." He looked at Kirk sternly.

Kirk was all set to roll out a list of often used rationales for breaking vows against intimacy but stopped. There was absolutely no opportunity for a dalliance here. He could continue to bark up this tree but this pussycat would still not come down. Still, what cheek! Who did this pup think he was yelping about remaining chaste?

52

"Oh, really? Well as it happens, I am more Christ-like than you are. Perhaps you have forgotten that Christ had twelve very close male friends with whom he slept every night." Kirk was being a little snooty as well as a bit questionable with Church teachings. However, he acquired the desired effect.

Peter was astonished and repulsed that anyone would say, let alone think such a thing. He briefly fought off the urge to remain silent. "That is not what The Church teaches."

"The Church?" More scoff from Kirk. "The Church is whoever is in charge of it at any given time. Just because all the queer popes have never been brave enough to allow the truth as dogma does not mean the truth is not the truth. Look at all the pictures of The Last Supper. Ever wonder why John, the youngest of the twelve sits next to Our Lord and has his head on Christ's shoulder? Ever wondered what his hands are up to?"

***

The encounter had a substantial and lasting effect. Although Kirk had failed to bed Peter, he did do some serious screwing with the young man's thinking. Kirk had seriously smudged the Church Hierarchy. Up until that point, while he knew all the gold and stuff was wrong, it had never occurred to Peter that The Church itself-its teachings-were wrong or could be the product of political manipulation. Cynicism was a teeth-crunching pothole on his road to Rome.

This series of incidents is also one of the finest biographical examples that show how Peter's mind works just like his bowling scores. He tells Vincent to seek advice from an elder (Strike). He tells him to confide in someone who is more than willing to jump on his bone (Gutter ball).

Thus began another long, muted period for Peter. The time he formerly invested in theological chats was now spent on his knees at the altar railing. Technically, he did not abandon his friends. He just stopped talking to them. They could see he was troubled but were not about to pry. They knew he had pulled a boner.

# 7
## ORDER UP!

Peter was getting ordained! After one simple, slightly painful ceremony, he would be able to perform all the magic tricks for which priests are known: Make a cracker Christ. Wash converts and newborn babes' souls sparkling clean. Marry a man to a woman (only) for all eternity so they must make babies. Arrive on the scene of a fatal car crash and get to the dying people at the last minute to pour some oil on their forehead to keep them from going to hell.

Peter was about to make the solemn vows of poverty, chastity and obedience. Just as Sister Evelene had taught, the only way to achieve perfect love for God was to take these vows. Doing so made a person more like Jesus.[56] Odd, considering the fact that while Jesus kept Himself pretty busy busting people for the way they behaved, He never told anyone to act like Him. Unlike most leaders of large groups of lambs or lemmings, He was characteristically vague about the specifics for getting into Heaven. Dismas was the exception to that.[57]

The life of Jesus absolutely reeked of poverty, chastity and obedience. With the exception of those who think that Jesus never actually existed, nobody has ever doubted He was as poor as leftover beans and hand-me-down undies. In that order.

He obviously made a sacrifice when it came to having loot. Since His Father, God, could do anything, wealth should have been a piece of cake. Instead, the Guy who created gold lets His Kid be born in a barn with only the breath of a cow to keep Him warm.[58] As an adult, Jesus chose to forgo the Best Middle Eastern and instead slept on the dirty desert sand with twelve equally poor men who smelled of Pee You de Carp.

Artsy paintings of Jesus all dolled up in satin, gold and diamonds have confused many into thinking He did quite well financially and was nailed to the cross not for being King of the

Jews and starting an insurrection, but more likely for failure to include some insignificant bit of information on His tax forms. So much pain in life could be saved if people only knew that most artists are drunks and the rest are idiots and neither group cares a fig about an accurate representation.

Jesus never had sex and never thought about it either. That alone should prove that He was God. Oh sure, there was talk about Him and Mary Magdalene, a prostitute he saved from stoning. The most they (They?) ever did was when she rubbed oil on His Feet then wiped it off with her hair. While admittedly kinky, it is unknown how He Reacted.

Then there was the whole "twelve guys leaving their wives and hanging out in the desert" with Him question. And yes, Judas kissing Him on the Cheek to identify the Troublemaker and Soon-To-Be-Sacrificed, has raised several eyebrows. However, these are incriminations believed by the same type of person who insists that Lee Harvey Oswald acted alone.

That covers chastity.

As far as obedience goes, He may have been God, but Jesus was none too bright when it came to getting along with superiors. He could have been nicer to the phony Pharisees and Jewish leaders in the Temple, too. Instead, he had to show them how much smarter He was and how His understanding of Jewish law was better than theirs. He could have been nicer when Mom asked Him to change the water into wine, too.

However, He more than made up for His occasional Bull-Headedness. His Dad, Who art in Heaven, told Him to die on a cross. True, He did spend a couple of hours whining about it in the Garden of Olives the night before his death. Nevertheless, that had more to do with the poorly digested, rich Passover meal He had just finished. When the decisive moment arrived, He went after the saving of personkind like, well, ever heard the expression "Just like leading lambs to slaughter?" It is impossible to be any more obedient than that.

People who have enough money not to worry about it, spinsters and "gay bachelors," and low ranking members of the military or any combination of the above, did not love God as perfectly as priests because priests formally promised God not to get rich, not to have sex, and to follow orders. That made priests superior and guaranteed them an upper bunk in Heaven.

These vows were part of a formal consecration ceremony and there was a catch. If the vows were broken without a special dispensation, the priest went to Hell.

In spite of that, or maybe because of the challenge it presented, most priests, as thinking humans, had their own ideas about the application of their vows. It may seem obvious to most people what each of these vows mean. In reality, the range and intensity of commitment varied. The only thing more common than a penny is the tendency for humans to rationalize things they should not be doing.

At first glance, poverty seems simple to define. Impoverished people are poor. They have no money or at least are obviously not living high off the hog. Jesus Christ was poor. With His typically clever turn of a phrase He once told a guy that because of all his moolah, the man would have better luck trying to push his camel through a needle hole than of getting into Heaven. Jesus, back off!

A typical picture of poverty is simple: Wear rags; beg for money; be homeless. Nobody in their right mind would expect that from priests. What about a car? A priest would need a car to go visit the sick and dying. Should some poor soul go to hell because the bus is late? Or a house? Had to have a house so poor people could sleep on the sofa once and a while. Had to have a kitchen so the priest could cook up a little something for poor people when they stopped by. Had to have a CD player and color TV so the poor people would not get bored. For that matter, a priest had to have cash in case poor people showed up asking for just enough money to buy a bus ticket back to Buffalo where a parent was, say, dying of cancer.

If Jesus were alive today, what kind of car would he drive? Did poverty obligate a priest to only buy an old Chevy with a sun-faded paint job? Or did it allow a new, mid-sized Ford with an AM/FM/Cassette but no power windows? What about a B.M.W? What if your parish was in a nice neighborhood? Only so many positions available in the ghetto. What if a rich person donated a really nice car that did have power windows? See how it works? Where does what stop? That was the question. Peter's trouble with his vow of poverty started somewhere just past the Chevy and simple bungalow with no electronics but would end irrevocably at the Vatican.

Look at any pope. With a few exceptions, most were former priests. Many vowed poverty yet lived in The Vatican, which are some of the poshest digs in the world. How did they dig themselves out of that hole?

This is how. It is ludicrous to think that popes inherit sins from prior popes. Not even God was goofy enough to accept that idea. Who bought all the artwork and glued gold to everything in sight? That pope is the one who maybe broke his vow. MAYBE you justifiably scream! How does a pope papal bull himself out of this one?

Very simple. Very, very simple. The ostentatiousness was-get this-for the greater glory of God. Worshipers could only fall on their knees so often, burn so many tons of incense before God got bored. Poverty bored God. Wealth inspired creativity for what to do with all that money.

God, it was believed was giddy for gold. Surely, a cage for the Holy Spirit (That is the little white birdie?) must be gilded. If God is going to pay attention to any human it is going to be the pope, so they have to make things nice for when He shows up. Since the pope has to have a church of his own and a place to live there is a certain sense for The Vatican to be the confluence of all The Church's booty. See how it works? It was a good idea to have explanations all worked out prior to judgment day.[59]

It should be noted, for those who have never visited the Vatican, that there is plenty of crappy artwork both on display and in storage there. "The Vatican" looks real good on an artist's resume.  Much of the trashy stuff was donated and so The Church got what she paid for.

In fairness, most of the early Christians and their immediate ancestors, those who maybe saw Christ or knew someone who claimed he did, were dirt poor. They heard Jesus say things like "Abandon your favorite things because poor people get cooler stuff in Heaven." And "Poor people country is God's country." And "Poor people will run the world." That kind of talk really torched those poor people or, at the very least, made them feel that life was not so bad and death would be a hoot and something to look forward to. That is why Peter looked forward to being dead too.

The vow of chastity was directly linked to the vow of poverty. During its first several centuries of the church's existence, clergy could get married. It was not until The Church started owning property and dipping their churches in gold and marble that trouble started. Blame the women.

In spite of an intense life-long love for their Redeemer, sometimes a guy and a gal just wind up hating each other's guts. Early rule-makers figured The Church would be on its way to financial Hell in a hand basket if divorce settlements started including the local cathedral. Consider the court jam as divorcing nuns and priests battle over who gets the candelabras and who gets the votive candle stand, to say nothing of the da Vinci original.

The Church developed all sorts of bizarre biblical proof to support its insistence that priests and nuns not have sex with each other or anyone else. They did not X out sex because some Church leaders found it scary or disgusting. Although that could be the reason millions of men and women figured "What the Hell" and made the vow. On the other hand since an unknown quantity of them who took the vow did have sex, it is not unreasonable to surmise that vowing not to and the Hellish consequence made doing it that much more delicious.

Jesus never encouraged a healthy sexual relationship. On the contrary, He told His buddies, the apostles, the original priests and pope, to "live like angels." Obviously, that meant that if a person wanted to be closer to God, as the angels were, they could not have sex. It is doubtful anyone close to God would even want to have sex. What with Him watching and all. It is also extremely difficult to imagine a couple of rutting cherubs.[60]

Because sex is dirty, people who vowed chastity figured it would increase their purity. The vow gave them extra grace, grace that vowless people would never have. Grace that got them several steps further up the stairway to Heaven.

Obedience is the only vow that makes sense. Just think how much easier a business would run if everyone vowed to God to be obedient. Bosses would have two clubs. One to fire people with and the other to remind them where they were going for not making this month's quota.

The vow was not invented solely to make it easier to push people around. There was a pervading sense of submission in Catholicism. It was based on the notion that the sacrifice of Jesus was one He willingly submitted to. Thus, all humans should willingly submit to discomfort through mimicry of the crucified Christ.

Jesus was the "Word Made Flesh" of the New Testament portion of the bible. His Dad was Le Grande Fromage of the Old Testament. God the Father never sacrificed squat in the Old Testament. He never asked. He ordered people to do things. God would never say "You might try not coveting your neighbor's wife." Or, "Do you really think killing someone is a good idea?" By the same token, "I'll think about it and get back to you" was not a suitable response to any form of communication from God. God cut people no slack. There were no negotiations. Groveling was the only acceptable response.

Obedience was supposed to smother pride. "Me first" attitudes were to be extinguished. The community of The Church could only exist with cooperation and complete trust of leaders who, of course, were selected by God.[61]

Standing in line to accept these vows first required Peter to meekly prostrate himself on the floor of the cathedral as he waited to receive the sacrament of Holy Orders. His nose pressed to the cold marble floor. His arms stretched out, his right hand perilously close to the center aisle. Peter floated placidly on the floor, a submissive lily pad.

This was the last ceremony that Archbishop Evans Logan would officiate. He was retiring in two days. He was 82. It was time to toss in the miter. The whole of his archdiocese, twelve churches with twenty priests, twenty-two nuns and thousands of parishioners were invited to his going-away party at the Fort Wayne Convention Center. Jewish and Protestant church and civic leaders were expected to attend. The love and admiration he attracted was not limited by theology.

Large of heart, and belly and body, this frugal shepherd stood on opposite ends of the field from Peter. One was in search of a flock, the other was about to let the flock wander. Speaking of wandering, that is exactly what Logan's mind was doing.

Normally his very soul would embrace the ceremony at hand. The very essence of his grand bulk would act as a conduit between God and the small fry below. Logan was dedicated to The Church.

His mind was not on the party next week and the inevitable accolades. He was just humble enough to be shy about such things and old enough to respond with appreciative tolerance.

Somewhere north of his nose, Logan had already skeedaddled to Michigan where his brother's lakeside cottage waited for him in South Lyon.[62] There a room waited for Logan. Logan's thoughts were closer to the end of the dock that stretched sixty feet out into Sandy Bottom Lake with his immense bulk straining a reinforced lounge chair and a baited hook dangling invitingly for a lake full of unsuspecting fishies than he was to the ceremony he was about to perform. That is why he failed to notice a hand on the floor in his path.

Archbishop Logan waddled as he walked. He occasionally experienced an odd little sensation of being off-balance. It caused him to compensate by breaking stride and shifting a foot suddenly to the left or right. Waddle waddle shift. Waddle waddle waddle shift. Waddle shift. He was also diabetic, so the sensitivities in his extremities were far from par.

Peter's hand had no business being where it was. All the other priests-to-be rested their heads on their hands as they waited for the grand finale of their lifelong inculcation. (One was Vincent! Congratulations!) Peter, as usual was busy being pious. His nose crinkled into the freshly polished floor. Trust being a not-too-distant cousin of piety, it did not matter if he knew his hand was in the road, he assumed others would not tread there.

Archbishop Logan did, of course, tread there. The shift part of his waddle waddle shift landed squarely on Peter's right prehensile. Only the thumb survived intact. The fingers busted between the knuckle topping the palm and the first finger knuckle. Logan glanced down and mumbled excuse me. He had no idea what he had just done and felt slightly embarrassed for that alone. Peter opened his eyes but he did not say anything. Not even ouch.

By the time Logan had waddle/shifted to his position several steps up to the altar platform he had loosed himself from the moorings on the Michigan dock. He glanced warmly at the half-full church. He looked to the attendants. Everybody smiled in formal anticipation. If anything had happened, no one seemed to notice. No one had seen anything because Logan's extravagant dress had draped the incident. He dismissed the idea that he had done something to someone and instead began to wonder if he had done something to his foot. However, what he could feel of his toes moved just fine inside his wingtips.

The intensity of the pain astonished Peter. He did his best to pray it away. On cue, he and the other supplicants rose to their knees. Logan mumbled some mumbo jumbo. Then Peter stood and walked forward. Time to do a little writing.

It was not enough for priests-to-be to say they wanted to be priests. They had to put it in writing. What better time to sign the contract than during the pre-game ceremony? Luckily for Peter, he and the others hand-wrote the declaration earlier. Still there were the John Hancocks.

Logan sat on his bishop's throne as Peter knelt before him. An assistant handed the document to Peter on a silver platter. No kidding. Then a miracle happened.

Peter accepted the pen handed to him. The miracle was that he did not scream out as he bent his fingers around it and began to scrawl his name. It was not really his name. There was something that rather looked like a capital P with a flattened aftermath. The rest of it was a fine, barely visible, totally unrecognizable bit of scritch. Same with the last name. It was supposed to be a capital B. It may have been. But that was no o that followed. It was the penmanship version of road kill.

Bishop Logan noticed beads of sweat formed along Peter's forehead. He still failed to put two and two together. It did occur to him that this candidate might be "sweating" signing the proclamation. That happened.

Logan also noticed Peter's crappy handwriting and somewhat crumpled paw and did consider, for longer than a moment, if Peter might be impeded or have an irregularity which would disallow him from the priesthood. It was Logan's responsibility to consider worthiness.[63] But Logan trusted the seminary and had met with Peter earlier. If Peter were impeded or irregular, surely he would have been weeded out by now.

In spite of pain severe enough to make him see lightning bugs, Peter felt on the verge of an exquisite ecstasy greater than he ever had or would for some time. His life of prayer and studies turned him into a photocopy Christ. Now his soul was supposed to be receiving more grace. Grace glowed within him. He was pumped. He was ready to do God's work.

Because of this ceremony, he would be able to save souls. Those bound for Hell could end up going to Heaven instead because of actions Peter took. Those were the thoughts performing a tutti chori pas de deux in his mind. Though his hand hurt like a mutha.

Logan had the liberty to add or subtract just about any part of the ceremony except one. He could not mess with the Laying On of Hands. Like having a pope or doing good deeds to gain access to Heaven, laying on of hands is something which distinguished Catholic priests from their ministering brethren in the Heresies. Baptists, Lutherans, Methodists, et al, could pray their brains out and would remain inferior in the Eyes of God because they would still not have this major Jesus connection. So the Catholics believed.[64]

Like a huddled team before the start of the big game, Logan's hands went on Peter's head first. Then, all the ordained assistants, several monsignors, a pile of priests, thirteen including Logan piled up their hands. Obviously if two hands were good, 26 would be better. Never know where there might be a week link in the hands-me-down chain.

Logan's hands were cool on the bald spot of Peter's perspiring head. The cool hands were a result of Logan's diminishing blood circulation caused by his diabetes. The sweat was a combination of Peter's excitement and swallowed pain.[65] The bubbly sheen of perspiration did not surprise Logan. He had lived his entire adult life sharing living quarters with men. The law of averages dictated a wet one would pop up every so often. Peter's white pallor did give him a twinge of passing concern, though.

During his sermon, Logan gave the impression to the congregation that he had known the ordainees since birth. He was good at that. Actually, he had met them the previous Friday. Logan was interested in other people. He paid attention to them when they spoke and, because what they said was important, he retained it. After one leisurely dinner with the priests to be, he soaked up enough information to do ten interesting minutes on each.

The congregation chuckled when he relayed the "unnecessary but understandable" concern of Vincent's parents because as a twelve-year old their son tried on one of his sister's dresses and started singing like Ethel Merman. The mirth was sincere, if not somewhat guarded, as Logan added it was a one-time incident.

Aware that both comedy and tragedy were stock ingredients of compelling preaching, Logan also mentioned softly and with sincere regard the deaths of Peter's parents and all eight of his brothers and sisters in a fiery car crash.

It was a sign of an exceptional preacher that after Logan concluded his sermon there was a smattering of quickly hushed applause.

Peter and the other practically priests promised obedience to the bishop and to their order.[66]

The ceremony continued and Peter's pain grew. It became increasingly difficult to avoid expressing it. Peter was not long to this ceremony.[67]

Peter received his priestly duds: a stole and a chasuble. Even though the bishop was a big shot, as was the custom, Logan dressed him.

The next part of the ceremony was the beginning of the end for Peter. Logan reached for the blessed oil. The plan was to anoint Peter's hands.[68] An assistant held a small gold bowl of chrism for Logan. Logan had an assistant for every action he took during the ceremony. Somebody would hold the book with the prayers Logan would read. Someone else would turn the pages. Someone would hand him the holy water sprinkler. Someone else would hold the incense thingy and make sure the fire was hot enough to burn the fragrant crap that Logan would sprinkle upon it with a tiny gold spoon. There was even a guy to lift the vestments away from Logan's butt, so they would not wrinkle when he sat down. All part of the ceremony.

The portly bishop dipped his chubby, short fingers into the chrism then dabbed it on the backs of Peter's hands. Peter winced. When Logan opened Peter's prayer-postured hands and dabbed the oil on his outstretched palms, Peter let out a barely perceptible "Owa, owa, owa."

The pain was undeniable at that point. Still Peter chastised himself by thinking of his Savior. He envisioned a Roman mallet the size of a number ten can driving huge spikes into the willing hands. Jesus did not bat a Godly eyelash. You can bet the farm on that. Instead, He probably looked at his torturer with a steady, loving, forgiving gaze.

A tear rolled down Peter's cheek.

Bishop Logan noticed.

"My son, are you having second thoughts?"

"No Eminence. I was thinking of our Lord."

Logan smiled at that and continued with the next step of the Oiling Of The Hands process. He wrapped Peter's hands snuggly in strips of linen.

Peter passed out.

# 8

## NOT JUST SOME SHITTY LITTLE ISLAND

In 1685, the Italians discovered Merdette, a tiny stool-shaped island off the coast of South America. They named it for its shape and the peculiar aroma that wafted about its residents like a swarm of wanton flies. The discoverers stayed only long enough to name it.

Naming a newfound island is usually a source of pride to the discoverer. However, Eno Nabalogne, the captain of the vessel, thought it would be funny to call it Merdette. So visitors would blame the French for not leaving the place uncharted.

Scientists in modern times, proudly oblivious to previous reports, landed then abandoned Merdette quicker than a skunk's frightened glance. They muttered something about a preference for sulfur fumes as they gagged into their hankies and grabbed for the door of the airplane from which they had just hopped off.

Because Merdette is inches from the Equator it is hot as Hell. When it was not hot as Hell, it was humid as bejeezes. When it was not humid as bejeezes it rained like screaming banshees.

The people of Merdette were small in stature and robustly flatulent. The only reason this lackadaisical, ill-tempered tribe rarely strayed from the island was that their personal stench was unbearable elsewhere. Leper colonies shunned them.

Merdette had been a cold sore on the gums of the Eustachian order since the island's discovery. A Eustachian priest was on-board the original ill-fated Italian vessel. Much to the dismay of his superiors, Peter volunteered for a mission there.[69]

Peter stood before his superiors and humbly whispered his hopeful request. What could they do? This kid was a keeper. However, this was a situation where the boy could actually die out there. They weighed the merits.

There were considerations other than the propagation of the faith out in Bumfuck. Maybe putting this Holy Roller, whose reputation preceded him like the Pamplona Bull Run, in a decent neighborhood church would make normal people uncomfortable. Holy? No doubt. But Mr. Meditation could not preach his way out of a paper sack. Had anybody heard him say two sentences back to back? How would he fund raise?

Jesus saved the day for Peter.

"I wish to be as Christ among the least of my brethren." Peter's superiors, four septuagenarians, nodded with solemn annoyance and with a grudging "Very well…" sent Peter packing for Merdette.

The plane dropped Peter off more than a little unceremoniously. The co-pilot quickly shoved out Peter's supplies, which included a pallet of communion wafers and a thirty-six-roll box of toilet paper. Peter did not object as his hosts quickly commandeered the later and used it as a decorative item: hanging it on trees, huts and each other.

The stink of Merdette failed to revolt Peter. By the time he was ordained, his highly developed sense for spirituality had nearly destroyed his normal human senses.[70]

Peter was the first "out-ee" to make a favorable impression on the Merdettes. They were amazed that this tall white man did not vomit or even appear to be struggling to hold down his lunch at anytime since his arrival. Within a week, Peter had christened fifty of the one hundred, forty-seven residents with the holy (and somewhat locally murky) waters of Baptism. They wanted to see what the host tasted like.

Just because the people of Merdette smelled like shit did not mean that is what they had for brains. In contrast to their bad attitudes was a natural curiosity augmented by a propensity for insisting upon detailed explanations. Questions usually continued long after a thought or process had been explained and re-explained and torn apart, explained backwards and sideways. In many ways the Merdettes' form of reaching an understanding was a lot like a typical meeting of any school board in America.

There was no native religion. They did not worship the sun, moon, sea or Rush Limbaugh. These were godless heathens in the finest sense. They took to Peter's praying lessons quickly for pragmatic reasons. What better way to kill time and in the process avoid chores?

They also admired Peter's silence. These naturally querulous people were extremely impressed by someone who said little, and never ever argued, let alone raise his voice.[71]

It took Peter about a month to pick up a few short phrases in the local language.[72] "Let us pray." Peter would say in English.

"Yay house puh hay." They would mimic, then slap their temples and fall to their knees in groveling somewhat excessive imitation. Considering Peter's appreciation of the church's history of self-inflicted pain and death, he was equally impressed with the Merdettes.

While Peter's 'less said the better' approach endeared him to the Merdettes, his bowling Jones eventually elevated him to the status of saint. After they nearly killed him, that is.

The Merdettes were obsessed with increasing the size of their penises. For as long as everyone remembered, both women and men were involved in an activity, which with persistence, could increase the length and girth. In addition to the visual and stimulatory benefits, a big one was a source of pride. A dead man laid out for a half hour viewing (That was about all a body could take in the heat.) would be dressed in a grass skirt specially designed to reveal what he had accomplished in his lifetime. Those who the family thought to be not totally pumped up would opt for a closed skirt ceremony. However, that was rare.

Sometimes for hours at a time, depending on a man's stamina, to say nothing of his self-control, a woman would stroke him to fullest possible erection. The idea being that a penis is at its largest state just prior to ejaculation. Kept at that state long enough the penile skin stretches and the tube eventually becomes longer and fuller.

The Merdettes were not in the baby-making business. They were not imbeciles. The length of the island could be walked in four hours the width in less than one. There was limited space and resources.

Most of the women were eager, to oblige in the task at hand. Except when with a wife or serious other, it was considered bad form to ejaculate. Some of the men were equally eager to return the favor for the woman. Both for the woman's pleasure and to enhance their own arousal.

No doubt, all this unresolved crank yanking and monkey spanking contributed to the Merdettes somewhat antsy attitudes since they were all in a near-constant state of arousal. It was not unusual to see men walking around with hard-ons, or, to see a helpful female casually and publicly stroking a flagging member. Take the occasional muffled cries of someone in the next hut very, very, very, very, very, very, very, very, close to finishing off, add in

66

the nearest bowling alley being about ten-thousand miles away, and you wind up with one frustrated Peter.

Many nights he spent in his hut caressing a coconut. Occasionally a small band of mesmerized Merdettes would watch, quietly grunting and slapping in wonderment as they debated what the hell the white man was up to.

On the fateful day, Peter was standing outside his hut near the outer perimeter of the main section. One of the local habits he had picked up was to just stand in place and stare. In this instance, Peter's unfocused gaze had drifted toward the main "square" – the middle of the village. He fondled his favorite coconut as he stood there figuring.

Scattered about the well-trampled area were groups of gourds left to dry in the sun.[73]

Peter stood. He stared for a good long while. He experienced the same sense of loss, of desolation, that curious tug at the heart that a bowler feels when they drive by a closed bowling alley. A skier feels something similar when looking at green slopes or golfers seeing those first horrible flakes of snow.

Some type of idea was gurgling in the saucepan that was Peter's imagination. The gourds stood in groups balanced on their fat bottoms. The gentle slope to the neck with the slight fattening at the head inspired an irresistible urge within Peter.

He looked at the coconut in his hands. He noted its heft. No sixteen-pounder, but it was certainly heavy enough to do the trick.

Peter went into the stoop in preparation of delivery. He began his approach and after tippy-toe steps brought back his arm then quickly forward again, and, to the horror of a group of constant followers, rolled a perfect curving arc along the sand path into a group of unsuspecting gourds.

Strike! The "pins" had barely stopped rolling into disarray when he had already grabbed another coconut from a nearby pile. The beast in his loins, if not calmed, was at least distracted.

Dizzy with excitement he lined up his shot and heaved the ball with inspired force and accuracy. This time he managed to not only crush the front three gourds and knock down the other ten behind them, but the ricochet bounced into another group and knocked down six more.

His back was to them as he plunged into the nearby pile of coconuts looking for new balls. When Peter was finally satisfied with his armful he straightened and turned.

The faces of the normally happy to see him Natives now wore expressions several miles down the road past disapproval. The Merdettes grabbed Peter and hurried him to a vacant hut, threw him to the floor and fastened tight the door. There Peter remained for three days and three nights.

During that time, when the rain did not drown them out, Peter would hear the Merdettes bickering in the shelter of a nearby copse of trees. The discussion seemed to be between two essential factions.

The side angry with him for his sacrilegious insubordination made its argument with shrill voices and loud insistent slapping. They were by no small coincidence made up entirely of the unconverted.

The opposition hoped with quiet patience for two things: to mollify the others and to make Peter the king, or god or whatever.[74] The pro-Peter people hoped elevating him would insure a steady stream of communion wafers, of which they had become quiet fond.

Peter supporters numbered just under half of the population. These quieter, less slaphappy folk had accepted the Divine Trinity, the virginity of Mary and her position as Mother of the Son of God, the infallibility of the pope and Jesus Christ as their savior. They were clueless as to what any of that meant. None of that had been explained to them, though it was implicit when they received Baptism. They simply liked Peter and wanted him to pour water on their heads and give them a treat.

Though no one on the tiny island had ever been intentionally killed, the non-Catholics wanted Peter dead. Hitting the sacred gourds with a coconut was bad enough, but for intentionally smashing three, his goose should be cooked. The non-Catholics intended to subject Peter to a slow painful roasting.

The battle would have gone on forever, but after three days, everyone was hungry. Gathering and gourd processing had ceased during the discussion. Nobody wanted to miss a thing. In addition, even these politic-crazy folk eventually ran out of things to say. Many of the more outspoken types began to complain of killer headaches from all the heated head slapping. All suffered from arousal withdrawal.

Due to the shoddy construction of the hut they stuck him in, Peter could easily see through the walls. He watched as the Merdettes piled a heap of compost around a pole they had stuck in the ground. Assuming he was about to become a martyr, he prayed with increased fervor for strength. A thought that they might want to fatten him a bit before the kill also skittered across his heaven-bound request. Peter was hungry too.

A last meal was not to be. The angry Merdettes pulled Peter from his prison hut. Although, now that they had this evil man in hand, they seemed almost shy about their intent. They stood uncomfortably around him mumbling and no more than flicking at their heads.

The Catholics stood by in a group. Their arms folded across their chests. The non-Catholics had defeated the Catholics simply by the virtue of talking louder and longer. The losers, embarrassed with their lack of defensive action, scowled self-effacedly and scratched at the muddy ground with their toes. They felt like the caller on the receiving end of a talk show host's diatribe.

Complacently, Peter allowed himself to be herded to the post in the middle of the compost. Though unbound, it was clumsy work getting the convict to the center. Once there, Peter backed up to the pole and faced the heathens.

Peter knew what was supposed to happen next, and suspected (correctly) that the Merdettes did not. He felt in his pocket for his lighter. A package from the home office given to him before he left included a lighter and pack of menthol cigarettes. Peter had lost the cigarettes long ago, but had put the lighter in his pocket. He had found no use for it until that moment. Taking a step into the jumbled collection of bramble, Peter handed the items to a Merdette then returned to his post.

While most of the rest of the planet waddled along in modernity, the Merdettes remained flint-bashers. Most of the time they managed to keep at least one fire burning constantly. That one, though, had gone out during the "discussion." Nobody could remember who used the flints last or where they were. In addition, at this point they were all nearly paralyzed with the stupidity brought on by hunger and fatigue. Deductive reasoning was the last thing any one on the island was capable of doing.

The poor man looked at the lighter a moment, figured it was some type of white guy memento, nodded his thanks and put it in his animal skin fanny pack.

Peter was experiencing a slight yet growing sense of impatience with his ill-executed execution. He was ready to receive his heavenly reward. He motioned to the man to hand back the lighter. When the man refused to surrender his prize, a nearby fellow elbowed him, performed a couple of grunts and head slaps on himself and, being considerably larger than the first, managed to convince him to return the Bic.

Peter stepped to the perimeter and crouched down and set fire to some twigs. He hopped over the small fire back to the pole, but in the process kicked a large log onto the fire, putting it out.

The thought that he was technically committing suicide never occurred to Peter. He bent where he was at the post, lit some flimsy kindling, then straightened and gazed skyward, prepared to meet his maker.[75]

While in his prison hut, Peter had spent most of his time on his knees. Eventually fatigue compromised his posture. He wound up with his butt resting on his ankles and his forearms against his thighs. With the wind whipping the rains through the aforementioned shoddy construction, the only part of his habit kept dry was indicated by parallel lines up the center of his thighs, which met, as his legs did, just above his crotch.

The flames were having a hell of a time with the damp wood. Up on the pyre, what seemed like eternity to Peter was actually about five minutes. Since he was standing about a foot deep in nature's trash, his bare feet were protected. The flames eventually made their way to him licking at the damp part of his tunic like a dog who has reached the bottom of the bowl: to no effect. Then sluggishly they hit on the threadbare front. The dry area formed was sort of an apron impression on the front of his habit. Ignition!

Peter felt the heat and wondered how much longer it would be before he would see the face of God, know the secrets of the universe, be embraced into the warm bosom of the Blessed Virgin who would cool his soon to be scorched skin in the healing waters of the Jordan River yadda, yadda, yadda. He was distracted from his holy reverie by mumbles of astonishment and giggles.

He opened his eyes (That much avoidance he had taken.) and looked at the Merdettes. Their mood had collectively changed. The will to kill had evaporated. The women were smiling appreciatively and the men were looking at him with what could only be described as admiration. Well, they were not looking at him exactly. They were looking at his genitals.[76] Though the Merdettes had made significant gains with their penile augmentation exercises, nobody had ever seen a pecker that big.

Most of the women (and a couple of the men) openly leered at Peter's appendage. Others squirmed in obvious delight.

70

Peter noticed this with a degree of shyness. That turned to embarrassment as his grand tool began to rise in response to his objectification.

Several rushed forward to spread the smoldering brush and branches of the failed martyr's pyre lest it might suddenly catch fire again. Nobody wanted to see this wienie grilled now. In addition, who does it hurt to maybe get a better look?

The Merdettes that had made up their minds not to become Catholics, immediately decided it would be a great idea to join the flock. The men, to a tee, assumed the big sausage was part of the spiritual advancement process (hence the priest's serene state). Those who had already converted assumed such growth might take time and so were struck proud with their forward thinking.

The same plane that dumped Peter on Merdette would deliver supplies every four months. It flew in from the closest inhabited island with an airport, Pissoirette.[77] The pilots would fly by at a low altitude and kick the goods-a crate of communion wafers and two packs of toilet paper- out of the side door. On the same pass, it would snag a mailbag containing a single letter in it (Peter's report: "All is well. Praise God."), drop off an empty mailbag and fly away. If something was wrong with Peter ("It appears I have a tumor the size of a grapefruit. Please advise.) it could be several months before the pilot picked up the information, stamped the envelope and sent it on to Rome.

There were two reasons the hired plane did this task so quickly. First, the smell of the people actually wafted up into the atmosphere for some distance around the island. Since it permeated everything the Merdettes came in contact with, the pilots would dangle the bag on the hook during the four-hour flight back to Pissoirette.

The second reason was that when they heard the plane approaching, the Merdettes would race down to the shore with bags of rocks that they had collected earlier in preparation.

The plane, a Grumman Goose, was one of those relics with the constitution of a steel drum and the plated sides of blindingly reflective corrugated metal. When it swooped down for its pass, the island folk would heave the rocks at it. It is an understatement to say these people resented being shunned. As is the case with so many aggressive nations, this was their method of displaying their hurt feelings.

71

In turn, this action not only hurt the feelings of the pilot and co-pilot, (Imagine being pelted with rocks just for trying to do your job!) but occasionally one of the rocks would actually hit the plane. (Imagine trying to hit a twelve-ton flying target approaching you at approximately 110 m.p.h.)

The pilots felt compelled to retaliate. Buzzing the village seemed like a good idea until they discovered that it was the confluence of the island's odor.

Instead, the pilots took to seeing how close they could get to the stone throwers and still pick up the bag. A menacing looking tilt of the wings during approach did little to deter the Merdettes. Though it did cause most of them to throw too soon so they would have time to duck.

On this particular day, the pilot was circling, as he always did, to reconnoiter. When low and behold, instead of the rag-tag group busily passing out rocks, down below on the beach he saw what appeared to be rows of midgets all neatly lined up about 100 yards from the pick-up bag. He wondered if he was witness to some native ritual where people face the sea while buried to the waist in sand. In reality, the Merdettes were kneeling thus giving the impression that they were buried to their waists in sand. It was an effective decoy.

Curious, the pilot slowed a bit more than usual and flew in to make his normal pick-up pass. Just after the plane cleared the last stand of trees at the far end of the island and headed into a long clear area the sniper made his move.

Nibawarumbedeecotta (ear pick) ran from his cover behind a bush. Though scrawny, Nibawarumbedeecotta (ear pick) had the best arm in the bunch and as it would turn out an impeccable sense of timing. Moments before the plane passed over him, Nibawarumbedeecotta (ear pick), using both hands and a surprising amount of strength, tossed up a rock the size of a soccer ball and scored a direct hit in the plane's starboard engine.

Meanwhile Peter was having sex.[78] Ys (wiggle index fingers) had found him napping in his hut. Ever since the aborted attempt to make Peter a fryer, Ys (wiggle index fingers) had been thinking about his splendid piece of equipment. Night and day she thought of that mighty pole waving in the breeze. As a good Merdette, she knew, with her tender ministrations, that she could coax it into being even huger. Generations that followed would sing the praises of Ys (wiggle index fingers), the girl who made a man, truly, all that he could be.

72

Since it was an exceptionally hot day, Peter was nearly naked, his robe draped about his privates in a (now) useless attempt to keep them that way. Ys (wiggle index fingers) crept close to the mat where Peter snored softly. She slowly pulled away the robe. Though completely disinterested for the moment, Peter's pecker was easily the most impressive one Ys (wiggle index fingers) had ever seen.

She lay down next to him and admired it for a moment. Well maybe a half a moment. At least a couple of seconds anyway. Unable to resist any longer she stroked its length. That in itself took a moment. Before her tiny hand reached the head the Mr. was already up and throbbing. Stifling a pleased giggle, Ys (wiggle index fingers) grabbed IT and issued a tender squeeze. Peter stopped snoring and moaned softly but apparently continued to snooze.

Ys (wiggle index fingers) was no virgin,[79] though she had a reputation for being a tough sell. She seemed to give the impression to most of the men of Merdette that she was born to bigger things.

Ys (wiggle index fingers) felt an itch. The itch turned into an ache. The ache turned into burning desire. Desire turned into action. This steed screamed to be mounted. Ys (wiggle index fingers)'s accommodations were soupier than the pots at a Campbell factory. Parting her grass skirt,[80] Ys (wiggle index fingers) straddled Peter and began to install him with microscopic nudges. She was determined not to wake him. It was known that no one on the island had made intimate contact with the priest. It was assumed that being an outsider he was repulsed by the Merdettes. Ys (wiggle index fingers) took no chances.

To say Peter brought Ys (wiggle index fingers) pleasure in those brief moments would be like saying the pyramids were big gravestones. Though Ys (wiggle index fingers)'s simultaneously sending a franticly delicate Morse Code on her muffin may have assisted her arousal a wee bit. Eventually, it was Ys (wiggle index fingers)'s extremely high-pitched, staccato squeals that woke Peter. Above him, he saw her face flush with excitement and tinged with a softness he did not understand.

People report all sorts of fantastic allusions when describing what their orgasms were like. Some of the most common are the cork popping from a frothing bottle of champagne, or a train racing into a tunnel, the waves crashing against the rocks or a smoke-emoting missile launching. For Peter and Ys (wiggle index fingers), the simultaneous moment of truth was accompanied by the actual sound of a plane crashing.

Peter arrived on the scene just as the pilots, wearing gas masks, stumbled out of what was left of their Grumman Goose.[81] The two trudged up the beach to the kneeling, giggling Merdettes. The closer the pilots got to the group, more and more of the Merdettes burst into giggles. By the time they were a few feet away, the whole lot of them were in hysterics.

It was the gas masks. The Merdettes had never seen them. Considering the severe limitations this would put on ear pulling, eye rolling, nose twisting and head slapping, this was tantamount to people in another country walking around with bags on their heads. Like humans everywhere, ignorance begat derisive laughter.

Thinking they might just beat up a couple of smart-ass Merdettes for laughing at them, and downing their aircraft, the pilots dropped their meager provisions and ripped off their masks. One sniffed tentatively, then bravely inhaled deeply.

"Shit! What's up? It don't smell like shit anymore."[82] Exclaimed Roger the pilot, as he slapped himself on the forehead in disbelief. Though a Yale graduate in economics, evidently Roger's language skills had fallen on hard times. Or maybe there was something in the water in his hometown of Crawford, Texas.

Unknown to Roger, he could not have made a more gracious gesture of good will to the Merdettes if Henry Kissinger had prepped him.

Though lacking some of the island subtleties, "Shit-what's up?"-or something that sounds like it-followed by a smack to the forehead roughly translates into the local parlance meaning "You people are the greatest thing since sliced bread." or words to that effect.

The islanders stopped laughing. They pulled themselves up from the sand and while chattering and bonking themselves, stretched their aching legs and backs (Though naturally lethargic, kneeling was none the less a new and uncomfortable position for them.) and slowly began to surround the pilots.

Ned, the co-pilot, a strong silent type[83] looked at Roger and observed nonchalantly. "Huh." Then, with a simian gesture that aped intelligence, he scratched his temple.

This drove the natives nuts. This was actually an ancient communication-similar to Elizabethan English-which meant, "I am come to rule you kindly." or something like that.

Ever willing to be acquiescent, and now actually having a reason, the Merdettes fell to groveling at Ned's feet. Those unable to get close enough to Ned quickly fell to the ground near Roger, who unwittingly was telling them, roughly, "Me too." As he scratched his head while whispering, "Damn."

Peter approached the pilots and explained they should use caution when putting their hands to their heads, since there was no telling what they might be saying.

The pilots quickly settled into an island life of eating garlicky tasting squash and getting hand jobs from any woman within reach. It only took four slaps in the face for Roger and twenty-six for Ned to figure out that while a woman would tug for hours at a time, ejaculating was considered an insult.

In spite of having crashed in jerk-off heaven, for a while after the plane went down, Roger was deathly afraid. He had recently been diagnosed with total cholesterol of over 300. What would he do now without his medication? Would he suffer a slow, artery-clogging death, or just have time to realize that spike in his chest was a heart attack?

One day while rummaging through the Goose he found some medical test kits that were intended for delivery to a clinic at the next planned island stop. His fear turned to jubilation, when one month after the crash, he had sliced his numbers in half. Roger wondered if there was something about life on the island that had lowered his cholesterol. Sure, he had shed a few pounds, but it could not be just that. If he ever got back, maybe he could get some doctor to figure it out.[84]

Six months later Peter's order eventually realized they had not heard from him in some time. Shortly after that, with the order's insistence, Roger and Ned's dispatcher sent out a plane to retrace their route and to check on Peter. Seems that her and Roger's parting had been less like "sweet sorrows" and more like "take a long walk off a short pier." Not that Roger was holding any grudges. He was enjoying this time out.

Roger looked down at his longer schlong. The women here were sure swell. And he had learned a thing or two about making them happy too. He believed that for the first time in his life, right here on Merdette, he had witnessed, had been an accomplice to an unfaked female orgasm. Maybe he could start excursions to Merdette. Millions of guys would pay out the wazoo for a reappraisal of the family jewels after a month of short arm stretching and a couple of pointers on foolproof methods for tickling a girl's fancy. Of course, that would make him a pimp. He watched that idea float out to sea like a never-to-be-found message in a bottle.

Ned had not learned how to communicate with the Merdettes nearly as well as he thought he had. The important thing was that he was convinced that he had and that made his life peachy plus. For the first time in his existence he felt intellectually superior not to one but to a lot of people. Ned felt he was smarter because he could speak English naturally and they could only do so with great effort. Though lofty, Ned was benign.

Since the Merdettes had no government, no leader and no inclination to try to figure out who should be in charge, Ned created a constitution and told the people that he was making Merdette a democracy. He easily convinced the Merdettes to raise their right hands when asked, "All those in favor of making Ned the king, raise your hand and say 'Aye.'"[85]

The remainder of Peter's days on Merdette passed without incident. Ys (wiggle index fingers) remained at the ready for a second coming. She knew better than to be a pest. She kept her distance while keeping in range. It only seems like she was stalking him. Truth is, frequently Peter would look at Ys (wiggle index fingers) and smile. It was not a smile of invitation. It was a smile of acknowledgement, and she thought endearingly, gratitude.

Peter forgave himself for the transgression. Then forgave himself for repeatedly reliving the moment. He did not understand why he felt transformed when he should have been feeling guilty. They did not teach this stuff in the seminary.

In his note that went back with the rescue plane, Peter wrote, "All natives are now Catholics. Need additional communion wafers. Am told island no longer offensive smelling." A month later Roger and Ned returned (gladly, this time) with Peter's replacement and orders for a transfer to a place worse than Siberia.

# 9

## COLD CASH AND FROZEN ASSETTES

To visualize the location of Peter's next assignment, imagine placing a bare right foot into a pile of dog excrement. The foot represents the Sea of Okhotsk. That splooge between the big toe and its neighbor? That is Magadan in the Russian Far East.

Magadan is so far east in Russia that it is east of Siberia. Magadan was one of Joseph Stalin's favorite destinations for dissidents, criminals, nogoodniks, people who were members of one of the Soviet Union's vast array of ethnic groups, capitalist lackeys, intellectuals or those with an intellectual disability, purse snatchers, rapists and sometimes their suspicious "victims," people who stood still too long or were short, tall, thin, fat, hirsute, bald or cross-eyed as well as anybody who might be useful for the next big project. Sick and starving in wretched squalor, these bad men and women's fiercely chattering teeth was just what they needed to stop them from jabbering about personal freedoms or other such nonsense.

Misha Cszt, dead for some time, while alive, was one of thousands of the Russian infantry surrounded by more thousands of Germans in 1941. Misha was a straggler. He was one of many who hid from the Germans and then later miraculously managed to sneak back to his Russian comrades where he told his superiors all sorts of useful information that he had noticed about the Germans on his way back.

A hero! Not exactly. Because he was a mason by trade and masons were in demand for the never-ending list of projects built by the labor camp inmates, Misha's comrades decided-since he knew so much-he must be a spy for the Germans.[86]

Misha survived his ten-year sentence as a mason. (Handling cement when it is twenty below zero is in itself a tremendous accomplishment!) Misha stayed in Magadan as a "freeman."

Misha's home was in Moscow, but when he was sentenced, he lost his right to live there. It did no good to sneak back the thousands of miles to Moscow because his papers would not be in order. If caught, he would probably be awarded another sentence. Attempting to get a papers snafu straightened out had led others back to the camp. It was enough of a miracle he survived ten years. Few did. Better not to push his luck.

Misha married Voytka, a local girl. Voytka had a dumpy, cramped, tiny apartment in Magadan and Misha had little money, fewer prospects and, as a typical comrade, was understandably void of ambition.

Voytka never talked. Voytka always yelled. She claimed this was a habit she could not break. It developed, she would holler, when, as a young girl until well into her twenties, she took care of her deaf grandmother.

Inspired by his barren and painful life so far, when he hooked up with Voytka, Misha became convinced that there was no God. If there had been, He was punishing him for some sin Misha was damned if he could remember committing. With Voytka, the punishment switched from physical to mental. Misha stopped talking. He became silent.

Misha found Voytka physically repulsive. Her large rectangular shape reminded him of the male cook at the labor camp. She also had the same strange pushed-in looking face and large nose. At least she had no mustache.

Avoid being misled by Western attitudes of love and relationships. At the time, life simply did not work that way in Russia and certainly not in the Far East. Two people rarely married out of affection. Financially on her own, Voytka was miserable. With Misha, she was maybe a little less miserable. It was also reassuring to have Misha around as a guardian against strange noises in the middle of the night.

A decade of sleeping head to toe with men in the Gulag and Voytka's uncanny resemblance to a brick shithouse was not quite enough to drain all the lead from Misha's pencil. Misha and Voytka had a baby. They named their only child Ivan.

As a boy, Ivan Cszt appeared to be a pleasant sort. Close association revealed him to be a clod. Ivan was also the most gullible person ever born anywhere on the planet.

In spite of his innate imbecility, he sailed through school quickly. His lack of brains and his constant grin sickened his teachers. The last thing they would do would be to hold him back and be faced with his face another year.

Fellow students enjoyed the company of Ivan Cszt for only one reason. He was a simple dupe: an easy target for practical jokes. When they wanted a real good laugh, they would push Ivan Cszt until he got angry. Though a rare treat, an angry Ivan was a hoot and a half to witness. Drool and snot flew as his harmless fists flailed the air.

Years later, as an adult of sorts, Ivan Cszt managed to weasel a job as spokesperson for the Magadan mayor. Somebody higher up somewhere was punishing the mayor. Ivan brought a zealously overstated lack of credibility to the lies he relayed to the media.[87] For its part, the media had no expectations for the truth. If anything, choosing an obvious fool for a spokesperson had an ironic twist that local reporters appreciated.

When it came to being the butt of practical jokes, age brought neither maturity nor wisdom. As village idiot, Ivan Cszt was still easy pickings.

One day a letter arrived from Rome, from the pope, maybe, hard to tell what it said exactly, it was in Italian. Ivan Cszt took it to the mayor.

Mayor Matvei Berman was a long-time Communist Party chief who switched horses in mid-stream as the Soviet's power disintegrated. Since then, Berman's swarthy good looks had gone to seed. With age, his former Kruschevian posture and in-your-face antics were much less imposing. He never lost his fondness for glaring at people. One eye was just a hair crossed, which telegraphed his ability to give insane orders. Mayor Berman stood in his office with Cszt and his two top cronies. In unison, they rubbed their chins sarcastically.

Ivan Cszt pointed out two words that appeared to be 'Magadan airport' and what further appeared to be that day's date. The big shots rubbed their chins in muffled appreciation. The idiot may have a point. In addition, 'Reverend Peter Bondeo' appeared to be someone's name.

"Well Cszt. You had better get moving. Don't want to keep the Pope waiting." Berman nodded towards the door.

Nearly consumed with glee over such an obviously important assignment, Cszt performed a sort of cough/burp/spit routine.

"Should I take the Mayor's car?"

The mayor looked at his cronies. Unison disapproval followed.

"Nyet. Nyet. Nyet." Berman responded. "Wouldn't look good. Don't want the Pope to think former Communists have money for a fancy car. Hitch a ride. You will do fine."

"For an emissary from the Pope? Hitch a ride?" Cszt was so pathetically disappointed the mayor and cronies almost lost it. "I don't-" Cszt made a quick kopek check. "I have only sufficient fare for one way."

Nataly Frenkel responded. Frenkel held the Magadan purse strings. During his seventy-six year life, nobody ever told Frenkel his little mustache make him look like an older, fatter Adolph Hitler. Always wearing that stupid little leather cap. Many wondered silently, does he take it off when he bathes?

"Good." Frenkel declared gruffly. "We don't want to spoil this Pope fellow. Get the guy used to paying his own way. You have enough to get you out there. Let him spring for the ride from the airport."

Then came the kicker from Lazar Kogan, Chief of Magadan construction. What a wheeler-dealer. Always with the pencil in his mouth, he eventually died from lead poisoning. Before closing his coffin lid, the undertaker forced a number two between Kogan's waxy lips. In life, many people did not recognize him without a phone glued to the side of his head. Kogan always spoke in a soothing, conspiratorial tone. Even when asking where the can-opener is. He put his arm around Cszt's shoulder as the three led him to the door.

"See here Cszt. During the war, I used to speak Italian. Some of it is just now coming back to me. It says here in the letter "We are bringing a box of money to spend on the poor people of Magadan. We expect to pay our fair share for housing and transportation." The crony smiled encouragement. The snorting did not begin until Cszt closed the door behind him. The old saying goes "he wore his heart on his sleeve." In Cszt's case, he wore his brain on his sleeve. The other old saying also comes to mind. "You could read him like a book." Cszt could be read like a comic book, or more accurately, like a one-panel cartoon.

When Peter arrived in Magadan, there was still evidence of Stalin's victims of the Gulag. Finding them might involve doing some digging in unusual places. Survivors report that crushed human bones were used as a foundation for the roads.

There were no bones under the runway at the Magadan Airport. When it was built, Stalin was deader than a two-kopek nail and Democratic Reforms had arrived. There were large cracks, holes and areas of general disintegration in the two-year old runway. Democratic Reforms did not influence the natural Russian tendency towards half-assed construction.

After landing, the Aeroflot steward gave no greeting over the public address. Passengers were in Magadan. If they did not know that, then they were in for a surprise. For big city Muscovites and Saint Petersbergers this area was the Far East. What could the steward be expected to say anyway? "Welcome to Magadan, gateway to the slave labor camps where sixty million poor souls lived lives the rest of the former Soviet Union dreaded and feared?"

If knowing the local time of day and temperature were so important people could find out for themselves soon enough. There were no announcements for catching connecting flights. Why should the stewards care if anyone was going anywhere else? Was that supposed to be their business? They were not paid to give out such information. Passengers should feel grateful. Remember the Aeroflot motto is "If you arrive alive, consider yourself on the better side of a bottle." Besides, the p.a. was busted.

The airliner slowed to a wheezing, flatulent halt at the end of the runway and stayed there. None of the passengers moved. Five minutes. Ten minutes. Twenty minutes passed. Peter looked out the window. There was a hill nearby and, through the haze, a suggestion of mountains. The wind occasionally made faint, swirling little eddies. The snow was not white, but gray.

Anyone else on the planet Earth, including those who lived in Magadan, would find this place bleak. Peter found it more comforting than anyplace he had ever read about or seen, including the packed dirt hut floor he slept on in Merdette for five years, because Peter found it humble. Squalor brought relief even when frozen solid. Peter felt rewarded for this chance to suffer.

An hour and fifteen minutes on the tarmac and there was some stirring forward. Sure enough the captain stormed out of the cockpit wearing his heavy woolen coat and one of those goofy but functional fur hats. Peter had no coat. His ticket came with his marching orders from Rome.

Peter was unaware that the Russian Far East was one step beyond Siberia. On the contrary, since he fared as poorly in geography as he did in Latin and Greek, Peter thought he was going to the East Indies and another set of dark-skinned, barely-clothed natives. It was not until he saw the captain's coat that he realized he did not have the proper clothing and that he was correct in his initial impression. That was snow out there not sand.

The Lord would provide. That was Peter's heartfelt mantra as Arctic air blasted through the opening hatch. Passengers scurried for their heavy woolen coats and goofy fur hats. Peter would offer his suffering up for his Savior. His Savior was about to get a hell of an offering. The temperature was ten degrees below zero, Celsius.[88]

Part of the reason it took so long to open the door was because the departure ladder was one of those old fashioned type on wheels. Someone had left it to the side of the runway in open mockery of government regulations. Someone else was left with the responsibility of digging it out.

That poor slob[89] rode his bicycle out to the end of the runway, saw what needed to be done, rode his bicycle-through the wind and snow-back to the terminal, rode back to the plane as he balanced the shovel on his handlebars, dug out the drift, attempted to wheel the damn ladder onto the pavement, watched the damn thing fall over, threw his shovel at it, and eventually dragged it-on its side-to within proximity of the exit door. He abandoned attempts to right it when he saw the crew in the cockpit laughing hysterically at him.

He shook his fist at them, got on his bicycle and rode off. The crew stopped laughing. After a quick discussion, they realized one of them would have to hop down off the plane and set up the ladder or they would never make it to Vladivostok before nightfall. Nobody wanted to land at Vladivostok at night. The pilot was about to restart the engines and leave-Magadan-bound passengers intact- when he realized that the ladder was in the way.

The crew drew straws. The captain picked the last straw, which also happened to be the short straw.[90] Surprising as it may be to the rest of the never-been-a-Communist-country-world, in spite of his additional responsibilities and training, the captain made only a few more rubles than the rest of the crew. His shirts were just as rumpled and threadbare as theirs. Democratic reforms had yet to make him a social superior.

The captain deployed the door's inflatable emergency exit chute. There was a hissing noise followed by a groaning noise followed by a popping noise. The chute flapped flaccidly in the wind. With urging from his fellow crew members and the forward passengers, he crawled ass-backwards out the doorway, then allowed his body to slip out. Accompanied by his own grunting and groaning as well as a steady stream of advice from the crew and passengers, he eventually found himself dangling precariously from the bottom of the doorway. It was easily a twenty-foot drop. The longer the captain held on the more difficult it became to let go. It was not until a passenger loudly suggested somebody step on the captain's fingers that he let go. Luckily, he fell into a snowdrift that had formed.

The passengers filed slowly out the hatch and down the precariously icy ladder on to the frozen tundra. The terminal was visible, but it was over a quarter-mile away. A bus emerged. The revenge of the ground crew! Now it was their turn to yuck it up. They had radioed the airline crew that no bus would come until the last person was out the door and on the ground!

Belching black smoke, the filthy bus eventually squealed and slid to a stop a good fifty yards from the plane. Boy, this was funny. The Vladivostok-bound passengers waddled slowly off the bus (They were not in on the joke!) to the ladder and up into the plane. The bus driver slapped the doors shut and made as if to drive off. He stopped only when the terrified Magadan arrivals screamed after him, waving their arms and cursing.

This was Peter's introduction to Russian Far East humor. Though he was not in a very receptive condition to either notice or respond or appreciate it. He was blue and bug-eyed with cold by the time he climbed on board. He had been the last person in line, of course.

The only advantage to the inside of the bus was the lack of wind-except near the busted-out window. Guess where Peter stood. The passengers huddled together at a reasonable distance: enough to placate their innate Russian Far Easterner's sense of isolationism.[91]

They waited another twenty minutes as the driver, and several impatient passengers, transferred the luggage from the belly of the airplane to the cage on top of the bus.[92]

By this time, Peter's physical condition had deteriorated into a full body shiver. Everything on him shivered. His hair shivered. The curls straightened and then vibrated. An old babcha took pity on him. This was to be his fate and the cause of a good deal of embarrassment during his tenure in the Russian Far East. Little, chunky older woman, shocked at his skin-and-bones frame and warmed by his exotic washed-out Italian good looks, took it upon themselves to baby him.

"Yaba goorrits koo dahm poreski vits doo bo." Or some such Russian gibberish she cooed in mock annoyance as she dragged him inside her woolen tent of warmth. It was all Cyrillic to Peter. Her mashed potato physique radiated a Merdette-like heat that melted away at the fringes of his frozen physique. As part of her attempt to warm him, she rubbed her breasts, as large and soft as worn out oven mitts, against his stomach. As the bus began to move, Peter's pecker popped up into her armpit. Her eyes widened.

"Pyasht nokla bree oosht!" She announced good-naturedly to the rest of the bobbing bus passengers. Something to the effect of, "He is frozen stiff." Some smiled. A few chuckled.

"Tak croom dahsh me yetah vill koom!" The shrieked topper killed 'em. Something to the effect of "And "it" is thrust in my armpit! It is bigger than a breadbox." Everyone roared with laughter. Peter's weakened attempt to pull away resulted in a more vice-like embrace and renewed guffaws and rumbling chortles.

The bus lumbered and belched its way to the terminal. The group's natural mordant state returned. The babcha's gaze glazed with a far-off mistiness as Peter's short-arm continued saluting in its newfound home. It took the driver's slamming on the brakes and the fishtailing bus to separate him from her armpit.

Now that is service! The bus had swerved very close to the terminal door. So close that the wider-bodied passengers, such as Peter's babcha buddy, found themselves squeezing through the partially opened folding bus doors. Accommodating fellow-passengers helped by shoving and mumbling. Far Eastern Russians mumble a lot.

At least it was not windy inside the terminal. However, there was no heat. What. Should heat be provided? Was this a hotel? A fancy dacha? Were people staying here a long time? If it is cold, they will move along more quickly. Employees should be grateful to have work. If they need to thaw out a bit, they can always build a fire outside in an empty-repeat EMPTY-jet fuel drum.

Since Siberia was a bit too exotic for even the most jaded tourist, there were no multi-lingual signs. A sign in Russian, Spanish, and English would only mock the locals.[93] Peter had only one bag and was clueless as to where to find it. He was wearing his sandals, and was sock less, no less-Peter followed the natural inclination that travelers more savvy than he used. He followed the crowd.

84

The Magadan terminal was a small rag-tag building about as sturdy as the average mobile home. Nevertheless, being small, at least everything was close and it would take a real effort to get lost. The herd bustled to the far side of the building.

No rotating gizmos or carousel gently popping out luggage for Magadan. Baggage claim consisted of a twelve-foot long, waist-high crudely cut hole in the wall. Anyone fool enough to expect baggage politely handed over was in for a surprise. The shuttle driver kicked it off the roof of the bus down to the frozen, filthy ground below. He relished this part of his job.

Another advantage to the impoverished Magadan traveler-and ironic contrast to the socialist collective-was the individuality of luggage. Samsonite? Ha, ha, ha! That is a good one! The only similarity was that most of the luggage was handmade out of worn chunks of carpet, canvas or anything approaching sturdy, pliable material. The few manufactured pieces were purloined military, or else looked like some type of thin metal or pressed wood assembled pre-World War II.

The crowd, to a one, pathetic to the bone, picked through the mess and slowly went to Customs before going on its way. Each on to his and her own life. No hurry. As Magadanians were want to say after several licks of the local vodka: "There is no life in Magadan. Only tomorrow."

Peter was left standing alone. His American Tourister was nowhere in sight. The bus produced a parting shot of thick diesel exhaust as it pulled away from the building. Now what?

Well. Christ had urged the have-nots to be like the lilies-of-the-field. They toiled not for earthly goods yet bloomed into beauty beyond compare, or some such silliness. People no better than wild flowers. Jesus! God would provide. Christ! Easy to say when your Dad is God and You are the Word Made Flesh!

Peter inched along in the line for customs. He shivered and waited and offered gladly the discomfort up to his God. It took an hour for him to make it to the head of the line. A person would have to be exceptionally stupid to carry on contraband. However, the Customs officials were not only thorough, they were nosey and they enjoyed harassing travelers. Power to the People!

All Peter had to show was the cassock on his back and the passport, which he now extended helpfully. The guard studied it for five minutes. There was no stamp from Merdette, so the previous destinations section was blank.

The customs guard wore the very heavy, very warm-looking dark, dark green soldier's uniform. His soldier hat matched in color and bore the outdated red Russian star.[94] The brim was fiercely black and shiny. It looked like polished ebony. Uniforms for customs officials and the Russian Army were one reason the Soviets never had a problem with recruitment. Not until democratic reforms, when the government stopped paying soldiers.

Professional looking uniform aside, this particular guard was a little prick. He looked at Peter's picture then sternly, suspiciously, peered out from under the brim.

"Hey officer? You gotta problem? Search him. Make him lift up his skirt. What's with all the cloak and dagger? You think that creep face of yours is gonna make the faddah crack? Come on!" That type of discourse was of course never heard in Magadan. Not until American visitors became more frequent and introduced an unknown emotion: outspoken impatience with authorities. This guard would hear none of that from Peter, of course.

Ivan Cszt stood nearby watching with the patience of a person with fifty-six years of no life only tomorrow. Strange how even strangers reacted to Cszt like pigeon dung plopped onto a shoulder? Find a way to wipe it off and be done with it. Maybe it was his vodka-bottle bottom eyeglasses nestled on the beak nose just north of the idiot grin.

Cszt was barely aware of how people would take one look at him then veer quickly away. The world smeared before Cszt like a French impressionist's daydream. Decent vision care was years away in the Russian Far East. What was there to see?

That said, Cszt had no trouble picking out Peter. He would have to be blind not to be able to figure out which one was the Visitor from Rome. Peter wore a robe with a wooden cross dangling on his chest. For Cszt, that worked as well as a pointing arrow on a neon sign that said "Guy from Rome."

Cszt walked up to Peter and stood there for a moment staring at him and waiting for him to say something in Russian. Though several potatoes short of a full sack in the brains department, Cszt had enough sense to know that he held a nearly non-existent command of English. Besides, he could not remember the word for hello. Silently, he held out his hand to Peter.

"Hello. I'm Father Peter Bondeo." Peter reciprocated warmly with his icy hand. For a minute or so, they blew frosty air into each other's faces. In addition to his litany of quirks and repulsions, Cszt had a habit of standing too close to people.

With neither able to scale the obvious language barrier, Cszt resorted to body language. Cszt wore what he figured was his most ingratiating facial expression: a somewhat withered smile that made him look as if he was in the habit of cleaning out his earwax with a screwdriver.

He clenched his fist horizontally and made an up and down gesture with it to indicate luggage. No less civil, Peter, in between an ongoing series of vibrant shivers, shrugged his humble shrug in response. The gesture was almost lost between an ongoing series of vibrant shivers. Peter held up one finger. Then shrugged again. This caused an expression of knowing disgust from Cszt. This pouting grimace made him look as if he was in the habit of trimming his rather thick mustache and nose hairs with a pair of pliers.

Mumbled, cautious gibberish to the Customs guard brought an annoyed, curt, spat response. No deterrence to Cszt. It was surprising that his tongue never blackened from a lifetime of bootlicking. He turned on the charm full blast issuing the smile of a guy who gargles with paint thinner. Annoyed, but without reason to stop him, the guard grudgingly allowed the two to pass back to the hole-in-the-wall baggage claim.

"Toop de doopteh?" Cszt stooped and sang atonally through the hole.

"Da." Somebody's annoyed response from the other side.

At this point Cszt started yammering away at length. It is not known or necessary to understand what was said. But, since he was the very model of a modern mayor's representative, it is a pretty good guess he recited a long-winded explanation of the importance of this new arrival to Magadan, and how important he, Cszt, also was as representative of, not only the Magadan mayor, but, also, perhaps, the Peoples of Russia. In addition, how important newly forming relations were with, not only the United States, but also the Vatican, with all its power, and dare say money-
.

Peter's American Tourister flew through the opening, skipped along the floor, and then slammed into a corner. Cszt muttered the Russian word for thief under his breath, then without another word to the hole in the wall, they retrieved the bag and returned to Customs.

Peter and Cszt would have been out of there in five seconds or less. However, Cszt made a point of pointing out this was a bag full of money intended for the use of the People of Magadan. The guard allowed Cszt to ramble a moment then held up his hand to halt him. Peter's luggage was not locked. The guard opened it slowly and he and Cszt peered inside.

The contents of the valise included Peter's three robes and a scant, tattered supply of socks and undies. The guard thought the lack of winter apparel was maybe strange and probably stupid. Cszt meanwhile displayed the incredulity of a man who realizes that a blowtorch is an overstated tool for the removal of lint hair. Where was the money?

The guard continued to rifle the contents, (a bit warily as he dealt with the undies). His eyebrows raised in discovery. Dramatically, he revealed a little black case the size of two packs of cigarettes. His look dared Peter as he unzipped it. Cszt hoped for a small gold brick.

Inside the priest's version of a doctor's little black bag,[95] the guard was very pleased to find a stole and a small silver jar. Probably contraband. There was a little crucifix on top of the lid. Clever disguise, perhaps? He held it cautiously with his thumb and index finger then shook it slightly next to his ear. No explosion. He began to slowly unscrew it. Cszt hoped for diamonds. Peter made the sign of the cross.[96]

Inside the container was a short stack of communion wafers. Jesus in a jar! Cszt heart sank. His mustache tips drooped from the ten and two position to a miserable seven and five.

Other than a few anonymous visitors to the camps, Peter was the first Catholic priest in Magadan since 1926. However, the guard knew damn well what the hosts were. Yet, he slowly, carefully dumped the dozen or so cracker Christs on to the table between them and methodically picked them up one at a time and examined them closely. Radio transmission devices?

The official held one up to the bare light bulb dangling from the ceiling. Then another, then another and so on. The last one he flexed slightly between his thumb and finger. A little harder flex and the host cracked falling in two pieces to the table. He picked one up, held it to his nose. He sniffed it, looked at it again and bit off a teeny, tiny bit of the edge.

Having squeezed all the blood out of those beets, he turned his attention to rifling Peter's robes. Peter looked at the spilled hosts for a moment then began picking them up. One at a time, he ate them. He had no choice. The guard had committed sacrilege. He had treated the hosts with irreverence. Peter was obligated to "destroy" them.

Since Magadanians, and Russians in general, are never astonished by anything, Cszt and the guard stared at Peter's action with tempered disbelief. If the same incident had occurred before the end of communism in 1991, the guard would have choked the hosts out of Peter's throat and turned him and the gummy remainder over to the K.G.B. However, that was long ago. Why bother? There was nothing of interest to a spy in Magadan anymore. The guard knew this. He turned his attention back to Peter's suitcase. Let the priest eat the hosts. It is probably the last digestible thing he will put in his mouth for a while.

Cszt saw Peter's causal snacking somewhat differently. His fantasy of a bejeweled papal emissary, an emissary that would elevate his stature not only in the Mayor's office, but also in the eyes of his family and fellow Magadanians, the Russian Far East and the nation as a whole was a vanishing mirage. Instead, he saw himself now in yet another humiliating situation. The mayor and his cronies had tricked him! Maybe Peter was in on the trick.

Cszt had expected elevated stature. He had expected a box of money. Yes, to be distributed to the people of Magadan. However, he, Cszt, would be the one doing the doling. Instead of bejeweled emissary, it is an American wearing an absurdly thin robe and a wooden, a WOODEN cross. This representative of the richest church in the world has less money than a street drunk! This smirking upstart fool does not have the sense to bring boots, gloves and a hat to the Russian Far East! And now he was Cszt's responsibility?!

The frustration came to a boil quickly.
"What?" Clipped and said quietly, it was the only word of English Cszt was confident enough to say aloud. It picked a scab and Cszt shouted.

"What?" That felt good. The next time he screamed at the top of his lungs.

"What?" Half the people in the terminal stared at Cszt. The other half pretended not to look. Then, empty palms up he pleaded quietly with Peter.

"What?" In Cszt's mind, what his 'what' meant was "What do you have? What do you bring us? What (sic) should I help you for? WHAT'S IN THIS FOR ME?" What is this, more embarrassment and humiliation? What is with the no money? What (sic) are you trying to make a fool of me for?"

Because Peter was Peter, he interpreted Cszt's 'what' to mean something more primal in the theological sense. Peter figured Cszt wanted to know: "What is there to live for?" Peter responded warmly and with easy confidence to Cszt's desperate tone.

"Hope"

"Hope?" Cszt did not understand the word. Peter offered his open hands palms up. He lifted them head-high. Peter looked above the three of them towards the rusty, frosted, ceiling supports in the general direction of heaven. Their eyes followed his. The guard looked too, though a bit more skeptically.

"Hope." Peter repeated knowingly.

"Aaaah." Peter and Cszt smiled at each other. Cszt was quick to cool. That is part of what made his anger so amusing. He also had no idea what they were talking about. It did not matter because Cszt and Peter now shared a bond. Peter was the first person ever in Cszt's life (Including Misha and Voytka.) to show sincere interest in him. So Cszt would accept the responsibility of this situation. He was a fool. He did not care. He had a friend. His first friend.

The guard watched all this calmly. But he had other, better ways to waste his time. He opined a cluck at the stupidity of people who come unprepared to a vast frozen wasteland. Peter continued to shiver every so often.

Since the guard was obviously in charge of Peter's life, Cszt figured that also gave the guard the responsibility for his health. Maybe Peter had no box of money. He was still an important person and should be treated that way. Cszt figured the guard should find a way to dress Peter so Peter did not freeze the moment he stepped back outside. The logic of superiors being responsible was a hold over from the old Soviet days.

A short exchange of Russian gobbledegook ensued. The guard was pissed that this skinny creepy guy was pressing him into solving a problem. At the same time, there was an undeniable ego boost for being assumed the superior person of the three. But eventually it was annoyance, the stepmother of invention, which led the guard to gather up a robe from the suitcase and toss it at Peter. The official wiggled his fingers about his head and shoulders indicating Peter should put the additional robe over the one he was already wearing.

The wool, though cold, promised Peter warmth. He put the robe over the robe he was wearing, but continued his little Morse Code of shivers. The official motioned for Peter to put on the other two robes and two pairs of socks. Slowly, the chattering subsided.[97]

On their way out of the terminal they were forced to walk through a group of milling people. People often stand still and do nothing in Magadan. What's odd is that they are not trying to kill time, necessarily. Time there is not a commodity and certainly not as precious as it is elsewhere in the world. Some of them were there an hour or two before their job at the airport began. Not out of eagerness to dig in. Just because. Others waited for relatives who would not land for hours. Others had dropped someone off hours ago. Russians in general spent a lot of time waiting in lines. Maybe this was practice.

In most situations, Cszt would join this "Queue for nothing in particular." However, he had seen a movie where a government bureaucrat, (quite like himself) picked up an important diplomat at the airport then rushed him through the terminal and ducked into an idling limousine. On film the awe of the crowd being knocked out of their path was palpable to Cszt. Odd now how the waves failed to part for Cszt and Peter the way they did for the guys in the movie. Instead people were annoyed with the pushy guy and the priest.

"Watch out for my corns!" and "Step aside everyone! It's the guy who owns the airport!" and, ironically, "Oy! What is the Pope doing in Magadan?"

Of course there was no limo idling outside for them either. Not even a taxi. In a sense, everyone who drove a car in Magadan was forced to be a taxi driver. Fuel was just too damn expensive. Whenever anyone drove anywhere they would stuff the car with as many paying passengers as they could fit. Passengers would then toss the driver a ruble or two. People would stand on the curb and peer into approaching cars. If a car with room inside passed you by you were justified-no obligated-to curse at the driver. "Your mother's menstruation is similar to that of a German Shepherd," was an old, colloquial favorite.

Cszt stuck his head inside a couple of cars and begged sympathy for their luckless situation. This was futile and Cszt knew it. He promised the money at the end of the ride. He would run up to his office-next door to the mayor's-and get the money- twice he cracked his head as the car drove away before he could finish. A half-hour of wailing and slobbering for mercy outside the terminal yielded nothing but insults. No surprise, though. It was silly to ask. Who would trust a comrade with a free ride? Especially a government bureaucrat.

The frigidity crept up Peter's skirts and the sequence of shivers returned. Cszt noted his companion's hue quickly returning to blue. The presence of Peter, obviously an important man, an American, a holy man, had not affected the way other people saw him, Cszt.

His ears burned with the scorn of the crowd who failed to see his or Peter's obvious superiority. Resentment gurgled up his long heavily wattled turkey neck. He was not a nobody! If these peasants didn't realize that, they could suck sheep fur balls for all Cszt cared!

Cszt began to walk. The angry trudging inspired more never-before-thought thoughts. Peter followed, looking like a tightrope walker as he attempted to avoid slipping on the windblown hard packed thin layer of snow. Sandals did not suit the Siberian terrain.

An observation, the only one Cszt had ever experienced so far in his life, nearly knocked the wind out of him. He slammed on the brakes and Peter rear-ended him.

Cszt turned to Peter. Frustrated and a little frightened by these strange emotions, the source of which he did not understand, yet still he knew that Peter was somehow responsible. His mouth gaped open and closed like a fish. He put both hands on the priest's face. As he did with printed material, Cszt craned his neck until Peter's countenance could be more clearly read. Yes, it was now nearly purple with the cold, but Magadanians learn to look past that. Looking deeply into Peter's eyes, Cszt was astonished to see exactly what he had expected. No fear.

The Communist Party had been out of power almost a year. The Party, but not it members. It was still the same wolves wearing sheepskin, from the bigwigs in the Politburo to little twerps such as Cszt. The populations at the labor camps surrounding Magadan had dwindled to almost nothing during Gorbachev. The snitches, who with a word in the proper ear could send an innocent off to thirty years of the worst sort of misery, were gone now, or at least silenced. The snitches had nothing to snitch about and nobody to snitch to. What had he Cszt to fear? By the same token, was there any reason to continue licking boots?

Cszt returned to his trudging and Peter followed. Sixty kilometers. Bah! They'll walk. It was suicidal but who cares? If they die the pope will kick some ass, for certain! What was there to live for anyway? The mayor had not paid him in three months! His wife, a black marketeer who horded her profits and shared only occasionally with him, held little more than scorn for Cszt.

His daughter, his little daffodil now eighteen, wore so much make-up, it made him want to vomit. Her late night returns featured vodka breath, disheveled clothes and male companions up to no good that was for certain. One actually spit on Cszt! Then they laughed and went to her room. She did not even respect him enough to look at him with the contempt Cszt knew she held in her heart. Cszt had recently swallowed this bitter pill.

Cszt and Peter continued their foolish stroll perhaps two kilometers. The airport shrunk into the distance. A few cars passed, all loaded with people. Maybe they could walk all the way. That would teach them all a lesson. A few more cars passed, one beeped in derision. Cszt waved at them in disgusted annoyance.

Dusk approached and they tramped on. The wind died down. The setting sun transformed the distant haze into a transparent gold orange band revealing the snow-capped mountains lining the western horizon. White near the sun, the sky blended from pastel azure to a deep Prussian on the eastern horizon behind them.

The movement helped to keep them from freezing. The isolation and discomfort put Peter at peace. This was God's country he thought. Unaware that, within a thousand square miles, he was the first person ever born to experience that thought as a first impression of the Russian Far East.

Berkeley Caldecott was too busy dreaming of making money to bother with the meteorological transformation and God's possible involvement in the terrain. The two-million dollar Alaska Lottery winner had driven out to the airport to pick up a case of canned fruit cocktail. Relying on the Russian postal system would cost the fruit, and Berkeley, a month's delay. That's if somebody didn't liberate the goods. This was good stuff too, Del Monte, still in the original box. Russians loved American logos more than the products inside.

Berkeley arrived in Magadan one month before Peter. He was there to make more money with his money. Why waste time on maybe investments in America. He knew the Russians would make great capitalists. He knew they were ready to spend, spend,

93

spend and shop till they dropped. The time was ripe. The former ad copywriter frequently fantasized his photo on the cover of Forbes Magazine, goofy fur hat and all, smoking a stinking Cuban and grinning like Gates or Turner. "Russia's New Czar from America" was the fantasy headline.

What Berkeley would have trouble realizing was that Russians, their grandparents and grandchildren, do not and never did dream the American Dream or anything like it. Russians do not know the difference between a job and a career. Why should they hustle? For a ruble? A worthless ruble? To spend on what? A more expensive brand of toilet paper?

The Russians had no exposure to the thrill of wasting money on junk at shopping malls. Other than the criminals, they completely lacked initiative. Keeping one's body breathing was more important than keeping up with the Joneskis. The poor slobs horded everything especially their near worthless rubles.

He had been slowly bleeding money since his arrival, but, like the compulsive gambler in Las Vegas, Berkeley insisted success was in the next roll. The Russians' lack of economic enthusiasm threw Berkeley only momentarily. That's why he was spending so much of his own cash. He greased every wheel he could find. That's what the fruit cocktail was: wheel grease. He thought, somewhat smugly, that he was like the drug pusher at the school playground. Give the unsuspecting kids a few freebies, get 'em hooked, then before you know it, they're killing for it! Berkeley could smell profits. Berkeley was experiencing olfactory hallucinations.

This long drive inspired Berkeley to consider developing his own delivery service: R.P.S. for Russian Postal Service. No. Russians wouldn't use it because R.P.S. sounds too much like a government agency. Maybe V.P.S. for Vladivostok Postal Service. Has sort of an exotic ring to it. Most Magadanians think there is grass in Vladivostok and that it's greener.

The 'V' could be made to look like a 'U' in the U.P.S. logo. Instead of the string wrapping the package put a bow on it. Wait. Why rip off U.P.S? How much would a franchise cost? Does U.P.S. franchise? That would probably call for several investors. Where to find them? Where to find enough trustworthy drivers? Where to find one trustworthy driver. Didn't he grab the fruit himself instead of trusting a local? That put the kibosh on that idea. Maybe in the near future when he'd have investment capital to burn. Besides, in spite of the oil and gas fields up north, fuel costs were obscene. And what about repair costs? Replacement parts?

Berkeley's brain purred and hummed along in his bulky, white Slatya as Peter and Cszt continued to tramp along just a kilometer or so ahead of its headlight beams and their collective fates. He chuckled aloud and tsked at the field of opportunities available here in this wasteland. There were so many that he found entertainment value in dismissing a good one.

This image of himself as the neophyte entrepreneur invigorated Berkeley. He felt like a big shot. He loved filling his pockets with connections. Sure he overpaid for the Slatya. But he was adjusting to the backfiring and the grinding gears. Anyway, the guy he bought it from claimed access to a fleet of cars. That's good to know. The cost of fuel was obscene but his connection at the filling station promised deals during certain hours at certain locations where the purchase was made directly from the tanker. Berkeley lived in the finest (relative to Magadan standards) hotel in downtown Magadan where the manager promised him deals for eventual visits from C.E.O.s from Kmart, Sizzlers and Starbucks.

Berkeley planned to be the regional wet nurse for capitalism. Once he had hooked a clientele, he would import anything and everything from Anchorage and sell it at tremendous profit. He was also making overtures to manufacturing corporations. When the Boeings, Nikes and Kenmores got a look at the many vast empty warehouses, dirt cheap lease rates and Third World labor costs he'd scouted for them, Berkeley's fortune as a consultant would be made. Too bad it was another six months and million bucks in "wheel grease" before anybody told him the Magadan port was frozen solid eight months out of the year. He already knew how reliable Aeroflot was. Also too bad for Berkeley: he ran into Peter.

Almost literally. Like everyone else in all of Russia, Berkeley drove slowly. The better to conserve on gas consumption. But the sun was all the way down. The miniscule amount of heat the blacktop had retained during daylight vanished within seconds of its adios behind the mountains. The dry, windblown snow quickly lost all traction. Berkeley (see above) was not paying attention to the terrain. Though he stared hard at the road, with his lack of concentration, he may as well have been staring at a pie chart. The frosty trekkers popped into the brief range between the car and the edge of the Slatya's headlights. Without thinking, Berkeley slammed on the brakes

The rear-end swerved into the oncoming lane. The enormous bulk of the sedan stopped. It faced the two humans who looked more like startled sparrows. Although one seemed a little pissed. Berkeley jumped out of the car.

"Are you alright? You surprised me." Berkeley's Russian, by the way, was better than most Russian's Russian. A Russian's Russian is all spitting, mucous sucking and throat clearing. Mr. Caldecott's Russian was smooth and resonant. It actually made the language sound attractive and not so proletariat. Maybe that was the way the Czar spoke Russian.

The impeccable tone and lack of dialect caught Cszt off-guard.

"Am I alright? Yes. As for this one. He speaks no Russian. Probably English. He's a Bishop from Rome." To illustrate his own importance, Cszt had decided on the spot to elevate Peter's rank. "He's a holy man."

"Are you alright?" Berkeley asked Peter in English.

"Yes. Are you okay?"

"Yes. Please, may I drive you into Magadan? It's awfully cold. And it's going to get colder. You don't really plan to walk another 20 kilometers do you?" This last question Berkeley translated for Cszt.

"Thank you. But we have no money."

Caldecott waved that excuse away. Suddenly very cold, the three skittered into the car.[98]

Introductions followed. Peter and Cszt were pleased to finally learn each other's names. Berkeley smiled openly at this serendipity. A mucketymuck from Rome and a guy who sounds like he might be the assistant mayor. If he had not been the cautious driver who keeps both hands on the wheel, Berkeley would have been rubbing his mittens together with glee.

"Do you know the person I should talk to about building codes, zoning and such?"

"Yes. Of course. Yes. I can answer all of your questions." Cszt responded with the diffidence of a stinky man insisting he bathes regularly. Although technically not lying, Cszt was not telling the truth either. He did not know what this word "zoning" meant.[99]

"Good, good, excellent." Berkeley, without batting a lash swallowed the hook, the line and the sinker. "And you, Excellency, just visiting? I ask because as you probably know, Roman Catholic clergy are quite rare in these parts."

"God willing, I am here to establish the Church in Russia."

"Oh?" He is going to need a building for the church. From scratch or an existing structure. He is going to need pews, an altar, statues; all those fancy priests' clothes, all those gold ornaments and (!!) a safe to lock the valuables in, a house, probably servants, a car. For Christ's sake, the guy's a bishop! That means some kind of regional headquarters. Berkeley could smell a school. He could taste a hospital.

"Where are you staying? With a family?"

"That would be very kind. I seem to have misplaced my money."

That Peter was a totally unprepared sheep pleased Berkeley to no end. Though he was not squeaking much. It was obvious this wheel could do with a bit of grease.

"I have a room for you. I'll take care of it. At Matryona's Izba. It's quiet nice. Not like anything in Rome, of course. But, a very pleasant hotel by local standards.

"That is very generous. But I can't allow you to pay for me."

"I insist. Think of it as a donation. If that bothers you, you can pay me when you're on your feet. Or when your superiors send money to you."

"Thank you for your generosity."

"I'd like to assist you even more, Excellency, there are only two churches here. Both are Russian Orthodox and though they are small congregations, both churches are being used. There is also a Jewish synagogue and that is in a basement in the business district. What I'm saying is there is no surplus of churches here." Yet another brilliant idea was erecting itself inside Berkeley's head. A thirteen-story idea.

The next morning Berkeley walked down the four flights of stairs to Peter's room. The elevator was still not working. It had not been working since Berkeley arrived at Matryona's Izba. Strange that. Stranger still that Peter' room was in the basement. He found the room, B-14. The door was slightly ajar. He could see dusky light through the crack. He tapped lightly.

"Come in."

It was Peter's soft voice. Berkeley opened the creaking door with some effort. The hinges were rusted. The interior, even by Magadan standards shocked Berkeley.

Peter knelt at the side of his bed: boxes-not even all the same height-with an unseemly looking blanket on top of it. He motioned for Berkeley to come further inside the room.

"I'm almost finished." Peter returned to his prayers.

If Peter had not been so engrossed in meditation, Berkeley would have screamed. What is the meaning of this?! I told them the best room in the house! This is some type of storage room. Look! There is a rattrap! With a rat in it! What is in these pails? Look at the dirt! The filth! When Peter closed his prayer book, Berkeley did ask him those very questions but quietly. Something about the beatific smile took the wind out of his sails.

"This is fine. I asked for it. The first room they gave me was much too fancy. It's quite warm. These pipes must be from the furnace."[100]

"You are an important religious leader. This is a rat's nest. Did you see the dead rat? You will be meeting with other important people. Do you want them to have to put up with dead rodents?"

"I am a priest. Not a bishop."

"Oh. I must have misunderstood Mr. Cszt. In any case, please reconsider." Berkeley knew what a brick wall was as well as when he was up against one. "Here I have a coat for you. And a hat. Oh. That fits. You have a rather small head. Can you see?" Berkeley was briefly puzzled when Peter did not offer to pay him. A gesture to fork over the cash eventually might have been nice. But then, Berkeley realized ruefully, there would be bigger bullets to bite.

"Thank you."

"You're welcome." It took both of them to close the door. Not only was it rusty. It had run ajar. There was no rail along the stairs leading from the basement. Berkeley took care not to brush against the wall.

"I think I have a building that I hope will be suitable for the Catholic Church to establish itself in Russia." Berkeley and Peter were in the Slatya winding their way through central Magadan.

"Thank you. Where are the houses?"

"A good question. There are only a handful of houses. The Communist Party leaders lived in them. Now the local government heads do. Not surprising that means there has been no change in tenants." Berkeley wondered if Peter thought he was making all this effort for the love of God. These Catholics can be tricky. How else could they afford to own so much gold stuff? Better to straighten that out now. Time to lay it on the line.

"Just so we understand each other, Father. I am willing to help you in every possible way. While I am not asking for money right now, I do expect to be paid eventually."

"Would you run the business end of the church for me? Take out whatever amount you think is fair for yourself. I'm afraid I have no mind for business. It will be a great challenge to express that joy to the people of the West Indies."

"…?" Had this guy taken a wrong turn?

"I seem to have misplaced the address of my superior in Rome."

"You realize you are in the Russian Far East? Are you supposed to be in the West Indies?"

"I meant Russia." Peter smiled at his poor geography. "If you spend what ever of your money is necessary to help the church get started, then perhaps you could pay yourself back with money taken in from collections. Is seventy-five percent reasonable? That includes donations and bake sales and bingo. If ninety percent is more reasonable, then make it ninety percent."

"…?" The goose was asking Berkeley how large should the golden egg be? Berkeley had taken for granted he would do well. But this was exceeding all expectations.

"I'll draw up a contract." Berkeley pulled the car up to the curb. "Meantime Father, say hello to home." The two exited the Slatya and stood before the empty Magadan Communist headquarters.[101] From the ground the utilitarian structure hunkered eerily in its stark simplicity. Tiny slits of windows elicited claustrophobia, even from the outside.[102] That was part of the architect's plan: To give the impression of living in a state of strangulation.

Berkeley led Peter around the fenced perimeter. They ducked under a large dog-ear ripped out at a seam in the fence and entered the building through the busted out front door. The joint was trashed. Workers took whatever building ingredients they could carry. But the Youth of Magadan had obviously made a visit or two. They had punched holes in walls; shit and peed wherever convenient-or suited their artistic inspiration; yanked moldings, and pulled up tiles. There was no graffiti. Spray paint is a luxury outside the grasp of the Russian Far East vandal.

"A bit messy." Berkeley chuckled. This was his first time inside. Cszt had been smart enough to show Berkeley the blueprint instead of the building.

"Is there a smaller building?" Be there anyone so humble? There's no one like Peter.

"I'll show you where the church will be. But I'm thinking of more than just a place of worship. I'm thinking more of a Russian Far East Center for Worship and Care. We have the church, yes, but we could shelter the poor, the invalid, the homeless."

Sure they could, but would they? Better check your contract, Father. A shelter was just a cherry bomb of a plan Berkeley tossed to Peter. In fact Caldecott's imagination exploded with a thousand smart bomb ideas. Peter's idea of survival on bingo and borscht sales was a wet fuse.

Berkeley imagined attracting the faithful from all over the free world. All those people who listened over the decades to the popes' warnings that only prayer to the Virgin Mary would avert an all out nuclear confrontation with the Soviet Union. Well it worked! Take that you cynics. Mary, the Mother of God Triumphant, has crushed the head of the heathen communist snake between her virginal toes! Berkeley made a mental note to check on all Catholic hyperbole before including it in advertising campaigns.

The prayerful conquerors will come with their Thick Wads of American Dollars, their Yummy Euros and Yen, their Dollops of Dolares, and yes even the occasional Patronizing and Proud Pounds. The prayers worked! All that burned incense and tossed holy water worked! Now the next step! Convert these poor, sad, misadvised, freeze-dried atheist Russians into Catholics! Knock down the statue of the devil-look-alike Stalin! Replace it with the crucified Christ! Berkeley jotted another mental note to fish around for a fire and brimstone Baptist, just in case this Father Peter fails to hook the locals.

Anyway. Visitors wishing to witness the birth of Christ's Only True Church in this Heathen Wilderness would need a place to stay-that would be in the southern wing of this here building. The northern wing would house the administrative offices of Berkeley Enterprises. Visitors to the Russian Holy Land, as it would surely become known, could experience the thrill of sleeping in a building meant to house Commies! They will need conveniently available transportation and lodging packages. This little office off the main entrance will make a swell souvenir shop. "My parents visited the Gulag and all I got was this lousy blood-sweat- and tear-stained t-shirt."

That room there can be the office for the bus and flight seeing tours of the nearby labor camps. Maybe hire locals to dress up in rags. Buy mannequins and leave them frozen-looking, dead and blue leaning over a wheelbarrow or against the barbed wire, maybe a hooves-up horse for effect. Build a ski area-have to talk to the Japanese about that. Of course, major investors will not line up on a long shot like this until it's proven to be viable. Berkeley needed more than a good sales presentation with impressive charts. He needed facts: lists of profits. Maybe go slowly. Just keep reinvesting the tub loads of profits. Then when he tired of this worn out wasteland, sell the whole damn kettle of fish heads-Wait! What an idea! A restaurant where you can eat gruel just like the prisoners!! Maybe a one-day overnight excursion spent in the dormitories. WITH THE COTS STUFFED WITH STRAW ALL ON TOP OF EACH OTHER AND NO HEAT!!! Why not? People pay good money for that hotel in Norway carved out of ice. Here is a real adventure! Experience what it's like to live in a Siberian Labor Camp. Maybe have Hollywood celebrities appear as guest star commandants!! Don Knotts! Barbara Eden, Sean Connery, Nancy Reagan. He would have to check to see what stars from the Soviet era were still alive. A short fat guy and tall skinny woman as Boris and Natasha!!

Berkeley and Peter stopped in front of two solid, heavy, gunmetal grey doors located near the center area of the building. The ceiling was so low it made breathing a conscious effort. Berkeley pulled a key from his pocket.

"I don't believe there is anything else available, Father. You could check, be my guest, but it's a very tight market." Technically, this was not a lie. After Cszt told him about this place, Berkeley did not want to know of other options. He would pay later for that.

Berkeley fought with the rusty key for a moment then opened the doors. Cszt's description of the room was inadequate, to say the least.

"Yow." Berkeley remarked with quiet awe.

"Oh, my." Peter countered.

The monstrous room was a backwards fan shape before them. Two, maybe three thousand cushy looking, blood red seats-chairs really- sat with small writing tables attached at the right armrest. Left-handed Commies were out of luck. Down at the end of the sloping floor before them, the stage ran the massive width of the hall. Berkeley and Peter strolled down the center aisle towards the front. There were two more aisles to their left and two more to their right. The hall was easily three times as wide as it was deep. And it was pretty damn deep.

"I never thought there would be this many important Communists around here." Berkeley mused more to himself than to Peter.

Before reaching the stage, they turned to look up. The ceiling rocketed away to cap a rotunda. Eight floors above them through the window slits in the ribs of the urinal drain they could make out the statue of Lenin, on his pedestal, obstinately unconcerned with the cold winds as well as the brisk breeze of political and humanitarian reason.

"Look at that old rat, Lenin up there, Father. Wouldn't you like to replace him with a statue of Jesus?"

"Actually…" Peter confessed. "I must admit. When I saw the statue? I wondered if it would be possible to replace him with one of the Blessed Mother. Perhaps with her arms outstretched in welcome? The place for Christ is in the sanctuary."

"Father, consider it done. Mary tops the rotunda. Jesus gets the inside."

The window slits allowed a surprising amount of the yellowish, half-hearted light of winter into the auditorium. The room was painted white. Monstrous copper friezes of brave, strong-looking workers cluttered the walls. Even to a person who does not speak Russian, the slogans on each looked demanding, if not a little threatening. In truth, the sayings were pretty much consistent with a theme of "All for one, and one for all!"

The two stood at the apron and faced the stage. The dais must have been one hundred feet long.

"Will this be too much for an altar? Do we need to cut it down a bit?"

"Yes. Please."

Oddly enough, the platform was raised only six inches above the main floor. Peter knelt on the edge of it. He crossed his arms across his chest and closed his eyes. After a minute of this, Berkeley began to feel a bit uncomfortable. Should he go or should he stay?

"I guess that's a pretty good height for kneeling, eh?" He looked at the blood red carpeting on the floor of the auditorium. He compared it to the flooring of the stage. As a testimony to bad choices for interior decorating, it was covered with linoleum. But not just any linoleum. Well, no. That is exactly wrong. It was obviously any linoleum. It was all mismatched colors, shapes and patterns. Perhaps any large amount of any one design was tough to come by in the Russian Far East.

So anyway.

"What do you think of this floor, Father? Have to do something about that. I guess. Yep."

Berkeley wondered if Peter was in some sort of trance. Though he could not be certain, he was pretty sure Catholics did not go for that stuff. But what about that movie about the little girl with the twirling neck who spewed green vomit and obscenities? Or were Protestants the ones in a trance? Or was it the Methodists? Holy Rollers? No. Those were the women with the big hair. C'mon Father, we got an industry to get running here.

"I am praying to Saint Barbara for guidance." (Not to be confused with Saint Barbra.) Peter was looking to the heavens for a word of wisdom from the patron saint of architects and builders.[103] He was not expecting contact. He was looking at a building. He knew Babs to be the patron saint of buildings. So he was more or less dropping a couple of quarters into her meter. Just touching base. He was a child of God who bore watching in her neck of the woods. To Berkeley, Peter was beginning to look like a fixture.

So as not to disturb the holy guy, Berkeley walked lightly around the dais to get a closer look at the imposing curtain hanging on the wall behind it. Jeez what a piece of cloth. He gave it a feel. Thick. Heavy. Red, of course, and monstrous it ran the length of the stage and upwards to a height that just about lined it up with the top of the fourth floor. Dead center, (What else?) a twenty-foot in diameter embroidered hammer and sickle.

"Ahh Ha!" A muffled rasp as recognizable as an audience member burping just prior to the third act climax, Cszt was here! "This is for a good church? Yes!"

Peter turned, saw it was Cszt, crossed himself, stood and smiled. "Dah goobra morngen."

Cszt looked at Berkeley for an explanation. All he got in return was a pair of raised eyebrows.

"Good morning Mr. Cszt. I must tell you that I am under contract to represent Father Bondeo. He is a priest, by the way, according to him, not a bishop. No. No. It's a trifle. More importantly, since I represent the Roman Catholic Church, I am responsible for all financial arrangements. We are impressed with the building. Have you spoken with your superiors about our occupancy here?"

Cszt's little chest inflated with pride. He anchored his hands on his hips and grinned foolishly. He tipped his head an inch to the left, then an inch to the right. Left, right, left, right, left, right. Cszt looked like a middle-aged man who discovered the joys of masturbation ten minutes ago.

"The building is yours."

"The building is…?"

"Yours. This building is yours to have for you!"

"How much money? Exactly how much money?"

"Money?" No. No money. The building is yours for no money."

"That's impossible."

"No. Not impossible. Communism. Before end of Communism, everybody, all people, own everything. Nobody owns just one thing. One building or two buildings. Communists pay for buildings. People live there. Communists pay for heat and electricity. Now, no more Communists. Building is free. People pay for heat and electricity."

Berkeley controlled what his impulses screamed: to jump for joy. But, a good businessman controls himself.

"When do we take occupancy? Eh. When do we move in?"

"Today. Right now. The building is now church."

It couldn't be so easy could it? So financially painless?

"Doesn't the city of Magadan want some money from me to prove I will pay for the heat and electricity? A contract? Where is the contract? Something to sign? There must be something to sign."

"You visit Electricity Commissariat. You pay him money for six months. He gives you electricity for six months. After six months, you do not pay, Electricity Commissariat turns off switch. You have no electricity. You pay double. He gives you electricity again. Communists very smart."

Yeah. Well, they couldn't do everything wrong.

"Simple. Also visit Heat Commissariat. Same things to do. Same rules. I think you will like it here in Magadan."

"But I-we must insist on a contract."

"Contract with what people?" Cszt showed the exasperation of a man who, after three unsuccessful digs, realizes he will have to blow his nose into a hanky. He was beginning to

104

believe what the Communists had said all along. That Americans were clucks. Good thing the Soviet Union was around to win the War Against the Fascists.

"With the current owner of the building."

"Communist Party owns the building. Communist Party is kaput September 1991. People of Magadan say, "Who wants Communist Party building? You can have for nothing. You want building for holy man. You can have. You must pay for electricity and heat. Please." Cszt held out his hands. He looked a lot like a weasel, or perhaps a ferret. No, no, a weasel.

Berkeley did get his contract. Cszt took him to the mayor's office. The mayor and his cronies were very nice, very attentive. They listened to Berkeley's plans and seemed caught up in his excitement and were impressed with his use of the Russian language. They scowled at Cszt and chorused "A contract! Of course there must be a contract!"

They sat at the splendid conference table in the mayor's splendid conference room (both relative to Magadan standards) and within three hours hammered out a deal. It was four pages long and said, in effect, the building was Peter's at no charge. He was expected to pay for electricity and heat. The building would now be called the Russian Far East Center for Worship and Care.

The mayor and his cronies were happy to give Peter the building. It was an eyesore and a reminder to them, former communists all, of better days. They were now saved the expense of demolition, or even simpler, of making a decision on what to do with the building that would not get them into hot water with their bosses.

As for Berkeley, they would save their honest thoughts for later. Save the contract and use it for your dupa. Toilet paper has more value in Russia than a contract. Let us say you fix up the building very nice. Let us further say that it proves to be a moneymaker. Let us take the next step and say the City of Magadan and its Honorable Mayor realize they must confiscate the building for any reason they see fit. What will you do American? Wave the contract under our noses? Hah! What you obviously do not know about Russian law would fill the Sea of Okhotsk and overflow into the Sea of Japan. Just which court will you plead your avowed injustice to? A contract court? Ha, ha, ha. And best of luck finding a contract lawyer. The closest one is in fucking Fairbanks, Alaska! On the other hand, do not worry. Since your silly scheme is doomed to failure.

Peter sat quietly during the contract talks. After they concluded, he did not accept the proffered shot of vodka. But he did shake hands. He accompanied Berkeley to the departments of heat and electricity where he watched his business manager fill out stacks of forms before turning over a pile of money. Berkeley was taken aback a bit during his visit to the Commissariat of Telephones. No new exchanges for at least one year. Is there a waiting list? The answer? "What is a waiting list?"

Berkeley decided to continue to live at his hotel. It would be easier to organize remodeling with a phone. Peter insisted on moving on site immediately. It was not his choice for a building but it was obviously God's will. They went to what passes for a department store in Russia where Berkeley paid for essentials for Peter: blankets, a lamp, cooking items.

Berkeley was surprised to return to the Center the next morning and find Peter in the auditorium on his knees shivering in the cold.

"There's no heat." Peter did not respond. "Why is there no heat? I paid for the heat. We should have heat." Leaving Peter to his Lord, he picked up the lamp and carried it to one of the plush little chairs. He plugged the lamp into the floor socket. He turned the switch. Nothing. He checked the bulb for tightness then turned the switch again. Nothing. He took the bulb out and shook it lightly. No sound. "Why is there no electricity?" Berkeley did not like this kind of surprise.

He helped Peter stand then escorted him out to the car. The shivering stopped just before he parked the Slatya in front of the city offices building. Inside, suffering gladly the sauna conditions, the workers wore suits. They would be shivering soon enough when they went home.

They stood and waited for fifteen minutes as the two officials on the other side of the counter did their best to not look at them. Berkeley was torn between the rage a typical American consumer would be expressing and his reluctance to shoot himself in the foot with these foreigners. Finally it appeared they were moving for the back door.

"Please. May we talk?" His tone of voice landed in the no-man's land between authoritative and desperation.

"No. We are going to lunch." The Heat Commissioners responded with a calm disregard well inside the border of indifference.

"Perhaps then I will go and wait in the Mayor's office."

The two commissioners looked at each other. Expression disappeared from their faces. They looked like twin Henry Kissingers minus the perfect hair. Their haircuts appeared to have been performed with hedge clippers. One harrumphed subtly. "Tell him we said hello." They left the room.

Berkeley had shown his hand. Now he had no choice. He must see the mayor. He and Peter found their way back to the office and peered inside. As luck would have it, no one was there but Cszt. Cszt listened to the story. He wore the knowing smirk of the professor who lectures with his zipper down. He sighed a great expansive sigh. A sigh that betrayed his fondness for herring.

"Come. Excellence, too, please come." Peter and Berkeley followed Cszt's trudge back to the Heat Commissariat. "Please wait. Please sit, please." Cszt went around the desks to the escape hatch. He tapped so lightly his knuckle produced no sound. Cszt then slowly opened the door and peered inside wearing the grin of a man forced to be entertained by holding a baby who was slicing into the insides of his cheeks with its tiny, sharp fingernails.

"Comrades Thesauruski and Dichunarivitch! Greetings!" The door closed on the mumbled discussion that followed. Apparently from the drawn out sentences and occasional phony laugh, Cszt was doing most of the talking. Shortly, the door opened. Out ambled the bureaucratic bookends. Cszt sulked behind them looking a bit like Tricky Dick himself.

"You have paid for heat everything is in order." Dichunarivitch growled.

"But there is no heat." Berkeley decided it was time to step over the line. He arched an eyebrow suggestively. "Is more money necessary?" He had the good sense to stop short of a wink.

Tweedles-Dum and Dee exchanged a glance. A Thatcher-like smile tickled the corner of Thesaruski's innate frown. "No. You have paid quite enough already. You must save your money for coal."

"For what do I need coal?" Berkeley knew though already. "I paid the money. The city provides the heat."

"No. Communist party, with great wisdom, has separate furnace for headquarters. Necessary in case of earthquake or other natural disaster." Just a microbe of amusement sidled up to Dichunarivitch mouth.

"You must keep money to pay for coal." Berkeley knew Thesauruski was talking because he was fairly certain he saw his lips moving.

"And the money I gave you yesterday? Will you give that back? Now?" More questions for which Berkeley already knew the answers.

"All persons in Magadan pay for heat. Money from yesterday permits you to have heat in Magadan. You must pay to have heat in Magadan. Very simple." Dichunarivitch must have taken a Logic course at Magadan Tech.

"So you expect me to continue to pay you for something you are not going to supply?"

"No. We say very simple." Thesauruski loved talking down to people. "You do not pay? O.K. You have no heat. Commissariat of Heat says you must have permit to buy coal…" Thesauruski also enjoyed the occasional opportunity to introduce a moment of high drama. "…from…Commissariat of Heat."

Cszt's lower lip looked as if it were attempting to coax his upper lip into his nostrils. Caldecott gave Peter a shorthand version of the conversation. "They are bribing us. I think."

A thought crossed Peter's mind. He knelt down slowly. "Let us pray to Saint Nicholas von Flue."[104]

Several thoughts crossed Berkeley's mind as Peter knelt there mumbling. He realized that he desired and longed for all the things those creepy big-shot religious guys had: Pat Robertson's TV empire; Jim Bakker's trophy wife; Jimmy Swaggert's swagger; and a Billy Graham sized stadium filled with ruble-dropping Cszts. Did he share these men's ethics? Before he could consciously answer his own question, Berkeley Caldecott began to make a fatefully inaccurate translation of Peter's prayer for the former Communists.

"Dear God, we ask that you punish thieves who attempt to steal from you. We only wish to spread your love. We are greeted instead with contempt and the hands of atheists in our pockets searching for lone rubles and lint. (This is one of the harshest Russian insults.) We wish to feed and clothe the poor, homeless and starving. These animals wish only to put us out naked and freezing into the streets. Will you crush them for us please, dear God? Because You are our friend. They are Your enemy. They hate You. You Who could destroy the world in a twinkling of an eye." Berkeley noticed a crumb of concern appear on the Kissinger Twins. He picked up the pace and the threats. "Make their genitals withdraw into their stomachs. Dearest God make large warts with long black hairs sprout from their faces." He paused. "That is to say make additional large warts with long black hairs sprout from

108

their faces. Make their skin flake. Make all food taste like excrement."

Berkeley Caldecott, who had never experienced anything more than a vague sense of the monotony of parentally mandated attendance at the Methodist church back in Denver as a child, now felt a delicious rush of godly power coursing through his veins. His grand baritone, normally a soothing, dark, deep, lyrical Rachmaninoff now sounded closer to a disturbed Shostakovich with just enough Scriabin thrown in to inspire thoughts of "Oh, please just make it stop."

It should be noted that while thinking about his future, on several recent occasions, Berkeley experienced thoughts of the non-positive nature. Skating around the perimeter of his Ice Capades Success fantasy was the pipe-wielding Tonya Harding of an idea that he could lose all his money and wind up penniless in fucking Siberia. Desperation lurked in the parking lot.

"Dearest God our friend, take the measly, fetid hearts of these two men from their flabby chests and squash them in Thy Mighty Hands!"

Trembling and blubbering, Thesauruski and Dichunarivitch reached inside their sweat-soaked jackets and pulled out their soggy wallets. This guy was scarier than Khrushchev. Cszt stood and watched, relieved to be on the winning side of justice.

They handed over their shares of the heat deposits. Berkeley counted quickly. "What is that you say Lord? You want more?" He leaned over a bit towards Peter, as if to hear more clearly The Lord's Commands. Peter meanwhile continued his mumbled intercessions to St. Nicholas von Flue.

They turned over their remaining rubles, and, having fallen to their knees, showed Berkeley the empty wallets, and then began digging into their pockets for loose change.

"No." Berkeley suddenly softened. "There would be no lesson from the Lord God if the Lord God turned around and stole from you. Would there?"

Thesauruski and Dichunarivitch missed Berkeley's point but quickly nodded agreement anyway. They had somehow stumbled into a brow beating. A lifetime of authoritarianism had taught them at least one thing. The easiest way to weather the storm is to duck your head and wait until it passes, hoping you are not struck by lightning.

Berkeley reached into Peter's armpit and lifted. Peter crossed himself and rose compliantly. Muttski and Jeffski rose too. "It seems there was a slight misunderstanding, Father. All is well. The city extends a generous welcome to the Holy Catholic Church."

"Bless you, my brothers." Peter shook their hands warmly. Both found the floor more interesting than looking directly at Peter.

"The father-the holy man says, continue to cooperate or he shall tell God to shove your fat heads into your own furnace?" Berkeley's smile was lathered with malicious inquiry. Cszt stood to the side filled with pride over his part in brokering another successful transaction. He looked like the preening actor, who after winning the Oscar inspires the huge television audience to simultaneously wonder, what drug he was taking that day.

That night, Thesauruski and Dichunarivitch told their wives all about their dances with death earlier that day. It was a good excuse to open a second bottle of vodka. The wives poured.

In spite of the coal discussion, the next day heat was pouring into the Russian Far East Center for Worship and Care faster than the annual per capita consumption of Vodka. Great billowing, invisible clouds of the stuff wafted out the busted windows of the first four floors. Much of the heat found refuge in the remaining, unoccupied nine floors. In the auditorium, now a chapel and center for correct worship of the Supreme Cheese, it was downright toasty. The heat reminded Peter of Merdette.

Peter perspired as he busied himself with an attempt to pull the huge flag down off its mast on the great wall behind the stage. He thought he heard a knock. He stopped. He listened. It was several knocks. Several people were knocking on the big, bulletproof doors.

"Please, come in." Peter answered quietly. If Peter ever shouted or raised his voice in his life, no one witnessed it. The knocking continued. He put two and two together and walked up the aisle to the door. He opened it. There stood a group of little babchas. Little grammas. All short. All substantially chubby and all topped off with colorful babushkas double-knotted beneath their chins under their weird fur hats.

With a sedate but friendly wave of his arm, Peter invited them into the chapel. Initially they oohed and aahed at the impressive majesty of the communist forum as they stripped down to their dowdy skirts and aprons. Then, an editorial cluck or tsk

110

sounded here and there. Such a big room those big shots build for themselves! And, Duck's Blood, it was hot in there!

Peter ushered them towards the dais. All carried a welcome gift of some sort. Gossip travelled faster than the approach of winter in the Russian Far East. That was proven true by the gifts of clothing that many brought. Several had tins with food. One offered a can of colorful fruit cocktail!

Like a flock of birds that makes a sudden turn, they magically migrated as one to the stage left side. Each set down her offering and chirped or gurgled an effusive Russian explanation to the non-comprehending Peter. He sweetly smiled his gratitude.

Cows' Lashes he was handsome. So tall, so thin. And his eyes were not the least bit bloodshot. Now that is something Russian women rarely see in a Russian male over the age of twelve. Put passion out on the back stoop, fool! These gals swooned when they saw the whites of a man's eyes.

Peter stood, hands clasped in relative comfort, as the gaggle giggled girlishly. Whispered accusations were exchanged, the Russian equivalent of the childhood charge "No he is your boyfriend." This game lasted an hour or so. Peter was as good or better than any Russian at standing around and doing nothing. Gradually the lovesick grammas tired of this and one by one decided to test the comfort of the chairs in the great hall. Eventually all of them were sitting cooing on their perches in comfort. Slowly they tired of this and just sat there and stared at Peter. A group of ten ducks lined up in two rows.

It had reached a point of less than nothing being done. Peter smiled at his new group of friends. He turned and walked back to the grand curtain, grabbed it and, with all his scant 150 pounds or so began tugging. Prior to the Babcha brigade's arrival, he had managed to free the great rag from only one of its moorings. There must have been another 99 more to go.

The girls, en choro, each raised a furry Andy Rooney-like eyebrow. Sure, there was nothing much left of the communist theory but a few road apples back in Moscow. But the pretty priest's yanking held out something of the revolutionary. They flocked to the stage and, at first, spread out, each grabbing on with chubby, weathered and wrinkled fists. No need for a "1-2-3-Go!" Ten women who have been menstruating simultaneously for fifty years have no such trivial needs for coordination. They put their weight into their grasps and tugged. A groan escaped the supports to the left center and right. This could be dangerous if the whole batten came down on their heads, they thought silently.

They grouped around Peter, pressing into him. Groped. He stood above them like the crane in the frog-laden lily pad. Innocence turned suddenly intimate, as it was boner time again! As shame reddened his cheeks, he mumbled a prayer to Saint Agatha.[105]

Peter was not privy to the flock's silent communications. They yanked and he was a second or two behind them. The rod, already loosed from its moorings fell in a heavy, red cloud upon them. Since Peter was the tallest, the rod glanced his noggin before making a louder muffled clank on the floor.

He was out like a light, although his switch remained in the on position. Moments later, he gained consciousness and found himself in a nest of deflated melon breasts and saggy, flabby underarms. Slowly he stood. Slowly he realized he was in Russia. Slowly he remembered where in Russia he was and why these women, three or four with tears in their eyes and one with a beatific smile adorning her wide face, were gathered around him. Slowly he realized his penis had maintained its proportions, but also that Saint Agatha had failed to halt a volcanic eruption. Must have been busy in Peru somewhere. One woman smiled conspiratorially-more a leer actually-exposing her one remaining incisor and two bicuspids.

Peter closed his eyes and made a confession to God. He admitted to the sins of lust, non-procreationism, hedonism, carnalism, eroticism, onanism, oedipalism, adultery, fornication, dirty thoughts and dirty underwear. Peter believed that when it came to telling Daddy you were naughty it was better to overcompensate.

When he had opened his eyes the girls let out a massive sigh of relief. They thought he was swooning. That happened to younger men after their first time with older women.

Peter found the approximate middle of the curtain. The babchas spread out along the edge and, with a good deal of huffing and puffing, pulled the grand drape out over the seats. Peter walked over to his things and picked up a small pair of scissors. He measured off an arms length, then put them to work gnawing away uselessly at the hem. At this rate the next revolution would come and go before Peter could slice the curtain into functional blankets, as was his intent.

The grannies, all experts at recycling-Communism and its deflation of a competitive marketplace does that to people-raised a ruckus. They dragged Peter over to a chair and forced him to sit. The leering grandma sat in the next chair and held his hand. The rest huddled. This was an unusual situation, so they talked. Shortly, they put on their coats and put their funny fur hats on over their bandanas (which they had never taken off). They gave Peter a "wait here" gesture and left.

They were not gone long. Maybe an hour and a half. With them they brought scissors, all types: pinking, cloth-cutting. One wrinkled chubbette pulled out two pairs of foot-long sheet metal cutting scissors. The rest laughed at her lack of daintiness. That is until they watched her rip through the curtain like butter, while they inched along.

Soon the work was done, supplying a pile of lovely red blankets, or rugs, depending on one's politics. Most were roughly 6x8 feet. The oddball was the 20 X 20 with the hammer and sickle on it. In a festive mood, Little Miss Smiley wrapped it around herself and filled with the joy over having given Peter a hand, and to boast about it a little bit, began dancing around.

"Fa la la. Fa la la." She warbled the Russian equivalent. The others watched. They gave no visible reaction, although they may have been glaring a bit because shortly Smiley slowed. "Fa la…" She stopped.

One of the ladies, a tank of a woman sporting a cheek wart the size, color and texture of a Marin County raisin from a good year, marched over to Smiley. Smiley at this point became Mopey. She stared at her boots. Wart woman pulled the cape off and flung it ceremoniously to the floor. Her cheeks began to twitch as a wet, rumbling snore rumbled her sinuses. Wart woman was digging for oysters, scratching up every patch of lung and bit of bronchial gum she could muster. She paused and formed her mouthful letting it congeal on her tongue then reared her head back, slowly back. Her skull catapulted sneeze-like, and the loogey sailed moist and massive through the air. It slapped into the icon dead center.

In seconds the others, Mopey included, joined in the snore, wad and hork fest. Some began stomping their heals into the symbol of what was left of their past. The vehemence reached a peak then quickly ebbed. Two or three began to sniffle a bit. One began to weep. Then two more, then another two more joined in as the bitterness turned into tears.

Peter had been folding the blankets, but stopped to watch the extravagant emotional display. He approached the group tentatively, and then put a consoling hand on the nearest shoulder. It was Wart Woman. She turned and embraced him, her gushing nose (All those wasted loogies!) pressed into his shoulder. That was all the others needed. Group hug!

Once again, Peter failed to respond appropriately to the physical contact. At least, due to his earlier emission, the root sprouted more slowly, but no less turgidly. Better to nip this bud before it blossomed. He pulled-tore himself away from the gals. They dissolved into sheepish giggles.

"Let us pray." Peter faced the now blank block wall. He knelt on the short edge of the stage and put his hands together, closed his eyes and bowed his head. The ladies quickly followed suit. None had prayed in decades. But once performed this bizarre submissive act is never forgotten.

The clank of the doors did not disturb them. Berkeley and Cszt had been watching. The two had witnessed the whole outburst from spit to giggles. Cszt had clumsily leaned against the door, which, up until that point, was slightly ajar. They walked slowly towards the backs of Peter and the ladies. The scene astonished and inspired Berkeley. Cszt, ever on the look out to act like a blowfish, began puffing up for the citizenry.

"Dear Jesus, please forgive our anger." Peter whispered.

"Oh Great Godhead high above us." Berkeley augmented in Russian. "We beg You to bury the-" Berkeley noted the gobs and heal marks on the hammer and sickle. "-enemies of your love. Bury the former regime in the mud of spring and let it fill their noses."

"Help us love our enemies."

"Fill their throats and stomachs with the dung of cows and the urine of plough horses."

That got Mopey's attention. She turned a wondering glance in Berkeley's direction. Wart Woman regained her attention with an elbow to the ribs.

"They have been misguided by Satan. Forgive their transgressions."

"May they eat worms through eternity. Or chop the beasts into little pieces and feed them to the snarling hogs for they lied to us and horded the fruits of our labor unto themselves."

"Teach us how to be kind and generous as You, sweet Jesus. Forever and ever, Amen."

114

"Show us how to be good capitalists and send the evil socialists to Hell to burn in pain. Forever. Amen." Berkeley paused a second. "Please respond by saying… Amen."

"Yay-min." Close enough.

The gals stood and listened raptly as Berkeley explained what Father Peter's Russian Far East Center for Worship and Care both needed and wanted to do for Magadan. Father Peter was not asking for sacrifices from them. Father Peter knew their lives were already very difficult. But Father Peter hoped to fill this former den of the godless socialists with the love and charity of Jesus. So, if they had any belongings or food they could spare, or (wink, wink) connections with someone who does, Father Peter would see all items would be put to good use.

This man was also very handsome also with clear eyes. Perhaps Americans did not drink vodka? The ladies nodded 'yes' they would also attend the service on Sunday.

That first Sunday a fairly impressive flock showed up and filled the 'church' to half capacity. The following Sunday it was packed. An extra later service was added and that also, week after week, filled the house. There were only a dozen or so men in the crowd of one thousand. The women enjoyed the way Father Peter-as filtered through Berkeley -told of God's scorn for the recently deposed regime. The sermons/tirades awakened their long dormant sense of superiority. He called them the true heirs of the monarchy. Although God was obviously superior to them, they were obviously superior to the atheist dung heads who did not believe.

Peter maintained an air of bliss, an air of innocence as he babbled Catholic Kumbaya that Berkeley ever more and more zealously misinterpreted. Though somewhat harsh or more often rabid, Berkeley spewed a theology typical of all religions.

Prior to Berkeley's misinterpretations, the only thoughts held by these intellectual quarantinees were of their own pathetic hopelessness. With their intellectual necks craned and philosophical mouths gaping the chubby chickadees hungrily swallowed Berkeley's wormy theology. It was a dive-bomb approach to catechism. They learned not only of God's love for capitalism, but gobbled the lessons on how to be capitalists. The few moldier oldies, who had attended church in their youth, were too addled to realize how little religion and how much economics Berkeley-that is to say Father Peter- was shoveling down their eager throats. Were all American men so pretty? Or was it just the Catholic Capitalists?

One of the lessons of the Bible the congregation learned was about consignment. Berkeley instructed people to take beds, blankets, or the odd bit of excess food they may have stumbled into possession of, as well as tools, weapons and appliances, and bring them to the Center. Berkeley would sell the items and give a portion of the profit to the person who brought the object. He also allowed trading. But traders handed over a stipend on the way out. Money was exchanged only at the coupon kiosk. The coupons were exchanged for goods. Berkeley constantly monitored the kiosk.

Berkeley, for now, gave up the idea of trying to figure out what these people would or would not buy. While taste and a desire for something nice was mostly non-existent, he could not count on these people to only want junk either. Some of the items he added to the stalls sold, such as Barbie dolls. While worthwhile items such as Tupperware collected dust.

There was no explaining either the tastes or needs of these people. He saw one ancient crow put down too many rubles for a bathing suit. A man's boxer style bathing suit! One man traded a perfectly good coffee percolator for a tape dispenser. It was empty! Where would the man find tape to dispense? What did he have that needed taping? He certainly did not have another coffee pot at home.

Berkeley relied on Cszt to display the items. Cszt held a shocking sense of order and how to separate things. Though bizarre, it worked. Put the flowerpots on the washing machine. (There were only four in all of Magadan and two of them were kaput. Previous communist party chiefs had owned all of them. The machines were vintage era 1940s with the squishing rubber rolling pins wringer and electric washtub. Of course there was no spin cycle. That was what the rolling pins were for. Oddly one of the machines a 1948 Hobart was worth 300 thousand dollars as an antique collectible back in the States.) Cszt would drape a tattered, old Oriental rug over the armrest of a beat-up old sofa. The colors and patterns clashed more often than matched. Some exotic form of Russian Far East logic made the rug w/sofa sell together and more quickly. A shovel lay perfectly centered on a Formica topped kitchen table. The buyer bought both together. The grossest but most successful combination was putting that rarest of Russian commodities-toilet paper-with the canned foods. The display consistently brought in twice the black market price.

Berkeley made the mistake of putting the dishes, cups, saucers and kitchenware on tables. Sales halted abruptly. Sheepishly Berkeley watched the turnover re-ignite after Cszt put everything in neat little rows back on the floor in a corner.

Soon products were spread out in more than twenty rooms. The east wing of the Russian Far East Center for Worship and Care was beginning to resemble a flea market. Berkeley was making a lot of money. Not good money. These were Russian Rubles after all. The merchant of trade spent the next to the last of his precious real American dollars on a very expensive telephone system, fixing the busted windows and turning sixty of the eighty west wing offices into forty hotel rooms. The last several thousands paid for advertising in the Travel section of the New York Times. The ad ran every Sunday for two months. One adventurous vacationer made a reservation. But he cancelled the day after it was made.

Berkeley could have saved a few sheckles on his office/room. Regardless of whether or not they can afford it, important people must live and work in an impressive looking environment. One does not need an M.B.A. to figure that one out. The only thing lacking was an equally impressive view. Berkeley installed large windows and too late realized that in Magadan there really is not anything to look at that constitutes a view. Frozen squalor does not constitute a view.

Peter survived happily in his three hundred square feet next door to Berkeley's several thousand. He had a bed with nightstand (which also doubled as a little shrine to the Virgin Mary), a wooden straight-backed chair. There was a tiny closet that was more than Peter needed and a small bathroom.

In the beginning, the little old ladies took turns (fought over) feeding Peter. He ate like a bird. It was several months before they gave up trying to force huge meals on the handsome holy man. A few tablespoons of borscht, a heal from a loaf of tasteless black bread, a sip of tea. Any more that that and Peter turned green and groaned and to look at him, you would think someone had shoved a cow down his throat. The additional reward to feeding Peter was doing his laundry.

So. Even though Berkeley's previous plans were miles down the crapper[106] along with every last American dollar, there was no denying the Center was a success. The Church and

117

Berkeley were rolling in rubles. Though it was all Berkeley's doing, word got back to Rome of this Siberian (sic) spiritual leader-Peter-who was once again a long-shot success.

Word got back to Rome via a threat eventually made good. Seems Russian Orthodox Church leaders, who had spent the last seven decades hiding in basements, were more than a little miffed at this interloper from the Roman Church. The R.O.s problem was that Peter was absorbing money and worshipers who should have been supporting the Orthodox. Their services attracted nobody. Not even their own nuns!

"Replace your Peter! Or we will make trouble." They threatened somewhat convincingly. Rome scoffed at the idea that Peter should leave. "It is a free country now. People can do whatever they want." They chuckled sardonically over cappuccino.[107]

That attitude is what led to Peter getting his holy butt booted out of Russia. Not, as some believe, by the atheistic communists. They had all donned lamb's apparel to do the free enterprise dance. What would they care about some piddly-dink preacher in Podunksky?

Could it possibly be the work of those wacky, bearded, incense jiggling, overdressed-including headgear that makes the pope's look normal, icon-venerating Russian Orthodox? Duh! The R.O.C. won an uncontested battle in Moscow that made itself the only sanctioned religion in Russia. Uncontested because it lobbied the effort and nobody from Rome, or anywhere else, showed up to oppose it because nobody from Rome or anywhere else knew about the proposed law.[108]

Peter and Berkeley could have continued business as usual for some time. If not for Cszt. At this point in the narrative, Cszt proves to history that if they had elevators in Magadan his would never make it off the ground floor. For it was Cszt! Of all people! Who read the tiny little story in Pravda about the bow to the Russian Orthodox Church! And then! Tells his boss the mayor!

The mayor liked the sound of this. He interpreted the new law to mean that the Roman Catholic Church was no longer allowed in Russia. This would mean Berkeley and Peter were no longer allowed to continue propagating in Magadan. While not even close to the spirit, let alone the letter, of the new law, the mayor's interpretation allowed him to acquire a nice, recently refurbished building to move into along with a profit-turning business inside it. Characteristically happy as a clam, ignorance

118

being the chief negotiator for bliss, Cszt continued to run the consignment shop.

These developments led Berkeley Caldecott to decide that enough was enough. Imaginative enough to invent new business ideas, but not perceptive enough to smell the manure spread among the rose bushes, he figured he would liquidate his several million rubles and head back to the states, maybe spend a month or two in Las Vegas. Una problema. Rubles were not allowed to leave Russia. Oops. It took nearly a month for the look of astonishment to wear off Berkeley's face. He wore it for another month when he realized that he had no contractual recourse. The mayor could indeed take back the building and pay nothing for all the improvements made and paid for by Berkeley.

Oh what was Berkeley to do? What to do? True enough, he had more connections than Siberia has useless acreage. True also that the Center, and all his investments in it, belonged to someone else. Yes, he was a rich man by Russian standards, but that was what was wrong: He was rich by Russian standards. In Magadan, no less.

Magadan, where that day's headline in the paper reported the wild dog pack had claimed another victim. Magadan, where the Diabetes Center announced its research department will discontinue transplanting pancreases from corpses, dead cows and other dead barnyard animals. Magadan, where the lack of heat is responsible for frozen sewage in toilets. Magadan, where people whisper about the new Russian Mafia and the 150 police it killed. Magadan, where the permafrost is one mile deep.

It was one night, deep in despair as well as his second bottle of vodka, that Berkeley imagined he heard the voices of the banished and the dead. The past wailed in his ears like some horrific personified tinnitus. As he dipped into the jar for another pickled egg, some type of crossed wires in his brain also made him think of his friends. His Russian friends. His Russian capitalist friends. Not all that hard-working or industrious. But where did hustling ever get a Russian? Maybe what Russia needed was someone just the opposite of Old Uncle Joe Stalin. Someone who offered hope instead of fear.

With that thought, relief washed over Berkeley. No more sermons threatening banishment to the non-believers. Good thing he had not burned any bridges with the mayor. Could still be some possibilities in a meeting. Berkeley screwed the top back on to the vodka bottle and fell asleep.

The next morning when he woke up, his plans for resuscitating relations with the locals vanished as quickly as the rumor of a Siberian hot spell. After squaring things with Peter and seeing to it that the priest had communicated his plight to Rome and that he would be taken care of, Berkeley packed his clothes into one bag and his rubles into another and bought a ticket on the TransSiberia Railroad.

He travelled the country for a year soaking up ideas about its people and their plight. He wound up in Saint Petersburg, which he liked the looks of, were he paid a radio station to allow him to host a radio show. He sold his own commercials and made a good deal of money. The number of listeners grew and when stations in Moscow and other major cities got wind of his success, they signed him up to a national syndication. Seems the Russian people could not get enough of the golden-voiced American who audaciously made fun of politicians who did not do things the way that Berkeley Caldecott thought they should.

As for Peter, he was about[109] to go from the frying pan of Merdette to the freezer of Magadan to the fiery sands of the Middle East.

# 10
## PETER. DIG IT

For thousands of years the Negev Desert has crumbled monumental rocky stands as it shifted its weighty sands. The winds merely caressed others, allowing them to offer proof to the whimsy of nature. Through the ages, all sorts of secrets have been covered and uncovered. Peter was about to stumble on a big one.

Prior to Peter's arrival, the last important historical figure to visit Wadi Rum, in the south of Jordan in the Negev Desert, was Lawrence of Arabia. Decades later a glut of tourists from Italy, Germany, the United States and Japan followed.

Peter received a letter from Rome ordering him to Wadi Rum. Peter did not question or wonder about the orders. He saw they came from the Eustachian office at the Vatican and so followed them religiously. No explanations were needed. When someone in a position of authority said "March!" Peter would respond with "How high?" Not that authority was ever an issue. As has already been exhaustively demonstrated, Peter would unquestioningly take orders from a wino on a street corner.

Anyone with foreign travel experience would take one look at the itinerary for Peter's cross-continental journey and quickly assume it was intentionally designed to prolong the agony of the trip with what could be seen as excessive layovers. In fact the wisdom becomes clear when considering Peter's trenchant for getting lost and not knowing one continent from another. He also had a tendency to wander or stand around until someone told him to move along, or worse, to direct him to the wrong place. He was truly a sheep. The orders compensated for anticipated detours. That was the reason for the long layovers and the complete lack of ambiguity in directions.

"Immediately after you board each flight, cross it off the list with the provided pencil.

-- 3, May, at 0515, Aeroflot Flight 4 from Magadan to Vladivostok. Wait in Vladivostok until 5, May.

-- 5, May, at 1825, Aeroflot Flight 9229 to Tokyo, Japan. Wait in Tokyo until 7, May.

-- 7, May at 1250 Turkey Air Flight 805 to Bushville (Formerly Kabul), Afghanistan.

-- 8, May at 2120 (Only twelve hours between connections. No time to dilly-dally.) Iran Air Flight 425 to Tehran, Iran.

-- 10, May at 1450, Egypt Air 1432 to Cairo, Egypt."

A less patient passenger would have been ready to cut his own throat, or someone else's by then. Not Peter. If it were not for a rather large desert in the way he could conceivably have walked from Cairo to his destination Aqaba, Jordan faster. Instead, as with all his previous layovers, Peter stayed where he was dropped off in the airport. He did not move to Customs. He could see the signs pointing to Customs. He could read them. They were written in Arabic, English, and German. It did not occur to Peter that there was plenty of time between flights to visit exotic sites outside these airports. Instead he would disembark the various planes and simply stand or sit in the retaining area. Eventually a security person would take it upon himself to ask Peter what his business was, check his passport and boarding pass and then, luckily, send him to the correct gate for his next flight.

Peter's longest layover-an eye watering, ear digging four days-was in Cairo waiting for his flight for the last portion of his flying journey to Aqaba. The itinerary had reached its end prematurely. From Aqaba, it noted, it would be Peter's responsibility to find his way to his next assignment, Wadi Rum, Jordan. There, Peter was to establish a church and preach the word of the gospel to the Bedouin in Wadi Rum. Good luck.

Peter was aware that he was in the Middle East. He also knew that put him some where near the Mediterranean. Though, frankly, his mental picture of the location put him somewhere closer to Morocco. That did not matter. His boarding passes had pointed him in the correct direction so far. He was certain that Jesus had lived in the land where he was now headed.[110]

The Cairo Airport was dark and dingy. Clean but not spiffed up. Nothing pleasant to look at: Mecca of utilitarian architecture. As he had during other layovers, when he was not conked out on a chair dozing, Peter took to his knees and began to pray.

Ahmed Salah had been dozing in the chair next to Peter. Ahmed, a Muslim, half dreary with snooze, seeing someone wearing a robe on his knees in public assumed Peter was a fellow

Muslim performing one of the five daily ritual prayers Muslims performed in order to consider themselves good Muslims.

Ahmed whipped his portable prayer rug from his carry-on valise, kicked off his shoes and otherwise began to prepare himself for prayer. But wait a minute! Had not he just prayed before dozing off? Could it be possible he had slept so long he missed his prayers and his flight as well? Ahmed studied his watch. It certainly was working correctly or at least appeared to be correct. Yes. It matched the clock on the wall. He tapped Peter on the shoulder.[111]

"Khhrup sherrup kadrrukhhah melchh hhabbah?"[112] Peter thought Ahmed was having difficulty clearing his throat and so offered this stranger his hanky. Ahmed considered the gesture for a moment before bursting into operatic gales of laughter. "You speak English. You do not speak Arabic. Is that correct?"

"Yes." Peter did not get the joke. By the same token it was not the first time someone, even a complete stranger, had unexpectedly exploded in laughter at something he had done. So in reply, Peter offered a completely unsuspecting, if not somewhat wan smile.

"I apologize. I have interrupted your prayer. We Muslims pray at appointed times. I thought you were a Muslim praying at the wrong time so I was letting you know. That is why I laughed in such a bellicose manner. But, forgive me. I continue to interrupt."

"I pray to the Lord whenever I have the opportunity." Peter said rising to his seat. With that, he and Ahmed then planted it simultaneously.

Ahmed did most of the talking. But tossed in enough questions to discover his current gate-mate would be married to this uncomfortable airport seat another three days and, to further his astonishment, Ahmad also uncovered the admission that Peter had no idea where Wadi Rum was or how he was going to get there and-the oddest part- did not seem particularly concerned about it.

"God will provide."

"What will God provide? A bus ticket to Wadi Rum from Aqaba? Or will God provide a new pair of sandals to replace the-pardon me for saying so-strips of the underside of a camel's tail you wear on your feet now. Those will not survive a walk of seventy kilometers from Aqaba to Wadi Rum. You will be lucky if the Bedouin do not capture you and murder you."[113]Peter's shrug contained no challenge. Peter had made his point. His complacency irked Ahmed.

"I cannot be a party to foolishness." Ahmed fumed a bit. Breath like that of the fiery desert wind scorched in microbursts from his great fury nostrils as he settled on inflexible. "I cannot allow this. I will take you in my limousine from my resort in Aqaba to your accommodations in Wadi Rum."[114] Ahmed expected at least cursory objection, but received none.

"Thank you."

"Ah! But I have an appointment this evening and you are planning to camp here yet another three days." Bemusement itched at the edges of Ahmed's fully expressive face. "But I would wager you have no tent for this camping. Am I correct?"

"This is what I have." Peter pointed to his travel-chafed American Tourister.

"This is all that you have brought with you from America. One small box?"

"I did not come from America. Not recently. I have come here from Siberia."[115]

"Siberia? That would explain this heavy winter coat you wear. You won't have any use for that in Wadi Rum. What work did you perform in Siberia?"

With that question Peter talked on at length.[116] about his adventures and the people of Magadan. As with many of the great communicators throughout history, it was not so much the substance but Peter's tone that moved people. So it was with Ahmed.

"You are a holy man. Not as holy as Lord Mohammed-peace be upon him. But, pretty holy. I, a deeply religious Muslim man, am moved to assist you a lowly infidel Christian. I will arrange for a ticket for you on this next flight to Aqaba. I am flying first class but I will see that you have an economy class ticket. Why do you look at me so? Very well. I will purchase a first class upgrade for you."

So it was that Peter experienced his first first-class flight. Though he would have been just as satisfied stowed in the water closet.

Jordan is a nice enough country. Once the Jordanians stopped arms wrestling with the Israelis over this or that patch of sand and settled down into the business of figuring out how their former enemies were so good at making money in an otherwise barren dessert.

Sure a kibbutz is a great idea on paper or when witnessing the greener grass on the other side of the border. But the kibbutzim took a great deal of "share the wealth" mentality the Jordanians found foreign. Instead they decided to ape the way the Israelis bottled the Dead Sea's endless supply of beautifying salty mud. Once fears of terrorist attacks were allayed the Jordanians found success sucking money from the pockets of tourists in resort towns such as Aqaba. Also, the Japanese and German governments stood in line waiting to give the kingdom money to uncover and eventually restore the acre after acre of buried ancient ruins scattered throughout the desertside.

Though most all of the residents of Wadi Rum are Muslim, instead of offering daily prayers to Allah, they should get down on their knees and thank their lucky stars for Hollywood. Wadi Rum is the area where the movie Lawrence of Arabia was filmed. The land boasts a moonlike desolation. It has absolutely nothing going for it but sand, sand and more sand and just enough rocky buttes to break up the monotony. These monstrous rock formations tower a thousand or so feet with nothing better to do than wait around for wind erosion.

The Americans of the late twentieth century brought along their penchant for backpacking and rock climbing as well as demands for Coca Cola and Doritos Tortilla Chips. The Bedouin who had wandered the area for centuries were more than willing to supply snacks as well as horses, camels, 4-wheel drive vehicles and tents. Anything needed to comfortably survive a rugged vacation in the desert.

The Bedouin were scattered all over the Middle East. They wandered areas everyone else deemed uninhabitable. As tourism increased, the Jordanian government's concern grew that foreigners perceived the Bedouin as poor, stupid people forced to live in the desert instead of in the cities. The government decided to spruce up that image by providing the Bedouin with housing. In truth, the Bedouin preferred a tent in the desert. Though anyone who has seen the squat, square little white boxes the king provided could easily understand the preference.

The king promised not to kick the Bedouin off the tourist attraction areas if they lived in the housing instead of the tents. The Bedouin, the older ones especially, did not care for this new way of living. After hundreds of years of wandering about in the desert pitching a tent where convenient, the whole lifestyle was more than a little ingrained. Often the older Bedouin, hearing Death tapping on the front door, would request a sojourn away from the Jordanian version of the trailer park, to spend their last days watching the desert winds flap the flaps before kicking the bucket. Oh well. Life is full of trade-offs and tourist money was easy money.[117]

On the drive to Wadi Rum Peter was transfixed, not so much by the barren beauty of the desert, but by all the trash scattered and blowing across it. In order to keep the desert clean people needed to put trash in a receptacle. That receptacle needed to be emptied. Why bother? Throw the trash in the desert! It is dirt. Dirt is dirty already! Who cares about a few Twinkie wrappers tumbleweeding their way across the desert floor?

As they drove along it seemed that perhaps Ahmed was peeved. Peeved at Peter for being an object of charity. Ahmed's charity. Ahmed ruminated the length of the 75-kilometre ride from the Aqaba Airport. What was the reason for carting this Christian heathen across the desert? A Roman Catholic priest, no less! Had not the Pope's armies murdered his Muslim brothers centuries ago? And though time heals all wounds, a series of slaughters is tough to forget. Thus it was that Ahmed Salah's mind wandered about in circles as surely as his '75 Ford Fairlane made a beeline for Wadi Rum.

Though Ahmed gladly filled his Muslim requirement to be kind to the less fortunate, how in Hell's Bells could charity apply to an Infidel? Perhaps it was Ahmed's unintentional confession that brought on this current discomfort.

It had started as a brag. Ahmed told Peter that perhaps since he was going to be in Wadi Rum anyway, he might just as well stop and see his Bedouin girlfriend. Kaliflahwa was not as attractive as his girlfriend Allanala in Jerash. But neither could hold even a birthday candle to his Turkish seductress Birpa. What a little pistol that Birpa was. Ahmed went on and on until Peter asked him if he ever intended to get married.

"Married?" Ahmed replied. "The stone wheel I hang from my neck in Aqaba might object. Twenty-three years. I barely believe it myself."

Peter said nothing but Ahmed heard a thousand words.

"What?" Ahmed demanded. Do you think I have sinned because of an occasional indiscretion? I am an Arab man. I am strong and virile. This is how we have our relationships with women. Do you doubt that my feelings are any different than any Arab man? You should go to Syria! Or worse! Watch a Syrian when he goes to Egypt! It would disgust even me! And I have a strong stomach! It is like watching a wild beast being uncaged. What? Do you dare to judge me?"

The car skidded to a dusty stop with the skyline of Wadi Rum clutching vaguely at the distant horizon. "Out!" Ahmed spat a bit too vehemently-considering Peter had not only not passed judgment on him, he had only a vague notion of what Ahmed was talking about.

After making a U-turn and roaring up the road a bit, Ahmed slammed on his brakes, tossed a business card out the window then blasted off. Peter shuffled up to the card, picked it up and read it.

"Ahmed Salah... Realize Your Destiny... Archaeological Excavation... Modern Renovations... 24-hour Plumbing Services... General Contractor... Hauling... Delivery Services... Laborers Both Dependable and Cheap!" Then it gave Ahmed's phone number. On the other side of the card the same information in Arabic, German and Hebrew!

Left on the side of the road with his single suitcase, Peter considered the card for a minute then put it in his pocket and began walking. In the wrong direction. It may have been the mind-numbing result of his long trip, being berated by Ahmed, or the fact that Peter was simply not paying attention that led him to take this wrong turn into a great coincidence. Most likely it was a combination of all the above.

Peter had not noticed the teeny Wadi Rum skyline in the distance. It was now dipping below the heat-drenched sands behind his back. It also did not occur to him that following Ahmed's car would most likely take him in the opposite direction from his assignment.

Peter walked for an hour. During that time two very nice looking cars sped by him heading towards Wadi Rum. Peter stopped. He turned and looked back over the stretch of highway he had just trodden. He touched his burning forehead. He had never been so hot in his entire life. Forget the nonsense about desert heat is a dry heat. 105 degrees Fahrenheit is 105 degrees Fahrenheit and it feels like 105 degrees Fahrenheit with or without humidity.

Peter heard the sound of a motor. He looked back and forth on the roadway but saw nothing coming from either direction. Yet the sound was getting louder. The motor noise was getting closer and closer yet was unseen on the roadway. Peter looked up in the sky. Maybe it was a plane. No. No plane anywhere.

At the last moment Peter turned around to face the vast desert just in time to see an ancient jeep come to a sand-kicking stop barely inches from him.

Peter remained motionless and so did the driver. Bechkded Amalamalak wore a white ghutrah, a typical Arabic headdress, which nicely framed his desert-chiseled features. It was a good look. Though only in his mid-forties or so (Difficult to say with any accuracy since not even Bechkded Amalamalak knew. Didn't keep track. What is a birthday to a Bedouin?) Bechkded Amalamalak had the wrinkles of a seventy-year old. He was leaning forward, his right arm draped along the top of the steering wheel. They stared at each other for a full two minutes. Finally, Bechkded Amalamalak tapped the horn. The loud bleep startled Peter. He jumped a little. Bechkded Amalamalak got out and motioned for Peter to enter the car from the driver's side. Peter grabbed his American Tourister and dragged his dehydrated carcass across the driver's seat to the passenger side.

Bechkded Amalamalak slammed the car into gear, hopped it up onto the highway then bounced over into the desert on the other side. Every so often as they sped across the sand, without slowing down, Bechkded Amalamalak would turn a big droopy-eyed stare at Peter. On three occasions he did this while piloting the Jeep up and over a very steep sand dune. Peter reacted to this heart swallowing display of driving prowess with little more than a raised eyebrow. The minimalist response made the eyebrows of Bechkded Amalamalak sharpen into right angles and caused his foot to press down a bit harder on the accelerator.

In Central Wadi Rum also known as downtown Wadi Rum, or the Wadi Rum business district there stood four restaurants. Not surprisingly, all offered authentic Jordanian cuisine. The two petrol stations were both priced a full dinar per liter above Aqaba's most expensive outlets. The four kiosks all begged to differ with each other. Theirs offered the best prices on authentic Jordanian T-shirts, local spices from Jerash 150 miles away, delicious snacks, and, most importantly, much, much more. The two camps both offered the most comfortable and spacious pup tents for an unforgettable night under the desert stars of LawrenceofArabialand. The price of using the showers and toilets was included in the very reasonable rate. All totaled, this grand city took up less space than a football field. Maybe a football field with the end zones clipped off. That, thanks to Peter was about to change.

Bechkded Amalamalak tooled his way through the street of central Wadi Rum. He brushed precariously close to several groups of his pedestrian friends and relatives. None took it personally. This is the way everybody drives in the Middle East.[118] He brought the Jeep to a slurred, sandy stop in front of his in-law's little tavern: "The Wadi Rummy." His father-in-law Mahmumed Belijer peered out at them from under his ancient kaffiyeh.[119] With careful aggravation, Mahmumed Belijer pulled at his agal.[120] No matter how he adjusted the agal, a tiny wiry thorn poked him somewhere in the head. This current adjustment brought relief to his left eyebrow and discomfort to his right temple. As the only potential customer for two days, Peter was a sight for Mahmumed Belijer's withered, sore eyes.

Bechkded Amalamalak climbed out of the Jeep and paused to help his aging father-in-law rise from his squatting position. It wasn't just his age that slowed Mahmumed Belijer. A man with half his decades would be troubled when rising from a two-day squat.

Not wanting to seem high-pressure, the two stood at the front of the Jeep and waited for Peter to get out and follow them into the store. Peter remained seated, staring passively in their general direction.

Mahmumed Belijer grilled Bechkded Amalamalak in muted tones. "Why does he just sit there?"

"I don't know."

"What is his name?"

"I do not know. I did not ask."

"Why is he here? He does not act like a tourist."

"I do not know." and "Good observation."

"He sits there for another quarter hour in that tin can of yours and we will have to start basting him."

"Do we use his own juices? Or should we send for some of that mustard-based barbeque sauce from South Carolina which is selling cheaply on the Internet?"

"No. Cheap poison is never a bargain." Mahmumed Belijer mused as he hobbled to the window next to Peter. "Hello, friend. Welcome to The Wadi Rummy. The finest tavern in all the Middle East. Are you in need of refreshment?"

Peter turned to face the two, and smiled as far as his parched, shriveled lips would allow. Which was not very far.

"Faygo? Mellow Yellow? Water, which has been sifted from the well of Lawrence of Arabia?"

At that Peter nodded slightly. Mahmumed Belijer failed to help Peter open the creaky Jeep door. He deferred with a disgusted huff to his son-in-law who reached behind Peter and pulled a handy-dandy crowbar from the seat's back pocket and pried the door open far enough to allow exit.

The two Bedouin walked into The Wadi Rummy. Peter wobbled not far behind them. Inside the air conditioning was turned off. Without customers, why bother? The room was thick with dark heat. A good twenty degrees hotter in the lavish Quonset hut than outside in the sun.

Mahmumed Belijer and Bechkded Amalamalak propped Peter up on a bar stool conveniently located next to the window air conditioning unit. Bechkded Amalamalak turned the full blast on Peter. Peter turned his face to the icy onslaught and shortly fell off his bar stool.

It was sometime later when he regained consciousness. Peter was lying on his back. He could hear the argued whisperings of Mahmumed Belijer and Bechkded Amalamalak off to the side.

He opened his eyes but could see nothing save a pale, tan, gauzy light. He put his fingers to his eyes, then to the top of his head and then his face. Someone had wrapped Peter's head in some type of odd cloth that for some reason reminded him of the locker room back at the seminary.

The whispering stopped as Peter folded his hands across his chest. He sensed the presence of Mahmumed Belijer and Bechkded Amalamalak on either side of him. After a moment the cloth over his left eye separated revealing the faces of Mahmumed Belijer and Bechkded Amalamalak peering down at him.

"Are you feeling pain?" There seemed a note of suspicion in the voice of Mahmumed Belijer.

"Feelen sie pain?" Bechkded Amalamalak queried in his finest pretend German.

"He is not German" Mahmumed Belijer practically hissed. "His passport is United States."

"Perhaps. But he has not spoken in English either. Maybe the fall knocked the English out of his head."

Mahmumed Belijer nodded noncommittal. He would not argue another foolish point. "Can you speak?"

"Yes." Peter managed.

"Good. You speak English?"

"Yes."

Mahmumed Belijer leveled a wizened know-it-all smirk at Bechkded Amalamalak.

"Water. Please?"

"Of course. Water. Here drink up. You have been guzzling it for the last two days! In your sleep! We apologize for the bandage. Your head hit the floor first and began to bleed. We ran out of Band-Aid adhesives. They are on order. We shall now remove this 'Ace' bandage."

"It is but a small scratch." Slight bewilderment from Bechkded Amalamalak.

"It appears to be healed. Try to sit up. Please." Mahmumed Belijer suggested as chief caregiver.

Peter was slightly surprised to see he had been lying on the floor. He took stock of his surroundings. There was a sink, and an old refrigerator, which performed a task closer to storage than keeping food cold. He was in the back room of The Wadi Rummy.

Mahmumed Belijer and Bechkded Amalamalak could not very well leave him lying on the floor. Would not look good if another customer showed up to have someone lying on the floor with a bleeding head. And, though all of their accommodations were available, the savvy innkeeper must always be prepared for a sudden rush of business.[121] On that account, the small wad of rubles they had found in Peter's American Tourister was not very promising.

Peter sat up. His head was clear as a bell. He had been exhausted from the journey and wrung dry from his wrong way saunter along the Desert Highway. His body had not sweat much in the Russian Far East. It made up for lost time in the Middle East.

"You are not a tourist?" Bechkded Amalamalak hazarded a guess.

"You are a Christian? A priest?" Mahmumed Belijer perceived, having ransacked Peter's belongings the previous day.

"Yes. I have been sent here. Where is the Catholic church?"

Mahmumed Belijer thought for a moment. Then he extended an index finger at Peter's heart.[122] "Your Church is right here. Just as I am a Bedouin in my heart."

Peter responded with a loud rumble from his stomach. The trilling gurgle reminded his hosts of the sound a camel makes after concluding a long journey across the desert.

"You are hungry. We will feed you." Once again Bechkded Amalamalak displayed his powers of perception and, to his father-in-law, an annoying non-profit attitude.

"And what about a place to sleep? Where will you sleep priest? Do you have only Russian money? Are you hoping to convert some Russian Bedouin? That is not likely. I have never seen a Russian Bedouin in the eighty-seven years that I live in Wadi Rum."[123] Though his intent was not to be mean, Mahmumed Belijer certainly came off that way. Maybe his agal made him a bit scrappy.

"You are welcome in my tent." Bechkded Amalamalak took seriously, his Islamic promise to help the needy.

"Tsk." ceded Mahmumed Belijer noting the gesture as well as knowing the reason for it. "You are some Muslim, Bechkded Amalamalak." He directed this next very important understatement to Peter. "We are Bedouin of the Al-Mana'ayah tribe, a people with a proud history of rootless wandering. We no longer wander. We now have solar powered television sets and refrigerated beer imported from Germany and Egypt. We are like garbanzos on a plate.[124] In the olden days other people marveled at our ability to exist under such harsh conditions. I marvel that our bowels are now sewn to this one place."

"Be quiet, old man." Bechkded Amalamalak laid a comforting hand on his father-in-law's shoulder.

"I will include thoughts of you in my prayers. May I?" Peter was always polite, even to the point of asking permission for such a thing as that.

"Sure. My Lord is too busy for me. Maybe your Jesus has a minute to spare." Then Mahmumed Belijer had another thought. "You are welcome in my tent as well. It is the Bedouin way."

Though the offer of free housing was made out of a spirit of generosity, Bechkded Amalamalak quickly discovered a profit from Peter's visit. The priest was not what one would call a "hard" worker. But, he kept at whatever task was at hand until it was completed. In a way Peter's slow constant pace matched the old-fashioned 'take it easy in this heat' attitude suitable for survival in the desert of Wadi Rum.

Peter's willingness to volunteer to take on the drudgery others ran away from impressed Bechkded Amalamalak. After rising at sunrise and saying prayers, before breakfast, every morning Peter would head to the lean-to where the horses were kept, so he could clean up the road apples before anyone else had the opportunity. With that type of attitude, Bechkded Amalamalak figured Peter could stay as long as he liked.

Peter would quite literally keep his nose to the grindstone. The Bedouin used an old-fashion grindstone to shine pieces of worthless, yet pretty, stone, which they would later sell to tourists. On several occasions Bechkded Amalamalak pulled Peter back as he sat too close to the spinning wheel. A chunk could suddenly dislodge and fly off hitting him in the nose or eye.

Another chore Peter took upon himself actually increased profits at The Wadi Rummy. He policed the perimeter around the tavern keeping it clean of not only the larger pieces of litter, potato chip bags and soda cans and such, but also smaller scraps of paper and cigarette butts. The tidy atmosphere made the building more attractive than nearby competitors.

One day, having discovered a rake, Peter went after the sands of the desert to even out the ruts that developed. Bechkded Amalamalak stopped him and told him to relax. Would he like to go for a ride on a horse? Free! No charge! Thus the stage was set for another incident that would, once again, bring Peter to the attention of Rome.

Peter made no converts to Catholicism during his stay in Wadi Rum. Though towards the end, in the midst of all the hubbub, Mahmumed Belijer made an unsubstantiated claim to the media that he was so impressed with Peter's holiness that he switched his allegiance from Mecca to Rome.

More out of curiosity than interest, occasionally the Bedouin would wander over to the side of the horse shed where Peter eventually made his sleeping area, and watch him go through his prayers or daily mass. On one occasion Peter paused his ceremony and acknowledged their presence with a hand extended in invitation. The Bedouin turned and walked away. That was the closest Peter ever came to proselytizing the faith.

By the end of one year in Wadi Rum, Peter fell into a daily ritual that began with mass, then mucking the horses, prayers, breakfast, prayers, helping saddle the horses for tourists when needed,[125] collecting trash, prayers, cleaning the toilets and showers, prayers, lunch, prayers, assisting with repairs on the fleet of Jeeps (Handing a certain wrench, or holding up the oil drain pan while someone else tightened it, or loosening the bolts for a flat tire.) prayers, cleaning the Jeeps, prayers, odd jobs (Stocking shelves in the kiosk, etc.), mopping the floors and dry-cleaning windows, prayers, evening meal. Then, if all the tourists' needs had been met, he and Mahmumed Belijer and Bechkded Amalamalak would saddle up three horses and take them for a spin in the desert.[126]

In addition to recreation, the activity served a practical purpose as well. Several horses in the herd were pretty far over the hill: mangy-looking and a bit threadbare. Horsies as large as elephants or skinny as the Turkish rails, that even neophyte equestrians had the sense to turn down, Peter would take out for a trot. Every body needs exercise.

Shuffling along the waveless ocean of sand, Mahmumed Belijer, Bechkded Amalamalak and Peter would wander, sauntering aimlessly sometimes, sometimes with purpose to Jabal Burdah to gaze at the Rock Bridge or to wade along the shifted sands of Wadi Um af-Ashrin or to stand in the grand shadows of the Seven Pillars of Wisdom[127] : A bunch of big damn rocks stacked up side by side like bloated slices of whole wheat bread with the crusts pinched off, or perhaps that chunky cinnamon loaf? Or maybe a veal roast? The kind with the strings on it. But the strings are made of wire and pulled so tight they actually cut into the veal so that these big thick slices are sticking up. But there would have to be seven of them and it would be, without doubt, overcooked.[128]

When they had put Wadi Rum in the distance, the three would halt the beasts and inhale the solitude. The wind stilled. The parched air embraced them. The breaths of them and their beasts of burden slowed to near stopping. The vastness was infinite. Nothing moved. Eyes did not move. The desert was as quiet as the voice of God.

Mahmumed Belijer and Bechkded Amalamalak were under the mistaken impression these little strolls in the desert were a treat for Peter. Though Peter performed more of the drudgery than anyone else in Wadi Rum he was still considered an outsider. A foreigner. A tourist. Tourists paid big money for something like this. This was some perk, they figured.

In truth these moments made Peter very sad. The severity of the silence reminded him of what he would hear inside his head when he paused between prayers to see if he could hear God answering him. The void did not inspire him. In these times he often thought about the little game he used to play in school, and all the different ways he would flick a pencil across a desktop.

During one of these little excursions Peter made a discovery that thrust him (Or, at least his name.) under the searing spotlight of an international reputation.

Peter was riding a horse named "Bshht." Bshht closely resembled a rhinoceros, sans horn. No one in Wadi Rum, not even the oldest man,[129] could recall a day when Bshht was not around, hogging the feed of the other horses and intimidating anyone who had the nerve to look at her.

Though she could usually be counted on to follow the other horses, there were many times Bshht demonstrated that she had a mind of her own. While this made her unsuitable for tourists, (Along with her looks and demeanor.) Mahmumed Belijer and Bechkded Amalamalak decided it made her just right for Peter. Bshht needed to be exercised regularly or she became cranky.[130]

The three horsemen were four and a half miles due west of Wadi rum and a few yards from dead center of the Barra Canyon as it looks to the west and Sunset Point. No surprise, they had made the trek to witness yet another stunning sunset.

Mahmumed Belijer and Bechkded Amalamalak brought their horses to a stop at a promontory. Bshht decided that she and Peter needed to get a little closer and so wandered exactly thirty feet north-northwest to the right of the promontory and forty feet, following the same vector, down a twenty-degree slope.

A fierce windstorm earlier that afternoon had ravaged and raked the sand. Some of the flimsy filth still clung to the atmosphere beyond them to the west painting the horizon in flaming pastels.

When Peter had reached a distance of exactly 140 feet from Mahmumed Belijer and Bechkded Amalamalak he noticed that they were not with him and turned to his left, or South, to see where they were. In an unprecedented anomalous response from Bshht, she followed this subtle movement from her rider as an indication to turn in that direction. If this unprovoked brief spirit of cooperation between man and beast had not occurred, Bshht would not have stepped on the pinnacle of the ancient Nabataean temple.

Bshht is one of many horses that, over the last couple of hundred years, literally tripped over an as yet uncovered archaeological site. Unlike her predecessors,[131] Bshht did not break a leg and was not shot for her contribution to history. She did chip her left hoof. Bshht also dumped Peter as she tried to regain her balance.

Mahmumed Belijer and Bechkded Amalamalak watched in amazement at the site of the elephantine horse seeming to trip clumsily on nothing more than the sand. They exchanged looks of

135

concern after witnessing Peter slide off the horse and onto the ground. The tumble was not all that violent. But, as Peter rose to his feet, dusting the sand off his thobe, all three noticed a spot of blood appearing on his chest. Peter had fallen directly on to the tip of the highest point of the buried temple.

Mahmumed Belijer and Bechkded Amalamalak galloped down to the scene and dismounted. The temple tip appeared as a tiny sharp tipped pyramid pricking up out just below sand level. The color was approximately the same as the sand surrounding it. At first Mahmumed Belijer and Bechkded Amalamalak could think of nothing better to do than scratch their heads and look at it.

"What is it?" Bechkded Amalamalak asked the older man.

"And how should I know?" Mahmumed Belijer replied with more wonder than aggravation. "Perhaps it is a sign."

"A sign of what?"

Mahmumed Belijer looked across the great landscape of his nose and stepped directly into the vacuous quicksand pit of the eyes of his son-in-law. "Did you miss the part where I said perhaps? I did not say that it is a sign. I said perhaps it is a sign. Perhaps it is a sign from Allah. Perhaps it is a sign from this one's Jesus and now we are forced to convert to Heathenism. Perhaps it is a road sign pointing one way to Mecca and the other to Damascus. Perhaps it is a sign advertising Pepsi Cola."

Mahmumed Belijer looked at Peter's blood apprehensively. "Are you all right?" The bleeding appeared to have stopped. Or at least the stain was not spreading. The original dime-sized investment made by the tip was now up to a nickel.

Peter opened the plunged neckline of his shift and the three inspected the wound. It was slightly worse than a scratch directly in the middle of his chest. But it did not look serious. They glanced at Bshht who was daintily holding up her right front leg.[132] Seniority dictated Bechkded Amalamalak would inspect.

"A tiny chip missing from her hoof. The leg feels fine. She works for our sympathy." They lost interest simultaneously and stared again at the tiny pyramid.

After ten solid minutes, it became obvious to Mahmumed Belijer that staring at this thing would not help them to figure out what it was. So Mahmumed Belijer got down on his knees and hands and touched it gingerly.

"Humph." Mahmumed Belijer unsheathed his scimitar from its scabbard and scratched at the structure a bit. "Sandstone."

"We are wasting time. It is a piece of rock. If sandstone attracts you so, I invite you to scratch away at any one of the thousands of sandstone mountains not covered with sand." On the rare occasions Bechkded Amalamalak spoke as a smart Alec, he performed quite well.

"What is your hurry? Is there another special on cable[133] about Heidi Fleiss?"[134] Mahmumed Belijer shaming response is why Bechkded Amalamalak was rarely witty in the older man's presence. "Perhaps you are correct. I proceed too cautiously. If you would assist."

With that, Mahmumed Belijer began digging "doggy style." Peter and Bechkded Amalamalak joined in. Within a moment they had uncovered the tip of a rather obvious iceberg. The three bent over in the sand stopped abruptly. They had uncovered enough to see that this was obviously the top of a tower, a turret, or perhaps a minaret. They stopped because the sand they had carelessly thrown behind them was now sufficient in stature to drift back into the hole they were digging.

Mahmumed Belijer and Bechkded Amalamalak stared at each other and spoke in hushed, astonished unison. "This appears to be a significant archaeological find."

The initial assessment of Mahmumed Belijer and Bechkded Amalamalak turned out to be correct. They were at a loss on whom or what to contact about it. The easy assumption that the Jordanian government would jump right in and take over was dispelled by a quick call to the Royal Antiquities Department in Jerash.

"A new archaeological site in Jordan? So what else is new?" After the hilarity and mirth calmed down, the bureaucrat who also thought he was a comedian explained. "There are many sites in His Majesty's kingdom laying discovered but barely uncovered: Perhaps several hundred cubic hectares.[135] Have fun digging. Don't make too much the mess out there in the desert. Ha ha ha."

What to do what to do? Mahmumed Belijer and Bechkded Amalamalak knew that even if the structure turned out to be a dinky little mosque, uncovering it would entail a great deal of work. The rest of the citizens, or at least the men, needed to know about and discuss the possible consequences of the discovery. Mahmumed Belijer and Bechkded Amalamalak called a meeting.

Mahmumed Belijer and Bechkded Amalamalak pushed the sand over the tip and marked the spot with an empty beer bottle.

137

To increase the drama of the presentation, they erected a large tent over the scene.

At the appointed hour, their fellow Bedouin formed a large mumbling crowd at the tent.

"Why have you called us here Mahmumed Belijer?" Memdahd Kalijha asked. "Are you to announce your divorce from Bechkded Amalamalak?" This brought many knowing chuckles from the Wadi Rummites. All had witnessed the quarrels between the old man and his son-in-law.

"No not for that, Memdahd Kalijha. The reason that I and the husband of my most treasured daughter have requested your presence is to forge an alliance with you. We have asked you to this spot to mine the shafts of your wisdom and to share a wondrous discovery."

"Please tell me it is not some old ruin buried in the sand." All eyes turned to look at Feta Geeaza, a slight and shaky yet chatty fellow. "My brother Blooeh works in the fine jewelry trade[136] in Petra.[137]

Every other day the Germans and Japanese find another monstrosity to uncover. There is never any treasure left to find. Thieves picked clean every site in the Middle East hundreds of years ago. Then, if archaeologists don't displace your home with their machinery and air-conditioned Winnebagoes, a huge pile of sand does. Archaeologists kick up a lot of loose dirt making everything filthy and they pay the Bedouin poorly for our work-of which we do the lion's share. There is more money to be made selling Pepsi-Cola. My apologies to Mahmumed Belijer and Bechkded Amalamalak. But if there is a building buried under this tent, I vote we leave it just the way it is. Well. You can move the tent of course."

The mouth of Bechkded Amalamalak hung open in unadulterated astonishment. Mahmumed Belijer on the other hand regarded Feta Geeaza through his tightly knit caterpillar topped eyes. "Have you been peeking, Feta Geeaza?"

"Let us allow Mahmumed Belijer and Bechkded Amalamalak to have their say." It was the beautiful rumbling basso profundo of Ahmahd Desantez, de facto mayor of Wadi Rum solely because of his beautiful rumbling basso profundo and his law degree. "How large can the building be to fit inside this tent?"

Nodding and chuckling agreement, the Wadi Rummites followed Ahmahd Desantez into the tent leaving Peter,

Mahmumed Belijer and Bechkded Amalamalak outside momentarily wondering what the Hell just happened. It would only get worse.

Inside the crowd milled about mumbling and chuckling intermittently. One problem came instantly to the attention of Peter, Mahmumed Belijer and Bechkded Amalamalak.

"Where is the beer bottle?" It was barely a whispered croak as the wind in the lungs of Bechkded Amalamalak evaporated in alarm.

The mumbling, milling chucklers turned silent as they parted to reveal one man, Hem Mahnem, sitting contentedly in a corner of the tent with the bottle in hand.

Bechkded Amalamalak fell to his hands and knees in front of Hem Mahnem and made his pleaded demand nose to nose. "What are you doing?"

"Peeling the label off. It is a nervous habit, I know. But it brings me pleasure. I enjoy it more when the bottle is cold and the label is moist. The pieces of damp paper become lodged under my fingernails and when I use a knife to remove them it cleans all the sand and grit out. So this is more than a simple obsession, the activity has a practical application as well. You may have the bottle back if you like. Look. There is still some label left." Many was the time the people of Wadi Rum warned Hem Mahnem not to be outside in the sun without his ghutrah on.

"Do you... do you..." Bechkded Amalamalak fell back on his fanny and did his own sotto voce mumbling. "...remember where... you found..."

"It was in the middle, Bechkded Amalamalak. Right about here." Mahmumed Belijer dropped confidently to his knees and began wiping away at the sand with both arms cautiously at first then progressively more frantic. He went at it long enough to build quite a little pile of sand and to work up a sweat. "The building is here... somewhere."

"It must be a very tiny ancient ruin to be so easily lost." For this Ahmahd Desantez received numerous chuckles of agreement and encouragement. "Now it is lost again. When you find this great building let us know. One of you should stand atop it to mark the spot until the bulldozers arrive. Then we shall call it The Twice Lost Ruins of Wadi Rum. Has a nice ring to it, don't you agree Mahmumed Belijer?" Guffaws followed Ahmahd Desantez's exit from the tent.

139

It was a week before Peter rediscovered the tip of the ruin with, of all things his penis. He had volunteered to spend nights in the tent. Bechkded Amalamalak and Mahmumed Belijer held the not irrational concern that someone, most likely Feta Geeaza might move the tent while they slept and thwart their efforts to refind their discovery.

For security reasons, Bechkded Amalamalak and Mahmumed Belijer insisted Peter keep the tent flaps closed. So, because of the heat, Peter slept without a bedroll directly on the sand. Lately, Peter had been experiencing frequent erotic dreams. While in the midst of a gaggle of naked Russian aunties, a sharp pain in the tip of his penis yanked him back from dreamland.

Wearing only his flimsy night thobe, which had ridden above his waist, Peter had been drilling away at the sand when he struck the mother lode. He lit his candle and then felt around inside the large hole he had created in the sand. Sure enough, there it was. The temple tip. It was actually way over in the corner. Right about where Hem Mahnem had sat peeling the bottle.

Relieved for the relief it would bring his two friends, Peter sought to re-establish the presence but this time more thoroughly. He spent the rest of the morning sweeping away a good deal of coverage and uncovering more of the temple than the three had done the previous week.

After sunrise he waited outside the tent for Bechkded Amalamalak and Mahmumed Belijer. The two had become increasingly dejected the last couple of days. Mahmumed Belijer did not even scoff when Bechkded Amalamalak had mentioned the possibility of a temple being a result of a group hallucination. "Stranger things have happened." Mahmumed Belijer did not bother to press for an example. Such was the depth of his misery.

Another factor was the reaction of their fellow Wadi Rummites. To express caution or disinterest was one thing. Mumbling and chuckling was not a good reaction.

Peter ruminated on these thoughts as he saw in the distance the watery, wobbly approach of Bechkded Amalamalak and Mahmumed Belijer. If only he could figure out a way to help his friends.

"Peter. Perhaps you have lost your marbles. You appear to have been rolling around in the sand. You are coated from the large nails on your toes which are ready for trimming to the white curls on the top of your head." Mahmumed Belijer amused himself ever so slightly at Peter's expense.

140

"Perhaps you dream of one of our beautiful Wadi Rum women[138] and so wrestle passionately instead with our desert." Luckily for Peter the two approached from the west and so were blinded by the sun and could see only that he was covered with sand, but not that Bechkded Amalamalak's remark caused him to blush fiercely under the filth.

"Did you find the missing building of our dreams in your sleep...?" Mahmumed Belijer trailed off as he noticed the bulging sides of the tent. He turned to Peter and warmly placed his hand on the priest's shoulder. "You are a good man. For a heathen. Thank you."

"Did you find it? Did you find it?" Bechkded Amalamalak jumped up and down like a school child.

"No. He is installing a swimming pool. Did we neglect to tell you?" Mahmumed Belijer led the other two inside, scrabbled up the dirt and sat at the top with a sigh. "You have worked well Peter. Now. Now to finish the job."

The quandary of who would take on such a task caused the image of Ahmed Salah to pop into Peter's head. "I know a man in Aqaba who does excavations. Maybe he could help."

"That is very good to know. We shall call him as soon as we win the lottery. Bechkded Amalamalak is there a lottery in Jordan?"

"No, my father." Bechkded Amalamalak replied sardonically. This line of questions always taunted Bechkded Amalamalak whenever he announced yet another get-rich-quick scheme that included start-up cash.

So the three sat upon the heaped sand for quite awhile, chins in palms, considering the little pinnacle before them. What could they do to distinguish The Twice Lost Ruins of Wadi Rum from all the other sites?

"Did you know that Mohammed, The Prophet travelled through these parts?[139] The man I mentioned, the one in Aqaba, told me that. This was before the Angel Gabriel appeared to him. I understand he was a camel driver on the trade routes."

Bechkded Amalamalak said nothing but continued to cradle his chin. Mahmumed Belijer, however, looked as if the ghost of his grandfathers had just whispered a secret into his ear. After a moment he smiled a little smile to himself then turned to Peter. "Would you be so good to tend to the horses now? I fear the stalls are beginning to look frightful. You too." With that he swatted

Bechkded Amalamalak playfully on the back of his head, knocking off his keffiyeh.[140]

"I? Muck the stall?" He had not done so since Peter's arrival on the scene.

"Yes." Mahmumed Belijer's response was understated yet emphatic. A smile tickled the corners of his lips. He waited until he was certain the two had left before getting down to business.

Later the next day, the crowd of Wadi Rummites were gathered once again outside the tent. Though they made no mention of it, both Peter and Bechkded Amalamalak were surprised to see that the tent no longer bulged with the weight of the displaced dirt.

"Please come inside for the ceremony." Mahmumed Belijer urged gaily. Though the way he held a shovel would look menacing to someone who did not know him.

"What type of ceremony would that be, Mahmumed Belijer? It is not necessary for a formal apology for wasting our time last week." Ahmahd Desantez the de facto mayor of Wadi Rum was conciliatory but also warned. "However, it might be an honorable gesture if you do not waste our time again this week."

"I bring you here today to honor you Ahmahd Desantez, for the very perseverance of character which allowed you to return here in spite of the prior visit. Come." With that, Mahmumed Belijer led them to the far corner of the tent. There on the ground lay his prayer rug.

"Mahmumed Belijer, how clean is your prayer rug! Is this the first time you have used it?" It was not beneath the dignity of Feta Geeaza to make a catty remark.

"It could be the prayer rug of Bechkded Amalamalak. He is the only man among us who prays less than Mahmumed Belijer." Hem Mahnem meowed as he chawed away at a hangnail.

"For my sin, please strip me naked and abandon me in the arms of Mother Desert." It was always a waste of time to attempt to get the best of Mahmumed Belijer. He handed the shovel to Ahmahd Desantez the de facto mayor of Wadi Rum.

"Did you hope I would find your building for you?"

Mahmumed Belijer knelt next to the rug and turned to his fellows. "My hope is to honor Ahmahd Desantez with the formal first spadeful that will unearth unknown treasures which lay buried beneath us all these centuries. Ahmahd Desantez, de facto mayor of Wadi Rum, I, Mahmumed Belijer give to you and all the people of Wadi Rum and the world, The Twice Lost Ruins of Wadi

Rum." With that Mahmumed Belijer removed the rug. He had undone Peter's efforts so only the top three inches poked pitifully out of the sand.

"It is a very small ruins. I will say that much." This was the final joke Ahmahd Desantez or any of the rest of them would ever make about The Twice Lost Ruins of Wadi Rum.

With mock formality, Ahmahd Desantez dug in and then tossed aside a spadeful of dirt. The crowd clapped. Encouraged by their response Ahmahd Desantez dug in deeper this time and hefted a much fuller spadeful. The crowd clapped again. It takes very little encouragement to get a politician to shovel it. That is why Ahmahd Desantez continued to shovel and shovel. It got to a point where several of the Wadi Rummites left for lack of room in the tent.

Ahmahd Desantez uncovered three feet of the spire and, as a tired Lettermanesque joke,[141] every three spades full, or so, what was left of the dwindling group would let loose with a wheezing half-hearted cheer. Ahmahd Desantez would smile gratefully at them and shovel three more shovels full and that would be followed by another half-ass hurrah.

The spire was towering above him before he finally decided to call it quits. Ahmahd Desantez hoisted the shovel overhead. Several of the men helpfully grabbed it by the spade and pulled him out of the hole.

"Mahmumed Belijer we thank you for this discovery. I am quite certain from the looks of this fine spire there is a very grand building attached to it. You will bring to yourself and the people of Wadi Rum great honor and even more historical significance. I am certain many, many, many, many[142] people will come to Wadi Rum and all because of your discovery."

"Hey! Look! There is writing on it!" Hem Mahnem had walked along the bank of sand behind the sight, and unlike the others there, could see the side closest to the tent wall.

"What!" "There is writing?" "What does it say?" "Is it an ancient message or fairly modern?" A general hullabaloo of questions ensued.

"I cannot read what it says because the writing is very, very tiny." Hem Mahnem looked at the others with fierce seriousness, not necessarily an unusual expression for Hem Mahnem to wear on his face since he often wore an expression of fierce seriousness regardless of what he was doing. "But! I will say this! Whoever wrote it was writing not so much to defile the ruins but to instead leave a message!"

"What a wonder!" Mahmumed Belijer felt that he now knew what it must feel like to win the lottery.

"Get closer so you may read what it says." Bechkded Amalamalak insisted.

"If I move closer I will fall into the hole."

"You are slight of stature and deportment. I will easily hold you by your robe and you can lean in closer and read it." Ahmahd Desantez de facto mayor of Wadi Rum was just trying to expedite the process.

"No no no! You will drop me in the hole! I will not hear of it! No." With that Hem Mahnem ran away.[143]

"Then I will do it. Since my new eyeglasses arrived by Federal Express, my eyesight is now excellent. And, if it is written in an ancient tongue, I will also be able to decipher it." All eyes looked at Feta Geeaza suspiciously. Was he not the one demanding they all simply walk away from The Twice Lost Ruins of Wadi Rum for socio-environmental reasons?

"What? What are looking at me for? Would I lie about such a thing simply to force you all through treachery to follow my will?" The men, to a one, all nodded in the affirmative.

"Why do you not just spit upon me then, to indicate how you truly feel?"

There was one mucousey rumbling towards the back, but his fellows nearby cautioned Hakim Hakunguard to keep his opinion to himself. A loud swallow followed.

"Fine then. Be you so callous! Have Mahmumed Belijer read the fine print. He trained for a time in archaeological studies at the Tourism Institute[144] as well. I warn you though. Be certain, for he will put an entertaining spin on whatever is written here."

"I will not read it. I will also not stand here and allow you to besmirch the honor of a fine man such as Feta Geeaza. I share your insult upon him as surely as if your spittle dripped here on my sleeve. I must leave. Fetch me when you have regained your senses." With that Mahmumed Belijer made to exit in a huff. As he hoped, there were enough objections to halt him before he reached the flaps of the tent.

"Will you accept our profoundest apologies, Feta Geeaza, and read these grand words of history?" Ahmahd Desantez de facto mayor of Wadi Rum proved once again his innate ability to expedite matters. He also, time and time again, proved that there are attorneys who are good for something.

"I." Feta Geeaza patted his breast pocket. "That is I do not have my glasses with me."

A groan of understandable disgust passed through the assemblage.

"Fine. Then I will hold you over the hole. You are not much larger than Hem Mahnem. With that the mayor made his movement over the sand pile towards Feta Geeaza. As he made a move to grab the rear of the thobe of Feta Geeaza, the near-sighted instigator pulled away.

"I. That is I. I am not meaning to cause a problem Mayor Ahmahd Desantez."

"We know that you are not." The mayor made another grab for Feta Geeaza and again met with resistance. What is the nature of the problem that you do not mean to cause?

"It is simple. I wear my summer thobe today." Feta Geeaza defended himself with a look of chagrin. In addition to his thobe being of obviously thinner weave, it also had several lengthwise tears. It was obvious to even the most simple minded among them that the garment of Feta Geeaza would rent with very little persuasion.

"Mahmumed Belijer. For the sake of the sanity of those gathered here, will you honor us with a reading of the inscription?" The request of Ahmahd Desantez de facto mayor of Wadi Rum took Mahmumed Belijer by surprise.

"No. I will not." Mahmumed Belijer's thoughts stalled momentarily as he tried to come up with a plausible reason for his objection. "The Twice Lost Ruins of Wadi Rum is out of my hands now. It belongs to... Let Feta Geeaza go home and get his eyeglasses so he may read the inscription. Have not the words been there through the centuries? If so, then what is another half hour, forty minutes?"

The whole group squinted in puzzlement at Mahmumed Belijer. In response, he made several odd gestures in an attempt to make him look somewhat addled and senile. He rolled his eyes. He chewed on the side of his tongue. He scratched himself in inappropriate places.

"I suppose I could go home and get my eyeglasses. Although I am saving them for special occasions, I suppose this may be considered a special occasion. It may take me awhile as my sciatica is acting up and as it is starting to become warm. I trust you will all remain patient in my absence." Feta Geeaza underlined the delay they could expect by limping interminably towards the flaps of the tent. "Or... Oh never mind. It is a silly idea."

"Please, Feta Geeaza, feel free to try our patience with a silly idea." Ahmahd Desantez was beginning to realize that there were things in the world more tedious than a school board meeting.

"It is that it has occurred to me that if you were to fill the hole back in-not the whole hole-just the side where the inscription is, then I could easily step on the dirt and put my nose directly to the monument."

Feta Geeaza had barely released the words from his mouth before several of the men began kicking dirt back into the hole. They went a step further by stomping it down as they went, so that Feta Geeaza would not sink as he interpreted. As an added convenience Mezur Stehk, who was the same height as Feta Geeaza, sized himself against the structure so that the angle of his nose was lined up with the inscription.

Feta Geeaza held out both hands, primly indicating he wished assistance stepping down the three feet or so into the hole.

"Well...Let me see. Yes, Mahmumed Belijer your question seemed to be appropriate. This indeed appears to words well over a millennium old. Yes, indeed. A millennium and then some." Mahmumed Belijer looked furtively about and chewed on his tongue a bit harder

What Feta Geeaza did next is what some historians, toxicologists and DNA experts argue may have altered the history of the Middle East forever.[145] First, Feta Geeaza blew at the inscription. Then he wiped the palm of his hand against it as a whole, and then, using his little finger, wiped at some of the figures.

"Before I allow your fellow citizens to bury you alive, Feta Geeaza please explain what in the bells of hell you are doing." Ahmahd Desantez de facto mayor of Wadi Rum accurately expressed the irritation and curiosity of those gathered.

"Well. As many of you may have noticed, unlike all of you, my hands remain moist and soft, in spite of the fact that we all live here together in a very, very dry desert. Perhaps the driest desert in the world. Certainly the driest desert in the Kingdom of Jordan."

At this point, his fellows were too bewildered by yet another detour to be angry. They stood, mouths open in wonderment.

"Would you like to know my secret?"

No response.

"It is Ahava. Yes! A cream manufactured by the Jews on the other side of the Dead Sea. It really is quite wondrous, and, as you can see, quite effective as well. Here. Feel my hand." Feta Geeaza extended a hand to Ahmahd Desantez.

"Lovely." The de facto mayor turned to the others. "It really is quite astonishing how moist his skin is." He turned back to Feta Geeaza. "It will make it that much easier to peel it off your bones."

Feta Geeaza tilted his head back and looked down the razor's edge of his sharp little beak. "Make idle threats. Laugh if you like. How can I expect you to appreciate the irony that something ancient keeps my hands decades younger than yours."[146]

The cream also made a discernable effect on the inscription. The light let in from an overhead vent was fairly flat due to the day's haze. The indentations were quite slight: just a peep deep. The moistness Feta Geeaza applied brought the message out into relief.

"There! That is much better! Now I can read the message!" Feta Geeaza turned to see twenty-five sets of glaring eyes. "Let me see...that's an.... ah-ha...yes... very interesting. Oops." Feta Geeaza turned to his brothers of the desert. "Wadi Rum. We have a problem."

"Is it something of historical importance?" Ahmahd Desantez de facto mayor of Wadi Rum pressed.

"Historical? Yes. Social? Yes. Economic? Yes. Spiritual? Yes, yes, yes. This inscription appears to be written by Mohammed the Prophet. Peace be unto him. It says 'Here lies Palestine.'"

Several of the men, the more devout ones, fell immediately to prayer positions at the mere mention of such a thing, and began to offer up thanks, supplications and groans of wonderment.

"This is Palestine?"

"No. It says here lies Palestine."

"But how can this be Palestine? Palestine is in Israel. Isn't it? Isn't that why they fight all the time?" Mezur Stehk, Feta Geeaza's hole double, was not the brightest bulb in the batch. But he did mention the very point the rest of them were thinking. 'Wasn't Wadi Rum parked a bit far south to be considered Palestine?'

"Several some ones are not paying attention. It says here lies Palestine. That means that this is Palestine. Not up north. But right here at this site. Mohammed The Prophet, peace be unto him, says so."

"How do you know it is Mohammed The Prophet, peace be unto him, who says so?" Mezur Stehk scoffed.

"He signed it. Right here. Here have a look. See that? And this and that, that, that and this. That is the signature of Mohammed The Prophet. Peace be unto him."

"I do not believe it!" Mezur Stehk shouted angrily hoping to inspire others to form a skeptical band.

"Congratulations, Mezur Stehk on being the first to say so. Know that there will be many others well studied scientists and spiritual leaders who will agree with you." Mahmumed Belijer cleverly played the devil's advocate.

"Not that I should dare to declare that I told you so. But did I not mention this find would bring grief?" Feta Geeaza puffed out his little chest as he chirped out his admonition. "Though it is obviously not their intention, Mahmumed Belijer, Bechkded Amalamalak, and, most likely, the heathen Russian priest as well, have turned Wadi Rum into yet another "hot spot" in the Middle East. It is much worse than my initial, simplistic prediction of underpaying archaeologists and filth. Dust will surely fly, now. Camel dung is about to hit the fan. War will follow this discovery."

"War?" Mahmumed Belijer decided to put his two dinars into the conversation. "Who will fight whom Feta Geeaza?"

"Obviously, we will be forced to defend our homes against the Palestinians." Feta Geeaza explained with a patronizing patience that almost made his eyes cross.

"Ah, ha ha ha ha ha."[147] Mahmumed Belijer wiped the tears from his eyes, cleared the drizzle from his beard and hitched his underwear up from his knees. "What do you intend to use for weapons? Empty beer bottles?"

"Your lack of sophistication to the ways of the world is painful to witness, Mahmumed Belijer. There are many large governments willing to finance our defense."

"Humor my ignorance, Feta Geeaza. Which country would back us in a war with the Palestinians? Israel? Ah, ha ha ha ha ha." The thought pulled Mahmumed Belijer back into another two minute fit. "Of course if the Jews don't save us maybe the Catholics will. Father Peter! Please telephone your pope and tell him we need supplies!" Ah ha ha ha ha ha.

"There are forty Bedouin tribes in Jordan alone. Many of them are moneyed and well connected to the international community. They will come uninvited to join their brothers, bringing arms and death as well."

"Feta Geeaza, since you are speaking from both sets of cheeks simultaneously, I am uncertain as to what you are saying. Do you not wish to fight the Palestinians?" Ahmahd Desantez spoke for those assembled as the conversation took this surprising turn.

"My intention was to instruct you as to what I <u>know</u> will happen now. My hopes...my wishes have and will lay silent. Contact the Public Antiquities Department and begin our end."

"Finally a good idea, considering that what you have suggested so far is also found in the collecting basins of the commodes." Mahmumed Belijer's condescending smile was more effective than his best sneer.

The remark brought a chuckle from the rest. All but Peter. "Excuse me?" He crossed the tent for intimacy. No matter everyone eavesdropped. "Feta Geeaza may I have permission to pray that your wishes be granted?"

"Yes of course." Feta Geeaza replied dismissively. Though never approached himself, he had witnessed this permission to pray business several times.

A group chide ensued. "Feta Geeaza tell us your wishes, too please." "Better tell him what you are wishing for Feta Geeaza. Or else you may end up with a second wife even uglier than the first." and "Feta Geeaza if your wish comes to fruition, then I too would like free HBO."

Feta Geeaza kicked at a pile of sand angrily. "I will tell you what I wish for! I wish to stop living in these tin cans the Kingdom has forced us into. I wish to live the life of my father's father: out in the desert. I wish to escape your HBO and Coca-Cola and instead be entertained by heat visions [148] and to suckle from the breast of Mother Desert for sustenance. I wish to no longer write checks and keep a ledger. I wish to shake the sand from my thobe at the end of the day instead of wondering how long it will be until the Maytag repairman arrives. I see the vast emptiness beyond Wadi Rum. It beckons to me. I wish to wander. I wish to spend my life wandering."

"Many are the times that I have wished for the same, Feta Geeaza." Ahmahd Desantez consoled wearily.

Many of the others granted their quiet ascents as well. "Me too." "Here, here." "That makes three of us." "You bet." "Five on Fat Chance to show in the fifth at Hialeah."[149]

"Ahmahd Desantez, will you then be contacting the Public Antiquities Department?" Mahmumed Belijer needed to draw only a few more lines on the blueprint of his plan.[150]

"Yes, I shall. If there are no objections."

There were none of course. Who in the hell would volunteer to telephone a government agency except for Ahmahd Desantez? Yet another reason he was de facto mayor.

Mahmumed Belijer pulled a note out of his pocket and handed it to the mayor. "Be forewarned. I have already made contact with them and they scoffed at me. But, in any event here is the telephone number. This is the man I spoke with. Perhaps you can request someone else."

"I doubt anyone will be foolish enough to scoff at the discovery of Palestine. Perhaps I should contact a different agency?"

"No. That would lead to giving details to people who had no business knowing. Best not to alert too many agencies. Enough buzzards will be attracted to this carcass.[151] The Public Antiquities Department may be insolent, but they are competent as well. Who knows? Perhaps they will want to keep it quiet."

The Public Antiquities Department did not ridicule, scoff, or belittle Ahmahd Desantez. A team of investigators from Amman arrived four hours after the brief telephone conversation with the de facto mayor. Three busloads of Palestinians arrived in Wadi Rum an hour before them.

Initially the Wadi Rummites' hearts leapt gleefully inside their rib cages at the large group. Noticing they were Middle Easterners caused a slight depression in their joy. Middle Easterners in beat up buses were not usually big spenders. Fear took over as the Rummites realized the Palestinians had arrived.

"Did they drive all the way from Amman with their heads stuck out the windows like that?" Sometimes the wise cracks of Hakim Hakunguard raised interesting questions.

The group was quiet and peaceful. They looked more like a group of awestruck nuns approaching Saint Peter's Square than a bunch of terrorists about to run off the Rummites.

"We have no weapons. We only wish to visit the site of the Twice Lost Ruins of Wadi Rum." Belaam Belaamin, the Palestinian leader and driver in the first bus approached and addressed Ahmahd Desantez.[152]

We are relieved to hear that. Frankly, we are fearful of the possible results our discovery may cause."

150

"You have no reason to fear us. I have a brother-in-law who lives here. Bechkded Amalamalak. Hello."

Bechkded Amalamalak boldly stepped forward and the two embraced, kissed, and exchanged greetings. Mahmumed Belijer began chewing his tongue again.[153] Bechkded Amalamalak then made introductions all around.

"Some of us are devout. Most? Not so much. None of us are militant. To be perfectly honest, we thought it would be fun to be numbered as the first modern Palestinians to set foot on the site. Would that be possible?" Belaam Belaamin had a friendly cut-to-the-chase, no-nonsense approach that appealed to Ahmahd Desantez.

"It would be my honor and pleasure to escort you to the site."

"As you can see by our humble demeanor and impoverished state, we are not politicians. We are not here to claim anything. We are but poor pilgrims. We are here to visit."

"You are most welcome to do so. Tell me Belaam Belaamin what do you do for a living?"

Belaam Belaamin pointed at the steaming heaps behind them. "I own these buses. I am trained as an attorney. However I spend precious little time in the courts.

"Ah! I recognized by your excellent syntax your probable experience with the law. I thought perhaps you were a diplomat. I also am an attorney with few opportunities to use my training! The desert sometimes shrinks!"[154]

The two new chums led the others, Palestinians and Wadi Rummites alike, out to the site. They walked. They looked. They returned. In the mean time the tanks had arrived.

That was why it took the Kingdom's armed representatives and academics longer to reach Wadi Rum from Amman than it did the Palestinians. The tanks moved a bit slower than the buses.

Six tanks, one dozen assault vehicles and thirty Hummers loaded with His Majesty's troops, mortars, weapons and one general. Precaution, when exercised by a government, always looks intimidating. After all, what good is a governmental sign of precaution if it does not scare people half to death?

General Mechal Mustah stood up in the back seat of his Jeep and gripped the roll bar for balance as the vehicle swerved around the tanks: A cheetah rounding up the elephants. He punctuated his shouted orders with a swipe of his general's baton. Swarthy, dark, and trim, a crisp looking, pressed uniform, but with moderate sweat stains on his back and armpits, Mechal Mustah was the very model of a modern Jordan general.

Satisfied with the troop deportment, Mustah dismounted and walked through the settling cloud of sandy dust to chat with the locals. "Greetings from His Royal Majesty. I am General Mechal Mustah. I escort the experts from His Royal Majesty's Public Antiquities Department. Who is your leader?"

Ahmahd Desantez stepped forward. "We have no elected officials." His friends and neighbors tsked and groaned with slight annoyance. The de facto mayor rarely screwed up. But nobody thought there was any reason to give the general a hard time. "What? What? There has never been an official election. What?" The annoyed looks persisted.

Mahmumed Belijer stepped forward. "This man, Ahmahd Desantez is our de facto mayor. He studied law with Bill Clinton. That is when he learned to split hairs so well."

That tickled the fancy of the mustachioed general. "Good enough. A pleasure to meet all of you. Of course all of you certainly realize the delicacy of this situation. The methods we use to deal with this initially and the way in which all those involved respond will undoubtedly have long term ramifications." The general stopped and calmly eyed Belaam Belaamin and the way his group hovered behind him. "My guess would be you folks are not from around here."

"I am Belaam Belaamin. I am here with my family and friends. My brother-in-law lives here."

"I am Bechkded Amalamalak. I can vouch for him. He is indeed my brother-in-law. His sister, my wife, is in my shanty. I will introduce you to her. You will see the resemblance instantly. It is quiet startling."

"I look forward to that. In the meantime Belaam Belaamin, may I see some sort of identification?"

"For what purpose?" As an attorney Belaam Belaamin was always on the lookout for dangerous precedents.

General Mechal Mustah sighed, then stage whispered. "Because, looking at you, I would guess you are a Palestinian. Reportedly a recently discovered site, thought to be of tremendous importance to the Palestinians, has been discovered...near..." General Mechal Mustah looked about, turned his head around, smiled and pointed to the 'Welcome to Wadi Rum' sign, which hovered there. He asked in a loud voice. "Where do I find Lawrence of Arabia Land?"

The locals shuffled their feet, found sudden interest in their fingernails and mumbled. "Here." "This is it." One smart-Alach "At Disneyland in Paris?"[155]

"Come on, come on. I'm not about to bite you, or your identification. See that did not even hurt. Belaam Belaamin? My brother Ketchaah worked with a man called Belaam Belaamin during resettlement of the Palestinian refugees in Amman. He was very impressed with this Belaam Belaamin."

"As was I with him." Belaam Belaamin responded with the faintest hint of dejection.

"I will remember that, sir. So. Here are the two options I offer you and your charges. Board your buses and leave now, or board your buses and be guarded by my men until my ruler and your ruler come to an agreement. The later choice could be decades from now. The former… let me say that when "now" is, is a fluid thing. "

Belaam Belaamin chewed on that for a moment. A mischievous smile twitched a hair or two of his jet-black moustache. "What if we boarded the buses and parked down the road a bit within sight of the site, but at a far enough distance so as not to interfere with the big shots? It would also allow the soldiers the opportunity to play dice games or catch a cat nap instead of standing at attention in the hot sun with their guns pointed at us."

"Fair enough, Belaam Belaamin. However would you find it acceptable if I posted a sentry half the distance between you and Wadi Rum?"

"Ah! The closer we are to Wadi Rum, the closer we are to the sentry! All generals should have your wisdom. And soft touch."

General Mechal Mustah placed a friendly hand on the shoulder of Belaam Belaamin. "Thank you."

Before the sun set that day, Wadi Rum had become a major distraction for the whole world. All eyes turned to Wadi Rum. Television viewers abandoned 'Survivor XXIV, Palos Verdes to scrutinize events in Jordan. Billions of baby boomers wondered, would it be possible to live to see both the Berlin Wall fall and hostilities in the Middle East cease all in less than half a century?[156]

As for the Wadi Rummites, the occupation of the troops and the media was both annoying and profitable. Annoying because they made an absolute mess of the commodes. Profitable because they all ate and drank snacks as if the practice were about to go out of style.

During lengthy lulls in negotiations, troops and equestrian types from the media rented horses and wandered the landscape. Mahmumed Belijer and Bechkded Amalamalak later organized horse races: Not the groomed oval of their more "civilized" counterparts. The two savvy organizers flagged off a track ten miles from start to finish. The course included racing over the famous Natural Rock Bridge-only wide enough to accommodate one horse at a time- tip-toeing at breakneck speed. Other thrilling portions included coaxing the horse through a series of thistle patches and rounding a hairpin in front of a monolithic rock stand. The best observation points were roped off.

A massive glut of Palestinians began arriving within the first week after the story broke. They took their place behind Belaam Belaamin and his family. Most were prepared for a long stay in the desert. They took pity on and helped those who weren't. For a group with a prior reputation for being rock-throwing, exploding vest-wearing troublemakers, they certainly got along well with each other. Within a month, the camp of refugees (Or "Homelanders" as they preferred to be called.) straddling General Mechal Mustah's line in the sand just north of his imagined Wadi Rum city limits, stretched out on both sides of the desert highway as far as the eyes[157] could see. This sea of humanity in the desert quickly developed into the revered established settlement it is today.[158]

[159]First-comers would telephone relatives with lists of things to bring with them as they abandoned West Bank or Bethlehem homes for what had turned into permanent relocation in Wadi Rum. Slow moving cars pulling overloaded makeshift trailers clogged the desert highway. Within a very short period of time it was actually faster to ship something through the Suez Canal to the Red Sea to Aqaba than it was to drive directly from Amman to Wadi Rum.

Within a month the vast majority of the Palestinian population had extricated itself from every city apartment and country home in Jordan and set up shop in Wadi Rum. Repatriation from other countries was more gradual. But soon Palestinians began trickling in from other Arab speaking countries, as well as Europe, Scandinavia, the United States, Canada, Central and South America. Two million Palestinians came to Wadi Rum before the site was verified to be authentic. Such was the power of faith.

For the Palestinian population in Israel the announcement lit the fuse for an exodus explosion. Palestinians poured out of Israel. Along the West Bank and in Bethlehem and Jerusalem you could roll bowling balls down the once teaming streets and not hit a Palestinian. The famous Temple Mount mosque with its blinding golden dome, where Mohammed the Prophet climbed the great white horse and flew off to Heaven was all but abandoned. The last Palestinian out had unplugged the taped call to prayer message and taken the cassette recording and player to a mosque being erected in Wadi Rum.

The size of the crowd of Palestinians leaving Israel was so great that satellite photographs recorded the dust it kicked up. It was a happy crowd. As were the Israelis back in Jerusalem.

After six months holding the world in breathless anticipation, the international group of scientists, archaeologists and celebrities[160] under the scrutiny of bureaucrats and diplomats also from Jordan, Israel, France, Germany, Japan and the United States, declared the site to be built by the ancient Nebutian society. While impossible to say with absolute certainty, there existed only the slightest scientific doubt that the writing on the obelisk appeared to be authentic and that of Mohammed the Prophet. The talk of a "Jewish Conspiracy" was to be expected.

For the Palestinians who had already moved lock, stock and barrel, there was no need. The message was carved in stone and signed. Mohammed the Prophet wanted them to live there.

Belaam Belaamin became a celebrity of sorts. As other members of his family joined him in Wadi Rum, they built lean-tos against the buses. The three of which were obvious landmarks.

Conveniently (Or as planned?), Mahmumed Belijer and Bechkded Amalamalak faded into the background of the political tumult surrounding the early days of their discovery. Interest eventually turned to the exact circumstances of how the ruins were found. Though technically honest, they coyly disavowed being an actual part of it and instead held out their hands[161] in Peter's direction.[162]

Peter remained predictably humble. Though, upon reflection, what could he brag about? His inability to control an obstinate horse? His natural clumsiness on sand? His divining rod dick?

As to the Wadi Rummites, they packed up and left just prior to a meeting held by "officials" to "negotiate" a "settlement" between the Wadi Rummites and the Palestinians. The big shots had given the Wadis until the next day to draw a map of the area where they would choose to live and to give a percentage of profits they expected to make from taxing pilgrims. They also wanted to know who would run the police, who would tend to the sewage, who would start picking up the desert litter and on and on and on.

On the night before that was supposed to be decided, the whole former population and Peter walked a good distance from Wadi Rum and the Twice Lost Temple site which, they noted with chagrin, was now an around-the-clock explosion of klieg lights and machine- and hand-excavators. Someone built a fire and the hundred or so gathered silently around it.

"Sure is a big deal, now." This time Hakim Hakunguard was poignantly amusing. The group, to a one, turned to look at the mass of twinkling lights along the horizon then stared once again into the fire and sighed. Ahmahd Desantez stood and seemed to fumble with his thoughts for a moment before he eventually spoke.

"My fellow..." The de facto mayor usually would finish the salutation with "Wadi Rummites." This time he did not. Instead he addressed them. "My fellow tribesman of the Al-Mana'ayah. Please do not think me insane for saying what I am about to say. But I must. Look there and see Wadi Rum sparkle in the distance." Most craned their necks to look. The rest remembered what they had seen when they looked at it about thirty seconds ago. "Our homes. Our history. Our sweat. ."

"Our trash." Hakim Hakunguard just couldn't resist a classic set-up.

"Our buried loved ones. Our lives and our pasts are in Wadi Rum. Look out here into the dark, mysterious desert." Everybody looked at the desert. The stars, the moon glowing on the sand. It was real nice. So. "But..." Again words bobbed like an apple in the water-filled washtub of his brain escaping the sinking teeth of elucidation.

Just then Feta Geeaza jumped up. "I say we keep walking. Let's just get the hell out of here. We are Bedouin. We should be out wandering around in the desert, not being the next poster group of people making life difficult for the Palestinians. Let them have the ruins. Let them have Wadi Rum. I say let's just vamoose.[163]

Mahmumed Belijer and Bechkded Amalamalak practically peed their sirwal in relief.

Ahmahd Desantez de facto mayor of Wadi Rum stared with considerable annoyance at Feta Geeaza. "My thunder is missing. Has anyone seen my thunder? Oh. Feta Geeaza I believe you have stolen it. But I must admit. Our tribal dissident speaks for me. I plan to become a Bedouin once again. I hope many-I hope all of you will join me."

Hem Mahnem leapt to his feet all saucer eyes and flailing arms. "But we will all die in the desert. We will not be able to live there. There is no water. What will we do for food? How will we make money? And what about "Survivor?"[164] Yet another episode is scheduled to begin in one month! Don't we all love to watch "Survivor?" Don't we all love to discuss the people and their possible strategies? If we are in the desert the cable will not stretch that far. Not only will we starve to death, we will all die idiots!"

"Then you do not wish to wander?" Ahmahd Desantez did not want this decision prolonged.

"Of course I do. I will ask my brother in Petra to tape the episodes for me." Hem Mahnem suddenly realized that he cared more for his tribe than for some "real" person on television.

Ahmahd Desantez looked about for further comment. His eyes settled on Mahmumed Belijer and Bechkded Amalamalak who both immediately stopped smiling. His eyes narrowed microscopically. He knew Mahmumed Belijer. Would bet his wife the man had a preference for the desert life. Wondered if somehow Mahmumed Belijer was responsible for all of this. But how? Could Mahmumed Belijer have assembled the ruins covertly and buried them to be discovered later? Absurd thought! Or was it? Yes. It was an absurd thought.

"Ahmahd Desantez, please stop staring at me. I grow uncomfortable." Mahmumed Belijer then stood. "If you are looking for my support, you have it. You all know of my longing for us to return to our life in the desert." All nodded their heads in agreement. Though in fact none had ever heard so much as a peep from him on the subject. There was an unspoken consensus to expedite the discussion. He began to sit, hesitated, thought, stood to address, sat down then stood back up again. "I know of the rumors and they lack foundation." Mahmumed Belijer plopped down into his seat in the sand with excessive indignity.

Ahmahd Desantez was about to ask Mahmumed Belijer to explain specifically what the devil he was talking about. If he had, Mahmumed Belijer's response most likely would have spilled the beans. Guilt was starting to burn at the bottom of his kettle. Peter interrupted the exchange.

"I deeply regret the pain I have brought upon the people of Wadi Rum. I was sent here to offer you the Word of Christ. Now you are losing your homes."

Several of the Rummites mumbled back and forth about this. They always wondered what he was doing there. Initially upon his arrival, Peter was considered a fool. Who but a fool wanders aimlessly across the desert? Oh. Wait a minute. That was what they were talking about doing themselves. Never mind.

"You have even less to apologize for than does Bshht. It was better that it was you who discovered the sign from Mohammed the Prophet. The discovery was made more credible because a non-believer made it. Incidentally, though you follow an outlandishly foolish spiritual path, we all here appreciate your presence. Would you not agree?" Ahmahd Desantez looked about and received head nods of agreement. "You may join us if you wish.

"So much for that. Shall we all move on? Abandon Wadi Rum? Life will be rigorous. But like true Bedouin we shall survive. Anyone with second thoughts?" Pursed lips and negative headshakes responded. "Everyone is eager to go?"

"Yeah, sure." Hey, why not? "What the Hell" "I am so out of here." Hakim Hakunguard, of course, insisted on delivering the topper.

"Your enthusiasm is not very convincing. Ah well. Best to save your energy. Life is a walk." Ahmahd Desantez unwittingly dug his heals into the horse's sides by spouting an ancient Bedouin saying. The Rummites immediately began chatting, joking and joshing amongst themselves as they made their last walk as landowners.

Ahmahd Desantez stopped by the Wadi Rummy where the decision makers huddled over piles of plans and agreements, yelling, berating, challenging, taunting, teasing, seducing, and pulling their (own) hair out. He stuck his head inside the door. "We are leaving." That was all he said.

The big shots thought little of it. Perhaps it was Ahmahd Desantez trying to be funny. It didn't sink in until noon the following day when they dragged themselves from the paperwork to seek him out for the various decisions/demands that they realized the Bedouin had left. Lock, stock and barrel.

The Bedouin took to the desert like fish to water. Life was much more difficult but considerably more challenging and as a result more satisfying. They avoided civilization for three years. Until one of them, in passing conversation, mentioned that a Mars bar would really hit the spot right now. The desire for the rich nougat, creamy caramel and sinfully rich milk chocolate spread like a barn fire in Chicago. Two months later they stumbled upon an outpost. Luckily the owner had a case in the freezer. As they lazily chewed their longed for treasures, the owner filled them in on news about their former digs.

The excavation was for the most part complete. There were a number of buildings great and small, the man did not remember how many, but there were a lot. What he did remember was that the man in charge of the bulk excavation, Ahmed Salah by name, had noticed while flying over the site in his jet, that the layout of The Twice Lost Ruins of Wadi Rum resembled the Plain of Assembly on The Day of Judgement. Muslims believe the arrangement to be the same layout for the throne of God.

Peter stayed behind in Wadi Rum. Three months after the Bedouin exit his new assignment arrived. His order ordered him to Rome.

# 11
## THE DROOLING POPE

Few of his predecessors could match Pope Martin VI for lack of power, including spiritual, administrative or brain. The church had run amuck under his leadership. Feminist nuns, and their sympathizers openly flaunted their disgust over Martin's reactionary edicts. Organized groups of Catholics demanding democratic representation in Rome flourished in Germany, France and the United States.[165] Church shepherds apologized to Jews everywhere because Rome "forgot" to condemn Hitler for the Holocaust. Many found the gesture more mocking than moot since it came a half-century after the fact.

The flock bleated its demands for birth control and abortion. Dioceses sold massive chunks of church properties to pay for millions of dollars in reparations and court settlements with the victims of pedophile priests. Catholics were no longer the docile sheep of the past. Verily, though they found the Lord and the path of the righteous, they had also found education. These were thinking sheep.

While historians prefer to think Benedict XVI did not exist, Martin's predecessor, John Paul III was a flitty, indecisive man. His major failure made him unique-even-rare-among church birds. For he was a thoughtful, methodical, intellectual willing to listen to all sides.

John Paul III was kind, generous and gentle. So much like Jesus it would just make you sick to your stomach. When he kicked, after a gratefully short term, the College of Cardinals got together for the traditional shindig and did what electing groups the world over have an unfortunate tendency to do. They over-compensated and elected someone who was the exact opposite.

Martin, whose name then was Luigi Arabrustacelliano, held more chits to call in than an old dog has fleas. Behind the scenes, sipping sherry and whittling Cubans, he often impressed his contemporaries with his erudite ranting and raving about the lost purity of Holy Mother, The Church. In public, he was just as sweet and firm as Wisconsin butter. A good sign, his supporters nodded. He switched gears easily. Knew how to put on a happy face.

Many of the Princes of the Church, weary of J.P.III's wuss approach to poping, wanted someone with sacred sacs.[166] They wanted someone who would scare the pants back on to all those lust-crazed, sinful and wayward Catholics. Someone like Pius XII but even scarier! Coincidentally, Martin considerably resembled Pius XII: beady eyes staring creepily through steel rimmed glasses.

He was no shoe-in though. It took several days with two votes each day to settle on Martin. Apparently, the Holy Spirit was not moving amongst them. The age limit for voting cardinals is 85. With an average age of 75, the conclave lacked the wherewithal for an all out battle. It also lacked the conflict for a battle. It was a totally uninspired conclave. Other than the Swiss, Michel d'Indy, who was certainly competent but had not been around long enough, Martin faced only a half-dozen, half-assed wannabes.

If the Holy Spirit gave them a common thought it was more along the lines of "Oh what the hell...what's the worse Martin can do?" By day six of the conclave there were only 25 dissenters when the ballots were cast in the morning. The second vote that afternoon was unanimous for Martin. The white smoke curled above the Sistine Chapel, and the crowd below cheered.[167]

The Curia snickered about the new pope's choice for a name. Martin. Harrumph. Perhaps their wise decision might lead to a mending of the centuries old schism that led to Martin Luther's Lutherans. Brother, the Romans could use some of those televangelist's dollars! Too bad the cardinals did not see the name choice for what it was. Just a dumb mistake on the new pontiff's part: an early sign that the new papal paint was already starting to peal.

Seventy-three years old when elected to start stamping the Holy Father's seal, Martin faded fast. Five years into his reign, his ardent supporters were turning their heads away just at the sight of him. Bad enough his mind had to go, they whined (to themselves, though not infallible, cardinals do not make mistakes) but did he have to turn into such a repulsive ragamuffin. Oh well. Martin was fairly old. They consoled themselves. How much longer could he last? Heh.

One of Martin's many odd developments was the use of his Holy Father's refinery for wiping whatever needed to be wiped: a fogged window in the papal limousine; his nose; dust that had collected on the Louis XIV side–table in the papal bedroom; his chin during dinner; an old LP recording, and, eventually, his ass.

The College of Cardinals had elected Martin to be pope and was stuck with him. Not that it was impossible to remove an incompetent pope. That was provided for in Church doctrine. But Martin was, (A) not a heretic and, though embarrassing to be within spitting distance of, was, (B) not clinically insane. An additional problem with Martin, as far as public image goes, was that he would insist on having moments of lucidity, damn him. Also, the bad P.R. resulting from picking the wrong guy to represent Christ on Earth is one thing. But the College of Cardinals was fearful —and savvy enough— to know that once dumped Martin would probably go running to the media.

Imagine. "Tonight on 60 Minutes: The complaints of an ex–pope. All that and Andy Rooney." So the curia watched and waited and prayed for a rapid face-to-face meeting between the sitting pontiff and his Lord.

For a near–mindless dolt, His Holiness sure had a lot to say. He would not stop writing. Martin's assistants watched nervously as he penned edict after edict.

An old nun's tale has it that a priest, early in his career, is generally more feminine, or at least inclined to the typically held feminine attributes: more understanding; quicker to sympathize; more sensitive, etc. The theory goes on to postulate that the older a priest grows the more these qualities shrink, then gradually turn and sour. He grows more typically masculine in his tendencies, and not the better characteristics either. No sweet Nell to begin with, in his dotage Martin developed into a misogynist prick.

He had a special problem with nuns. He did not care for women in general. But he saved his most intense wrath for nuns. Nuns seem to have gotten under his craw.

Often assistants would cower-or giggle- at the sound of his shrill reedy pipes bouncing around the papal offices. "Those bitches! They called themselves sisters! Brides of Christ, Hah! Whores of the devil more like it." Martin especially liked that last one. "Whores of the devil!" He could be heard screaming to no one save the countless art treasures.

Toward the end, Martin honed a paranoia that all those who surrounded him were out to get him. This was of course completely justified because, to a great extent, it was true.

His electorate, which five short years prior had given him something just shy of an eventual mandate, now were nearly paralyzed at the thought that they should actually have to carry out his pontifical gibberish. God's right hand man on Earth notwithstanding.

Martin's inanities did have an historical ring to them. Some even made a certain demented sense, especially considering the times. One, which Martin sweated over feverishly for several weeks, offered instant (non–appealable) excommunication to any Catholic belonging to an organization that publicly challenged the pope.

Some of the Cardinals nodded their heads at what seemed to them the surprising good sense of the edict in progress. Maybe the coach was back in the game. Maybe the Church's tiller was finally touching the water.

The cheers in their throats turned to cries of anguish as Martin explained his new doctrine. With a rare voice of calm reason, he let it rip that anyone who insisted on continuing down the path of heresy would be executed.

Luckily, Martin was seated on the papal toilet as he made a few final corrections in grammar and spelling. He wiped his ass with the edict and flushed it away.

As his mind declined, so the pope's corporeal presence shriveled, and did so at a noticeable rate. Never a large fellow, Martin's frame seemed to grow smaller day by day and sometimes by the minute. One assistant, Cardinal Berrinelli from Naples, remarked that he witnessed the pope shrink an inch while in audience with the President of the United States. Berrinelli had used the seal behind Martin, situated on the papal throne, as the standard.

Just as it would with any tragedy in any other work situation, a series of whispered one–liner jokes made the rounds among the various clerics of the papal administration, with "Pope Martin" being the assumed punch line:

"What's a foot and a half tall, and Christ's representative on Earth?"

"What's smaller than a skunk and gives off four times the stink?"

"What wears white robes has two teeth, a load in its pants and is not yet an octogenarian?"

On the way to the grand sitting room for an audience to meet new staff at the Vatican, where Peter was waiting, Martin lifted his papal skirts and peed in the general direction of a potted plant. This was Peter's immediate predecessor, and, friend to be.

163

# The Vatican Stash

Although it had a few off years when the Huns sacked, Napoleon plundered, or the Allied troops bombed Rome, during the half-century before Peter became pope, the Catholic Church was loaded. It was so moneyed, that then Cardinal Secretary of State, Michelle d'Indy, with all twenty fingers and toes in every financial pie, did not know the exact amount.

There were billions of Euros tied up all over the world. Through its various agencies, the church owned, controlled or invested in banks, shipping, mining, textile mills, factories, food and goods companies, even drug makers. Some of which made birth control pills!

One chief advantage Popes had over the run-of-the-mill multi-national corporation greed buckets was that they scoffed at the idea of "opening the books" to public scrutiny. After all, why should the infallible stand-in for Christ feel compelled to answer to anyone? There were no government controls or restrictions. The Vatican was its own government. That was the result of a 92-million dollar wheel-greasing Benito Mussolini gave Pope Pius XI in 1929.

The Lateran Treaty solved a sixty-year old conflict between the Italian government and the Catholic Church. Over the centuries, the Church acquired or lost huge chunks of land all over Italy. Some was given. Some was taken or lost by force. The Popes had an army, a navy and, more importantly, friends in high places.

At one point, the Vatican States consisted of 17-thousand square miles. That spells revenue from taxes, rents and the license or permit to do anything. As part of the unification of Italy in 1870, Italy took it back. It left the Holy Roman Catholic Church with the 109 puny acres known as Vatican City. In a fit of papal pique, no pope left the Vatican grounds between 1870 and 1929. All insisted they were "prisoners in the Vatican."

The papal land grab started with the Emperor Constantine. Up until 313, Roman emperors treated the Christians the way Republicans treat the poor today: Insisted they did not exist or fed them to the lions. Similar to other bizarre turns in history, the then pagan Constantine had a dream in which the cross of Christ appeared. He woke up and ordered his troops to put the symbol on their shields. The next day Constantine won the battle and repaid Christ by making Christians legal. He also tossed in some land and money so the pope could get comfy in Rome.[168]

For the next thousand years, royalty bent over backwards to help the Church spread the Word of God. If that meant slaughtering a few yokels for a chunk of property the Pope had his eye on, so be it. Plus various kings felt more comfortable knowing the Pontiff would not damn them to eternal hell over some unsuspecting prince's lakeshore property.

There were also plenty of Dukes and Barons looking to squat before the papal brown-eye. A gift of a few acres could forgive a lifetime of sin and debauchery.

Mussolini correctly figured his fascist regime would never be "freely" elected unless he made kissy-face with the Pope. The pact included a provision stating the Church would remain neutral during a war. So why are there so many photos in history books of Pope Pius XII shaking hands with Adolph Hitler and various Nazi leaders?

Before Pius was pope he had a position in Munich. As Archbishop Eugenio Pacelli he handed over a bag of money to Hitler to help the up-and-comer in his fight against atheistic communism. Later in Rome, Pius showed astonishing duplicity by announcing to the world that the occupying Nazis where not harming papal property. At the same time he was keeping mum about the thousands of Jews hiding downstairs or at the summer papal residence in Castel Gandolfo. There are reports that the Vatican, through financial or political means, may have saved as many as 1.2-million Jewish lives. In addition to putting Peter's Seat in jeopardy, the Vatican spent approximately $7,000.00 per day on food. By the by, in spite of reassurances from President Franklin Delano Roosevelt, allied troops bombed the Vatican twice.

The church lucked out with an answer to the question of what to do with Mussolini's money. It had arrived in the nick of time: just as the world was withering into the Great Depression. Bernardino Nogara, a prominent international banker, told Pope Pius XI, essentially, to forget about losing the land. Land did not mean doodly when compared to successful investing. Though skeptical of Nogara, the Church trusted him with the fascist's windfall. A well-founded trust since Nogara made a mint for the Church.

Pius XI signed Nogara up to manage the money on the day the pact was signed. Imagine being a hot-shot investor walking into the Vatican financial offices-which were then run by clerics who knew next to nothing about investment-and being handed 90-million smackers to develop a tax-free international corporation.

During his successful reign lasting into the late 50s, Nogara wisely kept a low profile. He handpicked his own near-equally savvy pals to serve on boards of directors in companies where he plunked down Christ's money.

***

The joint astonished and overwhelmed Peter. It also made him dizzy and occasionally a bit nauseous. He had been in many churches and a couple of small cathedrals, but there was absolutely nothing he had experienced previously in his life to prepare him for standing inside the largest church in the world. With all its vaults and shrines, saints preserve us, this was where the saints were preserved!

Did statues of saints (all his favorites were there) harden his resolve to be more like them? Did the shrines to Popes past plant him yet deeper in the fertile soils of his own spiritual purity? None of the above. The whole scene caused his thought process to over-chew one simple thought: Isn't all this gold and stuff exactly what Jesus preached against? These thoughts occurred to him almost simultaneously as Peter stood at the back of a pack of tourists lined up in front of "The Pieta."[169]

Peter's first encounter with the diminutive Big Daddy was at a papal audience for new Vatican workers. Martin was plopped down into his throne exposing his fuzzy blue slippers. With a bothered wave of a bony hand Martin indicated he wanted to get this show on the road.

Martin's chore here was simply to welcome these recent arrivals, say a little prayer, then go do some more drooling in private. Always one to interrupt smooth sailing with a few surprise swells, Martin spotted Peter. There was something wrong about that one. What was it? He was young! That was it. Cardinals were supposed to be old, not young. Why he thought he was involved in a cardinal making ceremony is a mystery of faith.

"Come here."

Peter took a few steps closer.

"A little closer, if you don't mind." He said in a matronly falsetto. With a withered fingery 'come here' gesture, the Holy Father was doing his La Mama impersonation. This was Martin's way of being cute.

Peter shuffled a bit closer. Martin responded with something that twenty years earlier in his life would have been an expression of amused exasperation. Now it was just another goofy, inappropriate old guy face. Peter was standing directly in front of him. Martin had rested his fleece-covered tootsies on a luxurious footstool. The tips of his fuzzies were inches from Peter's shins.

"Come here." Martin barked (sort of like one of those little yappy dogs). Peter moved in so close he had to steady himself on a throne armrest. Martin grabbed Peter's ear and pulled him to within inches of his sour-milk smell.

A few assistants held their freshly brushed breaths and looked furtively to see if any of the invited non-Vatican guests had noticed. They were met with expressions holding no more suspicion than expectancy could allow. The assistants resumed breathing.

"How old are you?"

Peter tried his Italian. Numbers were fairly easy.

"What? You're not three thousand years old. I'm not even three thousand years old. Your Italian stinks. Speak English?"

"Yes Holy Father. I was born in the United States."

"Really? Ever been to Detroit? I had a wonderful time there. Visiting with Cardinal Dearborn. Do you know Cardinal Dearborn? We went to some interesting places across the river there. In Canada. It was called the Windsor Ballet."

"Yes, Holy Father. I'm from Lathrup Village. I have been to Toledo."

"Toledo? Spain?"

"No, Holy Father. Toledo, Ohio."

"Where is Ohio?"

"Just South of Michigan, Holy Father."

"Oh. I see. And now... where is Michigan?"

"That's where Detroit is, Holy Father."

"Oh. Good, good. I'm glad we're making you a Cardinal, son. You seem like a very sensible lad. How old are you?"

"Thirty-six, Holy Father."

"Well. That's a little young-" The conversation having attained a certain symmetry, Martin let loose of Peter's ear but stared at him for a solid five minutes. Eventually an assistant whispered something into The Boss's ear. Martin re-entered the land of the living and snapped an unconvincing "I know that." He looked at Peter again, and then whispered with purpose. "Come see me in my private office." Another aide motioned Peter to move along. The ceremony continued then concluded without further incident. Though formally welcomed to the Vatican staff, Peter still had no idea what he was doing there.

Martin took a shine to this new kid. An unintended accomplishment for Peter since Martin looked dimly on everyone, and especially new staff people with those smarmy, kiss-ass looks on their faces. Long-timers were just as bad. They always tried to manipulate what he was trying to do or telling him what he should say. As if he didn't know what he was trying to say! Saint Joseph's throbbing head![170] He was The Pope! This boy was cooperative. There was a certain distracted, vacant air about him that Martin enjoyed. He would be a nice change to have around here. Unlike most other orders he gave, Martin remembered his instruction to Peter for a private meeting.

Later that day, Peter was escorted to the secret office where Popes went when they needed to be alone. This large, strange room had only one long window set five feet above the floor. It only offered its spectacular view of Saint Peter Square to a standing viewer.

Standing there, staring out that window, turning grapes sour  (Most concluded he was too young and so lost The Big Sedan to Martin.) was Michelle d'Indy, Cardinal Secretary of State. As the number two fellow in the Vatican, d'Indy's job was to run the business end of the Church.

d'Indy turned as Peter entered and fixed him with a glare that could break down plutonium. The look also was meant to inspire subservience and fear in the receiver. Though miles from obstinate, Peter did not cower from the scowl. As always, Peter was just being Peter.

d'Indy was always moving and shaking, manipulating people, switching them around so he would always be one step ahead of his inferiors, which included everyone he came into contact with. d'Indy was a born big-shot. Birthed to be Boss. He wanted to be pope so bad it made his fingertips itch. He could almost feel the crosier in his hand. Not John Paul II's arthritic looking Christ on a stick staff either. d'Indy fantasized his grand stick as a powerful Son of God gleaming in gold and rubies. Gold and rubies. Simple yet stunning.

d'Indy was the one responsible for moving Peter to Russia and then to what he hoped would be a safe hidden place in the Vatican. Someplace deep downstairs just shy of a dungeon, where any type of success would be impossible. The old cardinals were a bunch of gossips. They loved to prattle on about things both wicked and wonderful. He had overheard several occasional jabbers from indiscreet cardinals about Peter's seeming success in Merdette and then the Russian Far East and Jordan. That bothered the easily threatened d'Indy. The withered old prune of a pope was going to fall off the branch soon. d'Indy could not be too careful.

The pope was seated behind his desk. Peter went around it and fell to his knees, in order to kiss the pope's ring. The pope was busy with other things. To be precise, he was completely committed to an examination of the crease on his left cuff.

Peter waited for the hand to be offered. He waited five minutes. He waited ten minutes. After fifteen minutes, he dared a sideways glance towards d'Indy, whose steely glare was now augmented by just the microscopic hint of a sneer.

The room was very dusty. That was the way Martin had grown to like it. He insisted that it be left the way he left it. One of the few marbles he had maintained rolling around inside the playground of his mind was dedicated to keeping housekeeping out of that room. He had it padlocked and he had both keys. He didn't need a reason. He was the pope ("For singed martyr's sake!")

Peter's sneeze awakened Martin's attention.

"What are you looking for down there?"

Peter looked up into the bloodshot, watery eyes. He thought not of the leader of the universal church but of Fettuccine Alfredo. Not without good reason.

"I was waiting to kiss your ring, Holy Father."

"Oh it's you! My new cardinal! The one who is not allowed to speak Italian in my presence."

"Yes, Holy Father."

"Go ahead then, kiss the ring. And what are you doing on the floor there, then? Are you looking for something?"

"He was there to kiss your ring, Holiness.[171] Now he's done it. Perhaps we can get on to the reason for this meeting?" Though Swiss, d'Indy's Italian was flawless, his bearing impeccable, his patience as thin as the pope's waistline.

"What is your hurry? You have a plane to catch? Oh-" The pope had amused himself. "I suppose you do. Well then. Whatever it is you're looking for, you can find later, son. We don't want to keep Cardinal...whatchamacallit waiting any longer. Sit down both of you sit down."

There was only one other chair in the room. Illustrating his notorious, political savvy, d'Indy quickly sat in it. Peter looked

169

around the room, came to a quick decision. He sat on the floor next to d'Indy.

"Now. The reason I have summoned you two here-. Where is he? Where-?" The pope sighted a hand being waved at the edge of the front of his desk. "What are you looking down there so diligently for? Well, never mind. Let's get on with it.

"Cardinal d'Indy, you have been given the sacred privilege of serving The Holy See as Papal Nuncio in the Reformed Republic of Yugoslavia. You leave for Belgrade immediately, if not sooner. This nice young man will take your place as my Cardinal Secretary of State." Martin held his hand out across the desk as he leaned back dismissively in his cozy pope chair. It was not necessarily an intentionally humiliating gesture, but, of course, d'Indy was not about to take it as an attempt at anything else.

He leaned across the great expanse just far enough to make contact with Martin's fingertips. Then made just the slightest of kissing motions with his lips. d'Indy one upped Hollywood for fake demonstrations of affection.

"Am I excused then, your Holiness?"

"Why not?"

d'Indy left in a huff. He wanted to take a moment to attempt to whither Peter with another glance. To no avail, Peter was in sort of a lotus position, head bowed and hands dug deeply into his flowing sleeves.

The door closed with excruciating quietness. d'Indy had read Ibsen, of course, and so always fancied making a dramatic exit topped off with the ironic ideal of a non-slamming door.

The Pope and Peter forgot about d'Indy before he was half way down the hall. Martin's thoughts (?) drifted off to the increasing comfort he found in never-never land. Lacking a pencil to flick, Peter prayed.

They sat there in their respective states of mindlessness for some time. It could have gone on for an eternity if Martin had not let lose a bilious cloud of flatulence. When the stench reached Peter he coughed involuntarily. If he had been breathing through his mouth, they could have been there for weeks.

"Who's there?" Martin warned suspiciously. "Stand up."

Peter stood.

"Oh, you. Did you find what you were looking for?"

"No, Holy Father."

"Well if you like you can come back some other time and look for it then."

Peter closed the door behind him and was pleased to see his escort, Father Cletus waiting for him in the dim hallway. Though he rarely had anywhere to go, what with no job until now, he got lost every time he went anywhere.

"Father Cletus, where is the Secretary of State's office? The Holy Father wants me to work there."

"Yes, Father. Cardinal Secretary of State d'Indy ordered me to escort you there immediately after you concluded your audience with the Holy Father."

The two traversed a couple flights of stairs, made a dizzying number of turns left and right, shuffled quickly down several hallways so long the ends were not in sight for some time, took several more turns then down a staircase and then up a half-staircase. Finally they accelerated into the final straightaway.[172] This grand hallway was decorated with grand draperies on the grand windows, the grand purple runner trimmed with gold, and several elaborate grand chandeliers with grand candles. Father Cletus opened the grand mahogany double doors, which made a grand squeak.

As a person who admires the Son of God because of His appreciation for squalor, it took all of Peter's effort to keep his eyes open, as he dog paddled in this ocean of opulence. For any otherwise normal person, at first glance the room gave the impression it existed for receptions. Which it did.

Over by the grand bay windows looking out on the grandest of all views, (Saint Peter Square, what else?) stood a baby grand piano. A flock of delicate yet richly appointed wing-backed chairs, floated on the marble-on-marble inlaid floor. Strategically placed tea tables performed impressions of bird feeders. Silver trays offered petits fours topped with (Oh please! This is food!) gold-tipped florets. Just the far side of the fireplace a mahogany wet-bar leaned discreetly against the wall, eager to minister to those in need of a gargle or two. Wonder what vintage d'Indy preferred for altar wine.

Father Cletus left Peter squinting at the rich Persian tapestries. Peter tried not to look at all this grand stuff. He hoped it would disappear. He was in the same building as ol' Saint Peter's Bones, Jesus's best buddy, and look at all this high falootin' stuff. It made Peter's skin crawl. It made his stomach twist. It made his temples pound. It made his bleeding heart squirt painfully.

Father Cletus sat behind his receptionist desk. His deck topped with computer, various blinking electronic gear and several phones in a variety of colors. This was the Vatican poop deck. Behind him and to the left, another set of elegant doors creaked open (what is it with the squeaky doors in the Vatican?). There stood d'Indy. Expressionless.

"Father Peter." d'Indy's slightly deprecating tone greeted the distracted Peter from his miserable reverie. "Thank you for coming so quickly. Please come into my office." Yeah. Right. Like Peter was in the neighborhood so he just dropped by.

"I want to talk to you about your assignment. Please sit." Peter sat. Another wingback as complex in its comforts as a 1973 Sauceet Merlot. d'Indy sat stiffly erect in his throne: gold with satin covered upholstery. There were griffons facing off on either side of d'Indy's head. Snakeheads lisped angrily under his hands.

As if Peter weren't miserable enough from having all this extravagance forced down his throat, now he had dread tossed on top his heap of misery. He could barely breathe. Work would be a great challenge. Still, if he was ready to gladly sacrifice his life to a band of smelly Merdettians, he could certainly offer God the pain of working in this den decorated by the devil.

"Eminence, I pray to do God's will."

"Good for you." d'Indy's tone of voice was kind, in stark contrast to his lamppost posture. He occasionally suffered from lower back pain. It was one of the drawbacks of wheeling and dealing all day while seated upon a golden throne. Sitting up, up way up seemed to take off some of the pressure.

"Perhaps you have heard that his Holiness is not feeling well?

"No, Eminence. I did not know that."

"Well he's not." d'Indy snapped a bit as a twinge bit his back about six inches above his right buttock. "Trust me, then. The Holy Father carries the spiritual weight of Holy Mother the Church on his frail shoulders. We all must do what we can to help him no matter how small or unimportant the task may seem.

"If his holiness wants me to be his Secretary of State, then God's will..."

"As I see it, God's will is for you to stay as far away from this office as possible. I can't believe your cheek." d'Indy had blown the ballasts on his reserve of civility. "You don't really believe you can perform as chief financial administrator of the church do you?" d'Indy shuffled Peter's apparent resume and read from it through a scowl. "Merdette! You are nearly burned at the stake for kicking some vegetables! Siberia you established Flea

172

Markets! What on Earth is a Flea Market!" d'Indy's resolve was weakening as the thought occurred that perhaps Peter could run the Church. "Fell off a horse and ended the conflict between the Israelis and Palestinians. Humph. I might add, after your brief encounters with the Holy Father, you don't also believe the pope can perform as spiritual leader of the church, do you?" Peter was one of the best people ever born to pose rhetorical questions to. Especially when the question's syntax was scrambled. The question was water off a duck's back. d'Indy would have to toss Peter into the lake if he expected a response.

"What little is left of the pope's mind cannot be trusted-". d'Indy caught himself. That was too harsh even for the confines of his private office. Huge as it was, a whisper bounced about like a miss-shot Ping-Pong ball.

"What I am saying is, it is up to us to interpret his wishes. I understand how you may have misunderstood him. He meant for you to <u>report</u> to the Secretary of State-to me-for your assignment.

Peter was amazed at the Cardinal Secretary of State's ability to interpret the Holy Father's wishes. Relief washed over him like Amazing Grace. He fell to his knees gratefully, repulsed momentarily by the dreaded comfort of the plush carpet fronting d'Indy's desk. The nap of which seemed to lick his exposed toes seductively.

"I pray for the humblest task, Eminence."

Peter's gushed relief and sincerity surprised and surprisingly touched d'Indy. d'Indy didn't get to be a big shot by not being able to judge people with some degree of accuracy. Few so completely lacking in a little skepticism made it this close to the top. However, Peter was obviously sincere.

"Well..." d'Indy harrumphed half-heartedly. "You are a world-traveled priest. So we can't very well have you scrubbing down the latrines."

"I would thank God daily for such an assignment."

"Hmm." d'Indy picked up and scanned a small pile of papers. He settled on one and tossed the rest aside. "The Vatican Archivist needs assistance. How good are your Greek and Latin?"

Peter responded with a slight smile and a slight lean of the head to the right. By this he meant to preface his admission that his Greek and Latin were horrendous. d'Indy took the gesture as a humble deference to having acquired a superior knowledge on the subjects.

"Good. It's settled." d'Indy referred to the paper again. "You are now Chief Archivist for the Vatican. But do whatever Father Acalanes,[173] Jerome Acalanes tells you to do. He is-was-the Chief Archivist."

Do not confuse the Vatican Archives with the Vatican Library. Tourists never saw the Archives because that was where all the Dirt was swept. Prior to Pope Peter only a select few high-ranking church scholars were allowed access to the stacks. Though calling it access is grotesque exaggeration.

Vatican Archivists passed on a rigid tradition of giving a hard time, tempered with Christian indifference and superiority, to any and all others who dared to seek out this treasure trove. Interested parties waited weeks, sometimes years, for a pile of senseless forms to fill out. That was followed by a (chuckle, chuckle) waiting period and, occasionally, approval for short, limited study.

There was no browsing. The archivist retrieved the requested manuscripts from the archives then, with an impatient glare laid them down on the study table before the visitor. Depending on their ranking, and time permitting, Acalanes, as well as all his predecessors, was fond of then standing behind them, and breathing down their necks impatiently. This foiled most attempts at concentration. There was no photocopy machine and laptop computers were not allowed until the late 1990s. There were no electrical outlets available. Better bring an extra battery if you don't want to handwrite notes. And no, there are no extra pencils! Does this look like a stationary store?

It took Peter perhaps two minutes to assure Acalanes he had no intention of taking over the administration of the Archives and was there only to serve his brother in whatever capacity Acalanes saw fit. Therefore, Father Peter's job was dusting the shelves. What else could he do? If Peter were on a sinking Greek- or Latin-speaking cargo ship, he wouldn't know how to ask for a lifesaver.

It took Acalanes perhaps thirty seconds to figure out Peter's lack of foreign language skills and thus lack of archivist potential. Only a couple thousand items were in English. Most of those were requests for nullification from marriage or priestly vows. The sorting was a mishmash of chronological by subject matter with all sorts of addendum shelves often added centuries later in a far corner. Vatican Archivists had to be church historians

174

to understand the arcane static juggle. A misplaced item could be lost for centuries.

Thirty miles of shelves containing millions of pages of more than a millennium and a half of history attracts a lot of dust. (There would have been reams more had not Napoleon liberated them.) Everything was in a constant state of slow yet deliberate decay. There were a few sixteen hundred year-old binders that needed to be handled with kid gloves.

Peter had a predictably soft touch. He fluffed about with his feather duster at notes from Inquisition interviews and lists of slaughtered heretics including the justifications of their murdering judges.[174]

Though Peter dusted daily, at roughly one-quarter mile per day, it was more than six months before he was back where he started. Just as well. The months gave the dust a little time to collect. There is no more useless occupation in the universe than dusting at a flimsy, barely discernable, ungratifying level of dust. Not that it would matter to Peter.

Not that it was work to Peter. It was prayer. Worship has no goal but adoration. Therefore the more mindless the work the more perfect the prayer. Peter kept up a steady pace. He did not dilly-dally. But his thoroughness included taking down off the shelf each tome, reference, binder or dinky, insignificant opuscule and cleansing it carefully.

Initially Peter had no idea of the history he held in his hands. It was all Greek (And Latin, Italian, German, French etc.) to him. Peter's hands held the pornography of the Borgia popes' incest. Gently he cradled and cleansed the filth off Church enemies such as Luther and Calvin. It was a centuries old battle to keep the Roman grime clear from the binder containing the divorce decree for Henry VIII.

There were also reams and reams of notes, centuries worth of collected evidence which proved the saintliness of various individuals. If you think it takes a long time to get in and out of the Department of Motor Vehicles, try getting somebody made into a saint. Then watch the paperwork pile!

There was a pithy rumor that the Archives stored a secret safe that held a letter from a Portuguese peasant girl to the pope. The Blessed Virgin, (Jesus' Mom) though dead floated down from the sky (This was before the invention of outer space.) and appeared before three shepherd kids from Fatima. The skinny is

She told them the date for the END OF THE WORLD! Too bad it was just a rumor.

If it had not been for Father Acalanes, Peter would have never known he was knee deep in the sins, real estate transactions, expense reports for Secretaries of State and written battles for truth of the Church.

While in the Archives, Acalanes attempted to pour all sorts of vile, anti-Catholic rubbish into Peter's brain. Some of it may have stuck. "Why, look here, Father Peter. This is the Book of Concord. Are you surprised to see the Book of Concord here in the Vatican?"

"I don't know what it is Father."

"Really? This is a collection of what those heretic Lutherans believe. They are under the misunderstanding that their sacred tract is stored in Dresden. But some German prince, or other, a good Catholic at any rate, pilfered this, the original, and substituted a forgery a couple hundred years ago. He he he."

"Shouldn't we send it back, Father? Since it is stolen?"

Peter's sincere question lacked any expected irony

"You are a lamb, aren't you?" Then Acalanes naturally scampish nature grabbed hold of him eagerly. "Let's see if we can't find the address."[175]

They were an odd pair, the wise, sardonic academic and the unquestioning cherub. But, the two became friends of a sort anyway. Acalanes had known love in his life and was quickly fond of Peter. Peter's simple understanding of God's world, oddly intimidated the cynic and Acalanes liked that. Peter, though loving in a purely Christian manner, was quaintly distant emotionally.

"Why look here Peter. It's a note about a Pope condoning murder." Acalanes, though eager to infect Peter with at least a touch of skepticism, was equally curious to see how the simple man would float his faith against the tidal wave of reality.

"I understand throughout history oppression sent many souls to an early heavenly reward." Count on Peter to put a kind spin on it.

"Tsk. Look. I realize you don't understand Italian. But this is a letter from Bloody Mary Tudor, a former Queen of England. She is thanking Pope Paul IV for giving her permission to kill Protestants in defense of Catholicism."

Peter sighed and gazed sadly at the sixteenth-century parchment.

"Look. Look at this." Acalanes cradled a large tome. "This is Paul IV's crowning achievement. It's called the Index of Forbidden Books. Because these books were heretical or dangerous to morals, anyone who read them would be banished to hell. And what's truly unfair is that you can read all these books today and <u>not</u> go to Hell for doing so!"

"The Church Fathers are obliged to protect the souls she shepherds." (Sic) Peter responded meekly.

"Yes. And to protect the bulge in its purse. This one right here. That's the Protestant Bible. Imagine that. If a Catholic during the Reformation wanted to read this to see what all the fuss was about, he would be doomed to Hell. If that's not enough for you, Paul IV also forced the Jews to live in ghettos. Three centuries later, Pius XII gave a sack of money to Adolph Hitler."

"But didn't His Holiness John Paul II embrace the head Roman Rabbi as a sign of reconciliation?"

"That's right. I had almost forgotten. He absolved the Jews of any involvement in the crucifixion of Christ. He should have thanked them. Otherwise, we would not have had a Savior." Acalanes slapped the book back into its place with a slight annoyance. "Next you will tell me that John Paul II was responsible for the disintegration of the Soviet Union and the end of communism there. In reality, the Soviet Union imploded. It would have done that with or without John Paul." Acalanes waved off a comment that Peter was not about to make. "Yes, he convinced Solidarity to avoid the use of violence against the communists in Poland. I'll give you that."

True enough that Peter never did absorb Acalanes's contempt. But, Acalanes did affect Peter. His major impact was to augment the doubt of this deeply spiritual person. The most searing question being "Is this Christ's Church?" The pissed priest cornered Peter forcing him to respond. To act. The proof for that pudding was born out when Peter put d'Indy in his place.

Pushing the Push-over Pope

After Acalanes, Peter's most intimate acquaintance in the Vatican was his predecessor, Pope Martin VI. More accurately, Martin befriended Peter. Though Martin no longer had the mental muscle to figure out that most of the big shots in the Vatican were repulsed at the idea of having to put up with him on a day-to-day basis, he could still hear a very faint voice from his own past telling

177

him that it is nice to have a friend. Martin also held a teensy weensy niggling notion that he rubbed people the wrong way.

Not this youngster though. Martin could ramble around in conversational roundabouts all day with this one without ever being redirected back to the main highway. He also noticed that Peter never challenged his long lapses of silence. Peter's patience was a salve to Martin's self-doubt.

This new priest made Martin's scrawny little chest swell with renewed sovereignty. Everything he would say now (or not say) would be important. Martin felt like a pope again!

It was one thing to be the infallible, life-long leader of a huge international spiritual organization. It was another to be directed in everything he did by d'Indy, the curia cadre, his cook and his valet. As his feebleness increased, Martin had less and less of the wherewithal needed to assert himself. More importantly, while he may have been led around by the nose, the fellows with his boogers on their fingers were the ones who actually took care of the myriad of Church needs and duties. The idea that he should suddenly become responsible for the Church scared the be-Jesus out of Martin. But now! He fancied Peter as his replacement. He had someone he could trust. After his own living and historical reputation, the most important thing to anyone wearing a crown is his successor. Besides, what could it take to run a multi-billion lire[176] church, for Christ's sake! Men dumber than Peter had run the Church! Some into the ground, true, but It always managed somehow to re-blossom.

When he was not dusting or praying or getting an earful from Acalanes, Peter followed the pope around. To be more precise, he spent most of his time pushing the pope around. Martin's poor little chicken legs were giving out. There was no medical reason given because, in a fit of Church of Christ Scientism, Martin declared that he would wait for a cure from above. Till that time came, he would use a wheelchair.

It was during this time that Peter received a real tour of the joint. He and Martin would roll around for hours. Ever read about popes, or other powers being kept under wraps during their last years? This is probably what Mao or Stalin was up to in their final, suspiciously inactive days: just screwing around.

The time was not wasted on Peter, though. It amplified and sensitized his repulsion for the extravagance. Would Christ live here? The question scratched and pinched away at his very synapses. The hoard of sculptures and acres of painting smothered

178

him.[177] The swirling, frozen-in-time robes, the gaudy colors, the grandiose poses, the gaudy facial expressions all tied his stomach in knots.

If Peter were ever forced to paint, draw or sculpt his Lord, his Lord's Mom or the Saints, he would literally draw a blank. Peter did not visualize his Redeemer and company. One does not depict the Creator. Not with any accuracy, anyway.

Then there was also the ongoing artistic license/rape of all Catholic virtues. Room after room, vault after vault, tomb after tomb, chapel after chapel, and every nook and cranny was crowded with ritzy looking martyrs, perfect popes, spotless ecstatic virgins, and high-class Jesuses. It was ironic sacrilege that this, The House of God, the shrine to poverty, humility and sacrifice should be smeared head to toe with so much top-drawer bric-brac.

And that's just the good stuff. Everybody knows about the Michelangelo's Sistine Chapel paint job and Bernini's bee-invaded canopy over the main altar. But over the centuries the Vatican had become a junkyard/repository (some say suppository) for every second-rate artist with a connection. Not only was there a lot of art, there was a lot of bad art.

Any prejudice against modern art will not be fed here. And it shall be easily proven that many creative geniuses have also, at times, produced bowel movements more commendable than the crap they have tried to flush into the mainstream of artwork. Gian Bernini was modern during the first half of the 1600s. Many fawning historians consider him to be the greatest sculptor/architect of the 17th century. The best argument against this was Bernini's Reliquary for the head of Saint Sebastian, which sat in the sacred Museum. It looked like a huge, gilded silver gravy bowl, or a large over-decorated heating pan one might find in a restaurant brunch table. The only difference being inside there was no brisket, just leftovers of the head of St. Stephen.

Too many tapestries hung everywhere. "The Mystic Wine from Flanders" depicted the angels and Jesus' Mom Mary and everybody looking as if they just stepped off the stage from a performance of Two Gentlemen of Verona. Everybody had a large hooked nose, including the Baby Jesus, who was helping to make the wine (Such a good baby. They don't come any better.) by squeezing a bunch of grapes into a chalice. Peter knew that never happened in the New Testament. He wondered why someone hung all these rugs on the wall instead of putting them on the floor where they belonged.

One oddly disturbing depiction was Antonio Canova's bust called "Portrait of Pius VII" which showed the pope with his mouth characteristically hanging open. It must have been unveiled after Pius VII died because no living pope would tolerate such a depiction. Another was the statue of loin-clothed Saint Peter with nipples that looked like golf balls. Another "curiosity" was Leonardo da Vinci's "St Jerome" in which a bony, near-skeletal St. Jerome teased a roaring lion with his own lack of meat. Federico Fiori Barocci takes the Stephen King approach with a piece showing God drilling the hands, feet, and side of St. Francis in "St Francis Receiving the Stigmata". That was so that Frank could bleed in the same spots as his Savior.

Was Peter filled with awe by the Raphael Sanzio depiction of "The Transfiguration?" No. Here one witnessed Jesus' physical body rising up into space. The limited amount of religious artwork Peter experienced previously, he had always assumed was there to scare him. As that did then. Christ looked too chubby to be floating on that cloud. And who where those other bearded guys ascending into heaven with him? They were not mentioned in the New Testament.

Evidently in Caravaggio's "Rest on the Flight to Egypt," St. Joseph and the ready-to-burst-with-Jesus Mary stopped at a Hooters restaurant. As the wispy-outfitted woman holding the menu for Joseph would seem to indicate. Supplementing this theory is the fact that Mary has her eyes closed and is grimacing in pain, embarrassment or both.

One piece in particular used to really bug Peter. It was a native icon of the Black Madonna: a gift from a bishop of Constantinople. Probably looking for a place to chuck the junk. This was no way to end the ill feelings between the Rome and the Eastern Rite. Peter wondered aloud how much it was worth.

"That? Oh that is priceless, Pete."

"But Luigi-" The pope and his secretary were now on a first/given name basis. "Luigi" had insisted.

"-it's ... ugly." Peter did not understand that the style of the icon is not so much representational as it is an outpouring of devotion from the peasant artist, in this case, the 15th century Hungarian Pest Schprivt. On the other hand, Luigi did understand all there was to understand about art.

"Now that you mention it, it is ugly. Look how big the Mother's hands are. Her head is slightly misshapen too. Well, there is nothing we can do about it. Can't throw it away, can we? It was a gift from Archbishop Hopabopalous-er... something like that. One of those Greek Orthodox patriarchs. They're already mad with the Catholic Church for making the bishop of Rome the head of the church. They won't pray for the pope. That's why they split with us you know. That and a problem with unleavened bread. No reason to add salt to that five hundred year old wound now is there?"

"Luigi? Could we sell it? Use the money to buy food for the poor." What a lug Peter could be.

"Do whatever you like. You can be in charge of the art. How does that sound?" Oh.

That is when it began: the medicinal bleeding to death of the One, True, Holy and Apostolic Church. Ever since Vatican II, there had been talk of returning the church to its poverty-stricken roots. Talk that was quickly bashed to smithereens with the argument that all of the riches collected were for the glory of God. In a flash that argument became moot.

Cardinal d'Indy did not take the news of Peter's little sale very well. Losing semi-precious art was a personal affront to his aristocratic ilk. Centuries of inbreeding had made him ill-tempered and added length to his already great nose. The better to look down upon others with.

The moment he noticed the paperwork for the $750,000.00 sale, he got himself to foaming at the mouth and, using his proboscis as a divining rod, attempted to attack the little squirrel in its nest. Peter was not in his office because he did not have one. The nose did not know this. This aerated d'Indy's lather.

He marched over to Peter's cell. Nobody home. He tramped down into the archives. All he came up with there was an annoyed look and a shrug from Acalanes. Acalanes did not scare so easy.

d'Indy found Peter in the garden of the Pinea Coteca dipping a bamboo fishing pole line into the koi pond. d'Indy lunged upon Peter like a Saint Bernard in the last stages of dementia.

"What are you doing?!" The saliva swaying from his fierce scowl underlined the immediacy of his demand.

In explanation, Peter lifted the line from the water. On the end of the string, instead of a hook, was a paper clip, no not opened, as one would expect a substitution for a hook to be, but still in its manufactured shape. A rubber band[178] hung from the clip in a none-too convincing imitation of a lure.

181

Peter faced the Canine Cardinal. The cardinal's nostrils were like the Grand Canyon during an earthquake of major proportions and intensity. The hands at the sides opened and closed like land-locked fish gills. The eyes turned into little, black raisins, the mouth was a dead ringer for a confused sphincter.

"Praying and fishing, Your Eminence."

"What do you think you're doing? You will not sell so much as a mouse turd without my approval. Do you understand?

"I was following the wishes of the Holy Father, Eminence."

"You do not take orders from that stinking sack of wrinkles. You take orders from me." Peter dropped his line and contemplated the koi who seemed annoyed by this intrusion. d'Indy fired up a pot of disbelief. The audacity! Peter seemed to be considering his last statement. "Do you understand?"

"I understand I live to serve the Lord and His Church."

"You-" Though he had no intention of one-upmanship, Peter had him there. "You may have Martin's ear. But I will have your ass." d'Indy huffed again with just the slightest twinge of frustration, then turned and left. Peter returned his gaze to the koi. He paid no attention to how pretty they were. At that point he could practically belch beauty.

Before d'Indy could do anything, the sale of the icon made the news. C.N.N. ran a kicker.[179] The reporter interviewed d'Indy. That sealed d'Indy's fate. Suddenly thrust into the spotlight, d'Indy pontificated that this was an historic occasion for the Church. He could not very well say what he was thinking: "I nearly killed the little prick who was responsible."

d'Indy also realized that many of his fellow cardinals, who would be voting for a successor to Martin soon, pray very soon, would see him. This was a great way for international exposure. May as well let the sheep see their next shepherd. d'Indy also let on that there was a consideration being considered to sell more art to help the poor. God, he loved being a know-it-all for the cameras!

The ramifications of the sale were missed. Everybody on the planet already knew the Catholic Church was loaded. So they're selling a few Michelangelos or something. So what? It wasn't like they're scraping the frescoes off the ceiling of the Sistine Chapel, was it?

Peter stood with the art appraiser, both their necks craned back as they assessed the situation.

"What do you think? Could they be safely removed?"

Theo Toupe, the appraiser, was sweating profusely. He could not believe the transaction being discussed. He had joked with one of his buyers about this just the other day. "You'll be the first person I call. Ha. Ha. Ha." His client had Ha Ha ha-ed him right back with equal gusto.

"I don't know, eh...Peter. It seems, for the right price, anything is possible. It might be possible. No one has ever considered it before. Ha! Not that we know of! Ha!"

Toupe was not surprised to see the American priest did not share his humor. The responding smile looked-well- not exactly forced. Looked more as if the guy just did not get the joke. But, what do you expect from the religious? They walk around mumbling about God and Jesus all day. Not much funny about that. Ha. Being in sales Toupe noticed everything about a client.

"You might be better off to just sell the whole chapel. As is. How does that sound?" Toupe wanted to reassure himself that he was not the butt of some joke. Handling the sale of the icon and then the other museum quality jimjacks was one thing. That was a drop in the bucket-or drops in the bucket.

Peter looked at Toupe for a moment. Toupe took Peter's lack of facial expression for inscrutability. Peter lacked a look on his face, though, because there was nothing for his face to express. He was simply following S.O.P. waiting for his next thought to materialize.

"Maybe that will come later."

"Good. Heh, heh. I hope you will keep me in mind. Heh, heh." Toupe knew a humorless guy when he saw one. So why would Peter be pulling his leg?

"The Holy Father is very pleased with the way you are handling the disbursement."

"Oh he is? How is the Holy Father? I guess he hasn't been getting out much lately. Rome misses him not showing up on the balcony. There are even rumors heh heh. Rumors, you know, they get started. They-how do you stop them? I don't know." Toupe shook and sweated, as was his way.

"The Holy Father does not feel very well, Theo. But he sends you his blessings and thanks."

"Oh. Oh. Oh, good. I mean, not that he feels badly but-tell him you're welcome?" Toupe twisted his torso to the right and then turned it back, as if he had to make this strange unrelated movement in order to ask his next question."

"Speaking of the Holy Father-may God bless him continually here and in heaven, if that be the case- ehh... Cardinal d'Indy's office has contacted me. They say-here I have the letter-" Toupe pulled it from his satchel and handed it to Peter who began to read it. "They want me to send the money to the Cardinal Secretary of State's office, Peter. No bones about that. Instead of directly to the charities you had listed? Heh."

Peter read the letter then handed it back to Toupe.

"I believe the Cardinal Secretary of State has changed his mind." Peter had watched the TV interview, Toupe had not. Toupe looked more than a bit skeptical. "Are you Catholic?"

"Yes, Your-Father. Yes. Very devout too."

"So you understand that the pope is on top. He is the highest one up?"

"Oh yes. Until death. He is most certainly in charge. I think that might be why there are rumors? And now this letter from Cardinal d'Indy. Well. It makes it confusing. I must admit, Father Peter, this business is all very wonderful. At this rate the money being spent on the poor will reach into the millions. Those are American dollars. I insist on dealing with American Dollars. Very little for myself too. Only enough to feed me and my wife and children. Maybe a bit extra to help pay the mortgage. It is the Church we are talking about after all. But it is all making me just a bit nervous. This letter."

"Theo. Would you like to talk to the Holy Father? Would that ease your anxiety?"

"Tremendously! It is not that I do not trust the Cardinal or yourself. But you can see my quandary. If you could arrange a meeting. That. That would be wonderful."

"Good. Let's go talk to him now." Peter touched Toupe's elbow and motioned to move.

"Oh. But I'm not dressed properly. I'm-. Okay. If you say let's talk to the pope now, then let's go talk to the pope now then."

Peter paused. He searched Toupe's eyes until the groveling suck-up began to twitch and turn away from him. Peter held up a hand, and then pointed a finger toward "The Creation" above them. That regained Toupe's fidgeting attention.

"Can you keep this under your hat for right now?"

Toupe was struck with a rare moment of existence outside of his otherwise constant sales mindset. A miracle easily the most difficult for people to accept.

"Excellency- eh Holiness- eh Father! You can't be serious." Then whispered with complete and total incredulity. "You would sell the ceiling of the Sistine Chapel?"

Peter gave Toupe a Mona Lisa smile. Toupe's mouth dropped in astonishment. He closed it with a zipper motion.

"Thank you Theo."

They went to see the pope.

They lucked out. It was a "good day" for Martin. This means he could talk (instead of mumble and snort.), eat (that is chew and swallow, as opposed to bite and spit), pray (the alternate being a shouting match with his visions of what he called "The Virgin C*nt") and hint politely that he wanted to be helped out of his wheelchair (much better than just shitting in his Depends. Imagine having the job of changing the pope's diaper!)

Not that any frame of mind would have mattered to Theo Toupe. He was face to face with God's Representative on Earth. A burp and a nod of ascension would have sufficed, he was that scared and filled with awe.

Sweating and shaking, he would never have stopped slurping at Martin's ring if it were not for Peter's eventual hand on his shoulder.

Martin was overjoyed. He missed his audiences.[180] There were problems with a controlled environment too.

Only the most understanding dignitaries were allowed a one-on-one. As Martin's bellicose outbursts became more frequent, and inexplicable, there was growing concern that even "sympathetic" dignitaries might be tempted to communion with the devil (i.e. The Media).

Peter bade Toupe to join him on the love seat facing Martin in his wheelchair. Though obviously infirm, cowering weakly under his blanket on that warm afternoon, Martin gave Toupe an engaging smile. Any friend of Peter's was a friend of Martin's.

"What is it you seek, my son?" This was a new one: Martin plays the yogi on the mountaintop. He leaned forward from the back of the wheel chair with apparent complete concentration and interest.

Toupe matched the Holy Father by moving forward on the edge of the cushion. His posture looked uncomfortable as well as silly. But then the pope inspires many things.

"Yur hanknig." What with Toupe's skin erupting in sweat, there was precious little moisture left for his mouth. Peter came to his rescue.

"Mr. Toupe is worried about the profits from the paintings, Holy Father. He got a letter from the Cardinal, Secretary of State telling him to send the money from art sales to the Cardinal, Secretary of State, instead of directly to the organizations we chose. So Mr. Toupe wants to know where to send the money."

Martin nodded his head and smiled sagaciously all the way through this. He did not understand a single word. His visage developed into one of world-weary wisdom. He looked to the ceiling. Toupe was startled by the thought that maybe The Pilot of The Holy See was preparing to tell him to not only go ahead and sell the Sistine Chapel artwork, but also the cherubs cavorting on the ceiling of this, the pope's private apartment, as well.

"What can we do? What can we do?" He looked at Toupe with the directness that accused Toupe of having the answer. "What can we do."

Whew. It was rhetorical. Toupe relaxed. That's right. This guy's the pope. The other guy's like his advisor. His right hand man. They have all the answers. What am I going to do? Accuse these guys of not being on the level? He's the pope for Christ's sake! Peter just laid out the whole story. Now I'm just causing trouble for the old fart. Look at that. He can barely scratch his own backside. The poor old geezer will have to jump on that hard ass d'Indy and it'll be my entire fault. I'm no sucker. I know Peter's on the level. Maybe he's a little goofy for thinking about going to ReMax with the Sistine. But hey! Great ideas are always crazy sounding at first. Jesus, he's farting like a machine gun. I gotta get the hell out of here. Say anything old man! I'll agree with it.

"May we continue with the disbursements as we have Holy Father? Or would you prefer for Mr. Toupe to send the money to Cardinal, Secretary of State d'Indy?"

"d'Indy?" Martin affected a scowl, then, for no particular reason, switched to sly grin. "Shall d'Indy make the reason?" Toupe took it personally.

"No no no, your Eminen- errExcelency! Certainly not." Toupe groveled. "What ever Father Peter here decides. I'll go along with." Toupe clenched his fists and teeth simultaneously with such fervor something should have snapped.

Martin nodded his head. What was actually a temporary weakening of the Pope's neck muscles Toupe took for a sign of dismissal.

"Thank you so much Excellent. I have taken up far too much of your time. I will let you get back to the business of being-..." Toupe paused and stared as Martin's right index finger dove two knuckles deep into his nose. "-err whatever. Heh."

"The Bucket Is Kicked."

The Grim Reaper did not whack the doddering pope down with one fell swoop of his scythe. Rather, he pinched and poked and provoked a slow decay. Decay that forced Martin's courtiers to yawn and check their watches through a six-month long deathwatch.

Except Peter, of course. At Martin's whispered request Peter remained in the pope's bedroom with the pope and his doctor. A regular rotation of Vatican muckety-mucks stuck their noses inside the papal chambers and sniffed around, mumbling amongst themselves.

d'Indy checked in twice a day. He was convinced that he could tell simply by looking at Martin how close the Holy Father was to the Pearly Gates tollbooth. Something about the amount of rattle in the breath and the sharpness of the inner struggle that misshaped Martin's face. d'Indy would listen and look for a minute, then exhale expansively. He would bend and kiss Martin's ring then leave.

Peter spent most of his time praying on his knees on the tile floor over in a far corner. He would catch a little snooze in a nearby high back wooden chair. Rarely, he would slip out of the room for a bite at the buffet set up in the next room. The pope's chef down in the kitchen kept a steady procession of goodies coming up. Never hurt to make a good impression. The chef assumed (correctly) that Martin's successor would be eating his efforts.

The papal suite was surprisingly lacking in obvious luxury. There was a small library, a dining room and a study attached to the bedroom. Pope Paul VI deglorified the digs. When Martin died the rooms had a sort of modern-Italian-from-forty-years-ago- look to them. There was teak furniture and the same green stuff used for pool tables covered the walls. The staff roomed just down the hall.[181]

Martin rallied just before his last breaths. He opened his eyes wide then managed to raise his left hand a bit. He motioned to Peter.

"Come here, sonny. Your name. What is it?"

"It's Peter, Luigi."

"That's right. Wheater. What an odd name." Martin had rallied but not quite all the way. "You are a priest, Wheater, correct? I have to make my last confession."

"Tell me your sins, Luigi." Every Catholic lived for the chance to make a deathbed confession of their sins. Entrance into heaven could be delayed by even a few minor infractions. A deathbed confession was a chance to wipe the slate clean at the last moment on Earth. What sin could a person commit prior to the last breath? Covet his neighbor's wife or goods? Not likely. Especially in Martin's case. Peter did not assume the pope to be spotless in thought, word or deed.

The doctor left the room. Not so much for the pope's privacy but to notify the big shots. It was, after all, dinnertime. They were not about to settle for that cold, air-dried risotto, the rubbery prosciutto, or the cheese and bread festering in the antechamber. Leave it for the flies and Peter.

"The angel of death is near. I'm frightened. I am pope. I should not be afraid to die."

"Confess your sins. Find comfort in the Lord."

"I have not been a good pope. I have not been a good man. I have harbored ill will to more people than I have loved. I have not carried Peter's Keys to the Church well. Not well at all." Martin sighed. There was a tear in his voice. There were tears at the corners of his eyes.

"I have neglected the poor. I have acted more like an American conservative than a believer in the most charitable being who ever walked on this Earth. I have not been compassionate to the disenfranchised. I have had no tolerance for people who do not believe in me or my church." Martin grasped Peter's hand weakly, meekly. "It is not the Angel of Death who comes for me. It is Satan."

"Ask Christ for forgiveness. He will forgive you."

"Sweet Jesus forgive my sins."

"Are you truly sorry, Luigi?"

"I-am." In the space of that hyphen Luigi lied. Then, just as quickly, there was not much time to waste as death darkened the room about him, he discovered the truth of his deep-seated lack of faith. "I-am-not-sorry. I am damned. Not sorry." Wow. So he was not forgiven. But at least Luigi would die honest. God cares less for the truth than for the bended knee and bowed head. No room for pride in Paradise.

"My life... a sham. Not a fight for Christ. A struggle for power. Burn in Hell, burn in Hell." Martin mumbled. "...with the rest of the popes."

"Luigi. What about your charity? You sold some of the artwork? Christ sees that."

"Are you a saint or a simpleton? Did that to put a bee in d'Indy's bonnet." Martin stared past Peter's face at the ceiling. His breathing slowed so much Peter thought he was dead already. He respectfully reached to close Martin's eyelids.

"Hold your horses. I'm not dead yet."

d'Indy infiltrated the bed room. The doctor and several high towers were close behind him. The optimism brightening d'Indy's face clouded over as Martin noted his entrance with the slightest of nods.

"Patience, Eminence. I'm almost gone."

"Holy Father." d'Indy knelt and kissed Martin's ring. Oddly, he stayed on his knees.

"Sorry to put you through this, Michelle. Hopefully I won't spit blood out my nose, or eat my own tongue. But I'm glad this little crowd is assembled to witness this." Martin turned to Peter.

"By the authority of almighty God, of the holy apostles Peter and Paul, and of our own, we make...what is your name again?"

"Peter, Your Holiness."

"Peter Yerholiness?"

"His name is Peter Bondeo." The future of the church would have gone in a completely different direction if d'Indy had not been such a know it all.

"Oh. Then by the blah, blah, etcetera, etcetera-Peter Bondeo cardinal, in the name of the Father and of the son and of the Holy Spirit. Kiss my hand Peterey. That's it. Now kiss my foot. That's so you know where you stand in relation to the Holy Father. Now let me kiss both your cheeks. There. Ta-da. Another prince of the Church." Amusement scratched the corners of Martin's slight smile as he looked at d'Indy. "He's your equal now."

Martin closed his eyes. "I don't care much for this. I wish I had died in my sleep." With that, Pope Martin VI took his last breath and held it. Forever.

The doctor moved closer. He held Martin's limp wrist and felt for a pulse. "The Holy Father is still with us." He muttered softly.

d'Indy rose to his feet and walked into the pope's study. He returned after a few minutes with a small fancy schmancy purse. He began to open it. The doctor looked at him with just a tick's worth of annoyance, then repeated. "The Holy Father is still with us."

"Oh." d'Indy was legitimately surprised and actually slightly embarrassed. "I thought you were speaking metaphorically."

"The Holy Father's most recent heart beat was fifteen seconds ago. Do you object to waiting another minute?"

"No. Of course not."

So they all waited. Martin pumped out three more heartbeats in the next two minutes. The doctor waited another three minutes before calling the game. "The Holy Father has left us."

Nailing down the fact that the Pope was really and truly dead was done with a hammer. A silver hammer. The camerlengo or acting pope, in this case everybody's pal d'Indy, tapped the hopefully dead Pope on the head and called out his childhood name. He did this three times.

"Luigi?" Tap. "Luigi?" Tap. "Luigi?" Tap.[182]

That was only the beginning of the silliness. Next d'Indy took off the pale Pontiff's special ring, which bore Martin's unique coat of arms. Big enough to be a decoder ring, d'Indy took a heavy-duty pair of silver (of course) scissors and defaced the insignia. Then, if that was not bad enough, d'Indy, as did all his predecessors, smashed the ring into smithereens. All is not lost. The chunks of ring were later tossed into the pontiff's coffin. Instead of police tape, they seal off the Holy Father's apartments with fancy ribbons.

Peter wore his priest robes to Martin's funeral. It was not until Antonio Cardinal Zerbi[183] of Paraguay noticed Peter was not hanging with the other cardinals that he looked into it. Zerbi was the Mrs. Cravitz of the College of Cardinals: always butting his button nose into everything.

Peter explained he received no salary and so he had no money to buy his own cardinal duds. Zerbi nosed around until he found His Eminence Joseph Cardinal Kolinsky of Romania, who matched Peter pound for pound and inch for inch. Zerbi bummed an extra outfit off the obliging Kolinsky.

Other than that, nothing much of interest happened at Pope Martin VI's funeral. It may be interesting to note that, among his staff, no tears were shed.

# 12
## THE SECOND PETER'S THE LAST

It was believed that Jesus Christ selected the first pope, the first Peter, when he spouted the words "Thou art Peter and upon this rock I shall build my Church. Whatsoever you shall bind or loose on Earth shall be bound or loosed in Heaven."[184] The Church, always one to take things literally as well as figuratively, decided that meant that Jesus put Peter in charge. A few decades later, they built Saint Peter's on top of his maybe grave.[185] The binding and loosing part is the rationale for the dogma of the pope's infallibility. To paraphrase Jesus to Peter: "Whatever you say, goes." That said, it took 1,870 years for a pope to put that bit of puffery in writing.[186]

In spite of the power that came with the gig, there were few prerequisites for becoming pope. Potential popes did not have to be baptized Catholics to be elected. However, they would have to be baptized and made a bishop before being installed. Popes also had to have a penis. They used to check.[187]

The pope's titles included that of Bishop of Rome.[188] However, very few popes did very little for The Church in that city. Someone else would handle the local duties. The title "pope" which is Greek for "father" did not surface until the year 304. The first to use it was Pope Saint Marcellinus. The handle "pontiff" came along in the fifth century. Prior to that, a pontiff in old Roman times was a bricklayer.

Twentieth-century popes hated communists because they were atheists. That makes the lack of democracy in The Church's structure difficult to understand. Especially when considering the papal elections. One-hundred-twenty non-elected cardinals selected by a pope would pick a new pope for as many as 600-million Catholics. There was at least one pope who noted the unfairness. Pope Saint Leo said, "The one who presides over all should be chosen by all." Not that Leo did anything about it.

Tough beans. Only a fool would expect a general population to select some one who would be considered infallible.[189] How could you run an international election for a position in which the candidates are prohibited from campaigning? It was just as well that a bunch of doddering celibates made the decision. They did so under the inspiration of the Holy Spirit. So maybe the Holy Spirit should receive the credit for the bizarre selection of Peter.

Discomfort of the electors was also a part of the tradition. Prior to changes made by John Paul II, the traditional accommodations were miserable. The cardinals holed up in the Sistine Chapel and surrounding museums. Windows were sealed and either painted over or covered. There was access to a small, enclosed courtyard, but otherwise not much was available in the way of fresh air.

First day handouts included: a roll of toilet paper; one bar of soap and two cheesy towels; a couple of cheap pens and a writing pad; a wooden chair; bedside plastic drinking glass and a two-bit bedside lamp. A slip of nothing for a mattress with creaking wire mesh underneath were included at no extra charge. Many prisoners slept better. The overall effect was a cross between stuff from the K Mart markdown bin and an antique shop in an Italian ghetto.

There was one toilet for every five or six cards. Imagine a half dozen of The Church's princes, standing next to each other at the urinals comparing N.F.L. opinions and Vienna Sausages. Imagine further, their purple robes bunched above their flies, rolling their eyes heavenward, praying the ailing prostate was not sending out another false alarm as his excellence from Denmark is exploding some satanic stink in a nearby stall. "Your Eminence Karl Cardinal Knudsen of Denmark," one may have commented, "Tis holier to bury the dead. Don't ya think? P.U.!"

Not that any of these select grand men would consider escaping the holy chore before them. Nevertheless, just in case, workers filled the outer doorways with bricks. A conveniently located nearby cafeteria prepared the food which then, following inspection, passed through a slit in the wall.

The reason for the lock-up came several centuries earlier. The cardinals had been bone-stroking their decision for over a year and a half. The Romans grew restless with the wankers taking so long, so they locked up the cardinals. That became par for the course. Other amenities were added. When a conclave took too

193

long, the food rations were cut back to hurry up the inspiration of the Holy Spirit. Evidently, the Holy Spirit was a chowhound.

The days of the lock-up ended after the election of Pope John Paul II. J.P. II provided the Santa Marta Hospice, which consisted of 107 two-story suites with bath and 20 single rooms with bath. The "conclave" following the death of J.P. II was not literally a conclave at all since the word means "under lock and key." Cardinals could walk the 350 yards to the Sistine Chapel or take the provided bus.

However, secrecy remained intact. No outside contact allowed. The Swiss Guard continued to use scanners and detectors. They checked for bugging and recording devices in the cardinals' rooms as well as on their persons. The reasons for the security concerns were based more in avoiding outside influence than in a distrust of the cardinals.[190] Cell phones or newspapers were verboten. Communicating in any way with the outside world could lead to excommunication.

Not that any of this made a peep of difference to Peter. The fact that he was a prince of the Church and would be in on the next election had not sunk in. After Martin's funeral, Peter returned to his dusting job and also went back to sleeping in his little cell, his little cubicle, the wider side of a closet, really, off of the Vatican Archives.

If it were not for His Eminence Antonio Cardinal Zerbi, from Florence, Italy and his pal, Joseph Cardinal Kolinsky, from Krakow, Poland, Peter would have remained at post, and certainly would not have been elected pope. Zerbi, tsking and clucking like the mother hen he was, scratched about until he found Peter.

Father Cletus, still important as d'Indy's assistant, eventually overcame his snuffling reticence and turned over the information about Peter's whereabouts.

"I did not know that my brother cardinals are also being accommodated in the cellar near the Archives."

Father Cletus's understanding of Zerbi's halting English was comprehensive enough. However, the little prick preferred to snort and sneer and shrug his superiority to his superior.

When Zerbi found Peter in his dusty, pathetic cubbyhole, the sight deeply moved him. It moved him spiritually in a way he had never previously been moved spiritually. Peter knelt on the cracked and peeling linoleum floor, behind the door, self-banished in his oblivious attempts to communicate with his God.

There beneath the marble floor upon which waddled the neck-craning tourists, was the only person in the Vatican not distracted by the 290 windows, 800 chandeliers, 27 chapels, 48 altars, 390 statues, 748 columns, or domes, the monuments, the relics and the petrified popes laid out for all eternity in their ritzy robes. People did not visit the 25,616 square meters of the Vatican to pray. They came to experience the artwork and the excess. This was supposed to be the spiritual key to heaven. The basilica was even shaped like a damn keyhole! Yet no one, save Peter, at that moment, was trying to communicate with his or her purported creator. Zerbi found Peter and his God at that moment.

Zerbi detractors insist he campaigned for Peter's election. Not true. Zerbi only shared the religious moment he experienced when he found Peter scrubbing away like a scullery maid at his own soul.

Before Peter's elevation, Zerbi possessed, more than anything, negative political influence among his 120 fellow princes. Ugly, in a cute sort of old man way, the roly-poly cuddly little man in red appeared more gullible than impressive. Maybe that is why Zerbi had the impact he did. Helps to be unassuming.

d'Indy, naturally, attracted a great deal of attention from his fellow cardinals. After all, they all dealt with d'Indy to get to both Martin and his predecessor. With a practiced, calm kindness, d'Indy greeted, chatted and schmoozed. There were ways he could have been more obvious and gotten around the "no politicking" rule. But, there was no reason to do so. No other cardinal knew the 119 gathered there as well as he. d'Indy knew which buttons of reassurance to push with each man. d'Indy's confidence was reasonable.

Zerbi became a topic of whispered conversations. Several cardinals had noticed something odd. The usually squawking little cherub was quiet. Distracted. Instead of nosing around in everybody else's business, he kept to himself off to the side praying his rosary. His lips mumbled the silent prayers. At previous get-togethers, the cardinals would avoid Zerbi because of the way he would glom onto a person; wasting time with the most trivial matters. Simple eye contact was avoided. Now they corralled themselves around Zerbi's buddy Kolinsky, who was as naturally, annoyingly restrained as Zerbi was usually noisy.

"Is he ill?" Inquired Kalorey Cardinal MacDonald, of Scotland.

Kolinsky batted his eyes once solemnly and twisted his head ever so slightly in the negative.

"Has someone offended the little- eh, him?" Ricardo Cardinal Luci, of Venice solicited diplomatically.

"Does his soul carry the burden of a great sin?" Hans Cardinal Spatula, of Bulgaria ventured suggestively.

Kolinsky's barely audible groan rumbled softly with nullification.

"He has taken a lover then?" Sanger Cardinal Deeva, of Croatia concluded this was some type of game.

Kolinsky lisped a tsk.

Attracted by all the sotto voce sibilance, another half dozen or so cardinals gravitated to the core-Kolinsky. The outer orbits received brief mumbled reports of the subject at hand. Interest spread easily as most had wondered, "What's up with little Zerbi."

"He is saddened by the death of the Holy Father?" Maki Cardinal Toohi's, of Cambodia's logic and compassion were impeccable though inappropriate.

Kolinsky initially raised his eyebrows as if to agree, then frowned disapprovingly.

"He probably is worried he will be selected Pope." Bedgiy Cardinal Cosmos, of Rumania's infantile attempt at humor rattled his fellow cardinals.

Kolinsky's squint and smirk aborted any possibility that Cosmos, clumsiness notwithstanding, had nailed the problem.

"Probably the food disagreeing with him." Kremmit Cardinal Pechez, of France, joshed half to himself as he rubbed his global belly.

Kolinsky joined the others' looks of surprise over this unjustified criticism.

"It could not be the accommodations? Compared to his home, Zerbi is living in the lap of luxury." Robert Cardinal Stahl, of Austria maintained.

Kolinsky paused. He had exhausted the considerable spectrum of his facial pallet. So he simply responded. "Nope."

"What is it then?" Meltzno Cardinal Widhotski, of Denver, Colorado, insisted. "What is he moping about?"

Kolinsky thought for a moment. He peered back at his peers peering at him. "Ask him."

Zerbi sat in a sunny corner of the grand courtyard. He fingered his beat up old rosary[191] as the buzzing swarm neared.

Zerbi's humble string-o'-supplications was old and made of wood and thin, cheap, stainless steel necklace chain. The black paint had been prayed off decades ago. The crucifix dangling on the end of the looped beads was held on with a piece of copper wire Zerbi had taken from a busted tube-type radio. It was the last thing he would touch every night after turning out his bedside light. Every morning when he awoke, he would reach first for his Rosary and then his eyeglasses. Eventually Zerbi would be buried with it.

As the gaggle closed in on Zerbi, to a man, it was surprised to discover, upon closer inspection, not the expected intimidation, not discomfort or pain. No, not even what all had misinterpreted from a distance as sadness or of something being wrong. Closer inspection of Zerbi's mug revealed that he seemed to be at peace.

"I have been awakened." Zerbi volunteered before anyone had a chance to ask. Peace made Zerbi a bit more clear-headed than he had been previously. Exuberant, spontaneous outbursts had taken a back seat to thoughtfulness.

The flock of cardinals stood about him, bobbing, tipping and twisting their heads inquisitively. Some puffed out their cheeks a bit with labored, skeptical breath. They were attentive. Their natural instinct was to peck at something they did not quite understand. Instead, oddly, they approached with a certain amount of reverence. One never knew when that weird heavenly shit would happen. Perhaps Zerbi was the victim of one of those Virgin apparitions.

"I have witnessed a holy man in communication with God." Zerbi stared dreamily into the group. Although to be specific, his gaze rested more or less in the direction of the grand belly of Brad Cardinal Box. "That is all. Do not concern yourselves with my well-being because I am well."

"Who is this holy man, Zerbi?" Queried the soft-spoken, watery-eyed Colin Cardinal Durr, of England.

"The last of us cardinals chosen by our late Holy Father."

The group responded with impressed, if not somewhat guarded "oohs" and "ahhs."

A lone cuckoo perched on the eves above them gave a forlorn, silly little lament then took to her wings. She had just laid an egg in a finch's nest and wanted to get while the getting was good. She hoped the finch would come back soon and would take good care of her offspring.

The group watched the bird fly off above them then wandered off into a duo, a trio and a quartet. Zerbi had not pitched Peter to the college. Zerbi had not even mentioned Peter by name. But an impression was made nonetheless. For lack of any other truly juicy gossip, that small group managed to spread Zerbi's little story to everyone. Everyone except d'Indy.

There is no such thing as electing a new pope. When the old pope dies, the cardinals get together to select a new bishop of Rome. That bishop of Rome is always the Pope.[192] It may seem goofy, but at least it is consistent.

d'Indy, as Secretary of State and camerlengo, was in charge of all the rites and formalities involved in selecting Martin's successor.[193] This was his golden opportunity to strut his confident junk, (And perhaps get them used to the idea of taking orders from him.) as he stood before his fellows explaining the procedure. Yes, d'Indy was the hard-assed administrator of The One, True, Holy & Apostolic Church. However, d'Indy was also a sincerely devout believer in that same Church.

There in the Sistine Chapel, above those gathered, floated Michelangelo's frescoed efforts: a posse of (mostly male) fat fannies. Behind d'Indy at the Sistine Chapel's main altar in ironic testimony to the cavorting on the ceiling was Michelangelo's masterful depiction of the end of all fun: "The Last Judgment."

Other than the pornography on the ceiling, the Sistine Chapel remains an otherwise unremarkable church. It is a long rectangular box with an altar at one end and an empty space girded by an iron fence (!) at the other. The side walls have uncomfortable wooden seats planted into them. They run along the space between the sanctuary and the cage in the rear. That is where the cardinals used to plant themselves during the conclave.[194]

Tradition, tradition, tradition, more sacred than the Savior's testicles. Every man there, save Peter and three other neophytes, knew the drill. That is why tradition dictated that d'Indy explain it to them. He did so in Latin since that was the only language they had in common. (Save Peter.)

"My brothers in Christ, we trust the presence of the Holy Spirit in our hearts to guide us in our decision." d'Indy's benevolent pause was sincere. "But we know that there may be those of us who hear the presence differently." d'Indy's metaphor did not mix in Latin as it does in English. Such are the marked differences between the two languages.

"We meet to vote in the morning after prayers and breakfast. Failing consensus, we meet again before dinner and cast ballots again. This will continue until we reach a majority of two-thirds plus one. We cast our first ballots now. Let us pray for guidance from the Holy Spirit.

"As we put pen to paper let us guard against our own curiosity and the curiosity of our brethren. Shield your writing with the other hand. When you have finished, quickly fold your ballot in fours. Let us vote, now." Yep. That is right. It was in the rules. Just as in grade school, the top drawer leadership would make a little blind with one hand as it wrote with the other.

One of the assistants, evidently a pessimist, passed out a half dozen ballots to each cardinal. In fancy cursive, each ballot has the phrase printed in Latin: "Eligo in Summum Pontificem." Which translates to "I elect as pope…" The cardinals then filled in their choice. Disguising one's handwriting so it was not recognized was encouraged.

d'Indy sat at his little table just south of the altar area and west of the table where the four counting cardinals sat. In front of them stood a small silk covered table with a large gold chalice-shaped urn on it. On top of the urn was a round gold plate or patten.

d'Indy watched the 119 men reach for their pens. He sat, paused, before slowly writing his choice. Then he looked up and saw that no one else, except Peter, had written anything. After Peter had written, he returned his pen to the groove at the top of the desk. His fingers were clammy so when he did not quite set the pen straight in the groove, it rolled down the incline toward him. Peter reflexively flicked the pen back up the incline where it paused a nanosecond before dropping into the groove. He repeated the action again and again.

d'Indy, like his Church, figured he had all the time in the world. He waited five minutes. He waited fifteen minutes. Peter continued to putt his pen. By the end of a half hour, the conclave was staring mindlessly at Peter's little game. Prrrrrrrrrrr-rtt? It went on for another half hour. It was against the rules for d'Indy to encourage anything, especially speed. Another fifteen minutes passed. d'Indy cleared his throat ever so softly. The cardinals began to write simultaneously.

The sight of the odd-looking chorus of moving pens tickled the back of d'Indy's neck eerily. It was downright creepy when everyone also finished and put down his pen simultaneously.

All having scrawled the same letters…the same name! Just like that. It came to them! Out of the blue! Out of HEAVEN! Could this be the Holy Spirit at work? Of course it was. It had to be. This apparent acclamation was more than just coincidence.

The ancient procedure continued with each cardinal, by rank, those closest to the pope or having higher positions first, standing, one at a time, walking to the urn, then holding his or her[195] vote aloft proclaimed aloud that this was his choice. A selected member of the voting staff then placed the folded paper on the paten and allowed it to slide into the urn. Peter was the last man made a cardinal, and so, in spite of his friendship or proximity to Martin at his deathbed, was the last to vote.

The next gesture was easily the most superfluous action taken to maintain the obsession with secrecy. d'Indy lifted the urn and shook it. That is right. So when the ballots are counted they would not be able to know who Peter-the last vote-or d'Indy-the first ballot on the bottom-had voted for.

Next, the scrutineer, in this case Yaba'a Cardinal Dabudoo, of Trinidad, stood, set the paten aside, took out one folded ballot at a time, did not read it, but, held it aloft for all to see. He then dropped the slip into another urn. Dabudoo, and everyone else in the chapel, counted the slips. If the final count did not correspond with the number of men in the room, the vote was void. In this case, there was the right number of ballots. Phew!

Dabudoo then sat. He and two other scrutineers each had before them an eight-and-a-half by eleven pad of paper to tally the votes. Considering the results, they could have made do with a three-by-five card split into three columns.

Dabudoo opened the first ballot, copied the name to his pad, put one hash mark next to it, and then passed the ballot to the second scrutineer, Habas Cardinal Sabah, of Madagascar. Sabah copied the name to his pad, put one hash mark next to it, and then passed it to the third scrutineer, Esau Cardinal Ayman. Ayman, of Ontario, Canada, copied the name to his pad, put one hash mark next to it, and then announced the name to the group.

Ayman had been chosen specifically for the third scrutineer position because of his incredible talent for pronouncing languages. Ayman could only speak English, Latin, and of course, French. But he could flawlessly mimic dialects from Bombay to Bodg and Petropavlovsk to Guadalajara giving the impression with his pronunciations that he was fluent in the language. This name was no challenge at all since it came from less than two-hundred miles away (As the crow flies.) from his hometown of Point Pelee, Ontario.[196]

"Peter, Cardinal Bondeo."

Though it had no impact on his pencil putt (He still drained it.), the surprise of hearing his name caused Peter to flinch. He turned, wide-eyed towards d'Indy.

At the same time, d'Indy realized that he had not been selected, and that Peter had been. Because, as Peter's name was announced, d'Indy noticed that every single one of his fellows seated before him staring at their scratch paper, simultaneously pursed his lips. This oh so subtle gesture told d'Indy that all 116 had voted for Peter. Not about to wave their hands or point at themselves, this tiny en masse lip tick was a controlled way of every cardinal shouting, "Hey! That's my vote!" The cardinals all wrote Peter's name on their pads. It was okay to keep score.

Ayman took a threaded needle and drew it through the verb "I vote." This was part of his job.

Panic seized Peter's belly. His intestines churned and rumbled in shock. A hot sweat moistened his forehead, the nape of his neck, his chest and his testicles.

Dabudoo reached for the next ballot, opened it, said nothing, but smiled as he put another hash mark next to Peter's name. The fact that he had not written another name was not lost on the conclave. Many murmured momentarily, then caught themselves and cut it short. Some suddenly sought interest in Michelangelo's paint job on the ceiling. More than half had added a hash mark to Peter's name before Kingsville announced it. d'Indy was not the only one with a talent for reading body language, ya' know.

Peter sat back and stared straight ahead, thoughtlessly scared stiff and looking more like a corpse than an anointed one. He stopped pencil putting.

Ayman reported Peter's name another fifteen times before he announced the single vote for d'Indy. That was Peter's vote. Twenty-seven more Peter's were called before another anomaly: One vote for Zerbi. That was Kolinsky's.

It was at this exact moment that d'Indy began to suspect God's intervention. When he had scrawled his own vote for Peter, (You were not allowed to vote for yourself.) d'Indy had chosen what he figured was the longest shot. If for no other reason than to draw out the process to let the conclave see a couple vote counts and thus give it more time to consider the enormity of their

201

decision making responsibilities. Now he wondered why he had written Peter's name and not Zerbi? Actual potential be damned, Peter had a reputation. Anyone who knew Zerbi avoided him. That made Zerbi the least desirable candidate.[197]

d'Indy was unaware of his colleagues' newly found high regard of Zerbi.[198] The point was mute. The die-vote-cast.

Believe it or not, at this point the scrutineers began to slow down. Unlike, say elections in America, this selection process was something to be savored. There was no rushing to make some know-it-all call before the votes are counted. The last ballot was as important as the first. Especially since a microscopic error would invalidate the count.

Still, as the magic number approached, in this case eighty-one being two-thirds plus one of one hundred, twenty, breathing in the chapel had slowed. Extraneous movement, ear-scratching, cuticle-tearing and wart-picking and the like halted. Peter was doing a strange, almost imperceptible, rocking/nodding sort of thing. Paler than a holy ghost, he was.

Every cardinal who voted for Peter took for granted that his would be the only vote for Peter. Could Zerbi's story have made that great of an impact?[199]

There was a real hesitancy in voting for d'Indy on the first ballot. For one thing, no one wanted to give him that satisfaction. For another, d'Indy did not inspire anyone. Sure, he was capable. He already emitted an air of infallibility. But he had no sparkle or pizzazz and not an eyedropper full of charisma. Nobody liked him. Every cardinal knew d'Indy would be the next pope. No one wanted to make it too easy. On the other hand, maybe the Holy Spirit was suicidal.

The first overt reaction the college allowed itself came when Ayman announced Peter's name for the eighty-first time. Subdued, sincere applause erupted briefly.

Yes, the college had surprised itself. Every cardinal assumed his was the only vote for Peter. They all figured they would get down to the real vote later. No, the conclave did not think it had made a mistake. Each cardinal knew this casual vote, made to stop killing time, had in reality been inspired by the Holy Spirit. The Holy Spirit moved in mysterious ways. So they knew. So they taught. Electing a dark horse, non-contender such as Peter was proof indeed. God obviously had plans the conclave was unaware of. The conclave could not have been happier. d'Indy, the closest thing in the group to a cynic, looked at Peter and smiled.

As for Peter, luckily he had eaten only one small piece of buttered toast and washed it down with a small glass of grapefruit juice for breakfast. That four-ounce meal just over two hours old boiled and churned overtime in his stomach. A couple of rancid teaspoons made its way up to the back of his throat.

Though the vote was about as obvious as a vote can be, confetti did not blast out the butts of Michelangelo's depiction above their heads. The election was not over yet.

Next, three "revisers," selected earlier, rose from their chairs and walked to the counting table. They recounted the ballots, inspecting each slip for possible fraud, such as two pinholes indicating a double count, or hanging chad.[200] They matched the hand count of the slips to the hash marks of the scrutineers. Not a big job. Anyone who could count to 118 could have accomplished the job competently in ten minutes. Since there was no hurry, though, it took the three scrutineers just over an hour. When they were finished two of the cardinals nodded to the third, Hehas Cardinal Bendardondat of Ethiopia.

Bendardondat walked down the center aisle and collected all the notes any of the cardinals had taken. Including doodles. As with all his predecessors, the scorecards of the scrutineers were later shown to Peter. As with all his predecessors they were then stored in the Vatican Archives.

The closest thing possible to a unanimous vote was useless without the consent of the candidate. There had been those who poo pooed a pope position. d'Indy, in spite of misgivings he held about the outcome, could not help but be moved by the obvious. The successor had been chosen fair and square even if he had come out of nowhere.

As he stepped off the dais and walked towards Peter, d'Indy also considered Peter's history. He studied the man "who had taken God's Word to the frozen Russian tundra, to the baking sands of the lands of Lawrence, as well as found his own weakness amongst the tropical tubers."[201]

"Peter. I have a question to ask you. It is the most important question you will ever be asked. It is the most important question any one man has asked another." d'Indy's lilting Latin was flawless. To Peter it was mostly gibberish. One man's Sistine Chapel artwork is another man's porn. "Are you ready to answer the question?" This d'Indy asked in English.

Peter nodded a nervous, slight affirmative. Using both hands, d'Indy ceremoniously held the packet of ballots before

Peter. d'Indy returned to Latin to deliver the ancient phrase offered a couple hundred times to a couple hundred men about to become Christ's representative on Earth. "Do you accept your canonical election as Supreme Pontiff?"

Peter half collapsed, but managed to recover by turning the motion into a kneel at the last moment. It was a natural movement for him. Anybody with twice his strength and bearing would doubtless do the same when being overcome with God's power.

Peter looked at the expectant faces of the men in red standing around him. They gave him little "yeah, yeah, go ahead say yes" nods of approval. Peter's gaze settled firmly on d'Indy.

"Yes." With that response, Peter was pope.

There are those with an elevated self-image of themselves as skeptics, who maintain that Peter did not know what he was saying yes to. These historians lean too heavily on their life's blood of politics. Peter was not bright enough to act the way he did on his own, they say. Those same cynics who are incapable of believing the Holy Spirit could move 118 cardinals to vote the way they did also insist that the Holy Spirit could not move Peter to act the way he did.

"What name do you choose as pope?" For this d'Indy reverted to Latin.

"Peter." That response is a matter of record.[202] Very few are aware of the conclave superstition that the last pope will choose Peter for a name, thus, it is believed, bring about the end of the Church. d'Indy had forgotten the old nun's tale. Besides, he had other chores to attend to. Peter stayed on his knees. The surrounding cardinals cut d'Indy a wide berth, as he walked to the far end of the chapel to the famous stove. Bendardondat followed him.

Slowly they began the methodical process of making espresso for everyone. Just kidding. They were there to send smoke signals. Bendardondat had the matches and the chemicals in a jeweled box. A brief skirmish ensued when Bendardondat insisted the chemicals to induce black smoke were the ones that were needed. d'Indy, noting the increase in the depth of wrinkles on the guy's face, put this bizarre assertiveness off to advancing age.

"Look. Is that a mouse?" d'Indy's distraction worked. The alarmed Bendardondat looked away from the ceremony at hand. d'Indy grabbed the proper chemicals, sprinkled a healthy portion on the ballots in the stove and put a lit match to it. The muffled cheer of the huge crowd outside the chapel, waiting in Saint Peter's Square, indicated d'Indy had chosen correctly.

Peter stood and looked around silently at all the cardinals. They looked expectantly back at him.

"Please be seated." Peter requested before leaving the room.

Since the cardinals were already exhibiting pin drop silence, the telltale squeak of the rest room door opening was easily heard. That brought a chuckle from several cardinals. The tension of the election was further alleviated by Hier Cardinal Thayer from Baltimore's observation that "When thou must go, thou must go."

The new pope to be did not have to wiz, however. Another squeak from the bathroom door prompted another chuckle. It faded like the last gasp from a deflating balloon as the college noticed their new superior had entered the room with an armful of towels and a basin of water.

"Please remove your shoes." Pope Peter looked around for what? Objections? Resistance? His warm, slight smile was returned, for the most part, by looks that reflected the shock of recognition. The cardinals realized, as one, the perfect impact of such an act of humility. They had made the correct choice.

Peter went about his version of this humbling chore slowly. There was no hurry. The world could wait.

Unlike Jesus, who had bathed the twenty-four feet of his twelve apostles over two-thousand years ago, Pope Peter was thorough. A dirty or long toenail was grouted or paired with a pocket clipper. Cuticles were scratched back to the skin.

A moment of levity was provided by His Eminence, Jeraldo, Cardinal Garzon of Spain. Garzon demurred at first, insisting that he was not worthy. Pope Peter tilted his head, looked at Garzon and waited. Eventually the Spaniard relented. As Pope Peter began to rub the Cardinal's foot with the warm wet towel, the reason for reticence became immediately obvious. Garzon began to giggle.

"I am sorry, your Holiness. I am very ticklish." The College of Cardinals clucked with bemused understanding. Pope Peter was off to a good start.

Peter was doing more than playing footsie with the conclave. Yes, he was giving them an unforgettable lesson in humility. However, he was also avoiding something. It is always easier to scuttle about with some relatively meaningless task than to get down to the real job at hand.

d'Indy was not about to interrupt such a significant gesture. After his footbath, he stood with the other prelates and waited. When Peter finished, he walked back to his seat and sat, pulled out his Rosary and started to pray. Most of the conclave followed suit. Save d'Indy.

"Your Holiness."

Peter looked up.

"Your congregation awaits you. First, you need to dress for the occasion. Father Cletus will escort you to the papal valet."

Peter stood on not the sturdiest of knees and wobbled off with the valet. They walked past the smiling cardinals towards the back of the chapel, took a left, then another left, down a long hallway which double-backed along the chapel. Then Father Cletus erred by making a right at the next hallway, causing the two to be lost for almost an hour.[203]

## Diane Butts In, Again.

Diane was headlong into her second package of Oreo cookies. And none of this double stuff crap for her either. Diane preferred the classic. Occasionally she flirted with the chocolate dipped ones, though eating a whole package of those gave her heartburn.[204] She also bypassed routines which included twisting and licking or chipping the icing or nibbling the saliva-washed cookie. Diane's habit was the most popular approach to consuming Oreos. The one the R.J. Reynolds Company scrupulously avoided acknowledging. Diane stuffed the whole cookie into her mouth and chewed until the dryness became almost insufferable. Only then would she pick up her quart of chocolate milk, put the spout to her lips, and allow just a bit to trickle into her mouth. Just enough to turn the cookie's mass into a pasty, chocolate mush. She then continued chewing, when necessary, swallowed and rinsed with a formidable gulp of the chocolate milk.

Timing was everything. She calculated with every chomp and gulp the balance needed to finish the last cookie and follow it with the last slug of milk. That slight veneer of apprehension only slightly deterred her enjoyment. Every time she sipped the milk, she would harken back to those white-chocolate beauties in Spain. The flavor of those cookies had been so intense it made her mouth water so much that she had eaten the whole familia-size package without a drop of anything to wash it down with.

The television slightly distracted Diane. Looked like they had elected a new pope. She found this vaguely interesting. Diane was currently swimming in a vat of vague. Vague about what to do with the rest of her life. Vague about what to do with the world. She had made a lot of money on the books and subsequent years on the lecture circuit. What to do. What to do. Hard to believe, but lounging around all day eating Oreos was getting tiresome for the woman who was the last Miss America and a former U.S. Senator.

Looked like everybody was waiting for the new pope to appear on the balcony. Diane wondered if it would be an American this time. Naw. They never picked Americans. She decided to switch the channel, but first consulted the TV listings. Good thing for history that there was nothing on the other 128 channels.


Eventually Peter and Father Cletus found the entrance to the Sistine Chapel Sacristy. The priest's cheeks burned crimson as two acolytes standing in the sacristy anteroom chastised him. He scoffed a reply in Italian before he escorted Pope Peter into a very large dressing room. The room had a nickname. It was called "The Room of Tears."

Peter saw three robes: One small, one medium, and one large. Of course the valet, like everyone else, did not know beforehand what the girth of the new pope would be. Best to be prepared. There was also the little white yarmulke (One size fits all.), the knee-high silk stockings and the luxurious red, velvet slippers embroidered with red crosses. Only one man on the planet wore a get-up like that. Peter looked at the outfit and began to weep. He was not the first to do so in that room.

Peter fell to his knees and continued to weep. He wept for half an hour. He sniffled another forty-five minutes. The water works went on and off for another twenty minutes.

Father Coughlin, the papal valet, approached him. Coughlin was a shy, deferring man except around popes. He knew everything there was to know about what the pope should wear for any occasion. Anyone who has ever noticed the multiplicity of outfits seen on popes, knows that was a considerable bit of knowledge to have.

"Holiness. Please stop crying. Get dressed and greet the people." Coughlin did not know much about the use of gentle persuasion with an upset person. He was not using tough love either. He was simply short with people, pope or no pope. Also, he spoke in Italian, which with Peter was more than useless. It was a little silly. Coughlin exasperated a sigh and left Peter in the Room of Tears.

He returned a moment later with d'Indy. Peter looked up watery- and red-eyed at d'Indy. He sniffed a final snivel and closed his eyes. He remained on his knees.

There was a little shrine to the Blessed Virgin under a stained glass window at the far wall. In front of it was a kneeler, beautifully padded for the knees and elbows and stuffed with Iraqi down and covered with the finest scab red velvet. If you are going to Hail Mary, this was the way to do it. Not one to prostrate himself on the floor, even if it was Italian marble hand-carved three hundred years ago, d'Indy dragged the kneeler across the room so it was facing Peter. He knelt before-if not a bit above-his new boss.

"Congratulations." More than anything in the world, d'Indy loved a bit of ironic understatement.

Peter looked directly at d'Indy kneeling above him. "I am not worthy of this."

"No man is worthy of this."

"But. What if I make a mistake?"

"I think you already know the answer to that question."

"You should be pope. Not me."

"That is what I thought. Until what happened just now. My soul today drank from the fountain of youth. Thank you for the vote, by the way. It was your vote, wasn't it? I assume you did not vote for yourself."

"I don't deserve this. I can't. I'm not holy enough."

"The Holy Spirit spoke to us in the conclave. I do not know if any of us had a mind to vote for you before entering that chapel. I know I had no intention to vote for you. None of that matters anymore. The Holy Spirit guided us. He spoke through us. Do not deafen your ears to the voice of God with dampers of your own insecurities."

d'Indy, by nature verbose, had no idea he was inspiring an epiphany within Peter. Suddenly, the fear over Peter's task at hand vanished. If the Holy Spirit had guided his selection, perhaps He would also guide what he would do as pope.[205]

"I think the most we can hope for is that we do God's bidding." d'Indy rather liked this new role of Father Confessor to the pope. Like Machiavelli, only in a good way. Though d'Indy was oblivious to what he was encouraging.

"Will you help me Excellence?"

"Please." d'Indy decided to be friendly. "Call me Michelle. Yes. I pledge my support."

Peter's next expression, one of steeled resolve, initially took d'Indy by surprise.

"You'll support me even if I- What if I sold the church and gave the money to the poor?"

"?" Though a very bright man, at that moment d'Indy looked decidedly stupid.

"The Vatican blasphemes the charity and beautiful poverty of our Savior. The pope who built this building was a money grubbing nepotist.[206] If it weren't a sin to be violent, I would set off a bomb inside it and blow it to smithereens. This terrible place was constructed with money suckered from the poor."[207]

"Holy Father, please!" d'Indy found his wits. "These beautiful buildings praise God! The works of the great artists are here to praise God! The-the-the." d'Indy stuttered to a stop, overwhelmed with terror, mostly at the realization that his cushy gig was coming to an end.

"The…gold…the…marble…my favorite…chair…with the…"

"The simpler the plan the better. Sell the building and give the money to the poor."

"Holy Father, that would be a very complex transaction. It could take decades to complete."

"We will not hold out for the highest bidder either. We should abandon it. But the money will benefit the poor."

"And what of the thousands of people who live and work here? You throw them out on the streets? Will they be made beggars to pay for what you perceive as the sin of your predecessors?"

"The sin of my predecessors? That would be like the sin of Adam, wouldn't it? Passed down to each generation, mankind languishes in the disgrace of Adam. Covered in the sin of Adam until God sent His only begotten Son to pay for that sin by dying on the cross. That hardly seems fair either. Does it?"

209

"I can't, Holy Father. How can tearing down this beautiful building be good?" d'Indy asked the question although he knew the answer. He knew that Peter was right. He had on several occasions admired the beauty that surrounded him and chuckled slyly at the realization that his life as a prince of the Church was a trumped up sham. But it never occurred to him that someone would come along and do something about it. Nothing in his wildest imaginings would ever lead him to guess at what Peter was about to say next.

"I am not talking about selling only Saint Peter's."[208]

Diane was several inches from a chocolate induced sleepy time.[209] The tide was coming in on her famous eyelids and a slightly brown froth formed at the side of her mouth. Her breathing deepened as her famous grand belly topped with her equally notorious cupcake sized breasts heaved against her flannel bathrobe.[210] Her copious grandeur sprawled against the leather sofa. The covering squeaked its soft, luscious, comfort.

The crowd on the television cheered and Diane sat bolt upright neatly knocking her chocolate milk carton on the floor. Oh look at that. It was the new pope coming out on the balcony. Something odd was up. Everybody seemed to be deferring to the one guy, bowing towards him and all. Diane and half the people on the planet who were watching had never seen a pope dressed like this one.

She pumped up the volume with the remote. The announcer was babbling about wondering what was going on and never having seen anything like this before. As she mopped up her mess with a doily, Diane wondered if some type of extremist from the Middle East had knocked off the new pontiff and was posing as the pope. It was a guy in a black robe. Slowly it dawned on Diane. The guy was Peter Bondeo. The holy kid from grade school.

Inspired by an opportunity to misbehave again on a worldwide stage, Diane was yanked out of her funk. She showered, shaved, packed a bag, grabbed her passport and headed for the airport.

# 13

## THE CHURCH PURSUES PETER'S PENANCE

Diane, and the rest of the world who watched along, were teased with only a brief glimpse of the new pope. He appeared, walked to the edge of the balcony, peered over, shook his head 'no', turned around and walked back into the room just off the balcony. The cardinals, priests and various assistants looked momentarily dumbfounded, then shrugged and followed the new boss back inside. The French doors closed behind them with an air of finality.

For its part, the crowd behaved quite well. Considering they were afforded only a glimpse of the new Pontiff, who had not bothered to bless them or so much as wave his hand hello, for that matter. They milled about a bit, bought a few more souvenirs and gelatos, then slowly dispersed.[211]

It would be a gross understatement to say that the throng of a half-million or so packed into Saint Peter's Square intimidated Pope Peter. Peter II was not a public speaker. He gave no more than a dozen or so sermons during his career as a priest. The mumbled moments in Merdette and Russia hardly count, since his congregations had no idea what he was saying. Though they made him nervous just the same.

Back in the room off that famous balcony, Peter II turned to d'Indy.

"Cardinal Secretary of State, d'Indy." Peter II paused to arrange his thoughts. "Would you address the crowd, please?"

"Holy Father, the people are expecting you. If I go out there, I am certain a misunderstanding will arise. They might think I am you. Perhaps you could hold an interview with the television networks. They are here from all over the world. I will have something prepared immediately."

Peter directed his gaze meekly at d'Indy. "No interviews for me. Please, when you speak to them say something about the plans to sell this church, to sell all churches and to live a life in imitation of Christ's poverty as an example to Christians everywhere."

"Holy Father, what a horribly heavy cross you give me to bear."

"Carry it joyously, Eminence. You have spent all of your life talking to important people. You are prepared for this. For me, I would be breaking God's first commandment."[212] Peter II grasped d'Indy tentatively by the elbow and steered him away from the others, the assistants at the ready to kowtow.

"Do you believe this is God's will?"

d'Indy's grand stature deflated about a whisper. Astonishingly, he paused to think. "I feel uncertain. I feel slightly frightened. I also feel a bit exhilarated." d'Indy regained his full regality as he grasped Peter's hands. "Yes…I believe this is God's work."

None of the Vatican insiders were surprised at how easily d'Indy took to his new role as Church spokesman. d'Indy conducted himself with what he considered an understated yet dramatic flair. This was a golden opportunity to enrich and expand his complex presentational palate.

There are people born to be "on camera." These people "eat the lens." Simply put, their features look good on that flat depthless screen. Oddly, many of these people have horrendous complexions, d'Indy included. Magically though, the glaring lights washed his face clean. The growths with little hairs poking out of them, the pockmarks, the dark circles under his eyes all evaporated under the kliegs. What was left was a rather handsome, elderly man, with solidly white hair, a bit thin on top, the white Vandyke framing a mouth no longer purple but a serious red. d'Indy's usual splotchy pallor evened out and deepened to a dapper tan.

d'Indy's insides also appeared to be transformed during these performances. It might be more accurate to say he projected a more positive sort of creature. Because, unlike his quietly menacing whispered commands to religious underlings, with the media, d'Indy expressed himself in calm, reassuring tones. There was a patient bemusement with the big-shot anchors as well as the reporters, all of whom normally displayed a naturally aggressive attitude. Most importantly, d'Indy was immensely credible to the viewers.

d'Indy created a creature and then became it, with media and religious colleagues alike. Through the perspective gained by historical reflection, it is possible to understand that d'Indy played the media like a puppet. His sheep's clothing fit perfectly over his wolf's frame. However, it was his appetite for attention that was vociferous, not his goals.        Obviously over time, d'Indy developed enemies in the media. "When the scales tip to the positive side, at least a few admirers are bound to fall off the bandwagon."[213]

"Greetings, ladies and gentlemen.[214] I will make a brief statement and then entertain your questions. Our new pope has important news. My name and title is Cardinal Secretary of State, Michele d'Indy (Lower case 'd' apostrophe, upper case 'I' lower case n-d-y.) pronounced dawn DEE.

"This morning a new bishop of Rome was selected. His eminence Peter Cardinal Bondeo, common spelling, born in Lathrup Village, Michigan, U.S.A. has taken the name Pope Peter, the Second.

"Because of his innate humility, and aversion to spectacle, the Holy Father does not wish to make a public appearance. Since I am, as it were, second-in-command, he has asked me to speak for him.

"Holy Mother the Church does not change. God and his commandments do not change. Our salvation through Jesus Christ does not change. The command of Jesus to spread his word to the world does not change. Unfortunately or not, what also will never change are the weaknesses of humanity. History bears this out.

"What does change is our understanding." d'Indy paused and looked about the media gathered before him. Several were taking notes, some snapped pictures. The television photographers each had an eye gummed against their viewfinders. The still photographers, stationed immediately below him, knelt, crouched or sat crossed-legged like a throng of kindergarten children. They were all paying attention. Good.

d'Indy raised his hands above his head and a dozen or so cameras clicked. "This building…" d'Indy extended his fingers both for illustration and dramatic flourish. "…was built to praise God. That is what previous popes said. That is what their successors maintained. The greater and grander the building, the greater and grander the praise.

"This Holy Father believes that his predecessors were grossly misled sometimes intentionally on this account. Too often they fooled themselves. The spirit of Jesus is one of humility and poverty. With a sincere, and yes severe newfound realization, we shudder to consider Christ's words to the rich man that it would be easier for him to pass through the eye of a needle than to enter the Kingdom of Heaven. Because of his wealth. "Sell all you have and follow me." Jesus said. Sell all you have." d'Indy lowered his arms.

"This temple, Saint Peter's and the Vatican, is an example of the sins that we as frail humans are subject to. With its monumental collection of gold, marble, priceless antiques, paintings, sculpture, works of artistic genius, the frescoes... the frescoes alone. This temple glorifies, not God, but the sin of pride.

"This is the understanding our Holy Father brings to us today. This temple..." Here d'Indy used but a single finger held waist high and pointing up. Then he whispered. "This temple glorifies Satan. The Holy Father wishes to sell Vatican City as a whole, and give all of the proceeds to charity."

Time and history paused briefly in the calm of the eye of this hurricane. There were no responses from any of the hundred or so people in the room. Not only were there no responses, physical or verbal, but very little in the way of thought process. For a solid ten seconds, they stood stock still in shock. This from people who had covered massacres, famine, assassinations and the fashion industry. Not a blink for the ten longest seconds in the history of the church. Then it hit the fan.

It started with the television people. Ironic, since TV reporters are legendary numbskulls. This one had help, though. TV network reporter Peter Scolare's producer screamed into his I.F.B.[215] This brought the millionaire journalist out of his stupor. "Cardinal Secretary...?" He blurted urgently.

"Please. Call me Your Eminence."

"Your Eminence, how much does the Holy Father hope to get for the Vatican?" Scolare's question opened the floodgates for the other reporters who all began asking questions simultaneously.[216] d'Indy held up both hands for silence and received it.

"I will point to someone and that person will ask a question. I will answer it as best as I can. Then I will point to another person. That person can then ask a question. I will stay here until all of your questions are answered. Then, I will ask you three times if all of your questions are answered. That seems fair."

Jonathan Muttles, the natural sounding international correspondent for Public Broadcasting Radio, asked his most important question, (Without waiting for recognition either.)

"What about follow-ups? How many follow-ups do we get?" The others chimed in as well: "We should get at least one follow-up." And "How can you not let us ask a follow-up?" and "Yeah. What she said."

d'Indy found this odd. "Forgive me. This is the first news conference I have ever attended, let alone been a part of. You there in the rumpled coat. What do you mean by a "follow-up?""

The media chuckled at this. Jonathan Muttles blushed and bristled a bit. His "rumpled" coat was an Oxwhine original that cost seven hundred American dollars. Unlike everyone else in that room, except perhaps this sniping d'Indy fellow, Muttles was highly intelligent with deeply developed background in every area he covered. "Eminence, the habit of the news media to ask "follow-ups" developed and was refined as a direct result of the responders lack of candor. That is to say, to deflect when the responder was evasive or instead, to answer a question that was never asked. This gave reporters the impression that interview subjects were often trying to hide something, usually because they had done something wrong or because, perhaps, it was not the right time to answer the question, because, perhaps, someone or an agency was being protected. Hence, the "follow-up" allows the reporter an opportunity to fine-tune the question and chip away at the defensiveness of the responder and therefore uncover the truth. People outside of the media view follow-up questions as "hounding." I think I speak for the rest of us when I say to you we believe it is a necessary evil."

d'Indy responded. "No follow-ups. One question from each person at a time."

Carla Sigorninia, the Roman TV anchor known for unbuttoning her blouse to the waist when the set "gets so hot" or prior to the arrival of the sports guy piped up. "What if we do not ask the question correctly the first time?"

d'Indy responded. "Perhaps you should write it down on a piece of paper prior to asking."

Hert Ziegel from "SHHpekelt whispered loudly in imitation of poor Sigorninia. "What if we do not know how to write, Eminence?" He and his fellow sexist pigs guffawed and snickered at that. Carla Sigorninia reached over two rows of lucky guys to slap at Ziegel with her notebook.

Kelly Kilt from Disassociated Presses was losing patience with all of this and everyone. "Eminence, what if you do not understand the question?"

215

d'Indy responded. "That will not happen."

Kilt loudly exhaled her disgust. d'Indy's saying it would not happen obviously meant to her that it would.

Jonston Baningtonerhand, BBC-3 camerafellowe, broke twenty-five years of silence[217] by asking something that, quite simply, had to be asked. "Eh, yer Emmynence. Say oym joost stanin' 'ere, moindin' me own pays en' kyows, an' thu blewdy bloke nest to may done kwoyt boomp intuh may, boot joost sarta noodges may a moyt. Joost uhnuff tuh crup up may shot, sorta. Wih yore indoolgence, could yuh moyt ruhpate ta ansuh oot layst? Joost ifen that should sorta 'appen?[218]

The bloke next to Baningtonerhand, Crant Fuhr, himself a fifteen year photog vet from Quebec, gave him a good-natured slug on the shoulder.

d'Indy responded. "Raise your hand and I will repeat my response.

Baningtonerhand's query inspired the concern of Mdlk Vlditsik from the Iceland Herald. "What if you do not understand the question because of somebody's accent?"

Bizano Biscotti from the Milan Miner added. "What if we do not understand the question because of somebody's accent?"

d'Indy responded. "Has this happened yet?" Each person in the group pursed his or her lips, thought a moment and then shook his or her head in the negative. The cardinal had a point there. d'Indy continued. "Good. Shall we continue?" The group nodded its assent.

The only person who had asked a pertinent question so far, Peter Scolare, was getting a headache from the voice of his producer who was still screaming into his ear. "Eminence? I believe I was first?"

"Yes. You wanted to know the "asking price" for the Vatican. The answer to your question is that I do not know. A figure has not been set. The Holy Father will not entertain bids either. He is not looking for the highest bidder."

Paval Urbanachek from Digestible Architecture Magazine Intl. raised his hand and d'Indy recognized him. "Eminence, is it possible that the Catholic Church might sell the Vatican to a person or company which would maintain it as a museum?"

d'Indy responded. "That is a reasonable suggestion. However, frankly, I do not know if he will want to travel that road. Our Holy Father is a very- is the most spiritual man I have ever known. Pope Peter the Second is the holiest man I have ever known. I hope eventually he will overcome his aversion to you and at least say hello. That is probably all he would say. The Holy Father is a man of very few words. He is an inspiration wherever he goes. At this point d'Indy "backgrounded" them on Peter's previous successes.

"When he pointed out the ungodliness of Saint Peter's it reminded me of Christ throwing the buyers and sellers out of the temple. If it was not such a malicious act, I believe the Holy Father would tear down these buildings brick by brick. The last thing then that he wants to do is to make selling it a profitable transaction. If and when someone approaches us, I will take that information to the Holy Father. He has not said as much, but I am certain he does not want to make a mockery of this place."

Kelly Kilt from Disassociated Presses was holding back a belly full. "Cardinal, did you know before you elected this guy that he would pull a stunt like this?"

d'Indy responded. "No, I did not."

Kilt then began a series of follow-ups. Raising only minor objection from the group, since she seemed to be on a fast track to getting the lowdown.

"Did any of the other cardinals know about selling the Vatican before they voted for Pope Peter?"

"I doubt it. Word of something that significant would have spread. My duties to the Church put me in a position to be in close consistently intimate, contact with the College of Cardinals. The first I heard of it was from the Holy Father himself just moments after his selection."

"What are the other Cardinals saying about it? Are they pleased? Are they angry? Some must be angry. A building two thousand years old-the new guy comes along and sells it? Come on Cardinal."

d'Indy responded. "I have spoken only with the Holy Father about this. He then asked me to tell you. You may question as many cardinals as are willing to talk with you. We serve at the will of the Holy Father."

Kilt pressed on. "What about the millions of Catholics who see the Vatican as the center of their church? Isn't Pope Peter concerned about their feelings? What about all the history in these buildings? Haven't there been miracles here? What about all these guys buried downstairs? Are you planning to dig them up and put them somewhere else?"

d'Indy responded. "I will answer your second series of questions first. I do not know what will be done with the tombs or sarcophagi of Holy Fathers entombed here. That raises a question of monumental importance. I doubt the Holy Father means to desecrate the graves of his predecessors. I will confer with him. Perhaps the other gentleman's suggestion about making this place a museum, when presented with your observations about disrupting the eternal rest..." d'Indy trailed off.

"As to Christ's flock..." d'Indy searched for a way to explain how he expected three hundred million people to respond to the destruction of the bitchin'est shrine ever built. "I pray that Catholics will learn the valuable lesson the Holy Father has taught us. That lesson is an invitation to follow in the steps of the Savior. The Savior Who lived a life of poverty. The Savior Whose tormentors attempted to strip Him of all dignity, made a mockery of Him, tortured Him prior to subjecting Him to the most brutal and humiliating of deaths: stripped Him naked and then nailed Him to a cross, taunting Him as He experienced a slow, agonizing death. I pray that Catholics who object to the Holy Father's action will reconsider that the true grandeur awaits them after death in Heaven. Jesus knew this as He hung upon the cross. This was His great lesson.

"The essential truth the Holy Father imparts today is that the Vatican does not praise God, this pomposity mocks Him." Surprisingly, d'Indy was wise enough to shut up at this point. Using the barometer of the look on Kilt's face, obviously, she and the rest of the media were buying this explanation.

Meantime Peter was having a slightly tougher sell with the College of Cardinals. They had waited in the grand room behind those French doors off the famous balcony. They had heard d'Indy announce Peter the Second as the next Bishop of Rome, Vicar of Christ, etc. etc. They heard the roar from a half-million throats. They listened expectantly through a brief silence, then witnessed their Holy Spirit-inspired choice duck back inside the grand ballroom seconds later looking for all the world like the weakest kid in gym class during a game of dodge ball. Inside the grand room crest had fallen like drops of sweat at the final round of a polka competition.

Peter II and d'Indy had whispered a few words back and forth. d'Indy had made to leave, then, at the door turned to look at the college. Considering the oddity of what had just happened, the eminences were surprised to see the only reason d'Indy had paused was to turn to them and smile. Then he left.

Peter motioned slightly in the direction of the French doors and the crowd. "I'm not much for public speaking."

The boys in red nodded and several smiled slightly. That was forgivable. They were all familiar with Peter's history. Not that they understood. Most of them were dyed-in-the-wool windbags who would kill anybody who dared to get between them and their pulpits. Peter II ducking his first speech was certainly forgivable, if not a little squirrelly. They could adjust to a pope who kept a low profile. It had happened with prior Papas. It would be a nice change of pace to have a pope who was not a super-hero in a published comic book.[219]

"Cardinal Secretary of State will talk to the media for me." Peter paused. The cardinals waited; looking more than a little like a pile of netted fish. Peter pushed himself.

"I believe the Holy Spirit has moved within me today. I am telling you that so you understand that what I am about to tell you about a decision I have made has not been done capriciously. I have discussed it with His Eminence Cardinal Secretary of State d'Indy. He is now meeting with the media so that word will be sent to the rest of the world.

"This is what he will say." Peter II struggled to face the faces of the college. He failed, so instead he quietly addressed the floor.

"The Vatican is to be sold. The money will be given to the poor. If our Lord and Savior were here now, in this room I believe he would do the same. I am surprised He hasn't shown up already to do just that" Peter paused. It was obvious the concept took a moment to gel in the gray matter of the red-robed men. (Same as what d'Indy was experiencing several floors below with the media.)

Ten of these cardinals, who worked in the Vatican, had just heard their world was about to be obliterated. Six more were Italians with districts that invested a lot of time doing business with the Vatican. For all of them, their minds dwelt not so much with the loss of the buildings, but with the personal repercussions. All cardinals were part of the pope's retinue. That included the cardinals from New Zealand and Samoa. They were the pope's

"A" Team. An air of disbelief spread through the room like the sudden awareness that someone has poo on his shoe.

Cardinal Zerbi was the first to speak. "Holy Father, where will you live?" Zerbi's sidekick Cardinal Kolinsky mimed his curiosity to an answer, as well.

"I do not know. God will provide. If the apostles can be like the lilies-of-the-field, then shouldn't we too?" Oops. That was another hammer blow. Just as darkness waned and the sun began to rise, Peter whips out another stunner.

Zerbi was not only a fan of Peter II. He was also a helper. "You are welcome to use my apartment, Holy Father. Since there is no installation, I will return home tomorrow and begin selling my churches."

"Thank you, Eminence."

Cardinal Bendardondat was the first to find his way out of the fog. "Holy Father, although I am almost afraid to ask, what do you mean when you say "shouldn't we too?""

"You should also sell your churches and properties and give the money to the poor."

Bendardondat gulped his astonishment and followed it with a chaser of anguish. "Holy Father, your predecessors have already burdened themselves several times in the past with the question of how far to go with our dedication to the poor. The question has been settled. The church, the benefices do better and will continue to do well because people know their money comes to the hands of the Holy Father, who can better see to the eradication of poverty throughout the world. And. How do I put this? I was born in poverty. Abject, horrible poverty. Trust me. Please. It is not something to pursue."[220]

"Poverty is a reward." Peter II walked to Bendardondat and put a hand on his shoulder. "Your Eminence?"

Bendardondat's mind was a running washing machine loaded with wet, heavy towels in the spin cycle with the agitator post dislodged from its center post mooring. "I…erhh…"

"There is no rush." Peter counseled.

"Holy Father, may I offer a comment?" The cardinals buzzed, hushed, then held their breath. What would the outspoken and outrageous and somewhat scary Cardinal Cosmos say?[221]

"Are you out of your mind? You cannot shut down the Vatican and sell it to Mark Zuckerburg! Christ built His Church upon this Rock. The skull of Saint Peter is buried several floors below, as are the bodies of so many sainted popes. This is a place of worship and a final destination for millions of pilgrims. This is the axis of the Christian world and the cultural center of Italy. Will you hang a price tag from the toe of the foot of the Savior in Michelangelo's "The Pieta?"[222] Will you hack away and sell square-foot sections of the frescoes covering the ceiling of the Sistine Chapel? Perhaps you can get one dollar a piece for the bees on the baldacchino!"[223] By this time, Cosmos was directly in Peter's face.

Peter II grimaced slightly, but still spoke softly. "Those are examples of the money driven whores who built shrines to their own decadence.[224] Bronze and gold, and marble and eh… paint don't glorify God."

Several veins on Cosmos's nose and cheeks rose perilously close to the surface of his pockmarked skin as he sneered. "Are you one of those American hippies? Anti-establishment? Down with the man? That type of thing? Explain to me, please. I am from former Soviet Union. Like my brother from Ethiopia, I also know the horror of poverty and the sin-the SIN of a government that restricts the reverence and the glorification of God. That is what you do here." An intellectual nor'easter blew through Cosmos's sails as he turned in a slow circle, arms outstretched. "My fellow cardinals! I call for the recantation of our selection of this man before the crown of Peter is placed on his head. He who tears down our shrines and sells our statues of the Virgin Mother in the street and preaches the desecration of the most glorious symbol of reverence to Our Lord and Creator."

Peter II waited until the boomerang of Cosmos's voice stopped bouncing around the Grand Hall.

"Uh. That reminds me. Cardinal d'Indy already invested me. In private." That elicited several nods of understanding and a few whispered queries from cardinals unsure of their understanding of English.

"You are very quick to act. But then the devil always is." The face of Cardinal Cosmos was beginning to resemble boiling tomato soup. "We are all familiar with the old nun's tail which says that no pope should take the name of Peter because it is believed that the name of the last pope will also be Peter. We must act quickly to preserve our Church. To preserve this rock upon which Christ has built this Church of His.[225] We must rejoin in conclave to select a true successor to our saintly Pope Martin VI.[226] Who will stand with me?"

Stanley Cardinal Szymanofski, from Ireland[227] offered. "Could he be impeached?"

Strombone Cardinal Terdmont, the ancient representative from the Carolinas, shuffled forward. A shock of his white hair ironically fell boyishly onto his forehead. He spoke to the floor in front of Cosmos, patiently, as if addressing a puppy that had misbehaved. "I do not believe we could divest this pope, Your Eminence, even if we wanted to do so." Terdmont shuffled back to his previous position.

Julio Cardinal O'Rooley, from Chicago, mistakenly thought he would bring the discussion to an abrupt halt. "What ever you want to call the action, this Holy Father, as is the case with every Holy Father, can not be fired. He has to commit a heresy or be obviously insane."

Cosmos jumped on that one. "Any pope who decides as his first act without consultation with us to sell the Vatican is obviously insane. We should vote now today to have him removed. He would not only destroy the greatest building that honors God's glory but also desecrate the graves of the sainted popes who came before him." Cosmos's basket of exasperation now carried anger, indignation and impatience.

Cardinal Sabah was saddened enough by the prospect to produce a single tear of premature regret. "Holy Father, what would you do with the bodies of your predecessors?"

Peter II's response surprised them. "The dead could suffer. And the living too. Cardinal Cosmos didn't mention the hundreds of clergy who make their homes here in the Vatican. The Swiss Guard will be sent back to …" Peter II's lousy sense of geography again surfaced.

"Switzerland?" Since it was his homeland, Slalm Cardinal Skywyz[228] naturally knew where the Guard originated.

"Is it Switzerland, really, Your Eminence?"

"Yes, Holy Father. I am from Zug, a bit south of Zurich. My father was a member of the Swiss Guard. We Swiss, more than anyone, will miss the Guard and their fancy pants. But, if it is your wish, to disband them, Holy Father, I support you. If you are insane, it comes as a result of a desire to imitate the life of Christ."

"Thank you, Your Eminence."

Rasurlik Cardinal Guillotine, from Luxembourg seemed to support Peter II. "I will say this, Holy Father, I for one have always found distress with the vendors selling all sorts of trash here. It sullies the essence of what a church should mean to the people. The gelato vendors on the Piazza Pio XII are a disgrace. What they ask for a spoonful of gelato should be considered a mortal sin. And are not we all bothered by the old man at the Sancta Porta[229] claiming to be the cousin of John Paul II. Who among us did not expect him to leave after Karol died? But did he? No! True, he does resemble John Paul II a little and he also speaks several languages fluently…" Guillotine suspected he was rambling and so stopped and, looking slightly ashamed, walked to a far wall, picked a chair, sat down and put his face in his hands. Just before he made this trek to Rome, his housekeeper took him quietly aside and told him to take care, because, ever since his recent seventy-fifth birthday, he had started to ramble. Guillotine quickly became self-conscious about it. Usually after he had rambled a little bit. Back home, his sermons had shrunk to five minutes or less.

Several of the elder cardinals looked after Guillotine enviously. After being on their feet for a solid fifteen minutes, it would sure be swell to relax in one of those big satin covered chairs. Several withered minds whittled away at possible long-winded arguments they could make before excusing themselves.

Quinto Cardinal Cinto was the first to come up with one. "Holy Father, perhaps instead of selling the Vatican we could instead dismantle it, put it on a boat and ship it somewhere where it could be rebuilt. Corsica perhaps."

That idea appropriated several guffaws and chuckles all round. Deopadre Cardinal Corrleone, from Sicily, explained why for Peter II's benefit. "Holy Father, I believe you may have washed his feet, but have you been formally introduced to His Eminence Cardinal Cinto from Corsica?" Peter II and Cinto shook hands.

"The Holy Father will not excommunicate me for trying, I pray." Cinto's groveling was more ironic than sincere and the humor touched off another round of chuckles.

Mordan Cardinal Zimmer, from Germany, decided he had taken about enough of this monkey business. His nasal whine cut through the mirth like bees at a honey tasting competition. "I find your amusement and folly sacrilegious. You giggle like novice nuns for a man who says he will destroy this magnificent institution. You barbarians seem to forget that The Vatican is more than a settlement of astonishingly beautiful buildings, it is also a city-state. It is its own country. As sure as Italy is the cradle of modern civilization, so Vatican City is and has been the hand that rocks that cradle." Several supporters mumbled quiet support saying: "Here, here." Or "Word of God, he's got that right." Or "Does that look like a men's room over there?"

Zimmer continued to simmer and steep. "I beg the Holy Father to let us know exactly what his plans are. Will he sell the building intact, allowing mercenaries to plunder the priceless works except those that are too magnificent to move?[230] Does he feel joy at the prospect of perhaps The Disney Company setting up kiosks over by "The Pieta" to sell t-shirts with pictures of the Blessed Mother holding a dead Mickey Mouse? Or will the Holy Father simply raze the buildings?"

Peter II paused then pursued without petulance. "That would be the best thing. Cathedrals are shrines to our spiritual insolence. But tearing down the buildings as penance for our sins- it- mocks the poor."

Michael Cardinal Easley from Dallas, Texas coughed slightly before remarking. "The heretics in my neck of the woods have this thing about putting their piety on bumper stickers and jewelry and the like. Everywhere I go I see "W.W.J.D." It stands for "What would Jesus do." I don't mean to criticize them, but it always struck me as a rather simplistic way for people to think that they are following the life of Christ. Since one thing Jesus would not do is buy expensive designer jewelry or even chintzy junk- especially if it had His name on it. I realize that I'm certainly preaching to the choir here, but what the Holy Father here is asking does seem like something Jesus would do."

Though Easley had made a compelling point, most of the cardinals were distracted by the sound of his voice. He sounded exactly like Jimmy Carter, a previous president of the United States.

The aged Bullfinch Cardinal Cowenheath, from Scotland, shuffled painfully to Peter II, fell to an arthritic knee, and made to put his leathery wrinkled puss to the new pope's ring. Peter II would have none of it. For another thing, he was not wearing any jewelry, let alone a fancy angler's ring. "Please Your Eminence. Let me help you stand. No more of this either. No more bowing, no ring-kissing, no assistance given in holding books and turning pages during church ceremonies." Peter II paused, gulped, and then continued. "Let us drop the 'Holys' and 'Eminences' because eventually there will be no more cardinals, bishops, monsignors, or priests. No more Church royalty." Peter waited a full minute for the brouhaha to run its course. "God's Kingdom is enthroned in the palace of the heart. That is why I say that I am the last pope."

A shouting match ensued led by those now suddenly convinced that the Holy Spirit had not truly inspired them to select such a demon: "No cardinals! You're mad, I tell you, mad!" and "Insane. I tell you he is insane." And "I finally raised enough cash for a new cathedral. Are you nuts?!" and the other guys who, more or less, supported Peter II. The cacophony carried on for a moment until Himblo Cardinal Tubeh from South Africa, a man who as a monsignor had sung in a professional production of "H.M.S Pinafore," loudly sang out. "A-men."[231] While many chuckled at this, others felt chills brought on by the severity of the emotion emoted.

Peter II turned hopefully to the over-ripened Cowenheath who had been barely maintaining his balance by holding onto the pope's hand. He looked affectionately into the old man's weathered face. "Please Your Eminence, do you have something you wish to say?"

The geezer smiled a tiny geezer smile, made a little burping noise, coughed louder than anyone there thought possible coming from such a frail little thing, then said slowly and almost inaudibly. "Holy Father, if you think I'm giving up my fine clothes, my limousine and my chauffer to some drug addict, then you are out of your fucking mind."

Cosmos shouted. "Here here!"

It was then that Peter did what any person with a half-lick or more of sense would do. He left. It was time to put up the For Sale signs.

Nobody better get in Diane's way when she's going somewhere. She plowed through Customs, eyeing the official with a stern squint that likely gives him nightmares to this day. A dandy stepped aside to let her take his cab after Diane trotted to the front of the line, and in the process, offended fifteen other potential customers and left the dandy without so much as a "thanks much."

Diane could bully her way into anything. Her problem there in Rome was that she did not know where to begin the bullying.[232] It was not like there was a sign somewhere that read "This Way To The Pope's Office."

She attempted to corner several nuns, both in groups and individually. All were so startled by her aggressive behavior and terrifying demeanor. The ones who could speak English acted as if they could not.[233]

Diane eventually Roman-collared a priest,[234] who, though his English was rather weak, understood her pressing need to visit with the pope. The man was smart enough to realize that Diane may have been just another cracked pot, or could well be an important person unable to find her way to the correct office.

Diane knew he had led her to the right place when she saw that the waiting room was absolutely monstrous. She had not witnessed this type of extravagance since her days on Capitol Hill in Washington, D.C. The grand doors miles away on the far side of the room creaked open. The sound made Diane tsk.

d'Indy walked through the doors. He motioned her towards him then began a sotto voce remonstrance of his assistant Father Tinitus. Diane strode forward, eyes on the two of them. They were a bit taken aback that as she walked towards them she was digging forcefully into her purse-not a purse, more like a satchel really-could it be for a weapon? The two men, eyes widening in terror, swallowed dryly in unison, as Diane whipped out her always-handy can of WD-40. She passed them and headed directly to the doors.

"Gimme a minute." She squirted at the ancient hinges, and then wobbled the weighty door back and forth a couple of inches. One hinge still refused to come into compliance. She gave it one more squirt, wiggled the now silent door, then pulled out a Kleenex and dabbed up the drippings that had formed under the hinges and down on the floor.

"There is just something about a squeaky door that sets my nerves on edge." Diane offered the Kleenex to the obvious underling, Tinitus, who accepted it with a combination of wonderment and disdain. "When was the last time you greased these things?"

d'Indy recognized Diane's face as that of someone with, if not an international reputation, at least one whose fame did drift across the Atlantic. He could not place it. "I believe the chances are quite good that is the first time these hinges have been lubricated since their installation six-hundred years ago."

"'Bout time." Diane extended her right hand. "I'm Diane Gillette. I'm looking for the Pope. Is this his office?"

d'Indy returned the gesture, noticing a firm if not somewhat slick grip. "My pleasure, Mrs. Gillette?" d'Indy noted a slight bemused scowl at the reference and guessed correctly that he had guessed incorrectly. "I am Cardinal Secretary of State d'Indy. The papal quarters and offices are one flight above us. I am responsible for approval of all appointments with the Holy Father. How may I assist you?"

"That's easy. Take me to his office so I can have a little chat with him. We're old chums from grade school."

"Really? How charming. I will see to it personally that the Holy Father is aware of your presence. Here. Please write down on this piece of paper where you are staying, how long you will be in Rome and any other information you may deem pertinent. Someone will contact you at your hotel. Was there something specific you wish to address with the Holy Father or is this, as you say, an inconsequential chat?"

"Is that an elevator there? Does that go up to the Pope's place?" Diane learned from her political experience that one is never obligated to answer a question directly. Evasion is after all a response. Just not the one the inquirer wants.

"The Holy Father is not available right now, Miss. He is outside the Vatican visiting with the poor."

d'Indy's tone of voice and determination over determining her marital status annoyed Diane at approximately the same level as the squeaky door. She stopped her cross to the elevator. A plain-clothes member of the Swiss Guard[235] moved lithely from his position near the entry doors to block her path.

"Hello handsome. What time do you punch out?" Diane's finest demure did little to distract the massive guard, who, as it turns out: a) did not speak English and b) was gay.

"Miss Gillette, please. Attempts to muscle your way around the Vatican are simply not going to work. I am surprised you have made it as far as you have without the proper escort, but, I assure you that you will go no further without my permission."

"Don't call me Miss. Don't call me Mrs. I introduced myself as Diane Gillette. You many call me Diane. You may call me Diane Gillette. You may call me Gillette. My status married or single is none of you business. Understand?"

As she spoke, d'Indy raised his right index finger in the direction of the guard, who immediately spoke into his wristwatch.[236] The guy was beginning to look like a menace. Diane made a quick resolve to try being nicer. "Say-what's your name again? Cardinal Dandy?" Men loved it when she smiled coyly after intentionally mispronouncing their names. "Listen. I do need to talk to Pete-the Holy Father. Maybe you could sneak me in sometime before lunch?"

d'Indy had not risen to stratospheric levels because of a lack of diplomacy. He could tell Diane was backing down a bit from her earlier display of head butting and so he too relented slightly. "I tell you with all honesty there is nothing I can do for you this morning. I hope the Holy Father will be… make himself available… soon."

"You're worried about him. What's wrong?"

The accurate assessment took d'Indy aback. Diane's face was coming into d'Indy's focus now as someone involved, somehow in politics. Perhaps she was the wife of an American politician. The name Gillette was not ringing a bell. For some odd reason, it made d'Indy think of scraped skin. Perhaps it was her aggressive personality. Women did not act like this in the Vatican. Oh sure, there was the occasional sharp-tongued nun complaining about stained sheets or excessive use of toilet paper, but they were easily dismissed. d'Indy's natural inclination was to dismiss Diane as well. Friend of the Holy Father or not, she had no business here.

Yet, at the same instant these thoughts scudded across his mind, so too did d'Indy's intellect begin to cloud up with what seemed to be a scary somewhat dangerous emotion. d'Indy felt compelled to talk with Diane. The last woman he had felt this warmly towards had been his mother. d'Indy wanted to sit with her. He wanted to be the one Diane came to see for a chat. He wanted to take her cool, greasy little fingers in his own hands. He wanted to gaze into her eyes. His world had been doing a steady topsy-turvy since Peter's selection a week ago. Now the new pope was missing. He had not reported that little bit of information to the media. They were all such chums now with their daily news conferences. The corps had gotten into the habit of applauding at the finish of the briefing. Applause! Imagine that. People clapped when d'Indy finished speaking. What topped that was being able to see himself not only on the local Roman stations (The one featuring the naked women reporters.), but on the national and international cable channels as well. d'Indy had been important for some time. But now he was famous! It made his head spin sometimes. It confused him. Oddly, the attention he swam in made him suffer for solace.

d'Indy felt slightly enraged and foolish simultaneously. Though joyous, his life lately exhausted him. During the vast majority of his six decades plus life, what few emotions he experienced he quickly set aside. The only emotion he relished, and did so frequently, was his sense of superiority. That seemed to have flipped a bit though. His usual robustly confident image was fraying around the edges, because now he simply did not know how to go about his business. Uncertainty was a great field leveler.

"You look like someone carrying the weight of the world on his shoulders." Diane opined.

d'Indy had no need to respond with words. He exhaled exhaustedly and seemed suddenly drenched in dismay.

Diane placed a hand on d'Indy's forearm. "C'mon. Got a minute? Let's sit down and talk. You look like you could use a sympathetic ear."

Diane's solicitude moved d'Indy. As he motioned the guard out of the room, he realized nobody had ever spoken to him in such a way. Nobody had ever understood that big shots need compassion every so often. Nobody had touched him so casually yet so seductively. Nobody had ever been responsible for inciting d'Indy's penis to erection.

As he turned his back on her to close the now silent doors, d'Indy covertly looked south. Boy, where did Father Johnson come from after all these decades? He was concerned that his response to Diane's touch may have been protruding. Not to worry. His cloaks were significantly weighty and his penis significantly insignificant in stature, as to not make its presence obvious. However, it felt bigger than a basilica.

d'Indy mused over the astonishing turn his life had been taking recently. A turn to turmoil. First, he had been made responsible for the leveling of the grandest church ever built. Now his penis was harder than a spring tuber. It shocked him both that his weenie was wanting and that he was enjoying the sensation. What was next, he mused.

Diane knew what was happening. After all, as a slut (in the best sense of the word) who had fucked thousands of men, many was the time she witnessed a man's facial expression turn puppy dog as simultaneously the skin turned white. That could mean only one thing: That the blood was draining from one head to the other. Seeing the pudding's proof was not necessary.

Amused that the old fart was falling for her, Diane figured that this must be a personal best for unintentional entrapment. He was sort of cute with those soulful bloodhound eyes. Wouldn't that be a hoot? Doing it in the Vatican!

Diane crossed to the vintage Toma Amor'te love seat, sat and playfully patted the cushion. Detectable to the naked eye or not, d'Indy was eager to hide what felt to him like an engorgement of monolithic proportions. So, after bunching his robes in front of him, he sat down next to her.

"So…" Diane exhaled and d'Indy could smell her breath. It was warm and musty, earthy yet delicate. He hoped she would exhale like that again and soon.

A claxon should have sounded by then somewhere in d'Indy's celibate brain. Since technically, considering the length of his desire, he had, by Church standards, already sinned, it would have been a good time to step back, take a look at the situation, realize that his growing lust was putting his immortal soul in jeopardy, and then back off. Instead he smiled at her and, there can be no other way to describe it, checked her out.[237]

d'Indy sat to the side of Diane which, as fate would have it, was the open side of her blouse. The side with the buttons. Casual in her dress habits, even for a visit with the pope, Diane had neglected to button the top three buttons. As a result, d'Indy found himself following a field of delicate freckles that led from Diane's throat down to a clear pink area. It was her nipple, of course.

As a resident of the Vatican, d'Indy could barely walk from one room to another without seeing at least one female nipple depicted somewhere along the way. However, oil paint and marble are miles away from the real thing. Usually artists depict nipples erect: Little bits of strawberry or red pencil erasers. Diane's famous (to Americans anyway) puffy sat there like an easily startled pink marshmallow. It looked alive.

Diane exhaled again. It was of the volume that might in any other situation indicate exasperation. But that was not her intent nor was it the way d'Indy took it.

She was fairly certain the cardinal had just ejaculated. It was mostly his body tensing briefly and the way his eyes crossed a little. She hoped it was good for him, anyway.

They both chuckled softly. Oddly, d'Indy felt little inclination to tidy himself. He did feel a strange urge to smoke a cigarette, though. Since he did not smoke, that desire went unrequited.

Instead, after a yawn, d'Indy poured out his heart to Diane. He started with the most obvious. While it was true that Peter was making the major decisions, it was also true that d'Indy was the one responsible for implementing them.

"How does one go about selling the Vatican? Do I sit here and wait for someone to come calling? Or do I fasten "For Sale" signs to the Leonine wall?"[238] He blubbered on for some time on that subject. During which time Diane looked directly at d'Indy, without challenge or any readable response and said nothing.

"…And then there is also the problem of liquidating the Church's treasury."

"How difficult could that be?" Diane encouraged.

d'Indy chuckled at this and for the first time in his life did so without derision. "I can feel history breathing down my neck." Then. "Can I trust you with a secret?" A question d'Indy had never previously asked anyone. His recent sexual release had relaxed his otherwise hardnosed senses to that of a smitten twelve-year old.

Because she knew that if she thought it was interesting enough she would tell the whole fucking planet the minute she stepped outside his door, Diane said nothing but touched his hand briefly. d'Indy raised his eyebrows. An understated reaction considering that what he felt in response was similar to a full body tongue bath given by any other woman. At that moment d'Indy's mind made the decision-without telling him-that he was going to screw his vow of celibacy and have as much sex with as many women as he could for the rest of his life. Diane had that effect on many men.

He smiled and enjoyed the swirling rush inside his insides for a moment before continuing. "No one, myself included, knows the exact financial worth of the Church. We may realize it as we tally the sale of parcels and assets here and there. My educated guess places it at somewhere close to fifty billion dollars. In a good year these investments reap an annual profit somewhere near 100-million. Unfortunately that figure mirrors our expenditures."

Now it was Diane's turn to raise an eyebrow. "You're chipping away at your principle?"

Now it was d'Indy's turn to remain sphinxily silent. That and now it was not only her breath he was enjoying but also a delicious aromatic heat that radiated from her.

Diane noticed the cardinal seemed to be squirming slightly. While she appreciated the lubrication she apparently inspired from him, any previous sexual notions she had entertained were sidetracked by a developing fascination for the three hair sprouting warts on his left nostril. "If anything then, it sounds like this would be the best time to sell, before the Church tanks."

d'Indy wobbled his head and pursed his lips indicating that Diane's theory could work or back-fire.

"Does Peter know about the financial situation?"

"No." d'Indy scoffed politely. He paused. "That is I don't think he is aware. I would have told him eventually, soon actually, and I will tell him, soon, but I doubt that it will make any difference. I could not approach the Holy Father's predecessor with this information for fear he would do something publicly that would jeopardize the Church and make matters worse."

"Peter must have surprised you with his decision."

"I thought he had been reading my thoughts. There was a possibility that the conclave may have selected me. Again, I confide this prideful confession. While considering this, I wondered what I would do with the Church's purses."

The Church was digging into its capital, he explained. The end would have come eventually. Though d'Indy admitted it took him close to a decade to figure out the financial state of the Church, he knew the financial end was at hand. He had considered the possibility that after his selection as Martin's successor he might have to go hat in hand and do a little begging from some big time financiers.

There were other things to occupy his time and mind: Meeting with the media; separating the wheat from the chaff (Cranks versus serious buyers), to say nothing of all the cardinals breathing hot and heavy down his neck.

And what of d'Indy's future after all these important issues were settled? What would become of him? It was not as if there was another One True Holy & Apostolic Church out there somewhere looking for a Cardinal, Secretary of State. Where would he go?[239] What would he do?[240]

"You don't know where he is, do you?" Diane inquired with a gentle realization. She stood and d'Indy followed her to the door.

"I cannot tell you for security reason. I could not say exactly where anyway." d'Indy stared at his feet. "Please do not tell a soul. It would cause a scandal. He has been gone… It is not as if he has been gone all that long."

They paused before the closed door. Diane noted the similarity to the awkward last moments of a first date with a fifteen-year old.

"I have another confession." d'Indy offered his hand and Diane responded with both of hers and a smile. "I apologize for my earlier rudeness. I thank you for speaking with me. You have helped me immensely in the approaching decisions." d'Indy stopped abruptly as he realized he was about to say something that might not be advisable

d'Indy made to drop her hands but Diane held steady with the touch as well as her gaze. She rather enjoyed this.

"You didn't confess, Eminence. That was an apology and a thank you."

It was not until that moment that d'Indy realized that a few minutes ago he had broken a vow and was now eagerly anticipating doing it again.

"Madam, you challenge my vow of celibacy."

Touched by this, Diane let go of one of d'Indy's hands and put her fingers lightly to her throat. As she did so, she noticed d'Indy go a little cross-eyed again.

By the time she hailed a cab outside Saint Peter's Square Diane had guessed where Peter would be. Bowling!

The driver looked as Italian as Diane's preconceived notions allowed. Still it did not hurt to ask. "I don't suppose you speak English, do you?"

The driver eyed her in the rear-view mirror. "Not only do I speak English, but I bet you are from the Midwest? Ohio? Indiana?"

Diane smiled. "Michigan. I'd prefer not to get any more specific than that about my childhood."

"Good enough for me. Where to?"

"That's where you come in. What's the closest bowling alley to the Vatican?"

"Bowling alley? There aren't that many, that I know of and I've probably been to most all of 'em. The closest one? Let me see… Oh! There's one over on the Via Ottaviano just past the Via Crescenzio. A lot of the priests, Americans mostly, from the Vatican go there. It's almost a hangout for American priests, matter of fact. Wanna go there?"

"Please."

"Yeah a lot of priests sure do like to bowl. Italians don't care for it that much. They have bocce ball. Fact now that I think of it, most of the bowling alleys around Rome are near Universities

233

or whatever where a lot of American students or priests are stationed. Ever wonder why priests like to bowl so much?"

"It subjugates the sex drive."

"Sure that's probably it. The ones who don't bowl end up fondling the altar boys. My name is Al Einstein. No relation."

Diane was conveniently rummaging through her purse/gunnysack and so did not have to do anything with Al's extended hand. After he withdrew it she noticed he was eyeing her in the rear-view mirror more than was advisable for safety's sake.

"I would feel a lot more comfortable if you would keep your eyes on the road, Al."

"Sure sure sure. I'm from Indiana. Terra Haute. Thought you looked kinda familiar."

Diane felt no compunction whatsoever to chat about why she might look familiar.

"Anyways you have a pretty good chance of finding your priest friend at this bowling alley. It's the closest one to the Vatican. I'm assuming you are looking for a priest friend, probably a relative who's in the Vatican here and you're on vacation so you came to see him. 'Course, it could be a nun friend. No. Nuns don't bowl. Not around here anyway. Not that I've seen."

Diane easily resisted the urge to set Al straight. Though he was a nice enough guy, it would not do well to have to put up with a gummy cab driver in a city where people drive "molto wacko." It would do more harm than good. "You're pretty close."

"Yeah. I'm pretty good with stuff like that. When I was a kid, I used to read a lot of the Peter Whimsey books, Agatha Christie and eventually Sir Arthur Conan Doyle. I have a pretty deductive mind no relation, heh, heh."

Diane's return smile was slightly strained. Just enough to make it clear that she was listening but not connecting.

"Here we go. It's down this alley. See the Budweiser sign near that t-shirt stand?"

"Yes, I do. Thank you."

"You want me to wait? You sure this is the one?"

Diane stepped out of the world weary Fiat and slammed the creaky door. She set aside an urge to whip out the WD-40. "Now that you mention it, it probably would be better if you do wait. Maybe we should work out a deal though."

"Sure. How about 15 euros for the first hour and 12 for each additional? Anything over the hour you pay for a full one."

"That sounds alright except for let's say three by the quarter hour over the first hour."

"Six."

"Five." Diane had learned long ago that it is always best to haggle even when the initial offer seemed perfectly reasonable. It is a wonder with her "grasp" of numbers, that she never went bankrupt.

"Deal."

"Good. I won't be long."

Diane was not long either. It took only a moment to see there was no Peter in the quaint little five-lane alley. An hour and two alleys later and Diane began to reconsider this haphazard approach.

"Is there one near a monastery or a church?"

"Monastery or church? There are churches all over the place here. Tell me something. I don't mean to pry or anything, but is this person you're looking for a little bit different? You know, not maybe strange, but well maybe let's say a bit strange, you know…?"

"Let's pretend the person is? Where would we go?"

"I was just thinking about the "bone" church."

"That sounds interesting."

"It is. Course the church itself is not actually made of bones. It's decorated on the insides with bones. The bones of Capuchins, dead ones of course, you know the priests who invented cappuccino coffee-not the exact priests-but members of the same group anyway. The bowling alley is a couple a blocks away. Hey, look there's the Trevi Fountain. Anyway, which first, the bowling alley or the church?"

Diane noticed nothing much remarkable about the exterior of the church. She did notice that it was in a neighborhood that included several embassies and could not decide if that was significant or not.

She walked up the stairs to the main doors of the church. Locked. That entrance was on the first floor level.[241] Below her, on the ground floor she noticed an unmarked door.

The door opened into a narrow musty-and something else smelling-hallway. It took a quick sharp turn to the left. Diane found herself in a little souvenir shop. Over in the far corner a Capuchin monk sat reading his prayer book. He did not bother to look up.

Diane noticed a little slotted donations box sitting on what appeared to be a cash-takers counter. She slipped a ten-euro note into the slot of the box. If the sight was worth more she would hit it again on the way out.

Near the corner where the monk sat was the only other doorway, other than the one she had entered through. She walked up to the brother.

"This must be the entrance?"

He said nothing but almost imperceptibly raised his right index finger from the corner of the dog-eared book.

She walked through the curtain and waited for her eyes to grow accustomed to the lack of light. She breathed through her mouth, since she doubted her nose would ever grow accustomed to the dusty, musty, somewhat rusty aroma that had grown stronger on this side of the curtain.

The floor was, surprising, made of dirt.[242]

She could not tell what the ancient walls were made of, contemporary concrete or some type of rock. She did realize immediately her natural inclination to avoid touching them.

Diane walked tentatively towards a dim light emanating from off to the left up ahead. She noticed three other dimly lit areas up ahead and in the furthest a man kneeling. The kneeling man was Peter.

In spite of her trepidation over tripping in a dirt rut, she quickened her pace, eager to see her long-gone chum turned pope. She was stopped dead in her tracks however, by what the dim light revealed to her as she passed a wall and stood in front of the first alcove.

The altar was fashioned out of bones. The cross in the center was made of bones. The candleholders were bones: thigh bones, unless she missed her guess. Human thighbones. Those were human skulls rimming the edge of the altar. Big bones used for structure and support. Small bones were for decoration. The whole of the alcove was decorated with bone arrays. It was amazing what could be done with several thousand finger bones.

Open-mouthed now with astonishment, she moved to the next alcove and another original human bone altar. From the middle hung an elaborate bone chandelier. On both sides of the altar two intact skeletons hung suspended (On what else? Bones.) from the wall. In their rotted robes, they appeared to be flying.

"Odd, isn't it?" Peter was standing beside her.

Diane tore herself away from the absurdly grisly scene to face her friend. My, my, my. He was the cutest pope she ever met. She looked at his kind face, the rosy cheeks, the kindest most understanding eyes on the planet, the hair, still amusingly curly and thick and blondish brown without a trace of gray that would otherwise be perfectly acceptable from a man his age.

A warm rash radiated from the bottom of her throat. Her breathing seemed compromised: not quite right. A whisper of moisture developed in her palms, her lower back and down south. All her favorite places. Her body was energized with a dizzy weakness.

Less than two hours ago, she had put d'Indy through something similar. A voice several miles in the back of her mind pronounced an echoed vow to never scoff, even sweetly, when she put someone through this.[243]

For Peter's part, he was yanked back into adolescence and also "going through this." Not since his partially unwilling dalliance with Ys (wiggle index fingers),[244] had these sensations coursed through his body.[245]

Unlike other men in the throws of physical desire, Peter was not in the habit of imagining traits simply by looking at a person's face. So he was not attracted visually in the same way other men would describe it. He was drawn by Diane's presence. He immediately experienced a sense of "right" with her that in comparison made any moral decision or judgment seem like puny potatoes. This feeling may well be similar to the one that cause men to kill each other over a woman.[246]

Though the catacomb altars were musty and cool, almost cold, a barely perceptible damp line developed along his forehead, the bridge of his nose and in the fold right where the inside of his chin met his neck. Like Diane, his breathing became weird. His knees and all the major and minor joint areas seemed weak. Three of his chest hairs straightened and he knew without looking that his navel was filled with lint. In addition, an eerie sensation made him suddenly self-conscious about the length of his toenails and the amount of jam stored both there and under his fingernails. His skin crawled or burned, depending on the location. His tongue grew thick and seemed coated. Oh. He was sportin' wood too.

While pungent and desirable, the sex syrup dripping through his being was resistible. In addition to being pope, Peter was also a priest with a life-long vow to not do-ever- what his entire body was trying to communicate it wanted more than anything. His desire for Diane was not greater than his believed need for redemption from the Savior and eternity with Him in Heaven sitting on clouds and strumming harps.

"Since you're the Pope, why don't you get rid of the celibacy rule, so priests can be a little more like real humans?" Diane, never one to subscribe to small-talk of the "how ya' been" nature, also did not suffer from the tongue problem afflicting Peter.

Peter knew there must be saliva hiding somewhere in his mouth. He smiled benignly.

"Do it on a trial basis. Priests, and nuns, can be off celibacy for a year. See how it works out. If problems develop, just go back to the way it was. Where is the harm?" Unlike Peter's, Diane's mind continued to function as the sexpot percolated.

Just a dab of spit, a bubble and a half's worth, showed up on the right side of Peter's tongue. It was sufficient to reduce the Styrofoam sensation a notch or two.

"Celibacy is a vow we make to God." Peter heard his voice talking and choked back the urge to giggle. Not that he thought the pronouncement amusing, but his chest and throat area were throbbing with giddiness. His suppression inched him into defensive territory. Though he felt like a traitor to the wonderful mush he had been floundering in, at least he had a hand back on the rail. That sinking feeling was exalting, but wrong. "The Church does not change rules on a whim."

"Why not? In addition to being occasionally whimsical, maybe The Church should try being a tad more democratic."

"Diane, you are still a trouble-maker, aren't you?" Peter's genuine smile gave him just an inchworm of relief.

"I try to follow my natural instincts, yes." Though to be truthful, at that point, Diane had the reins of lust yanked back tightly, as she thought how naughty and nice it would be to juggle the challenge of sucking on Peter's throat and investigating how kindly middle-age treated him underneath that pope robe.

But she had never attacked anyone and was not about to start now. There is also something to be said for the power of dozens of naked skulls and their staring empty sockets that strains even the most ardent passions.

"I have a cab. What say we go for a little ride? We'll get caught up on old times and you can give me a guided tour of the city."

"I don't know the city at all. So I wouldn't make a very good guide." The truth was, Peter could get lost walking to the corner and back.

"How about lunch?"

"Can we walk?"

"Let's try it and find out."

If it seems Peter is getting a bit chatty, it is true. In addition to experiencing a sexual tension strung tighter and more precarious than a circus high wire act, he now, for the first time in his life[247] found himself charmed. Chatting seemed to relieve the vertigo.

Diane paid off Einstein, looped her arm into Peter's and off they went. The cab followed at a distance. Behind it, on assignment for d'Indy, four Swiss Guard versions of Dick Tracy were crammed into a Smart Car. What were they planning to do with Peter when they found him? Tie him to the roof?

As they strolled past the American embassy, Diane gave Peter the run-down of her life since their last little get-together in the woods, back in the day, as they stood on the precipice of pre-puberty.

"Why did you leave the convent? You would have made a wonderful nun." Peter asking personal questions and making small talk. Now this was something new.[248]

"Let's just say that I developed an itch that Jesus could not scratch." She stopped and faced Peter. "Peter. I am a woman. I tried to hide from that, from my needs and desires, as the Catholic Church teaches, but I could not hide. Do you think I'm a whore?"

"Yes." Considering the answer, Peter's response came a bit too quickly, albeit, in a surprisingly non-judgmental manner.

Diane said nothing but her eyes began to squint a teeny weenie bit.

"But so was Mary Magdalene. And many believe she was the best friend of Jesus."[249]

"Well I guess if anyone is in the position to pass judgment on others and then forgive them in the next breath, it would have to be you."

"You are a tough cookie, Diane Gillette. You always have been and you always will be."

Diane was struck by the way Peter's mind seemed to have been formed several decades ago and had evidently not changed much since. Though she had only a vague recollection of the woman, she thought he might sound like his own mother, or maybe an aunt she may have met a time or two. Diane, excellent reader of others that she was, saw that inside the toe-head, Peter was chewing on something. She had never considered him a thinker, but now realized that he was. And strong too. There seemed to be a personal strength under the worry lines on his forehead and the fresh crows feet at the edges of his eyes were simple indications that he was resolved to carry out a difficult task that lie before him. Of course, there was always the possibility that outside of a few wrinkles Diane was imagining all this.

The only reason all this information about Diane is being included in this history is because of what happened next.

They passed several restaurants but continued to walk. Their lust had nose-dived like a Messerschmitt running out of fuel in a dogfight. Diane felt the need to leave but nature held her back.

"You hungry?"

"Yes I am." Peter paused. "But I don't have any money."

"Well. Let's stop by a normal church grab a gold crucifix, go hock it and buy some lunch. If there's any money left over we can give it to a poor person. Isn't that just about your speed?"

Peter laughed aloud at this. Something he had not done in a long, long, time.

"We can go to the Vatican. It's almost lunch time."

"I got a better idea. Let's just go to one of these "Elementries" or what ever they call them. They're all over the place. They have these precise-looking, perfectly formed sandwiches displayed in the windows. I'll buy."

They did just that. They found a little shop a short walking distance down the street from the Bones Church. As Peter ate a bowl of sautéed mushrooms, Diane filled his ears with all sorts of changes she thought he should make to Church rulings about abortion, birth control, celibacy, women in the clergy, etc. Peter listened. He listened very carefully.

# 14
## CHRIST IN A NUTSHELL

There are many fanciful stories surrounding the last hours of Peter's residency in Rome. Most of them have just enough of what sounds like the truth in them to spice up the credibility.

One popular ditty involves what is called the "Walk of Tears." This story is favored by the romantic novel crowd engorged on the irony of the final scene of the previous chapter in this book, but with a quart bottle of Wasabi hot sauce thrown in to it. In this version, the bosom-heaving, spunky maiden spurned her highly ranked, somewhat dull-witted, extravagantly slung exalted lover over a matter of his principles. It seemed there would be none of the requisite heavy, whorish breathing, lewd lip licking, followed by probing tongues slavering and, obviously, Roman hands and Russian fingers. Peter walked weeping back to the Vatican. His very soul so torn asunder that he gave up his ship. He was so distraught over the pain of Diane walking away that, as an ode to her, he followed all the suggestions she had made. He signed the last of the papal bulls and then walked tragically back to his lonely papal bed where, surprise! Diane lay all naked, coy and cute.

Another populist tale fancied by people who buy lottery tickets, is that Peter gave the keys to the front doors of Saint Peter's to an obviously distressed poor beggar man who stood on the side of the Apian Way.[250] The man, so the story goes, was just like his benefactor: too shy to step into the limelight and instead helped to organize the great Catholic Renovation, as it came to be known. He also scored himself some mighty fine gold, jewels and priceless paintings which d'Indy gave to him for all the fine work he had done.

The conspiracy crowd favored an inventive story of a lunatic who sullenly jabbed a gun into the back of the last pope and forced him to sign The Renovation Bull. The gun totter, d'Indy most likely, was a communist who simply wanted to spread the wealth around a bit. d'Indy took his walking and pointing orders from a seedy little unnamed fellow who seemed to whine a lot about the poor quality of Russian cigarettes.

Kind readers of this (May it soon be over?)[251] tome already know what truly happened because they just finished reading it. After Diane left in a huff,[252] the SmartCar pulled up. One of the Swiss Guard gave Peter his seat then flagged down a cab-guess who was driving- and they all headed to the Vatican. The car passed Diane and she was briefly moved to see Peter's face pressed up against the window. He seemed to be yearning for her. In truth, because it was such a tight fit in the car, his face was smashed up against the glass.

Peter then went to the chapel in the papal apartments and prayed for six hours straight. Diane, a little bit confused because she was experiencing profound doubt over her actions at the very same time was winging her way to London.[253]

There was a man she planned to look up there. A man whose name she has never revealed. This man reportedly was some sort of masterful Harry Horsecock type who "nursed" Diane back to the lovable scamp she was before the painful encounter with Peter.

Peter went to see d'Indy in his office. Though he was pleased that Peter had decided to address the crowd from the papal balcony, d'Indy was thoroughly distressed when he learned what it was that Peter intended to tell the crowd.

"Holy Father-"

"-Peter."

d'Indy did not initially understand.

"Michelle?"

"Oh. That's right. No more titles. Ehh. Peter, while you know you have my full support, I believe that if you follow through with this you will have gone too far. This is the grandest and obviously most debilitating decision ever made by a pope. A decision with irreversible consequences. You must call a consistory first to discuss this matter with the College of Cardinals. At the very least a synod of bishops. The best thing would be to call a council with both."

Peter sighed a bit. "They will only attempt to talk me out of it."

"But then you could instruct them on how to manage such a transition." d'Indy was close to pleading.

"I wouldn't know what to say."

242

d'Indy dropped all pretense and pleaded. "Please, please, please, please Peter! You cannot just throw away over two thousand years of prayerful thought." d'Indy decided to try a more natural tack by being slightly devious. "Has it occurred to you that it may be the devil who has been whispering these things into your ear?"

"God's will will always prevail. Do you have such little faith?"

d'Indy hung his head and nearly blubbered. "I- I am blind, perhaps. I am so confused. I... I have sinned recently. It weighs heavily on my mind."

Sure was weird what a pussycat he turned into once Peter became pope.

"Would you like for me to hear your confession?"

"Would you?"

"I would be honored."

Honored was the last word to accurately describe what Peter's reaction was to d'Indy's confession. Seems being juiced over Diane was weighing heavily on the conscious of d'Indy. He told the whole story of the "interaction" right down to the gummy details to a silent and thoroughly flabbergasted Peter. Though Peter had called Diane a whore recently, the idea that someone else was actively desiring her gave him the sensation that an ax was halving his brain.

Peter did not say a word even when d'Indy went on to confess that the image of her still floated like melted Swiss chocolate in his imagination. Although it was a minor transgression, the neophyte Lothario retold the incident as if it included panting, sweating, heaving bodies.

"You are forgiven. Sin no more." The sin, though someone else's, bore weightily on Peter. For him Diane, though "immoderately active," was still as clean, pure and perfect as Michelangelo's portrayal several floors below them.[254]

"Thank you Holy Peter. And my penance?"[255]

"Yes. Your penance." Peter appeared to be considering the penance weightily. Rather than slap him with a month standing on his head balancing two bowls of goldfish while saying the Our Father backwards, Peter decided to forgive not only d'Indy, but also himself. "Say a Glory Be[256] when you have the time." d'Indy, shocked, glared a little at Peter. "I have never been too hard on sins of the mind. Especially when it involves someone with a good deal of intelligence and imagination."

d'Indy's glare ratcheted down a few notches to an intense stare.

"It <u>was</u> all in your imagination, wasn't it?"

"Yes, it was all in my imagination."

"I have made your life very difficult lately."

"Yes, it has not been easy."

"Would you hear my confession now?"

"Yes, of course, Peter."

"I had similar thoughts. The difference is that I took action. I all but asked her to marry me. My grievous sin was an obvious rejection of my vow of celibacy."

d'Indy broke from penitential format and whispered furtively. "Is she some type of devil, this friend of yours?"

"Yes, eminence. She has always been a bit of a devil."

They both smiled a bit ruefully. Then, though he had already confessed earlier transgressions involving his scepter and orbs to an invisible God, in a bit of plaintiff one-upmanship, Peter now confessed to d'Indy. Peter after all had to maintain his self-image as the number one sinner. It comes with the territory of being the holiest. So he filled in all the gory details of his moment of ecstasy on Merdette, his long schlong events in Russia and even the fantasy of Sister Juleen back in the sixth grade, though Father Bob had already given him full remission for that commission of sin. Peter did however manage to neglect to mention the incident with Diane in the woods. Oh, he remembered all right. He just did not say anything about it.

This was turning into a Vatican version of locker room braggadocio, this reminiscing of sexual sins past. After Peter finished, d'Indy countered with his own childhood sexual epoch, quite similar to Peter's, of an inspiring nun back in seminary in Switzerland, though d'Indy's was not nearly so Felliniesque.

They concluded the little jam session with simultaneous "phews." It was then that d'Indy had an idea. He hated the thought of misleading his buddy the pope, but at the same time, perhaps he could buy a little time. He would be lying, there was no doubting that, but he would be lying for The Church. d'Indy brushed aside yet another internal argument over which was more important, what the pope said or The Church itself. Though the fight over present, past and, face it, the future, was tempting, not as tempting as Diane say, but pretty close to that, his mind's halls did not need another World Cup soccer match slewing mud all over the walls.

"Peter. There is a way in which you could address the people without having to actually look at a half million of them."

"No Michelle. I should really do this."

"Please do not misunderstand. You would still be performing the address and possibly millions[257] will hear you. You could use the Vatican Radio Station."[258]

***

Peter stood in a room about the size and shape of a large closet. It was dark save for the light in the center of the ceiling which shone down on his speech, which sat on the music stand in front of where he stood, just next to the house that Jack built.[259] One wall was half glass. He could see the engineers in front of their relatively modest mixing board adjusting knobs and levers. The headphones fit snugly on Peter's head. Looming out of the darkness, a microphone hanging from a boom pointed at him rudely. Earlier the engineer had adjusted the microphone, putting it right up to Peter's face.

Peter tapped on the microphone and said, perhaps a bit too loudly. "Hello. Testing. Is this thing on?"

He noticed the engineers in the control room wincing and scrambling to turn down the monitor volume in the control room. One of them turned on a switch, and his voice came into Peter's ears tinny, tiny and distant. "Holy Father, please do not touch the microphone. It is rather sensitive. By the way, the volume control for your headphones is on the wall to your left. You might want to adjust that to a comfortable level before airtime. Also if you wouldn't mind giving me a ten-count please?"

Peter did so, counting the wrong way up to ten but spoke sotto voce.

"Tell you what Holy Father. Just read a couple of sentences from the speech in your normal speaking voice. You're not in Saint Peter's so you don't have to yell."

Peter complied and the engineer was satisfied. The broadcast booth in which he stood reminded him slightly of a confessional booth, except of course for the window, the light, the glass of water, the microphone and the headphones and the fact that he was standing instead of kneeling.

"Thirty seconds to air time, Holy Father. You okay?"

"Yes. Thank you. Call me Peter, please."

The engineer nodded his head "Yeah, sure, right," then announced fifteen seconds, and then counted down from ten

245

finishing five through one with his fingers. On what would be zero, he pointed at Peter.

The silence that followed was the thickest most palpable silence Peter had ever experienced in his life. Cut it with a knife? Try a hacksaw. It was then that it occurred to Peter the enormity of what he was about to do, or more precisely undo. Who was he to do this? He felt he was a fraud. He felt frightened of the consequences. He felt afraid.

Everything he had done so far in his life, he had been fairly certain that it was the right thing to do. Yes, he had made mistakes which had weighed heavily upon him, but even as he swam into the roiling waters of rut-roh, he was still confident that what he was about to do was the right thing.

Perhaps this tortuous trepidation was brought on by the enormity of the action he was about to take. Then, as if from heaven, a voice whispered in his ears. "Ehh… Holy Father? You're on the air."

Trepidation be damned. Peter forsook the speech he had written with the insistent aid of d'Indy and spoke off his threadbare cuffs.

"Blessings to the children of Holy Mother the Church. I am Peter the Second. The last pope of the Holy Roman Catholic Church. I say this as a matter of faith and church doctrine.

"What I will say to you might seem like a surprise. But it's really the logical conclusion to the Second Vatican Council. It is based in the belief that the pope, cardinals, archbishops, priests, nuns and brothers and the laity are all equals in the eyes of God.

"You may have heard of my supplication to the college of cardinals to destroy the Vatican. There is a great deal of argument against this. So I leave it to you, the children of Christ to decide. This is what I think.

"The Vatican is a shrine to the godless worship of ego. Yes, holy men have passed through these doors, but then as if to squander their beautiful lives of humility and sacrifice, they have been buried in layers of marble, fine wood, laid to rest in silks with golden threads, entombed beneath acres of marble and tons of gold. Churches such as Saint Peters are sacrilege. The true glory of God is not expressed in cathedrals. Our hearts are the true residences for God.

"Regardless of what you as Christ's children decide to do with your palaces for cardinals and bishops, remember how Jesus told us to live. We should live lives of prayerful humid- humility.[260]

246

It is impossible to follow the example of Christ, the Sacrificial Lamb- it is impossible to be holy, and still believe there is anything good about these gold-encrusted, stain-glassed museums. So it is up to you whether or not to get rid of them.

"There are several major issues the pontiffs have been at odds with the laity: Birth control, women as priests, priests marrying and abortion. These issues are for you as Catholics to decide.

"This could lead to chaos. But remember, those who hear the voice of the Savior calling them to the greatest of all vocations: to live lives of love and sacrifice for others… those people have no need to argue over who is in charge.

"Before every action you take or word you speak, pray to the Lord for guidance. Also, pray for humility. Humility is the joyous penance we accept for our prideful sins of the past. Say a prayer before every decision. Care for the poor."

A decent speech that few heard. The engineer did not have the presence of mind to record it. There was one reporter from C.C.N. hunkered down studiously in his cubbyhole in the Vatican. Benito Nolobene not only had the professionalism to monitor Vatican Radio, he had the sense and presence of mind to hit the record button on his radio/cassette player, and, luckily, and also a better than passing knowledge of English, otherwise the speech, and its impact, would have been lost, possibly forever.

Unlike his comrades in the international press corps, Benito was not asleep at the wheel. As the content of the speech became quickly evident, Benito was clever enough to turn the volume down and had a story on the air and a photographer dispatched to the radio station in Castel Gandolfo before Peter was finished. As luck would have it, CCN had sprung for a second photographer for Peter's election. She met Benito out in Saint Peters Square for a live stand-up. Clever fellow that Benito was, on the way out of the press offices of the Vatican, he surreptitiously turned off the television set in the break area. So, while all his press pals were busy dozing or complaining to each other about what a boring gig the Vatican had turned into, Benito was reporting history in his live shot.

Back in the various home studios of networks and newsrooms all over the globe, competing news directors sat for a moment slack-jawed and droopy eyed as little Benito performed one of the grandest story scoops anytime anywhere. The other eighteen reporters phones all began ringing within ten seconds of each other. The fact that Benito had the only recording of the speech forced his competitors to give his network credit for the report as they cribbed from it to get the nuts and bolts. That tape was now sitting in the breast pocket of a currier who was racing to a studio on the outskirts of Rome to satellite feed the precious sound to CCN HQ in San Antonio.

Oddly enough, after finishing the speech, Peter felt like having a beer. Not literally, but his mouth was dry, he felt the warm exhaustion of having exerted himself to accomplish something substantial, and so his brain asked politely if it might have something cold, and alcoholic to dull its function just a little bit. Peter, of course, said no to this feeling. Instead he went bowling. And every time he got a strike, he thought, oddly, not of Diane or Ys (wiggle index fingers) or Sister Juleen. He thought of Sister Evelene. And that made him throw the ball a little bit harder.

After getting wind of what had just transpired, "behind their backs" and "without so much as a long-winded, wordy press release to warn them," the Vatican media turned into a nest of angry hornets. Senza Nolobene, they swarmed back to the pressroom where they assumed d'Indy, red-faced as well as red-robed, would show up and apologetically explain everything to them.

Print reporters sharpened their pencils extra sharp. Photographers tightened their focus to expose every wrinkle and blemish and instructed the lighting techs to make the lights as bright as their irises would tolerate. They fumed for about an hour, until Carla Sigorninia, the Roman TV anchor with the loose buttons, sighed breathily and announced "Jesus Christ it's hot in here."

Eyes turned to her expectantly. "Boys, boys you are all such sick little puppy dogs." She half giggled.

Kelly Kilt from Disassociated Presses groaned annoyance. "So where the fuck is Big Red?"

That got a laugh from everyone. It brought relief. If Kilt was pissed, it would be because she had missed the Big Story, just as they had. That made it a little bit more bearable. The media were, if anything, quick to forgive themselves.

With that relief of professional tension, some of the anger dissipated as well. Little groups of pals formed to chat amiably. A deck of cards came out. Newspapers unwrapped. Books snuck out of satchels. There might be quite a wait.

It is a good thing that these reporters were prepared to sit around and twiddle their thumbs for a while, because d'Indy was not coming. Peter told him the announcement on Vatican radio would be sufficient and there was no reason to talk to the media about it. Ha!

It was four hours after the swarm buzzed down in the Vatican media center than who should show up? The Pope!

Peter's driver had let him off inside the Vatican gardens, but instead of taking the stairs or elevator to the papal suite, he wandered about, taking what he figured to be his last look at the Vatican.

This was not aimless wandering. He wanted to see if there was anything-anything that would make him change his mind.[261] When he walked into the media center, he stood at the back and looked at the folks sprawled about in the news conference room. He had enough time to formulate the opinion of how out of place people look in an excessively decorated surrounding. Perhaps the opposition was correct. Maybe this did glorify God. Peter forced himself to focus on the idea. He stood there for fifteen minutes or so. He was not waiting to be noticed, and, not a surprise considering the group of Mensans gathered there, nobody did notice him.

Peter walked down the side aisle along the rows of chairs. There was not a glance in his direction. He made his way out the exit door just to the right of the podium and found himself drenched in the sunlight in the pinacotteca courtyard. He sat on a bench near a fountain and wished for a pencil to flick at. He felt somewhat weird too, and overly aware of his surroundings. His despair turned to, eh… even greater despair. The urge to capitulate coursed through his veins like some type of beckoning, sinuous opiate. It promised a dark joy, but also the coldest abandonment, then headaches, severe cramps, chills and most likely, eventually, vomiting.

Peter cowered as he faced the force of two millennium of organized oppression. Who was he to dare to doubt all these learned men? They suddenly stood before him. He almost jumped. Where did they come from? These rubber-stamps of their predecessors all done up in their fancy red outfits. Red like the color of the blood they had collectively over the centuries squeezed from so many turnips.[262]

How in Heaven could he claim to have any holy one-uppance over this valued group? The sourness of his current situation filled his mouth and lungs with the dank and disgusting short and childlike breaths of death. The sins of his past, though seemingly unintentional to the logical minds of liberal, kind-hearted, sympathetic readers, to Peter throbbed redly, like a dangerous sunburn, like the first tentative toe dipping into the pool of Hades, like the robes of the men who surrounded him. It was as if the pink tip of his rather large pecker peered lasciviously from his robes at them. Peter was every saint disgusted with his body.

And wasn't Peter just as bad as everyone else who had oppressed over the centuries? Look at all the lives he was directly and indirectly rerouting. Some would end up on the street. No doubt about it. Though selected by the Holy Spirit, perhaps Peter was the one who needed some learning. After all, Peter had always known that he was the deficient one. He was the one who had failed to understand the wily ways, the long and winding road, the how-to-preset-a-VCR-ways of God's thinking. They knew though. They must know. Maybe they only seem to know. Maybe they don't know anything at all about God. No. They knew.[263]

It was at the moment when he approached his weakest hold over his goals; a struggling grasp of what he knew was right but could never be: Just as he sensed the tentacles of defeat insinuate themselves into his sandals- it happened.

He saw Jesus.

The action was sudden, jarring and, since Peter did not have the imagination to imagine such a thing, obviously the truth. This was not a vision. It took place in less time than it takes to realize an itch, let go a cough, or blink an eye.

Peter found himself in a massive dark place. Black black black where off to the horizon eons away there was a thin stream of light bordering the edge of this place. The ground, the floor, whatever it was, glowed a disheartening blue and gave his feet the impression somehow that it was not safe. Just the slightest budge, lean or toe wiggle and a dizzy vertigo kicked into his system.

In spite of this, he knew that Jesus was below him and that he must look at Him for guidance. Peter forced himself to lean forward-only a hair-and immediately discovered that he had fallen to his hands and knees.

Directly beneath his navel, or thereabouts, he saw what at first appeared to be a pecan, or maybe it was an oddly detailed leaf. No it was not. It was Jesus. Jesus was all curled up in a tiny little pecan ball. A teeny black patch moved back and Peter realized it was Jesus revealing His face.

250

Tortuous despair ravaged His face. His tears were blood. Jesus uncurled his arms and legs as if for an embrace, but then, quickly wrapped them around his chest.

Jesus screamed. Anyone else would have blocked their ears, the scream was that wrenching and terrible, but not Peter. That was why he heard the scream. The scream became a part of him. Just as Peter thought it would drive him insane it not only stopped, but was replaced by a bolt of joy within Peter so severe, he though he might choke.

Peter's interpretation was simple and instantaneous, as well as thoughtless. Jesus was in despair. Jesus was relieved to see Peter because He agreed with him. That was Peter's rationale, his judgment. Peter was more than convinced. He was a physical part of the despair and the subsequent joy of sacrifice.

As quickly as it started it was over. Peter found himself once again standing face to faces with Cosmo and d'Indy with Cosmo not so surprisingly, halfway between the last word Peter heard before the vision and the word after the vision ended.

"-mistakes. Though they seem more like blunders." Cosmos finished with just a bit too much appreciation for his own wit.

"It is not a mistake." Peter spoke so softly several of the hard-of-hearing birds leaned forward, their faces transmitting expressions of "message not received."

Cosmos, sensing some support, inflated a bit more and queried facetiously. "Do tell us. What is it in your limited administrative resume that leads you to presume over the Church's fathers assembled here before you?"

Peter answered humbly. "Working through the Holy Spirit, you selected me."

Zimmer, a noted expert on Church law, intervened for Cosmos, a mere noted bigmouth. "Selling the churches and shrines, as you suggest, or knocking them down to pay for the sins of certain of your predecessors is not a question of faith or morals. You are not dealing with faith and morals here. You are dealing with simple, harebrained, monetary ignorance. We your brothers are here to guide you through the more difficult branches of your rule."

Cinto, perhaps still hoping for a chunk of the Vatican to reassemble in Corsica, as a noted historian came to Peter's aid. "I must disagree with my brother from Germany. There are countless instances recorded where the Holy Father made decisions in

251

regards to the Church and commerce. As you may recall, these building which surround us now were built with money the popes raised through selling indulgences. A matter that inspired a certain priest from your homeland?"[264] Other popes levied taxes on land acquired through force or as gifts from royalty. What is so bad if we give a little back?"

"Little!" Bendardondat did little to contain his shriek of indignation. "Perhaps my understanding of English is not good enough to understand some unspoken subtlety, but what is "little" about what he suggests?" Bendardondat underlined his question with a stern finger pointed at Peter. "In Ethiopia, we have spent the last ten years raising enough money to build a church in Whoduhwadopia! If I carry out this foolish order, I will be murdered for certain! My blood will be flowing before the words finish out of my mouth! Is this what my life of struggle to spread the word of the Savior has led to? My blood is down a drain for my efforts?"

Peter's suggestion would not sell well with Bendardondat or any of the others gnawing a similar bone, which they were loath to pick. "I will go to your country and make the announcement for you, Eminence. The greatest honor in life is to die for Christ, I will go for you."

Cosmos's smirk was audible. "Oh goody. Now he is suicidal."

O'Rooley expressed the less cynical reluctance being expressed by many of the others. "While I don't expect Chicagoans to kill me, we ask that you understand that while yes many of the Church's shrines are testaments to the vanity of the Church's fathers, even more were built with sacrifices made by the lay people. We all know that God is everywhere present, but our churches are places for reflection and inspiration. They show us, in a physical manifestation, of the goodness and glory of our faith."

Peter's lack of an immediate response drew their attention so that when he spoke, though again barely audible, there was no doubt. It was also pretty short. "No."

Szymanofski exposed his hand. "My situation in Ireland would be, I am afraid, quite similar to my brother from Ethiopia. With a major difference being that my death would be slow and painful and would probably include gasoline, in some way. And I would not blame my flock for tar, feathering and boiling me in oil; especially those who have lost loved ones fighting to express their faith. This decree will cause bloodshed. That much is guaranteed. Bloodshed, pain and suffering."

Peter looked to be carrying his own unexpressed pain as he responded to Szymanofski. "No person has ever suffered the way Jesus suffered. He still suffers today. Your objections cause Him to suffer, now."

Cosmos let loose another volley of derision. "And how do you know that? Are you on speaking terms with the Redeemer? Has He spoken to you?"

Several of Cosmos's comrades joined the others in tsking and hushing him as he had obviously gone more than a bit too far with this last crack.

Peter's answer shocked all of them. "Yes. He has."

Cosmos threw up his arms in an excessively dramatic display of pointing out the fact that he now thought Peter was cuckoo.

"That is why I shall not be moved."

Corrleone asked in awe. "What did Our Lord say?"

The others edged towards Peter. They stood there waiting, waiting and waiting some more. Peter seemed to have discarded all sense of the rhythm of dialogue. Eventually he told them of the apparition. He surprised himself with his thoroughness of detail except one fact.

Cosmos came to before the others and thought to ask, though with the snicker knob turned down several decibels. "When did this happen?"

"Moments ago."

"I knew it!" Everyone turned to look at Kolinsky. Just the idea that he was adding anything to the conversation was remarkable in itself. "I swear to you. I saw a light pass over his face moments ago. It Happened. I know it happened."

Then, with timing only God, or a Broadway lighting designer could have, a glorious golden light did glow upon the face of Peter.[265]

Cosmos was the first to fall to his knees. He hollered. "Lord Jesus forgive me. I only meant to protect your Church." The others followed suit crossing themselves and falling to their knees-with the more agile amongst them making it down faster.

Peter joined them on his knees and they prayed silently. After an hour, Peter rose. The flock stayed on its knees. "Please. We have a lot to do. We should get started." He went about offering a hand to the slower more wilted members of the group.

253

# EPILOGUE

Obviously, since most of the great cathedrals-and a good deal of dumpy churches-are still standing, Peter's dreams of demolition failed to materialize. His great success, however, was the bottom line hope that churches cease to be gold-crusted shrines to local egos. That said many churches, buildings and properties were sold and the money was given to the needy.

Catholics earned a new reputation as sincerely charitable. "Administrative costs" disappeared. The flock grew. What the Catholic Church lost in property it dramatically multiplied in spiritual capital.

A group of rich Catholics formed and is now known as The Buckley Foundation. It bought the Vatican, Notre Dame, Saint Stephens in Vienna and thirty other grand cathedrals throughout the world. d'Indy brokered the deal using his formerly nefarious connections. To his credit, the vast majority of the funds were distributed to the poor-primarily in Africa-but also to other Third World countries on other continents. d'Indy made it part of the contract that voluntary stipends could be collected from site visitors for maintenance and utilities, but that 99% of the money would go to the poor. The Foundation administration was in Pakistan, where every person on the staff, from janitor to CEO was paid a wage commensurate with the current minimum wage in the United States.

Of course there were complaints. However, "The Renovation" provoked very little in the way of violence. There were several noisy protests here and there throughout the world, but other than the occasional scuffle that caused a scratch or two, the amount of bloodshed would scarcely fill a teaspoon.

That is because before a single brick or beam was whacked, the cardinals, through their bishops and down the line to the priests held meetings with the congregations where it was explained that the Holy Father had ordered demolition of not only the churches, but of their positions as well. Not only their positions but also his own position as pope.[266]

Oddly enough, the oodles of people who held axes to grind with the Church Fathers before The Renovation cooled their jets once the opportunity to take over presented itself. Maybe they were sincere enough about their convictions to allow the other members of the "Mystical Body"[267] to have their say.

Many of the grumblers seemed to come from those dyed in the wool. Little grannies and grampies who wheeled their chairs to church. Somebody had to defend the way it was.

Not that objection to the democratization of the church was limited to the elderly. There were plenty of young pups yapping as well. However, objecting was as futile as eating fish on Friday to make up for sins committed Saturday through Thursday. Like his predecessors, many of whom Peter detested, he was the pope and what he said went.

Ironically, the praying field was now level. Peter filled the potholes and raked low the mountains and molehills along the Church's landscape. There was no elevation of anyone to anything. The cardinal who insisted on wearing the red even though it was blatantly anachronistic, had no more power than the blue-haired faithful who had lined the front pews for decades.

If any of the Church leaders ended up out on the street, homeless, derelict, sucking on a bottle of rotgut altar wine, nobody said anything about it. Zimmer, for instance, would seem like a loser before the starting pistol fired on this slow motion race to dismantle. Yet, surprisingly, history depicts him as one of the staunchest supporters.

His former chair was Saint Stephens in Vienna. Many wondrous occasions took place there. Mozart worked there as he composed The Marriage of Figaro, was married there and his funeral was held there as well.[268] That is just the tip of the historical iceberg.

Peter's declaration and Zimmer's subsequent carrying out of orders came directly on the heels of the completion of a fifty-year long cathedral restoration project totaling in the millions. When initially built, the church ran out of money towards completion before the second massive spire could be completed. The structure stood there for hundreds of years with one spire about one hundred feet shorter than its mate's. After years of twisting the arms of big business as well as the little people for donations large and small, Zimmer performed a spine cracking about face and announced the cathedral's imminent destruction. To say the least, the Viennese Catholics-and a good many of the non-Catholics-were pissed.

How did Zimmer get out his pickle? He borrowed a little something from Peter's bag of tricks. He asked his offenders to pause before their admonitions and pray with him. Zimmer was a sturdy, wiry little guy. He could park on his knees for hours. The objector would start to rise or fidget a little. Zimmer would place a kindly hand on the person's arm and ask for "just another little moment." If the pain and fatigue of a half hour on the marble floor of the cold, ancient building did not kill them, monotony would.

Zimmer also turned out to be the one who came closest to being a murder victim. While holding a meeting with objectors, he received the call from d'Indy telling him Saint Stephens would be one of the churches left standing.

Bendardondat got more than he had bargained for back in Ethiopia. It was tough enough to be a Catholic in Ethiopia. The more natural, sun/stars/moon/trees/snakes-based dogma of the various tribes looked down upon any bringers of new concepts as being heathens.

For a while, he maintained the status quo. He did not act one way or the other, but instead thought he would lay low for a few years. Who knows? Maybe it was just another fad. Bendardondat held high hopes that Cosmos[269] or one of the others who had opposed Peter would eventually come through with a solution that would keep things status quo. That was his delusion.

Word of what the rest of the world was up to eventually got around to Ethiopia. The media there may have been a little sleepy, but it was not dormant. Eventually the story picked up enough steam to turn into a scandal.

Editorials demanded. "Who was Bendardondat to keep the laity out of the decision making process?" "Does the cardinal think his flock are a bunch of stupid sheep?" Another insisted. "Come out of your palace and pray like a man!" Eventually an angry mob stormed his residence. They were there to run Bendardondat out of town. Luckily, he had the sense to remember Peter's suggestion to pray before taking action. Miraculously, the group stopped in its tracks and fell to its knees to join Bendardondat in a recitation of the rosary. Then they ran him out of town.

256

O'Rooley from Chicago suffered a similar fate.[270] O'Rooley had stepped on many toes since assuming his position. All in the Windbag City, including the non-Catholics, loved his predecessor, Stanley Cardinal Kilvanski. Though an alleged crook, Kilvansky's easy-going attitude included a laizze faire attitude towards morality. On several occasions, he defended his friendships with the criminal element as not so much consorting with sinners as more a simple attempt to lend a little moral guidance up close and personal. Sort of a spiritual trainer.[271]

O'Rooley was easily just as likable as Kilvanski, though more circumspect in his activities with the criminal element. Many of whom were deeply religious in their own suspect way.[272] These same people found O'Rooley's announcement of the demolition of Our Lady of Covenance Church something just the wrong side of intolerable.

Initial threats to destroy his family fell upon deaf ears because as an only child, now pushing eighty, O'Rooley had no one other than a couple of distant cousins whose names, he was embarrassed to admit to the "spike man," he was unable to remember.

The mobsters did have a point, albeit minor, that since they had donated the lions' share both in cash and forced unpaid labor, they should have a greater say in whether or not the buildings came down.

The conflict became public when O'Rooley invited the media to a news conference where he spilled the beans on the mob's attempts to sway him from carrying out the Holy Father's edict. Oddly, a few media outlets did not find the story newsworthy although several others chomped onto it like a puppy with a stinky slipper.

The bottom line was that no actual destruction was done to O'Rooley personally, however he was forced to use public transportation after the slashing of three successive sets of tires.

Mexico held out longer than any other country. Jesus, Cardinal Puerco remained adamantly silent on the issue.[273] Personally, Puerco liked the idea. However, the challenge of facing millions of staunch Catholics and telling them that the only beautiful thing in their mostly sparse lives was about to be ground into pumice overwhelmed him. Without a trace of foul play or explanation, he disappeared.

When it comes to Christian religions, the Catholics were always the smartest-no contest. Those who disagree have never read a papal bull, or leafed through the Catholic Catechism. For the most part, Church leaders erred on the side of intellect, as opposed to humanity, when developing their myopic methods for following Jesus Christ.

By the same token, it is simplistic to think the Church was hoisted by its own petard.[274] Sure it oppressed, plundered and Crusaded, but eventually it relented to the essential wrongness of its structure and history.

Peter was a champion of the inherent genius of the Catholic faith. With the added advantage that he did more than listen. He paid attention. Then he acted.

There are no reliable figures on how many of the faithful remained so following Peter's exit. It does seem though, that there are more people quietly going about, doing good deeds.

As would be expected, Peter kept a low profile. He spent his final days practicing one of the few things he preached: tending to the less fortunate. He subsisted on "in-kind" wages from the sympathetic owner of a bowling alley in Gaffney, South Carolina.

# ENDNOTES

---

[1] Blame Adam and Eve. The first culprits. The two blew a perfect existence in Paradise when they welched on a deal with God. He guaranteed they would never be sick, weak or weary, have cramps, blue balls, diarrhea, headaches, heartaches or hunger, and best of all, they would never die. The only catch was that they were forbidden to eat from The Tree of Good and Evil.

God leaves, barely turns the corner, and the Devil appears and convinces the soon to be doomed couple that if they eat from the tree they will be smarter than God.

Guess what their last meal in paradise was.

In the first of many Supreme Biblical Rages, God tossed them out of Paradise. Not one to forgive or ever forget, God slapped this sin on A&E's children as well as every baby born since. Since Adam and Eve were the originators, the father and mother of mankind, the origin of the species, and the first ones to both sin and get caught, it was called original sin.

Trying to be smarter than God is about as original as a sin can get. Only the waters of Baptism could cleanse the soul of this sin.

So, what in the Hell does this have to do with Peter's baptism? Well, he abandoned his papal position, in part, because he saw that in their attempts to be like God the church's leaders were stuffed with applesauce.

[2] Not the backbreaking dance from Jamaica. Limbo was a place where dead babies' souls went if they had not been baptized before kicking their little buckets. It is interesting to note that a few years after Peter was born, the Catholic Church decided Limbo did not exist. It gave no explanation for where the babies who had accumulated over the previous two thousand years went.

[3] People who died prior to being absolved for a mortal sin would go straight to Hell and burn for eternity. The nuns later taught Peter that committing a mortal sin is the same thing as nailing Jesus's hands to the cross.

[4] That was before anyone wondered where in the hell everyone was going to live, or for that matter, where the hell they were going to find enough jobs or food to feed everyone.

[5] Almost forgot to mention Joseph. Just like Jesus' step dad, also named Joseph, he was a carpenter by trade. That is not ironic. It is coincidence.

[6] In most Catholic churches, the baptismal font resembled a freestanding sink with no faucet and a larger bowl for holding babies over. Unlike the full submersion technique of the Godless Baptists, all that adult converts to Catholicism received was a dribble on the forehead. While we are at it, it should be noted that children were forced into Catholicism before they were old enough to speak or resist. Then later they were taught that if they left the Church they would go to Hell when they died! Today we call this child abuse.

[7] The nickname used by smart alecky kids who, because of their smart mouths, would probably all burn in Hell when they died

[8] Peter's parents' tragic death would not occur for another 23 years. The whole family-minus our hero-perished together when a bridge they were crossing collapsed sinking the entire Bondeo convoy. They were on their way to a friend of the family's funeral. Now that is ironic! Eh…wait. Maybe it was coincidence.

[9] There are Christian heresies that teach complete submersion into the water is necessary for a complete baptism, but, for Catholics, truly, a little dab'll do ya.

[10] There is a theory that several historians have floated stating that the fungus in the baptismal water infiltrated Peter's brain and affected his decision making process. But, it does not hold water.

[11] The fact that it was a Christian religion did not keep Lutheranism from being essentially evil. Lutherans hated the pope. The father of that particular heresy, Martin Luther, began his religious life as a Catholic priest. It might well be true that many devout Catholics evolved into some of the grandest anti-Catholics. Luther rebelled against the Church's practice of selling indulgences

(redemption coupons) to finance the sixteenth century remodeling of Saint Peter's Basilica in Rome. Since Luther and his Lutherans all ended up rotting in Hell, it was probably a better idea to sit up straight than to tempt fate.

[12] Most likely the devil's blood. Though it may have been the blood of children who misbehaved. The designer of the logo had taken liberties. While St. Mikey is usually pictured slaying a dragon (Lucifer), the sword rarely flames. More often he holds a scale (Used to weigh souls!) in his other hand.

[13] The only design allowed was sold in the basement at Hudson's Department Store.

[14] It would only lead to testicle fondling and eventually masturbation. Now, of course, boys are encouraged to do so because it makes them thoughtful.

[15] The formality of confessing to God a wrong done. The person must regret having done the act, known it was wrong and promised to never do it again. Most people reading the above passage would pass it off as just another dumb kid remark. How could little Petey know? Well, according to Church law, a person reaches the age of reason at the age of seven (A little older for "retarded" children) and becomes morally responsible enough to differentiate between right and wrong.

[16] This is not as far-fetched as it sounds. Several credible scholars have unearthed significant, though dubious, evidence of one female pope. Pope Joan managed to be elected sometime around 1300 with nary a cardinal aware that she was not only female but a pregnant female coming to term. Parading to her soon to be aborted coronation, she gave birth to a bouncing baby. The crowd along the route quickly realized it had been tricked. They bounced Joan out of her papal carriage and beat her to death. Christian charity, understanding and compassion had yet to be invented.

While the authenticity of the story of Joan has its detractors, it is fact that during that time the practice of checking a pope elect's gender came into being. Prior to coronation the pope-elect sat on an elevated throne similar in design to those found in outhouses. (It had a hole in the seat.) One of the junior cardinals would crawl underneath and confirm that the new pontiff's family jewels were the appropriate ones.

[17] The sanctuary is the sacred consecrated area of the church. It is usually elevated or otherwise architecturally set off from the rest of the church. It is also the area where the priest hangs and the people are not.

[18] The tabernacle is a cupboard for storing extra Jesuses. (More later.) Some cupboard! Many are gold, or decorated with it. The tabernacle at Saint Michael's was suspended with gold plated chains from the arms of the crucifix. Gold plated chains also ran from the four corners of the base of the box to the floor. That kept it from swinging in the wind while protecting it from priests dizzy from too much wine and burned incense.

The monstrance was not as scary as it sound. If the word gives you the heebie-jeebies, then call it an ostensorium. By any other name it was quite beautiful. The body was made of white gold. Precious gems dotted its form. Streamers of solid gold radiated from the round glass encased center. A single communion wafer rested there in a lunette. Rumor (or faith) has it that some time in the middle of the thirteenth century Saint Clare repulsed a group of heathens by showing them a monstrance. She would have held on to it with a cloth since only priests (men) were allowed to touch it barehanded.

Way off the subject, but interesting to note, on her deathbed Clare could "see" midnight mass being celebrated in spite of the fact that there were several walls in the way. For that reason Pope Pius XII made her the patron saint of television!

[19] Jesus Christ is credited with instituting confession as well as all the other sacraments (All seven will be discoursed upon at one point or another in this pulchritudinous tome.). The sacraments were a collection of rites, which gave Catholics yet another reason to feel superior to the other, less Christ-like, heretic, copycat Christians.

This is how confession worked: A priest sat in a closet. (That is like so ironic, isn't it?) To his left and right there were two adjacent closets, which, instead of doors, had heavy soundproof (Yeah. Right.) curtains. Since it could be tiresome to listen to the same old boring sins all Saturday afternoon, the priest sat on a chair. The penitents knelt facing the priest's ear. It would make for good, flippant fun to say sinners would eye the priest's ear. Fact of the matter was, the priest and penitent could not see each other until the priest opened a small, eye-level, screened door.

Sinners ratted on themselves, received their punishment, and occasionally a sermon, and then split. Saint Michael's, as well as many other churches open for business after the invention of electricity, had buttons installed under the kneelers which activated a red light over the confessional indicating to anyone under the age of 75 that someone already had a confession rolling in that booth.

[20] Explaining it now would interrupt the narrative. Bwaaah ha ha ha ha ha ha ha ha!

[21] If Peter had truly committed a mortal sin, then he was obligated to search for forgiveness in the confessional. A sincere act of contrition would take care of cheesy venial sins, but murder, rape and not donating enough money to the Church were crimes against God that needed to be forgiven by a priest.

Just as charm and social position would most likely get a hoity-toity kid into a better school, every soul must be in a "state of grace" to gain access to Heaven. On the practical side, maybe sin makes a soul heavy and would drag it down through the clouds into Hell. Hell, everybody certainly feels better, lighter, when they get something off their chests. Who knows?

It may be helpful to forget about all the different types of grace the Church made available (Actual grace, efficacious grace, justifying grace, sacramental grace, sanctifying grace and sufficient grace) and simply concentrate on regular old "grace" grace. God was picky but not that picky when people came knock, knock, knockin' on Heaven's door.

An absolute prerequisite for admission to Heaven was that the soul be clean when the body died. That is, in a state of grace. Ah ha! The smart Alecs say. Then I can steal murder and commit all the adultery I want until I get old. Then just go to confession and remain sinless until death. Many of those transgressors are burning in Hell right now.

During life, the soul must be clean all the time because people can die any second. Few people have the time or presence of mind to gasp out a sincere act of contrition while bleeding to death after being run over by a truck. Additionally, a little minor or "venial" sin, a slight soul stain (quarrelling with ones brothers or sisters) did not dictate a ticket to Hell, a layover in Purgatory was likely. After all, would it be fair to expect some spiffy, holier than thou soul to spend eternity with some filthy, smelly, riff-raff trailer trash soul?

[22] Only God can forgive sins. But, since God is God, He can go about it any damn way He pleases and that is how a priest had the power to absolve sins. Jesus reportedly gave his twelve apostles the original means to forgive sins. "Whatever you say goes." is a paraphrase of his orders to the apostles, who, by lucky coincidence, were also the first priests and the first men to interpret His words.

[23] Many people, hearing of the Father the Son and the Holy Spirit, assume that Catholics believed in three Gods. Wrong. The Father, the Son and the Holy Spirit comprise the Trinity. Three Gods in one was/were not correct either.

Around 200 A.D. some wise guy came up with the idea and decided everybody had to believe that each of these "God-heads" was separate, unique and equal but still floated around in the same being. In spite of that, the Father was not the Son and the Son was not the Father or the Holy Spirit. Since they/it was/were God/Gods they couldn't very well be human. Except Jesus who was a man, or "the Word Made Flesh" who came down to Earth to be crucified. He, Jesus, was no less or more than the other segments of the Trinity because of His stint in a body. Even though His body joined His Spirit before His final ascent into Heaven. That is right. Body and soul in Heaven. Up there. In the sky.

God, probably the Father, appeared to Moses as a Burning Bush in the Bible. Early Christians report that the Holy Ghost (Yes that is the same Guy as the Holy Spirit.) appeared as a White Birdie or a tongue shaped flame above people's heads and inspired them. Inspired? Spirit? Get it? Does that make either one/two of them more or less equal to one or the other two/one? No. Not when one is sodden with faith, or, a pitcher of margaritas.

This whole theological shebang, the Trinity, was a "supernatural mystery" that nobody was ever expected to understand. That includes faith-blinded believers as well as the guys who made the whole thing up. No one was ever supposed to understand it EVEN when they got to Heaven. Now <u>that</u> is a mystery.

It is important to remember that many of the first Christians were often educated, converted Jews, Greeks or Romans who had nothing better to do with their time than sit around and dream up theologies just as confusing as the ones they had recently abandoned.

Before receiving his First Holy communion, the Church required that Peter acquire a rudimentary understanding of its beliefs including the Trinity. The Trinity got top billing on the marquee of beliefs because it was so unexplainable. Since Jesus rose from the dead, he would be an "also starring." However, the feature presentation was called Communion. That involved eating a wafer that was Christ's body and blood. Really.

Thank the Jews for this peculiar, cannibalistic commemoration of Christ's Last Supper. That meal celebrated Passover, an ancient Jewish feast (Jesus was born a Jew.) that started in the Middle East several thousand years ago.

God supposedly told Moses to tell the Jews to butcher a lamb, smear the blood around the door and eat the lamb. That night the Angel of Death flew through the ancient Egyptian city where the Jews were being oppressed, and slaughtered the first-born child in every house that did not have blood on the front door. Conveniently, no one told the Egyptians.

Christians later called Jesus "The Lamb of God" because he sacrificed Himself on the cross for their sins.

How about that?

In a nutshell, Communion was food for the soul. Evidently high in fiber, it also cleaned out any venial sins that collected along the soul's bowels. The priest recited a blessing, which, because he used "supernatural power" got Jesus Christ literally, personally to enter the host/wafer/bread. After this act of "transubstantiation" although the bread (Styrofoam) still looked like bread, smelled like bread (dust) and tasted like bread (the priest's fingernails), it was, in fact, Jesus.

"God maintained the appearance of the bread looking like bread to enable people to eat the flesh of Christ without difficulty." It would be more than a little creepy, disrespectful and rude to be in church, walk up to Christ and bite off a hand or ear, or even an eyebrow for that matter. Transubstantiation also afforded the Living Savior the ability to be transubstantiating in innumerable locations simultaneously.

Christ was self-contained in every crumb of every host. As a result, the priest had to be careful not to drop any on the floor or people would be stepping on Jesus until the next time somebody vacuumed the sanctuary. Then all those microscopic Christs would end up in the trash.

Obviously, no one with a mortal sin on his or her soul could receive communion. That is why there was confession. Oh, sure they could waltz up to the priest all-innocent and act as if they were in a state of grace. They would be fooling only themselves as they smeared upon their souls yet another mortal sin. This time, the sin of sacrilege. Hopefully they did not get run over by a truck and die after leaving church that day.

People fasted from normal food for one hour before communion. It might be that Jesus did not mix well with oatmeal, eggs or pancakes. Water was okay anytime. Fasting was not necessary if someone was in danger of death. Not even the Church expected a dying person to lie there staring at their watch hoping they did not kick for another seventeen minutes.

Fasting could also be set aside in the event that the communion host needed to be saved from insult or injury. A good example, discussed in every second-grade First Communion class, was this: Suppose a bunch of atheists or angry apostates broke in during services. The priest could ask the nun playing the organ to help him hurry up and eat the wafers to keep the atheists from playing tiddly-winks with the hosts. The nun could do that even though she just ate a candy bar between songs.

This original "soul food" was not to be an object of gluttony either. It was verboten to receive communion more than once on the same day. The exceptions were someone who received at Christmas or Easter midnight mass, or, again, someone nearly dead. Because, for the most part, it took a day to digest this "Body of Christ."

Occasionally the priest consecrated too many hosts and there were a few leftovers. It would be silly to expect the priest to yell out in the middle of services "Who's hungry for Jesus?" just so he could get a head count and know exactly how many to parcel out and transubstantiate. In the event of large quantities of extra Jesuses, the priest put leftovers in a ciborium. The ciborium looked just like a chalice but had an airtight lid that fit snugly on top to keep these extra "Jesuses-in-bread form" fresh until the next communion.

A final note on communion: The Church obligated people to receive it once a year, following a recent confession, during a forty-day period around Easter. Catholics who failed to perform this "Easter Duty" not only committed a mortal sin but also were excommunicated! That meant they lost Church rights but sustained obligations.

[24] They were separated because one never knew when a couple of second-graders might burst into spontaneous sexual intercourse.

[25] Children who eventually grew up to run factories that paid workers a buck or two an hour to build computers for an American company that was the first to be worth one-trillion dollars. Prayers are funny that way.

[26] Fent later, though fortunately early in life, would die from heartily inhaling a line of powdered sugar a "friend" would tell him was killer cocaine.

[27] For instance, was Saint Stephen, his near naked body porcupined with heathen arrows, gazing heavenward in expectation and awe of the love of God? Or was he feeling a little woozy too?

[28] To "say" mass is an antiquated term. Vatican II's marketing campaign replaced the common phrase with "celebrate" mass. The idea being that instead of the priest (Whose title was switched to "celebrant.") saying/mumbling the Latin to himself and the altar boys, he would instead "celebrate" it with the congregation. Who, nonetheless, by a fifty-per cent margin, would still fall asleep.

[29] This was heresy. Diane was a girl. Girls were not allowed to assist the priest at Mass as altar boys or to become priests. Peter only knew Diane was capable, competent and available. For Peter it was the only thing to do. The Church taught that women were exalted by not attaining positions of prominence, because humble subservience would make them closer to Christ. Taking that thinking one step further, who knows what kind of wacky theology a bunch of educated women in charge would have introduced!?

[30] A solemn high mass was sung with a choir and, at the altar, a minimum of five bodies: three priests and at least two altar boys. A regular high mass was also sung but required one priest and a minimum of two altar boys. Sometimes Peter would draft a few of his little brothers or sisters, letting all the stops out for a mass with four altar boys. But the little ones inevitably started to fidget and quarrel with each other. That threatened the solemnity as well as Peter's insistence for straight rows.

[31] One priest. No altar boy was needed. No singing. Does not even deserve regular quote marks.

[32] More details on particular vestments are available in a later chapter. To put them in now would once again-tee hee, giggle, giggle-distract from the rhythm of the narr-Aaaaaahahahhahahaha-the narrative.

[33] Jesus and His Mom were the only people ever born without the stain of Original Sin. When Mary died, she floated body and soul up into Heaven. Then she started appearing to people. That's right. After she died. "Adoration in the Grotto" was the children's reenactment of these apparitions of the Virgin Mary

More than 300 years after Mary floated off into the stratosphere, she appeared in a dream of a rich Roman. The guy told the pope about it and the pope replied, "I had the same dream and she told me to build a church in her honor too!" They went to the spot their dream gal designated and there, in the middle of August, was a patch of snow on the hillside. And you thought impossible snow only appeared in Hell! The outline of the snow patch was in the shape of a church. Mary knew that tacking a blueprint to a tree would not be very miraculous. To this day The Basilica of Santa Maria Maggiore stands on the site.

Usually Mary appeared to poor, uneducated people somewhere out in Bumfuck. One instance in Guadalupe, Mexico involved an Aztec Indian named Juan Diego who found her floating (most likely vertically) by the side of the road. She told Juan to hustle the local bishop for a church in her honor. The bishop was not disbelieving but asked if maybe, considering the poverty level of the surrounding area, could Juan provide a little proof before he poured his pesos into a church? Long story short, Mary loaded up Juan's poncho with flowers. Juan drops it open for the bishop. The flowers drop out, but there is also a pretty impressive picture of Mary on the poncho. That sold the bishop. The practical side of this was that the church gained six million Aztec converts. Although considering how the Conquistadors were fond of slaughtering heathen Aztecs, the converts had little to lose and their lives to gain.

In spite of wondrous events and miracles included in such Mary Happenings, the Church often seemed overly cautious to lend its endorsement. There was reason to be slow on the draw. More than 150 phony Marys popped up following the Virgin's appearance at Lourdes in France. This was typical. Examples of shyster sightings abound such as Magdelaine of the Cross.

Magdelaine had an impressive habit of levitating while praying. She could tell the future and heal sick people. There you go. Obviously, Magdelaine was a saint. Not so fast. On her deathbed, she confessed that as a child she had made a pact with Satan! This was a tough but appreciated lesson for the Church to learn. You never knew when somebody's vision of "Mary" was simply the Devil in drag. The few who received the endorsement of the Church survived because the apparitionees' stories were consistent even following constant grilling by a short-tempered guy who looked like Vincent Price.

The Church preferred to wait until long after the visions had ceased-usually decades- before rendering a decision. That was just in case God popped into the pope's study and told him definitively, one way or the other, whether or not the visions were real. Imagine the infallible pope's humiliation if he had guessed wrong! Also, the longer they waited the better the chance of uncovering some type of devil deal.

[34] If the discussion were about the pose of the pop singer Madonna, the subject would wear a tasselled, conical-shaped bra and lie flat on her back, legs spread wide in front of several thousand people. There. Are we happy that we got that out of our systems? Actually, the author should not be so snobby. The Madonna pose consists of the Blessed Mother Mary holding the Baby Jesus. The author misuses the word Madonna here only to allow himself to chastise the reader for a sad joke that he, the author, insists on including.

[35] Middle aged women-no, make that women in the Middle Ages, used to wrap their heads in rags because they though it made them look classy. In The Sound of Music, Maria, who was "not an asset to the Aaaabey" used to wear curlers under hers.

[36] For the lecherous reader, the three never faced the dilemma of repeating their "Adoration of the Virgin" and its new "twist" because the grotto and the surrounding woods were bulldozed for a fancy new subdivision.

[37] Fallen away" Catholics were those who were derelict in receiving the sacraments and so would fall all the way into Hell when they died. The term originated when Lucifer, who originally was a big shot angel, had a turf war with God. Lucifer and his gang 'fell' from Heaven to Hell, hence, the whole etymology of falling from grace. As a snide side note, while many promise the perfect bliss of life after death in Heaven, no religion has ever addressed the issue of what would happen if another Lucifer shows up.

[38] Plenty of marquee saints were big time sinners prior to seeing the light (Or as in this case, running out of steam.). Saint Augustine whored around plenty with both men and women, and sired a child out of wedlock. Contemporary thinking may lead one to ask, "Yeah, so what?" When he was older and all poontanged out, Augustine became a bishop and one of the most influential theologians of The Church. He invented the idea that sexual desire is always bad and intercourse was only for married people and only to make babies. This Bishop of Hippo also came up with the notion of Original Sin (See page 1.). As the reader will read later, Peter's thinking took a U-turn at St. Augustine.

[39] Please remove your mind from the gutter.

[40] I said, get your mind out of the gutter.

[41] All right everybody. Into the gutter!

[42] An international charity, run by the Vatican that collected money for the maintenance of The Church. This is such a HUGE irony, considering what happens between these dust jackets.

[43] Blessed John Dun Scotus (1266? -1308? These dates are questionable. All that is known for certain is that he *was* born, and by now is most likely dead.) lived in Scotland, but also spent time in Ireland and England. The theologian and philosopher's backhanded nickname "The Subtle Doctor" was given because his writings were so complicated nobody knew what the hell he was talking about. Quite an accomplishment for a person whose childhood nickname was "Peabrain." That all changed when the Virgin Mary appeared to him and raised his I.Q. by several decades. He reciprocated by convincing The Church that Mary was so holy she was the only human born without the stain of Original Sin. (Jesus was a hybrid: half man, half God). Scotus represents the theologically formative years of The Church when every educated, well-read believer contributed to the development of Church doctrine. Every Tom, Dick and Harry (No gerlz aloud.) had a hand in it or, if they did not have a hand, they could get the ear of someone who had a hand, or, err, uh, an ear.

[44] Your own, not his.

[45] It was not until some thirty years later when a class action suit showed up on his retirement doorstep that Kirk realized he might have been imposing his desires a wee bit.

[46] Sniff. Sniff. Anyone smell hubris?

[47] This includes those ordained after the switch to English.

[48] Patron saint of seminarians, he had a speech impediment while still alive. Hopefully it was cured in Heaven or he could have held up the line at Saint Peter's Gate for eternity.

[49] This type of thinking made him an unflappable attorney after he left the priesthood in another fifteen years.

[50] Before Vincent's fate is revealed, those who experience satisfaction when dill weeds come to a violent end will be interested to hear what happened to Charlton.

After the Vincent incident, the cad was faced, or rather not faced, with the whispering abandonment of his troops. All the smirking and quickly changed expressions drove Charlton into a deep dark funk.

"Queer as a…" "…always grabbing somebody's…" Charlton heard as he walked in on conversations. Smirks would greet him now instead of the expected groveling, butt-kissing. Yep, a little pull or three on someone else's wank took the lead out of old Charlton's pencil. He had gotten quite accomplished at writing his favorite script: fear. Now everything was different.

Not that he gave a rat's ass. He became sullen. So what. Who needs these twerps. His silence ended up working to his advantage. His father, who had forced him into the seminary in the hopes it would take the kid down a notch or two, mistook Charlton's bottled up rage for some type of acquired depth or sensitivity. What a hoot!

Pops yanked his sire out of the seminary and put him in a famous, highly litigious prep school in Ipswich, Massachusetts. Charlton had learned a lesson in the seminary, all right. Keep your yap zipped, don't try to explain anything, and you can get anything you want from the old fart.

Eventually, Charlton lived the high life on his inherited fortune. At the age of fifty-two Charlton was gunned down in what the media reported as a senseless random shooting. He was at the peak of his economic success as the principle shareholder of a chain of 1,500 radio stations. A week after his funeral his wife married the pool cleaner. Let us not say she squandered the money. Let us just say she spent it all. No problem. She sold the radio stations. What remains exceptional about that is she only entertained buyers who promised in writing not to sell the station to a radio station conglomerate. If not for her ingenious generosity, three companies would own all the radio stations in the United States.

[51] The relic cost 12-thousand dollars. (Or as people who call themselves professional journalists would write $12-thousand.) That was a lot of moolah back in 1902 one year before the seminary opened. It was against church law to buy or sell relics. Bishop Giuseppe Cinqueterre, the seminary's first prefect (boss) stumbled upon it in Padua, Italy. He did not know about the rule and the Paduan monsignor who sold him the saintly contraband was not about to bring that rule to Cinqueterre's attention.

[52] The only other way would be to be dead and run into the saint in Heaven.

[53] These much smaller more intimate altars were not built to include the congregation. The rows of pews faced the main altar and so were perpendicular to the side altars. If a worshiper were hell-bent on following the mini-service, they would invariably wind up with a stiff neck.

What made these dinky altars distinguishable or potentially interesting was that instead of containing the oh so typical replica of the Slaughtered Son plastered to their rear walls, they featured shrines to various saints or the Virgin in one of her many regal and eternally innocent guises.

The side altars also served a practical necessity. There were a lot of priests at Duns Scotus and they all said mass every day. Can't have them squabbling to be the one on the dominant holy table. It is not like dibs on the mesa grande made a fellow any closer to God.

[54] The sacristy of a Catholic church was similar to the backstage area of a theater. That is where the priests and altar boys changed into formal prayer gear. The priest's area usually occupied the stage left side of the sanctuary with the altar boys holing up on the right side. In most churches, the sacristy was just immediately adjacent to the altar area. In larger cathedrals, such as Saint Peter's in The Vatican, it was a good five-minute or more trek from the altar to the dressing room.

[55] A cabinet or gold box acted as a miniscule garage where they parked extra hosts that had already been consecrated. It was usually on a pedestal directly behind the altar. What happens to the "Body of Christ" overnight was a mystery of faith. Because the hosts could be brought out even as soon as the next mass and served up for a hearty communion, proving perhaps, that Jesus keeps. Is he somehow taken out of the host and then re-introduced during the next transubstantiation? That is a tough call. In addition, what about all those fresh hosts still sitting in their shipping boxes in the sacristy? It is not as if they were stored in lead.

[56] Ergo, all priests are superior to all nonordained men and, of course, all women. All proselytizing Christians seem to suffer from this blind spot in their vision of The Truth. Other than the occasional, "I'm not perfect, just saved." bumper sticker that shows up every so often, they fail to realize that if it is better to be a Christian-because that is the only way to gain access to Heaven-then all other beliefs are inferior. This might be considered ironic, since Christ taught that the "meek and humble of heart" shall see God.

[57] The thief who hung on a cross next to the crucified Christ who asked Him if he could go to Heaven. Jesus told Dismas "On this day you shall be in Heaven with me." This should rankle Christians because the crucifixion took place on Good Friday and the Son of God did not make it to Heaven until two days later on the first Easter Sunday when He turned into a chocolate rabbit, climbed into a little basket, surrounded himself with jellybeans and cream eggs, and hid under the beds of the apostles. Just kidding. He rose from the dead and went into outer space. It is difficult to know for certain where exactly He went, since only the dead are allowed in Heaven and, as everyone knows, they tell no tales. For the same reason it is unknown if Dismas rotted for two days on the cross or was buried and took the same bus Jesus did on Sunday, or, if he got to Heaven on Friday before Him. Some know-it-all Christian scholar should look into this.

[58] Cheese! Not even a space heater.

[59] No one has ever explained how a pope commissioning a monstrous marble statue of himself and plunking it down inside Saint Peter's glorifies God.

[60] Did angels have genitalia? Tons of pin-sized penises are depicted (and that's a lot of peni!), but no depicted angel ever had a vagina. Depicted angelic genitals were always male and they always sported tiny little Vienna Sausages, as opposed to the New York Deli Salami. Therefore, if an angel did have sex, it would probably be homosexual and not very satisfying, although it would most likely rarely be painful.

[61] Anyone noticing similarities among Catholic leaders, royal families and the former Soviet Union has been paying attention.

[62] There is no North Lyon, East Lyon, West Lyon or Lyon in any direction relative to South Lyon anywhere in Michigan. When visiting, take care not to refer to it as South Lyons. Locals get miffed with a plural version of their town's name, though many of them make the same slip themselves. Check the web page.

[63] A man with a deformity or amputation, which would hinder his priestly duties, could not be a priest. The blind, deaf and epileptics would be shown the back door too. Although, it is rumored, that Pope Pius IX, the guy who on July 18, 1870 decided that he and his successors were infallible, was not only epileptic, but also insane. Since they never did autopsies on a dead pope, it should be easy to understand how no one is capable of even suggesting an examination of a live one.

Doctors could not be priests and continue to practice medicine. On the other side of the coin, murderers and abortionists would be directed to another career. Cynics would find it understandable why they would not allow elected officials to sign up for the priesthood.

[64] This is how it supposedly started. Jesus laid his hands on the apostles heads. The apostles laid their hands on their disciples' heads. Then each successive generation laid their hands on the heads of those all the way down the line to Logan's hands on Peter's head.

The Church insisted that gave it the right to claim a direct physical link between Jesus and a priest being ordained twenty centuries later. Following that logic, that means there is also a direct physical link between Jesus and anyone who touches a priest such as a heretic minister administrating a friendly handshake. Photos exist of Pope Pius XII shaking hands with Hitler as well as Mussolini. Did he wash his hands thoroughly following these encounters? We may never know. Following this logic, six people are the only thing between you and a relationship with Kevin Bacon.

Now we can understand why, in spite of all the efforts and hoopla surrounding the effort to rejoin the various heresies back with The One True Holy Catholic and Apostolic Church,

275

negotiations would stalemate when The Church maintained non-Catholic ministers would not be allowed to perform the sacred sacraments unless they were ordained. The ministers were not about to get ordained. They figured they were sacred enough. Also, who the Hell did the church think it was?

The Church's obstinate attitude is defensible. Many non-Catholic ministers not only did not receive Holy Orders, they never went through any ritual at all. They just hung up a shingle, said "I'm your preacher," and went about the business of saving souls and running people's lives. These non-Catholic heretics answered to no one. They vowed nothing, let alone poverty, obedience or chastity. The idea that moneymaking ministers of the twentieth century, such as Pat Robertson or Jim Bakker would consider a vow of poverty is absolutely laughable.

[65] The bald spot which spread a bit wider than the crown of his head was not natural. It was a result of an earlier tonsure ceremony, which made Peter a cleric. Peter was most likely one of the last to get this full-tilt hair whack. The practice was dying out just as Vatican II banned it.

Because it was a sign of meekness, Peter was inclined to go overboard. In a private little ceremony, Peter's superior snipped little tidbits of hair from the front, back, sides and top. Just enough to make it look like a bad haircut. Later that day, Peter went to the seminary barber to have the more radical procedure performed. The ceremony had passed down through the centuries from various brands of priests. Priests who made every effort to show off their humbleness. Perhaps they figured their chrome domes made it easier for God to spot them from way up there in the clouds.

[66] What? Two obedience promises? Yes. Though technically one is a promise and the other a vow.

Peter made a promise of obedience to his order: The Eustachians (Named after Saint Eustatia, the patron saint of good listeners.). An order is sort of a brand of priest. Priests not belonging to an order were called Diocesan. A Diocesan was a generic priest who reported directly to his bishop. The bishop would tell the priest where to go and what to do and settle stuff like border disputes. Order priests reported first to their order. Not that they would ever make flicking gestures from their noses at the bishop, because they had made a vow of obedience in his presence.

The religious orders specialized in running hospitals, orphanages and foreign missions.

[67] However, it is a fact that Peter was consecrated. Several witnesses on record not only say so but have also written successful books on the subject. After Peter became pope and caused the big brouhaha, there were accusations that his papacy was not legitimate because he was not a consecrated priest when he was made pope.

[68] The oil was a combination of olive oil and balm. Catholics loved to rub holy oil all over everything. It was not enough to make the sign of the cross or spritz holy water, or waft some incense over something to bless it. They rubbed or dripped chrism, as it was called, when consecrating churches or altars, chalices and church bells. Holy water was more than just water, by the way. They dripped a bit of chrism into it.

[69] The ranks of Catholic priests were steadily thinning at the time. The hierarchy was stuck in a rut at a fork in the disciple distribution road. Should they cater to the white, moneyed literate Americans and assure their own survival? Or go with the traditional mission: spreading the gospel to God's less fortunate children?

[70] His hand had healed quickly, by the way.

[71] Following his encounter with Father Kirk in the seminary, Peter's vocabulary rarely extended beyond: yes; no; thank you; you are welcome and let us pray.

[72] The Merdette's tongue did not stop with the mouth. It combined words and grunts with slaps to various parts of the speaker's head and body and included plenty of eye rolling and winking.

[73] The gourds contained a pulp the Merdettes considered precious. After the skin of the vegetable had dried sufficiently, it was peeled away to reveal its mustard colored innards. This meat was sliced into even rings and sun-dried, then eaten like chips. That and the coconuts, a few odd berries and the occasional dead fish that

would show up on the beach, were the sum total of what was available on the Merdette menu.

The gourds needed much tender, loving care to grow to their full size. Drying them was an art and iffy work with the wet weather. The preparation was left to a few skilled experts. The seeds were carefully horded and planted in the best spots. The Merdettes were fanatical about the maintenance of their gourds, since a bad crop could mean the end of civilization.

[74] The Merdettes had never in their entire history had an elected leader. They could never agree on whom it should be, let alone why he or she should be chosen or what they should be called.

[75] There were quite a few potential Catholic martyrs who spent their few remaining hours pacing their cells wondering if hanging on to a belief in God was really all that necessary. Others cowered in a corner, weeping and gnashing their teeth, as they considered recanting their belief in the Savior and in the process saving their own hide. "Jesus already died, so, then, why should I? Isn't waste a sin?" They may well have reasoned.

Others would be on their knees with head bowed in prayer. Prayers for forgiveness of their tormentors, prayers that they themselves be forgiven their own transgressions, prayers that someone will think to take care of their cat, now that they are dead. These are all possibilities.

[76] Coincidently, English and Merdettian have one word in common. It is "yowsa."

[77] Known for its oddly-hued yellow waterfalls.

[78] If sexual intercourse is what is considered sex, then Peter was not having sex. That was yet to come and so was he.

[79] In her book "No Big...Woops!" co-written by William O'Riley, Ys (wiggle index fingers) initially denies that the incident was a defining moment that determined her expectations from men. It was only after moving to the United States, joining then quickly leaving the Republican party and then twelve years of therapy she confessed that Peter was the yardstick (tee hee) by which she measured other men.

[80] The literal translation of the phrase "parting a grass skirt" in Merdette is "mowing the lawn."

[81] Out of the 345 distinctively styled Grumman Geese built between 1937 and 1945, this was one of six still flying. Er…make that five.

[82] Though scientists have studied the mystery of the disappearance of the stink extensively, the best they can come up with is the addition of communion wafers to the Merdettes' meager diet. Since they were in abundance, many ate them like candy.

[83] i.e. big and dumb.

[84] Fat chance of that. Roger ate only vegetables, primarily the gourd, and no meat and a meager amount of fish. As a result, he was ingesting next to zero cholesterol. It is funny that to this day doctors give patients diagnosed with high cholesterol, a pamphlet containing eating tips that are written by a drug company. Tips include: "cut down to one or two servings of beef per week. Instead eat chicken, veal or fish." First off, a "serving" of beef for a human is seven or eight ounces. That is two or three servings for a dietician. Second, eating fifteen erroneous servings of chicken is just as bad as over-doing it on the beef. Instead, what would happen if the drug company literature suggested that the patient strive to eat foods with a 0% cholesterol level on the nutrition label? Oops. Then nobody would need the cholesterol-lowering drug!

[85] "Say Aye" in the local lingo means "Throw sand at me, please."

[86] The K.G.B. assumed that stragglers were alive because they gave troop information to the Germans. Think about that. Hundreds of thousands of assumed, unproven informants.

[87] Cszt was one of many bureaucrats who managed to hang on to positions both during communist rule and later after "democratic" reforms.

[88] Which is really cold in English!

[89] Sure. Go ahead. Call him a ground crew member.

[90] They did really have straws. It was in abundance on the floor of the plane. A result of certain passengers being small barnyard animals.

[91] Here the author is being both ironic and verbose. However, this is the type of creative thinking that/which wins awards. Editor please fix that/which can never remember which is that xoxo AlSo

[92] Good idea not to carry breakables when flying Aeroflot.

[93] Oddly, standard EXIT signs were everywhere. Sometimes they did mark an exit.

[94] The new Russian Commonwealth (Ha, ha, ha, ha. Now that is funny! Commonwealth. Get it? Common WEALTH?) had yet to invent a new logo.

[95] The author went into a week-long depression after writing this sentence as it occurred to him that much of the readership under a certain age would have no idea what that was. In the middle of the last century, believe it or not, when people were sick, doctors would make what were known as "house calls." The little black bag contained a stethoscope, aspirin, bandages and the right drugs for the occasion.  This was a long time ago, before there were advertisements exhorting people to tell their doctors (in their offices) to give them certain drugs.

[96] When Roman Catholics made the "sign of the cross," they traced a diagram of Christ's crucifixion cross over their chests. Using their right hands, they would say "In the name of the …" and time it so they touch their forehead for "Father." Head south to between the boobies for "and of the Son. And of the…" "Holy" is on schedule for the left shoulder with "Spirit" or the antiquated "Ghost" on the right shoulder. Hands meet in prayerful respect for the "Amen."
	For someone trying to score big with God, this was no touchdown, but it was easily good for an extra point. Especially the way Peter used it as a sort of antidote against the poisonous

disrespect of the atheist customs guard. The sign of the cross was also used to begin and end prayers. It was a way to get God's attention and then to let him know the pray-er was signing off and the frequency was clear.

The sign of the cross is the reverse of a "blessing." Ordained guys, using the same forehead, breastbone, left shoulder, right shoulder format, would "apply" the blessing to a large group of people. The blessing hand was held out away from the body so they would not actually touch themselves. The higher in the pecking order the better the blessing for the receiver. The special pope's blessing equals a two-point conversion. A pope would blow off the head and shoulders routine and simply trace three little crosses in the air in the general direction of the "blessing" recipients. The dinkier and more casual the effort the cooler the pope. On the other hand, it could mean he was exhausted from being infallible, had very little gas left, and was going to die soon.

That said, the Russian Orthodox (A half-assed Russian version of the Roman Catholic Church, the R.O.s tolerated a revolving door policy with the various Soviet dictators. Sometimes they did what the pope said and sometimes they did not.) and Easter Orthodox and the Coptics (See an encyclopedia. Oops. Another dated reference. An encyclopedia is like Wikipedia but made out of paper.) reversed the shoulder-to-shoulder portion to right to left because they had the Holy Ghost part backwards. Thus the customs official, who had never seen a Roman Catholic bless himself, had reason for suspicion.

An interesting side note: With all his hopes for riches from Rome, Cszt had his fingers crossed. This gesture has two meanings. One is to indicate hope and I do not know how that got started. The other is to cover for a lie. The later is an old Christian custom said to have begun during the Roman oppression. When early Christians felt the need to make the sign of the cross but could not, for fear of becoming lion kibble, they would simply cross their fingers. Upon interrogation, when asked, "Are you a Christian?" to keep from getting a lance up the rectum, they could lie while they had their fingers crossed and it would not really be a lie. At least that was the rumor in Catholic grade school.

[97] Interesting to note that one of Peter's predecessors, Pope Innocent IX, caught a cold and died from it less than two months after he was crowned in 1591.

[98] From this point, please assume that Berkeley speaks Russian to Cszt and other Russians, and then translates into English for Peter what he or the Russians have said. In addition, perhaps obviously to some, the author freely translates or interprets items that are labeled, printed or posted in Russian.

[99] In Cszt's defense, the Russian people will always respond to questions regardless of whether or not they actually know the answer. It is their way of being helpful. It is similar to New England, where if you ask someone for directions they will tell you how to get there even if they have never heard of your destination. The comparison remains consistent in that both Russians and New Englanders give answers so complicated or convoluted that the inquirer is no better or worse off than prior to the inquiry.

[100] Peter was almost correct. Those pipes carried heat. However, they were miles away from the furnace. In Magadan, as in all Russian cities larger than a certain size, the city provides the heat from a central coal/steam-producing furnace. Scary, ain't it? Here is what can and did happen. In the late nineties, the system simply died through a combination of shoddy construction, poor maintenance, a coal shortage, bureaucratic squabbling, and pissed-off workers who had not been paid in over one year! The continued devaluation of the ruble meant that if they ever did get back-wages they would be worth one-third the value had they been paid when due. Common sense prevailed. While the workers could stay warm by burning coal at the heat plant, their families and extended families were quite miserable at home. The workers eventually fixed the furnace.

[101] This abandoned commie H.Q, the largest piss-pot in Magadan, had never been occupied during the decade and a half of its existence. Workers walked away from the project several months before it was supposed to have been completed in 1991 because the Soviets stopped sending money. At least nobody died during its construction. Unlike a certain one hundred mile long White Sea/Baltic Canal built on the whim of Uncle Joe Stalin at the cost of one hundred thousand lives. It was not until it was finished that the inaugural ship's captain realized the canal WAS TOO SHALLOW FOR SEA-GOING VESSELS!

Any man will immediately grasp the inspiration for the shape of the Magadan building's design. If a person were to hover over the building in a helicopter, facing the front, he would quickly realize that he is looking at a thirteen-story replica of a urinal. Including a statue of Lenin where the drain would be! Yuri Plepov, the architect, found his inspiration while relieving himself. He waited and waited and waited for a safe opportunity to express both his structural fancy and feelings about communism. He nearly peed his pants with excitement upon receipt of the commission to design the Communist Party Headquarters building in Magadan: an area where there were no sophisticated upper party members but where he assumed, (correctly) the crowd of banished dissenters might have a last laugh.

[102] Former Communist Youth Party members, who discovered a ton of unsupervised time after the Party's nosedive, busted out most of the glass of the first three floors.

[103] Although there is a good chance she never actually existed, her story is fun to tell because it is loaded with gore, violence and a lack of common sense from the Big Guy upstairs, you know, Whosee?

Before he left on a long journey, St. Babs's dad locked her in a tower. Perhaps it was to protect her virtue. That was the usual reason. The Church taught that all women were sluts. This doctrine was based on the bitter sexual rejection of someone important historically, or maybe, sour grapes.

Perhaps to disprove the slut theory, St. Babs did not use this "time out" as most good girls would. (To examine how many orgasms a clitoris can produce and tolerate.) St. Babs instead abused this golden opportunity by finding the Lord and converting to Christianity. This was fifteen-hundred years ago, so details are sketchy.

Accepting Christ also affected her thinking about the concepts of form and function. Somehow, she punched three holes in the wall of her cell. These windows were a proclamation of her newly found belief in the Trinity (Father, Son, and Holy Birdie? Remember?) and perhaps to air the joint out a bit.

Upon his return, Bab's Dad was predictably pissed. Enough to take St. Babs to court and accept the judges' decision that he, the father, should take her, St. Babs, to a mountain top and slew her because she refused to renounce her faith or fix the wall. Though many contemporary fathers have considered as much when "Princess" trashes her room, gratefully few follow through.

St. Babs's dad did though. Reports say that God retaliated on the spot striking St. Babs's dad dead with a lightning bolt. Though crude, the holes left in the wall stood as a reminder to architects suffering from builder's block. Architects who design buildings in areas with severe winters and insist on putting parking lots a mile's walk away from the building most likely have found inspiration in the dubious tale of Saint Barbara.

[104] Another good one for Peter. St. Nick (Not the same as the jolly one.) von Flue followed a successful military career with appointments to a city council position. God had different ideas and whispered in his ear to become a hermit and survive by eating hosts. Cynics say N. von F. was simply grasping any excuse to get away from his ten children.

[105] Again, this was another ingenious choice. St. Aggie is patron saint of volcanic eruptions. Her emblem or symbol is the hook. Aggie turned down the sexual advances of a Roman emperor who, in retaliation, sliced off her breasts, roasted her, and then rolled her body over broken pottery. Enough already!

[106] Another failed venture to note. Berkeley imagined that people who supplied public restrooms would want to update their squat over hole in the floor style toilets with fancy commodes that people could sit on comfortably. ("You can read the newspaper or a book while going about your business.") The responding looks on people's faces made Berkeley realize his cache of 200 Fitz-Prizer toilets were going to go nowhere slowly.

[107] Two interesting side notes: The word sardonic has its roots in a plant grown in Sardonia. It is said that people who eat the plant laugh themselves to death

Capuchin monks invented cappuccino. They must not have consumed much of it, or else it was decaffeinated. The Capuchins were known for their austere often cloistered existence as well as the habit they had of walking around with their habit hoods up over their heads. Capuchin monkeys have more than word origins in common with Capuchin monks. Their fur

(Referring to the monkeys' here. Though this probably also applies to certain monks.) grows up over the top of their heads down to their eyebrows. The monkeys' hair sprouts up the neck to the chin. Looks for all the world like a dark, little face peaking out of a hood. The monkeys' tails grow to be as long as its body: sometimes fifteen inches. The monks have no tail.

[108] Any resemblance between the workings of the Russian government and any government anywhere else in the world is the product of hallucination. Give notice of intention to consider a new law? What should government officials do? Place an advertisement in Pravda so people would know what their "elected" officials were up to? Perhaps they should also give the pope a call on the phone just in case he did not subscribe? What? Call collect? What for? Let him take care of his own business. The Russian government knows what is best for its people. The last thing they need is some meddling Polak. Although the current pope, was German, it was quite common for former communist big shots to refer secretly to the reigning pope as "The Polak." Many historians assume, probably correctly, that making the R.O.C. the one true Russian church was to get back at Pope John Paul II (Who was Polish.) because of his involvement with the Polish Solidarity Movement. That group's activities signaled the beginning of the peaceful end for communism. And what a pain in the dupa that brought.

[109] CLUMSY METAPHOR ALERT! CLUMSY METAPHOR ALERT!

[110] Nope. Though as a baby escaping death, he may have passed by a couple hundred miles to the West.

[111] Even considering his aggressive personality, this was a very odd thing for Ahmed to do. It is considered rude to interrupt a Muslim who is praying. Could it be that Ahmed sensed Peter was not a Muslim and therefore fair game for some type of jest or uncalled for rudeness? Or, was he, like Peter, dim-witted from too much travel?

[112] This is an unfair misrepresentation of a Jordanian speaking Arabic. It looks more like a representation of an Egyptian speaking

Arabic. When Egyptians speak Arabic it sounds as if they constantly interrupt themselves-mid-word! Jordanians on the other hand speak Arabic in what is to Western ears, a very musical manner. Jordanian enunciation is a classic form of the Arabic language. Ask any Jordanian.

[113] Ahmed obviously is trying to scare Peter. The Bedouin were more concerned with making a killing in the tourist industry than with killing a possible tourist.

[114] Here Ahmed classically illustrates the outmoded use of Middle Eastern exaggerated English. Ahmed's 'limousine' though a trustworthy machine with minimal missing parts, was a generic Ford several decades old. Knowing that, it is small surprise to learn his 'resort' was a time-share one-bedroom condominium a mile from the more pricey Red Sea beachfront property.

[115] Sic

[116] Perhaps thirty seconds. That would be 'lengthy' for Peter.

[117] In between terrorists' attacks, that is.

[118] In her fourth autobiography "Touring the World's Sandtraps" Diane Gillette wrote of a harrowing drive in the streets of Cairo thusly: "Traffic signals are mere ornaments. Signs indicating 'Yield' or 'School' are decorative. The lane striping is merely a suggestion that no one takes seriously. We sat in a traffic jam six cars wide. The street was marked for four lanes. After ten minutes my driver began a conversation with a passenger in the car to his left. At one point he reached over and helped himself to a cigarette from the man's shirt pocket. That's how close we were."

[119] The Kaffiyeh is another name for the traditional cloth Middle East men wear on their heads. Certain materials and colors or patterns hold significance for some. That significance has yet to be determined decisively. The expression, "Your Kaffiyeh reminds me of my grandmother's dish towels." by the way, is meant as a compliment

[120] That is the thingy that keeps the Kaffiyeh in place. It is made out of anything from braided silk to barbed wire. Depends on the owner's disposition.

121 Pup tents of course. They owned sixty in all. "Spend the night under the stars in Lawrence of Arabia land." What a luxury for an innkeeper: pup tents, no sheets or towels to clean, no maid to hire, no Koran to steal, no soap, mouthwash or sewing kit to supply. Those items could be purchased at the kiosk of course.

[122] Mahmumed Belijer had recently viewed the Kiosk's rental copy of "E.T. The Extra-Terrestrial."

[123] Mahmumed Belijer knew his actual age was seventy-two. But figured that tourists found a spry eighty-seven year-old more interesting than a spry seventy-two year old. Mahmumed Belijer averaged fifteen years above his real age for the last twenty years. He eagerly anticipated his eightieth birthday. So he could turn 100

[124] A Bedouin term for couch potato.

[125] Peter stayed back by the horse shed. Stories from people who claim a man dressed as a priest, wearing a Roman collar, helped them mount their horses are fabrications. Peter's one and only "monkey suit" disintegrated shortly after his arrival in Jordan. He wore traditional Bedouin garb after that.

[126] What about bowling? A fair question. Peter tried to create a makeshift alley using empty oilcans for pins and a "ball" of crushed soda cans someone had welded together. All attempts ended quickly as the "ball" refused to roll in the sand. A few of the locals heaved the "ball" at the cans for a while. But quickly lost interest. What Peter did to sublimate his sex drive, other than excessive prayer, is unknown. Wisecracks about his proximity to the horse barn have, by legitimate historians, been unappreciated.

[127] The Seven Pillars of Wisdom" is also the title of the book by Lawrence of Arabia that details his 'humble' assistance in the defeat of the Ottoman Turkish Empire in The Middle East and explains how (T.E.) Lawrence put the idea into the heads of the

various Arab peoples that they should develop as nations and unify. Nice going, Larry.

[128] To this day, in spite of rave-winning culinary advances, still the safest degree to order meat cooked in the Middle East.

[129] At that time that would be Mech Amouh who was almost ninety-nine years old. For ninety-eight and a half of those years he was deathly afraid of horses and so went out of his way to avoid them. Thus his recollection of Bshht's beginnings was dubious. Amouh claimed to be traumatized because his mother gave birth to him prematurely after being severely startled by a horse. After tolerating the chiding of friends and relatives for almost ten decades, Amouh conquered his fear, and climbed on a horse. The horse threw him. Amouh died from the injuries.

[130] Many would assume that a desert tribe such as these Bedouin would simply slaughter such an inconveniencing beast. But none of the Wadi Rum Bedouin had the heart or stomach for such a task. Frankly too, the horse could be rather fierce-looking. Luckily for them when Bshht eventually died of natural causes it happened out of nose-shot in the desert. The rider abandoned the horse and hitched a ride with a pal. Legend has it the expression on the horse's face was so scary that vultures left the carcass to rot. Legend also holds that Bshht's attitude worsened after the historic event with Peter.

[131] Two had tripped on tips of as yet undiscovered pyramids, another on a Roman obelisk. All stumbled in Egypt. This would be the first reported horsey find in Jordan.

[132] As all good statue experts know, a horse posing with one hoof raised indicates that the rider has been wounded. Also, in statue terms, when both front hooves are raised, the rider is dead. Both rear hooves raised means a human is headed to the emergency ward. One rear hoof raised indicates a horse that thinks he is a male dog.

[133] Of course the Bedouin had cable TV. Just after the turn of the century the demand for it down in Wadi Rum became so severe

that the King of Jordan had service installed from Jerash along the desert highway to the Red Sea.

[134] The famed "Hollywood Madame" supplied in the flesh fantasies for movie stars. Following her conviction she served her sentence in the Santa Rita Women's Correctional Facility in Pleasanton, California. Mahmumed Belijer's dour response chastises Bechkded Amalamalak for watching a program that includes on-camera interviews with allegedly former prostitutes. By the way, Saint Rita is the saint to pray to for marital problems and desperate situations.

[135] An hectare is almost 2,500 square acres, so this is a rather large chunk of cheese being discussed.

[136] Code for "He sells trinkets to tourists."

[137] After the pyramids in Egypt, easily the most astonishing site in the Middle East. Several movies have been filmed at the former capital city of the now-dead Nabataeans including one of the Indiana Jones movies. The site is more impressive in real life than reel life.

[138] One of many confirmed comments made either by Bechkded Amalamalak or Mahmumed Belijer indicating disrespect for Muslim thinking. Muslims were extraordinarily conscientious when it came to covering up a woman's desirability. Most historians of reliable reputation assume the two were Muslim in claim only. Countless regulars at the sole mosque in Wadi Rum swear upon oaths that neither of Peter's sponsors ever attended prayers there and also that although both owned prayer rugs both rugs were "clean enough to eat off." A sure sign in Wadi Rum of never being used.

[139] Yet another indication of the lack of Muslim conviction on the part of Bechkded Amalamalak or Mahmumed Belijer is the failure of both to say "Peace be unto him" when the name of Mohammed the Prophet is mentioned, as is the tradition.

[140] Yes, that is a different spelling than previously. It can also be spelled keffiyah, kaffiye, keffiya and koffiya. Pick any of the

variants and ask your Arab friend to pronounce it for you. He will invariable put a stress on a different syllable every time he illustrates the only way to say it correctly.

[141] Named after David Letterman, a late night talk show host. Later in life, Letterman developed a small but dedicated coffee house audience reading original, sad poems about dying flowers, lonely nights and three-legged puppy dogs.

[142] Boy is _he_ selling the impact short!

[143] Hem Mahnem was most likely more concerned that the others would not drop but throw him into the hole. Such things would often happen to him in childhood. Then as he grew older it would happen to him often in adulthood. It was one reason he rarely ventured outside of Wadi Rum. Several times, as an adult, people in the big city walked up to him and for no particular reason took one look at him and threw him into a hole.

[144] Any tourist guide worth his or her salt is certified by the government. As a result the Middle East has some of the finest tour guides of anywhere in the world.

[145] Other experts say, in that special bored tone of voice so many experts employ so often when they are unable to come up with a plausible contradiction, "So what?"

[146] This statement seems to lend credence to those in support of the theory that Feta Geeaza was in cahoots with Mahmumed Belijer. They say that the particular batch of skin cream Feta Geeaza wiped from his hands onto the inscription was from a very deep, very old mineral excavation sight. Therefore the basic DNA structure of the cream, because it was from ancient times, altered the carbon dating on the inscription and that Feta Geeaza falsified it when he wiped his greasy palms on it.

[147] Mahmumed Belijer laughed much longer and harder than the narration indicates. He cackled, burbled, bubbled, screamed, chortled and choked. After almost two full minutes he came to a sore-throated, wheezy stop.

[148] Mirages.

[149] That Hakim Hakunguard could be a real card sometimes.

[150] The weakest metaphor in this book.

[151] One of the many excellent metaphors in this book.

[152] It may seem odd to many, but another reason for the de facto mayorship of Ahmahd Desantez was his large size. He stood there like a big tank, yet, like a giant statue of Buddha, was eminently approachable.

[153] Certain witnesses in cahoots with certain experts claim that Bechkded Amalamalak should have been embarrassed or at least chagrined when it was discovered he had made such a contact with Belaam Belaamin. That he instead made a certain show of himself corroborates that the surprisingly quick arrival of the Palestinians was a result of his doing. Other speculation is that Bechkded Amalamalak brokered a deal with his brother-in-law to come unarmed or be met with resistance.

[154] Idiomatic for "small world, isn't it?"

[155] You have been warned about Hakim Hakunguard. He could joke with anyone under any circumstances.

[156] Sure.

[157] It took at least two eyes to see them all. There were that many.

[158] That would be "First Homelanders' Village." The name is more impressive sounding in Arabic. It looses a lot in the translation. That area though, became the place to live because of its historic significance. Other later developments closer to the site were not as desirable a location. Later, after the international airport was built, instead of making the traditional walk from Amman (Aqaba did not count. Since it had so little to do with history.) pilgrims would land, take a taxi to First Homelanders' Village and then walk the half-mile or so to the site.

[159] Or the urge to try to beat the crowds.

[160] No understandable reason was ever given, but famous actors Alec Baldwin and Paul Ruben showed up.

[161] A local custom. Wadi Rummites considered it rude to point fingers.

[162] The actual moment, edited for broadcast shows the two Bedouin shake their heads "no", hold out their hands to Peter, and mimic his clumsy fall off Bshht the cranky horse. Their gestures become more insistent as they point to his chest. That day Peter's thobe has a closed collar. Mahmumed Belijer then bends over seizes the hem and yanks it up to Peter's chin. Yes, sure enough there is an almost healed gouge in Peter's sternum. That day Peter had gone without his sirwal (underpants). There is also Peter's impressive (even at ease) pole exposed to a quickly impressed crowd. He had chosen that of all days to wash his undies. Which were at that moment also dangling in the breeze, back in the horse shed.

[163] Again the influence of obscure cable television channels on the Middle Easterners vocabulary is obvious.

[164] Hem Mahnem refers here to a popular television program. The producers strand a group of people in a remote area and force them to eat bugs and live by their wits. Everybody loses their self-respect, but the winner-the one who wittily manipulates and deceives his fellows- receives one million dollars in compensation. It is both ironic and a coincidence how similar this it to what the Wadi Rummites were going through. Except of course the part about the million dollars.

[165] Hah!

[166] Testicles.

[167] Not much of a sign, that. The last time a Saint Peter's Square crowd booed a selection was in the Middle Ages.

[168] By the way, it was Constantine's mother, Saint Helena, who built the shrines at all the Jesus historical hot spots. Helena rolled into Palestine on her jewel encrusted caravan, and announced she wanted to see the precise spots where Jesus was born and died so that she could buy the properties and erect huge shrines there. Several real estate agents were seriously injured in the fight that ensued as they tried to sell her their differing versions of the authentic locations.

[169] It was obviously "The Pieta" by Michelangelo. This sculptured pose, (Also executed throughout the centuries by other artists.) shows Mary the Mother of Christ holding her dead Son, Jesus, just after He was taken down from the cross. Typical of Mich's curious slant on life, she appears to be staring at His crotch.

[170] The spouse of the Virgin Mary, Mother of God and the unstated patron saint of cuckolds. After all, if a woman who has never had sex with her husband becomes pregnant and claims that God is the father. Come on! The throbbing head is an obscene reference to Joseph's penis. Since the Kid who slid down his virgin wife's chute was the Son of God, it is more than likely that the carpenter would not be allowed to subsequently nail her.

[171] The pope was addressed: Most Holy Father, Holy Father or Your Holiness. By calling him "Holiness," d'Indy is being snippy with the pope. On the other hand, perhaps he was looking at Martin's threadbare sleeves.

[172] And people wondered why changes from the Vatican took so long! Everybody spent all day walking to their destinations-literally-cross-country.

[173] Acalanes was named for Saint Jerome who was also an important book jockey at the Vatican.

Like most people born almost two thousand years ago, the story of Saint Jerome is spotty. Yes. He was a Dalmatian and big with the big books. He is known for his (Spotty? tee, hee.) translation of the Bible from Greek and Hebrew into Latin. He was (Here's another coincidence.) secretary to Pope Damasus. Jerome performed his monumental task in the Fourth Century. Copies of his Vulgate, as it is known, were made by hand, since this was more than one thousand years before Gutenberg (Inventor and comic actor.) invented the printing press. Incidentally, the Vulgate was the first thing Gutenberg printed.

For two thousand years the Church relied on this "Vulgate" or, common version, as the authentic translation of the Word of God. Is it possible that the first Jerome made any mistakes? This is not just mindless conjecture. Mistakes are one of the easiest things in the world to do. Even teeny-weeny ones can have a far-reaching impact.

Consider how many hundreds of hands Saint Jerome's Vulgate went through as copies were made of it over that one thousand year period before Gutenberg showed up. Know how many hundreds of arguments Church leaders had amongst themselves about what God's Word means? Any idea how many then went on to put it in writing? Answer: Quite a few. Think any of those boys had any theological axes to grind? Think maybe they fine-tuned a Psalm here or a Letter from Saint Paul there?

Ever see that children's game where they sit in a circle? One kid whispers to the next, then that kid passes it on. By the time it comes back to the first kid's ear, it is not even close to the original statement. Apply that to history. Old history especially, is about as reliable as the least credible television reporter. Plus members of a religion are the last people on the planet capable of objective reporting.

[174] Many are of the impression that the Inquisition was just a period of mindless slaughter of people who did not want to accept Christ's salvation. In fact, most defendants, even disbelievers in an afterlife, looked forward to a bloody conclusion to the torture of their endless days in court. Anything to escape the rambling judges and clerics defending the truth (i.e. The Church's teachings.). The endless list of uncross-examined witnesses included the butcher, the baker, and as many village idiots as could be rounded up to testify to the sorcery of the accused. These were no kangaroo courts. A long drawn out process was strictly followed before the inevitable death sentence was carried out. The only thing worse than being the accused was being the court reporter.

[175] All correspondence to the Pope, or the Church in Rome, wound up in the Vatican Archives, including tons of angry missives from nuns who wanted to be priests, requests for permission to take

birth control from already burdened, non-rhythmic mothers, and other assorted whiners.

After Peter's selection, notes of congratulations dribbled in from well-wishing, name-dropping friends. Childhood chums sent hate notes about Evelene. A surprising number of acquaintances made intimate admissions.

[176] The Vatican did, but Martin's mind never made the switch to Euros.

[177] Consider the legions of art critics driven insane by Baroque excess.

[178] That is an "elastic" for those who live in The Hub of the Universe.

[179] Those cute little useless bits of human interest used to conclude a newscast. Kickers convince the audience that, in spite of another suicide bombing, a president who lies to his country, or the gunman in the bell tower, it is still a wonderful, and sometimes kooky world.

[180] The appearances on the balcony were discontinued when a sudden fit of anger erupted within him, one day, and he flipped the bird to the sheep herded below. A five-minute monologue of flatulence followed. There was no need for discussion. All silently knew then, that it would be best to keep his Holiness away from crowds.

[181] Several popes had weird eating habits. Pius XII would sit on one side of a long table. If aides joined him, they sat at the ends. If guests attended, they sat opposite the pope. Pius XII, who ate like a bird anyway, would sometimes invite people to sit and talk to him while he ate but not offer them anything.

[182] This bizarre and barbaric practice is based on the reasoning that if the dead guy does not respond to his childhood name he must really be dead. So, why not say something like "Oh, Pope? Jesus is here to talk to you." Difficult to say other than it was probably a matter of faith.

[183] Cardinals' titles come after their first name. Like Stonehenge and the Moai on Easter Island, no one has ever given a sufficient reason for it. It might be a throwback to the Really Olden Tymes when men used their occupation as a second name: Joe Fisher, Joe Baker, Joe Pickpocket, Joe Cardinal. The other church ranks do not maintain that tradition because it would sound stupid: Joe Priest Smith, Joe Monsignor Smith, Joe Pope Smith.

[184] This statement is from the New Testament of the Bible, which contains among other things, four versions of Christ's life as penned by guys named Matthew, Mark, Luke and John. The books were written sixty years after the Crucifixion. Ask the best journalist or biographer, who is not depending on notes, a tape recorder or video camera, how dependable his or her memories of a person's whole life is sixty years later. The men who had the most to gain from its interpretation approved the eventual versions. The Church leaders. Having the authorization come from the horse's mouth makes it that much more tough to argue. (i.e.: The Bible is the inspired word of God.)

[185] Which came first, the church or the reported gravesite is a "fact" still under scrutiny.

[186] Although the Church frequently declared *dogma* to be infallible-not to be confused with impeccable, infallible people are exempt from error-It did not come out and say the pope was infallible-when speaking on faith or morals-until the First Vatican Council in 1870. The Council was a rubber stamp for Pope Pius IX. The longest reigning pope figured that if 32 years in the pope chair did not make him infallible then nothing would. It would be fair to conclude that his longevity also made him an interminable interlocutor.

Pius IX (This is like sooo ironic.) was not the first pope to set aside his piety. In the late Ninth century, Pope Saint Gregory VII declared that the Bishop of Rome was supreme over the other Big Bishops who were reigning over the massive congregations in Constantinople and Africa. P.S. Greg 7 was an upstart with royalty as well saying that "Only the pope's feet are to be kissed by princes." One hundred years later, Innocent III took those two concepts a step further when he claimed the Pope's authority over all The Church and the entire world. Huh.

[187] See reference to Pope Joan in Chapter 2.

[188] The pope job description also included that of: Sovereign of the State of Vatican City; Vicar of Jesus Christ; Successor of Peter or Successor of the Chief of the Apostles; Supreme Pontiff of the Universal Church; Patriarch of the West; Primate of Italy; Cheetah of Tuscany (I made that one up.) Archbishop and metropolitan of the Roman Province; Servant of the Servants of God. People have been known to die of laughter while considering the irony of the last title.

[189] Although, centuries before the infallibility bug bit, that is precisely how popes were elected. Or a version of it. Sometimes the emperor handpicked the pope. Other times the emperor nominated the pope and the lay people and clergy in Rome voted. Remember, the pope was the Bishop of Rome.

[190] Halliburton, after all, was everywhere.

[191] The Rosary carries an interesting history that includes Lady Godiva. Yes! The naked chocolatier equestrian! The tradition of repeated prayers probably started ions before Jesus, Catholics, and maybe even the Romans and Jews too. With the early Church, it began with peasants too uneducated to read religious tracts but smart enough to memorize and repeat a paragraph or two of devotion. They could memorize a prayer they heard, but not count.

Jesus had directed his followers to often say His prayer, "The Lord's Prayer," known colloquially as the "Our Father." Having never defined "often" a practice evolved of saying it 150 times per day. That is often enough to be an intrusion, thus proving earnestness, but not an investment that would take all day.

Early monks wanted to be certain nobody cheated God by skipping an "Our Father" or two or ten or twenty. They used ropes with 150 knots to keep track. Through the centuries, most of the Our Fathers were dropped to make room for "Hail Marys" and "Glory Bes." (A short invocation to The Trinity.) These additional prayers were tacked on as the devotion to the Virgin Mother reached and surpassed cult status. Besides, it is not a good idea to put all of one's eggs in one basket. Spread the worship around a bit. New prayers broke up the monotony, too. Eventually, specific spacing and designations for certain knots and groups of knots developed, thus indicating the order of the individual prayers. The ropes, too cumbersome to carry around, gave way to strung bits of wood, beads or beans.

Obviously, the rich could hardly settle for garbanzos when there were so many diamonds to show off. Lady Godiva was one of the first to own a Rosary made of fine jewels. In her will, she bequeathed it to a church with the charge that it hang around the neck of a statue of the Virgin Mary.

[192] Although in 1309, Pope Clement V thought it would be nice to move the papacy to Avignon in what is now France. Rome, at the time, was a dump. Who gives a flying fig for where Saint Peter's bones are supposed to be buried? Clements's six successors decided the luxury that royalty treated them to in France beat the pants off living in the shit-hole Rome had become. Sixty-eight years later, Saint Catherine guilted Gregory XI into moving back to Rome. She must have been a parochial school nun because she got Gregory to go by telling him "You are pounding nails into the hands of Jesus." Or, words to that effect.

[193] Another little nitpicking Catholic fact: Popes do not succeed each other. All popes succeed Peter. So let us simply call this activity "voting for the new guy."

[194] Another dropped tradition: Each of the seats had a little canopy above it. When the winner was announced all the canopies would slap up against the walls with the exception of the canopy still dangling over the pope nouveau. A little sight gag that made it easier for the truly old-fart cardinals to figure out who their new leader was. To a lesser extent, the canopy would also protect the new pontiff from possible leaks in that famous roof.

[195] Apologies to women everywhere. The narrator could not resist the absurdity of such a statement. It will not happen again.

[196] Most people do not think of Canada as having a southern most point. Nevertheless, there it is, Point Pelee, on the northern shores of Lake Erie. Sort of the Florida Keys of Canada.

[197] Per his publisher's threatened lawsuit: This paragraph is based on information gleaned from "God Retires His Servant" the fourth autobiography of Michelle d'Indy. Available in paperback in all fine bookstores everywhere.

[198] Another possibility, more realistic and less flattering to d'Indy is that a vote for Zerbi would have better stacked the deck in d'Indy's favor.

[199] Don't ask me.

[200] By the way the plural form of the word chad is chad. No 's' is necessary. Like snow.

[201] A direct quote from "His Word Is My Word" the second autobiography of Michelle d'Indy per settled court agreement.

[202] There is speculation that Peter did not know the significance of this response. Considering his downright laughable grasp of Latin, many think Peter thought that d'Indy was just asking him for his name as some type of formality. But every nitwit priest knows the pope changes his name upon election. True enough that.

[203] An easy mistake for anyone to make except Father Cletus. Cletus, another Vatican small-fry know-it-all, maintained that the new Pope insisted on the right turn when going straight ahead was the correct course. "Cletus all reetus all wrongus", as he was dubbed later that afternoon, like every criminal, dragged his version of the story with him to the grave.

[204] All her life she claimed the best cookies she ever ate was a package of white chocolate dipped Oreos she thought she had bought in the Madrid, Spain train station. She tried the same cookie when she returned to the United States but found them waxy. Her craving to relive the taste became so great that two years later she flew to Madrid and searched the train station there in vain. In fact, she had made the purchase at the train station in Barcelona where, to this day, the white chocolate dipped Oreos are still available.

[205] A logic used by many many many lesser popes than Peter.

[206] Peter refers here specifically to the Sistine Chapel, which was named after the Pope who built it, Sixtus IV. Sixtus allowed six of his nephews to suckle on the teat of Holy Mother the Church when he made them cardinals. That is a record.

[207] Peter is talking about the Church's practice during the Middle Ages of selling indulgences-forgiveness for sins yet to be perpetrated-in order to finance rebuilding the Vatican. The privileged class could buy them as well. The practice was one of many to raise the ire of Martin Luther.

[208] This appears to be an abrupt change in both personality and intellectual expressiveness for Peter. Cynics also harrumph at the suggestion that he could persuade d'Indy so quickly. Perhaps it is a matter of faith. In the author.

[209] It is true. There are people who do not get a caffeine "buzz" from chocolate. Diane was one of them. She could also drink a pot of coffee and nod off.

[210] Diane, for those living in a cave the last twenty years, was the last woman crowned Miss America. The decision followed public rancor because Diane stripped naked on live television after receiving her crown. The judges thought it would increase the legitimacy of "scholarship competition" if they chose a classically "ugly" woman with a "smart mouth." They were sure surprised as the Velcro came undone exposing their choice, right down to her clean-shaven labia. The public outcry that followed was a preamble to tremendous support at Diane's many public appearances (Not on broadcast TV. Nobody but the sexy cable channels trusted Diane and she would have nothing to do with them.) and through sales of her autobiography "The Last Miss America."

[211] Several savvy hawkers were ironing decals that read "Peter II" in the blank they had left on t-shirts pre-inscribed with "I saw Pope _____ first!"

[212] I am the Lord, thy God. Thou shalt not have strange gods before me."

[213] Tis easier to aim the arrow at a shining light than a dim bulb." From the book "Malapropisms of the Rich and Famous" by Kilgore Trout. Trout attributes these two quotes to Michelle d'Indy. All knowledgeable critics and historians take for granted these and most all the other quotes in the above title were written by Trout himself.

[214] For expediency's sake, only the English versions of d'Indy's first remarks to the news corps will be given here. There is very little difference between the English and the French, Italian, German, Russian and Spanish versions. Much ado has been made about the Japanese translations. d'Indy dismissed the accusations of the Japanese media, insisting they did not understand his "play on words" when he "cleverly used several dialects simultaneously."

[215] Nobody knows what the letters stand for, but it is the earplugs still commonly seen on television people. The "talent" can hear producers talking in their ears, updating information or telling them to "wrap up" a three-minute story in three seconds and all this is done without the viewer knowing. Reporters often respond to these tethers to Mother Earth by lightly touching the earpiece with one finger. That tells the producer to "Shut the hell up. I cannot concentrate with you yammering in my ear."

Many reporters find great amusement in broadening their smile while the producer screams an impotent threat that they are going to cut to a commercial break. These reporters, "live from the scene of the train wreck," instead of wrapping it up, smile even more as they relate an amusing story about their pet kitty.

[216] Often, people witnessing news conferences wonder why they are not better organized and why everyone yells questions at once. The reason everyone yells simultaneously is that, regardless of how inane their question is, they feel it is the most important one to ask, and that it must be done loudly. All are also afraid someone else will ask "a really good one." So they scream the first question that wanders into their brain, hoping it turns out to be a really good one.

[217] Silence imposed by his employers at BBC-3. They fired him immediately following this incident. Not so much for breaking the

code of photographer's silence, but because BBC-Too caught it all on tape and began using it in their promotional announcements.

[218] "Your Eminence. Say I'm just standing here minding my own p's and q's, and the bloody bloke next to me don't quite bump into me, but just sort of nudges me a might. Just enough to crap up the shot, sort of. With your indulgence, could you might repeat the answer at least? Just if that should sort of happen?"

[219] Pope John Paul II.

[220] Bendardondat spoke from experience. Born and raised twenty miles or so (There is no road, so he never measured the actual distance. A path lead from his village home to the town.) west of Mogor, Ethiopia, Bendardondat barely lived to survive the hunger, destitution and the occasional unwanted visits from Somalian rebels.

[221] Cosmos holed up in Bucharest, Rumania. He claimed to be a reformed criminal. Others, in and out of the Church, insisted the reformation adjective is dubious and his ascension through the ranks was through strong-arm tactics and, sometimes, literal arm-twisting or worse.

[222] The Pieta" is a classic scene used by many artists but the most famous version is easily the one sitting just inside and to the right in Saint Peter's. The scene is of Christ, freshly dead, taken down off the cross lying in his mother's arms. Sure, it is beautiful to see for its delicacy, strength, smooth lines and details. What annoys some though, is the lack of reality in expecting a 90-pound woman to be so easily capable of balancing a dead man's sprawling body. What disturbs others in this depiction is that Michelangelo (The Scamp) has the Mother Mary staring through all of eternity at her Son's (With God being the Dad.) crotch.

[223] The bronze canopy, the baldacchino, rises high above the main altar in Saint Peter's, is covered with cast, bronze bees. They have also been swarming for centuries on the cross that tops the canopy. Bees were the symbol for the family of Pope Urban VIII.

[224] Peter makes a valid, if not truncated point. Not only did Sixtus IV sell indulgences, (Pardon for sins yet committed banking on the grace of God and the Saints in Heaven.) he created papal offices and sold them. He used the money to build the Sistine Chapel, which he named after himself. He also kicked off the Spanish Inquisition and was involved in a murder conspiracy.

To his credit, Urban VIII rebuilt the crumbling basilica. He also created the ground rules for excommunication. That may have slowed successors from willey nilley condemnation of kings who do not cooperate. To his debit, he had a bad habit of appointing relatives to high church positions and declaring war every other week: a great way to deplete the Vatican treasury as well as the Roman population. People ran out into the streets and cheered when Urban VIII died.

[225] Last crack about Saint Peter being the rock and his skull and building the Church upon it. The Saint Peter's these boys were standing in was actually built directly over an earlier version of itself. The first Saint Peter's was built over the ancient Roman circus. Under that was "the apostle's skull." People who believe it truly to be Peter's skull also are easy prey for investment payments in the Brooklyn Bridge.

[226] This was an odd argument for Cosmos to make, considering that a healthy majority was glad to see Martin gain his heavenly reward. As to the outburst and call to conclave, there is no literature on the subject and it remains a mystery. Speculation is that Cosmos entertained the fantasy that he would be selected to replace Peter II or that the replacement would be so grateful he would toss Cosmos a piece of cake gig at the Vatican. Two years later, the Italian journalist Benchi Menooti mentioned Cosmos's name in relation to a drug smuggling ring. While there was never any proof given in any court, Menooti suspected that being able to hide drugs in the basement of the Vatican could be quite profitable.

[227] It is a long story. You do not want to read it.

[228] Skywyz was the only person historically to share the distinction of having participated in both a conclave and the Olympics: 2002 Winter Olympics where he won a bronze medal for the downhill

slalom, an event which was cancelled following its abysmal record for broken bones in a single day in a single event. Skywyz and the gold and silver winners were the only competitors to survive the competition with all their bones intact.

[229] The Holy Door is one of several massive doors on the front of Saint Peter's. The Holy Door used to be opened by the pope every twenty-five years for what was called a Holy Year. Holy Years were every 100 years until a certain greedy pope realized the celebration increased the number of money-spending pilgrims that he could tax. It was all down hill after that, with various popes playing around with the numbers so it would likely include a date somewhere in their term.

[230] Zimmer may be referring to the bas-relief carving on the sarcophagus of Pope Gregory XIII. Gregory's resume included the elimination of ten days from existence. Based on a mistake during the previous calendar reform in 45 CE., Gregory decreed that there would be no October 5th through the 14th in the year 1582. As a result, October 4, 1582 was followed by October 15, 1582. The carving is a depiction of that event. And it is a big one.

[231] Greek? Latin? Hebrew? For "So be it." The author needs a nap.

[232] An intentional choice of words by the author. "Begin The Bullying" is of course the grand opera by Sir Peter Townsend. Townsend states in his otherwise salacious memoirs, "See Me, Feel Me, Touch Me…" that it was this very moment in history which inspired the work. "The vision of this not-so-good-looking older chick (sic) storming the gates, so to speak, at the Vatican-not knowing which tree to bark up-but barking up a storm none the less. What can I say? I was transfixed and inspired."

[233] Sister Mary Artisan, on vacation from her assignment convincing racists in Alabama to destroy their confederate "stars and bars," remarked later in a press report: "She was scary. Scarier than a Klan threat. Scarier than the nun I had in third grade. And that's pretty darn scary."

[234] Roman-collared. Tee he he.

[235] Following the attempt on the life of Pope John Paul II, the Swiss Guard began special training for a plainclothes corps responsible specifically for the immediate personal safety of the pope's person and personal staff. In addition to being experts at hand-to-hand combat, these men were also packing. Obviously, this is not the type of position where colorful pantaloons, a big puffy hat, and a near useless, unwieldy spear would do much good.

[236] Okay. So their technology was slightly Dick Tracy. They were still trained killers.

[237] In defense of d'Indy, it has been reported in Cosmo Magazine, that countless men who have met Diane in person said that a simple introduction can be a thoroughly erotic experience. Most use a superlative in describing it such as: "the most" or "the best" or "grist for the old jerk-off mill." All state that what is usually considered innocent physical contact was part of the encounter and that Diane always initiated it. All went on to report a sense of being "enveloped" by her and uniformly insist that there were none of the typical sexy gestures such as batting eyelashes or winking, lip licking, or giggling inappropriately. In his Carolina Medical Journal article entitled "This Siren's Silent Song," Dr. Sybil Lance polled two thousand Carolina men (Diane lived in Charlotte for two years after discovering the genius of "buying up" from the sale of her house in California.) and discovered the above consistencies in all but three of the poll subjects. After the article was published, all three contacted Lance to inform him that they were homosexual and that they had volunteered for the poll under false pretenses. They confessed that they had never met Diane, but all three stated that, from what they had seen on TV, she seemed "really, really sweet."

[238] A wall that surrounds approximately two-thirds of the Vatican. It was built by (big surprise) Pope Leo. One portion extends to the Castel Santangelo, a fortress where popes would hide during Roman Sacks. There is a convenient walkway along the top of that particular wall. Many a pope was spotted racing for cover, ducking flaming arrows along the top of that parapet.

[239] Prague, The Czech Republic.

[240] He would write too many books. Subjects would include his childhood, seminary life, his sex life, four tomes from four angles on time spent with Peter, organized religion, women (Including an exaggerated importance placed on *his* "influence" of Diane.), ornithology and a best-selling murder mystery. Though nothing compares to living in the Vatican with a staff at one's beck and call, d'Indy lived comfortably.

[241] For American readers, it would be the second floor of the building. In Europe, it would be considered the first floor. Yet another reason (In addition to the election of Donald Trump) why Americans and Europeans will never understand each other.

[242] Diane would be more surprised to learn that the dirt on this floor was shipped from Jerusalem over five-hundred years ago.

[243] For the thousandth time.

[244] Who at that very moment was back in Merdette playfully scolding her ten-year old toe-headed son. (Sequel Alert! Sequel Alert! Sequel Alert!)

[245] Unless the encounters in Magadan with the Babushka on the bus and the covey of them reviving him after his conk on the head counted.

[246] Please expect nothing so repulsive here, though.

[247] All references to Peter doing, feeling, or thinking something "for the first time in his life" will, until the conclusion of this story be deleted. From this point, other than basic bodily functions, just about everything Peter does will be for the first time in his life.

[248] Oops. Sorry. Will not happen again.

[249] Saint Mary Magdalene was the patron saint of reformed prostitutes. In the New Testament, Jesus casts several devils out of a 'ho named Mary. After the exorcism, Mary gives up her evil ways. That may or may have not been Mary Magdalene, but why get fussy with dubious history? There are several mentions of Marys in the bible and they are either whores or the Mother of Jesus. There

is a kinky story about a Mary washing the feet of Jesus then drying them off with her hair. She evidently would be a babe the "business" missed. She then slathered the Lord's feet with perfume. For that reason she is also the patron saint of perfumers and hairdressers. The latter is a real stretch. There are theories that Mary was a wealthy businessperson. But, are not all wealthy business people whores?

[250] Cynics say the man carried a sign that read, in Italian, "Will work for drugs or booze. Ha Ha At least I'm honest." They chortle that Peter did not read Italian and assumed the sign read "Viet Nam Vet Please Help God Bless."

[251] Yes. We thank you for your patience.

[252] Insert your own joke here:

_____.

[253] A rare moment indeed for the closest thing we come to what resembles a heroine. Unless you want to count Ys (wiggle index fingers) back on Merdette. After all, her undertaking, though pleasurable, was certainly not heroinic. Anyway, the only other time Diane suffered doubt this severe was when she left the convent. Oh. Did I fail to mention that in her younger years, Diane studied to become a nun? Oh, I am so sorry.

[254] Though in Peter's rearranged memory, the Virgin Mother stared at her slain son's face.

[255] A little something the confessor gives to the confessee after confession. Usually depending on the scope of the sin confessed, sometimes the penance is light; say a couple of short prayers. Other times it is heavier. "Yes, the postmaster deserved to die for his cruelty, but you must go to the police and tell them all that you did the deed, and don't shoot anybody else on the way over." The punch line is that the sin is not forgiven until the penance is performed. This is one other routine that separated Catholics from the heathen Lutherans.

[256] A very short prayer, sort of a capper, which goes a little something like this: "Glory be to the Father and to the Son

and to the Holy Spirit as it was in the beginning is now and ever shall be, world without end, Amen."

[257] Technically d'Indy is about to lie.

[258] Guglielmo Marconi, who invented the radio, designed the Vatican Radio station. Marconi ran Vatican Radio for the last few years of his life. In 2001, neighbors close to the transmitter sight in Castel Gandolfo won a lawsuit that temporarily caused the station to be shut down. They complained it was putting out dangerous levels of radiation causing chickens to be born with two heads. But seriously, Vatican radio had a total listening audience of one or two people, depending on how many are actually inside the broadcast studio and are therefore forced to listen.

[259] I am truly sorry. My interest level is wearing thin, even as we rush towards the exciting climax of this epic …eh … thing.

[260] It was muggy inside the recording booth.

[261] What!? Change his mind?! After all he has already said and done!? Here the reader must realize that the pope has the same responsibility to make sense as say the king or queen of England. He can also completely reverse himself any damn time he likes.

[262] Believers.

[263] It should be noted, there is a very good chance that the mushrooms Peter had eaten for lunch were bad. Or, as someone who appreciates the affects of hallucinogens would say, "really good."

[264] Martin Luther.

[265] Good chance it came from noontime sun reflecting off one of many stain glass windows in the courtyard.

[266] Peter remained pope until his death. He never formally renounced the title. The curia had the good sense to keep mum. Many still hoped that eventually things would, if not go back to

being the way they were, at least they would get to keep a pope plugged in somewhere, somehow.

[267] This is one of many beliefs of the Catholic Church that reduces sophomoric non-believers to giggling fits almost as much as transubstantiation. All Catholics are supposed to be members of the Mystical Body. Nobody knows what happens to the excommunicated or quitters or "fallen-away" Catholics. Did the Mystical Body lose a lot of weight during the Reformation? Few would quibble with Christ as the Head. Especially considering all he had to go through to get there, getting beat to a semblance of marinara, sweating blood, and dying and all. After that, it is a toss-up as to who is what organ. Maybe the pope would be the heart or brain. That would make the curia the spleen. Who gets stuck with the less pleasant areas, specifically the one where the sun don't shine?

Which brings to mind another series of questions the aforementioned sophomores have squandered centuries ruminating. Did Jesus fart? Or did everything He ate "agree" with Him. Jesus must have had a penis, because the Church held a feast day in honor of his circumcision. That raises the next series of questions oft pondered by morons. How big was It. Did He ever sport wood or shake more than necessary? Did he ever write his name in the sand?

While we are at it, and since we are being paid by the word, there is something else a little odd about this Mystical Body. It comes from a dusty, ancient copy of "The Pocket Catholic Dictionary" Abridged edition of Modern Catholic Dictionary by John A. Hardon, S.J. Hardon (giggle) wrote "Moreover, the Roman Catholic regards herself as the Body of Christ." "Herself?" Does that mean the Mystical Body has the head of Jesus and the body of a woman? What happens when the Mystical Body gets Menstrual? Oh! THAT'S what happens to the "fallen-away" Catholics!!

[268] Cynical musicologists insist the last two occasions are somehow related.

[269] For awhile, Cosmos could be seen making the rounds at the high stakes tables in Las Vegas, Nevada. He later "accepted Jesus as his Lord and Savior" and became involved in the administration of the traveling faith healer circuit.

[270] It should be noted that Chicago had a larger Polish population than any city in Poland. Most of them were fierce, traditional Catholics After all, it was John Paul II, the greatest Pole since Kosciusko, who single-handedly kicked the Soviets out of Poland. (General Thaddeus Kosciusko fought alongside the colonists in the Revolutionary War. He went home and led battles for independence from the Russians. Imagine that! People deciding for themselves to throw off the yoke of their oppressors!)

[271] There is a joke in that mess somewhere.

[272] One fellow, Rudy Buddi, stuffed the Catholic criminal attitude into a nutshell in a quote taken from "Holy Mobsters" an article in the Chicago Sun-Times, by saying, "… so we's figures dat it don make no dif'frence if we's doin' bad stuff or not as long as we's able to make a soluble confession before we's dies." Later in the article, Mr. Buddi credits Kilvanski with his spiritual understandings.

[273] Puerco left the Vatican immediately following Peter's election. Had he been involved in the imbroglio of his fellow cardinals versus Peter, he most likely would have said nothing. Puerco was one of the largest shy people ever to grace the Earth. If it were not for the fact that he was a better than average writer, he probably would not have been selected to be a monsignor, let alone a Cardinal. He was in the habit of allowing seminarians to read his unaccredited sermons to the congregations at Sunday mass.

[274] An olden days type of bomb that had a reputation for going off too soon, killing the bomber instead of the enemy.

Printed in Great Britain
by Amazon

23716509R00182